THE KNIGHT GOES FORTH ON HIS FIRST QUEST

The Bookshelf
for Boys and Girls

Prepared *under the Supervision of*

**THE EDITORIAL BOARD
OF THE UNIVERSITY SOCIETY**

VOLUME VIII

Bookland Classics

THE UNIVERSITY SOCIETY, INC.

Educational Publishers since 1897

NEW YORK

ACKNOWLEDGEMENTS VOLUME VIII

Grateful acknowledgement and thanks are extended to the following publishers, authors, periodicals, and individuals for permission to reprint copyrighted material:

Curtis Brown, Ltd.—"Lassie Come-Home" by Eric Knight, copyright, 1938, by the Curtis Publishing Company and reprinted by permission of the author's estate. An expanded and novel length form of the story is published by the John C. Winston Company.

Grosset & Dunlap, Inc.—Illustrations by Donald McKay for "Tom Whitewashes the Fence," and "The Cat and the Painkiller," from The Illustrated Library Edition of *The Adventures of Tom Sawyer* by Mark Twain, copyright, 1946, reprinted by permission of Grosset & Dunlap, Inc.

Harcourt, Brace and Company, Inc.—"Peculiarsome Abe," from *Abe Lincoln Grows Up* by Carl Sandburg, copyright, 1926, 1928, by Harcourt, Brace and Company, Inc.; renewed, 1954, 1956, by Carl Sandburg. Reprinted by permission of the publishers. Illustrations by James Daugherty from *Abe Lincoln Grows Up* by Carl Sandburg, copyright, 1926, 1928, by Harcourt, Brace and Company, Inc.; renewed, 1954, 1956, by Carl Sandburg. Reprinted by permission of the publishers.

The Macmillan Company—"Sea Fever" by John Masefield, from *Salt Water Ballads*, by John Masefield, published by The Macmillan Company, New York. Used by permission of the publishers. Illustrations for Washington Irving's *Rip Van Winkle* by Maud and Miska Petersham from the New Children's Classics Edition, copyright, 1951, by The Macmillan Company.

Charles Scribner's Sons—Illustrations for "Black Beauty" by Paul Brown from *Black Beauty* by Anna Sewell, told in Short Form and in Pictures by Paul Brown, copyright, 1952, by Paul Brown. Used by permission of Charles Scribner's Sons.

Frederick A. Stokes Company—"A Song of Sherwood" by Alfred Noyes, from *Poems* by Alfred Noyes. Used by permission of Frederick A. Stokes Company, New York, owners of the copyright.

World Publishing Company—Illustrations by Fritz Kredel for "The King of the Golden River" by John Ruskin. Published by World Publishing Company in their Rainbow Classics edition and used with their permission.

A Word to Parents about this Volume

BOOKLAND CLASSICS

THE land of good books is the pleasantest of all browsing places for those who love to roam through that enchanted realm.

Many of today's children, however, have not learned to appreciate the delights that bookland has to offer. This volume, therefore, proposes to introduce them to those delights through well-selected samplings of books that thousands of children have loved and enjoyed to the full.

All these books have *something* about them that has made them appeal strongly to children — humor or sympathy or adventure or characterization. Most of them have remained popular with children for generations. Some have become children's classics in more recent times.

We have not, of course, included whole books. But we have chosen the most beguiling *highlights of books that have stood the test of time not only as literary classics but as favorites with the children themselves.*

Some of the earliest, such as "Robinson Crusoe" and "Gulliver's Travels," keep bobbing up on children's best-seller lists today, even though they were written over two centuries ago. So do "Heidi," "Little Women," and "Black Beauty" — books that many adults consider old-fashioned and sentimental but many children love.

In addition to such immortal favorites as "Alice in Wonderland" and "A Christmas Carol" and "Tom Sawyer," we have included a variety of books that appeal to children whose tastes range from the fairy-tale quality of "The King of the Golden River" to such an adventure story as "Treasure Island."

And we have included two modern classics: Eric Knight's "Lassie" (the complete original version) and a chapter from "Abe Lincoln Grows Up" by Carl Sandburg, surely a classic author, especially of stories about Lincoln.

The poems we have selected for inclusion have the same timeless quality as the books. Some are immortal. Of many another, as the great English poet Alfred Noyes has put it, "the music's not immortal, but the world has made it sweet."

There is something here for every taste and every interest. Some children will skip. Many will want to read everything in the book. Some will be led on to other great stories and poems through finding their own preferences here.

It is our hope that these samplings will sharpen our young readers' literary tastes and will so stimulate their appetite for more that they will want to read the whole of the original books to which this volume introduces them.

Table of Contents

	Page
Adventures of Pinocchio *From* PINOCCHIO *By Carlo Collodi*	1
My Garden *By Thomas Edward Brown*	20
Flower in the Crannied Wall *By Alfred Tennyson*	20
Out in the Fields with God *By Elizabeth Barrett Browning*	20
Heidi at the Alm-Uncle's Hut *From* HEIDI *By Johanna Spyri*	21
The Height of the Ridiculous *By Oliver Wendell Holmes*	48
Dorothy's Travels to the Land of Oz *From* THE WIZARD OF OZ *By L. Frank Baum*	49
The Mountain and the Squirrel *By Ralph Waldo Emerson*	70
Toby Tyler and Mr. Stubbs *From* TOBY TYLER or TEN WEEKS WITH A CIRCUS *By James Otis*	71
Three Things to Remember *By William Blake*	84
Be Like the Bird *By Victor Hugo*	84
Adventures of Black Beauty *From* BLACK BEAUTY *By Anna Sewell*	85
What Is Good? *By John Boyle O'Reilly*	97
Canticle of the Sun *By St. Francis of Assisi*	98
Little Daylight *From* AT THE BACK OF THE NORTH WIND *By George MacDonald*	99
Christmas with Queen Bess *From* MASTER SKYLARK *By John Bennett*	111
Hark, Hark! the Lark *By William Shakespeare*	118

v

		Page
Who Is Silvia? *By William Shakespeare*		118
Lassie Come-Home *By Eric Knight*		119
Abou Ben Adhem *By Leigh Hunt*		130
The King of the Golden River *By John Ruskin*		131
The Pied Piper of Hamelin *By Robert Browning*		144
Sea Fever *By John Masefield*		150
A Midsummer-Night's Dream *From* TALES FROM SHAKESPEARE *By Charles and Mary Lamb*		151
Forbearance *By Ralph Waldo Emerson*		159
The Tempest *From* TALES FROM SHAKESPEARE *By Charles and Mary Lamb*		160
The Christmas Story *From* THE BIBLE		168
Christmas at the Marches *From* LITTLE WOMEN *By Louisa M. Alcott*		173
Alice in Wonderland *By Lewis Carroll*		185
Through the Looking Glass *By Lewis Carroll*		214
The Green Grass Growing All Around *Author unknown*		256
Tom Whitewashes the Fence *From* THE ADVENTURES OF TOM SAWYER *By Mark Twain*		257
The Cat and the Painkiller *From* THE ADVENTURES OF TOM SAWYER *By Mark Twain*		267
September *By Helen Hunt Jackson*		270
Apple-Seed John *By Lydia Maria Child*		271
Robinson Crusoe's Adventure on a Desert Island *Retold from* ROBINSON CRUSOE *By Daniel Defoe*		273
Ozymandias *By Percy Bysshe Shelley*		283
How Arthur Became King *From* KING ARTHUR AND HIS NOBLE KNIGHTS *By Mary MacLeod*		284
England *By William Shakespeare*		288
I Wandered Lonely as a Cloud *By William Wordsworth*		289
Chartless *By Emily Dickinson*		289
The Year's Round *By Coventry Patmore*		289
Adventures of Don Quixote *Retold from* DON QUIXOTE *By Miguel De Cervantes*		290

	Page
Gulliver's Adventures in Lilliput *Retold from* GULLIVER'S TRAVELS	
By *Jonathan Swift*	307
Invictus *By William Ernest Henley*	322
A Song of Sherwood *By Alfred Noyes*	323
Lochinvar *By Walter Scott*	325
Rip Van Winkle *By Washington Irving*	327
A Christmas Carol *By Charles Dickens*	342
Ring Out Wild Bells *By Alfred Tennyson*	363
The Cataract of Lodore *By Robert Southey*	364
The Voyage of the *Hispaniola* *From* TREASURE ISLAND	
By *Robert Louis Stevenson*	366
"Peculiarsome" Abe *From* ABE LINCOLN GROWS UP *By Carl Sandburg* .	378
I Sing America *By Walt Whitman*	384
America *By Sidney Lanier*	384

Illustrators of this Volume

ELINORE BLAISDELL, *Canticle of the Sun; A Midsummer-Night's Dream; The Tempest; The Green Grass Growing All Around*

PAUL BROWN, *Black Beauty*

RAFAELLO BUSONI, *The Height of the Ridiculous; Christmas with Queen Bess; The Pied Piper of Hamelin; Apple-Seed John; Adventures of Don Quixote; Lochinvar; A Christmas Carol; The Cataract of Lodore*

JAMES DAUGHERTY, *"Peculiarsome" Abe*

FRITZ KREDEL, *The King of the Golden River*

DONALD MCKAY, *Tom Whitewashes the Fence; The Cat and the Painkiller*

T. MORTEN, *Gulliver's Adventures in Lilliput*

MAUD AND MISKA PETERSHAM, *Rip Van Winkle*

HARVE STEIN, *Toby Tyler and Mr. Stubbs*

MARY STEVENS, *Heidi at the Alm-Uncle's Hut; Little Daylight; Lassie Come-Home; Abou Ben Adhem; Sea Fever; The Christmas Story; Christmas at the Marches; A Song of Sherwood; Voyage of the* Hispaniola

FRANK SZASZ, *The Adventures of Pinocchio; The Wizard of Oz; Robinson Crusoe's Adventure on a Desert Island*

SIR JOHN TENNIEL, *Alice in Wonderland and Through the Looking Glass*

The Adventures of Pinocchio

By Carlo Collodi

This outrageously funny story, whose hero is a wooden puppet, comes to us from Italy. That should surprise no one, for Italy is the home of the world's best puppets and marionettes.

In this delightful tale, by the witty author who called himself Collodi, an old man named Geppetto carves a puppet out of a piece of wood. Geppetto calls his puppet Pinocchio and hopes to get some pleasure out of him. But, alas, Pinocchio gives poor old Geppetto a swift kick, runs out of the door, and sets off on a career of being a very impudent and daring puppet indeed.

He has the most fantastic adventures in the course of which he meets a Talking Cricket and the Blue Fairy who tries her best to make him tell the truth—but in vain.

How Pinocchio repents—for a while—how he becomes a real boy, and what he does then are among the liveliest parts of an entirely lively story.

Pinocchio does naughtier things than any real child ever did and he suffers more dreadful punishments. But through them all he remains gay and impudent and, somehow, lovable.

There is a laugh on every page of PINOCCHIO, and the chuckles and giggles of children who read it can be heard around the world. Here is part of the story.

O NCE upon a time a piece of wood was lying in the shop of an old carpenter. He was called Master Antonio, but because his nose was always as red as a ripe cherry, everyone called him Master Cherry.

No sooner had Master Cherry set eyes on the piece of wood than his face beamed with delight.

Rubbing his hands together happily, he said, "This has come right in the nick of time. It will just do to make the leg of a little table." With that he picked up a sharp ax to peel off the bark and shape the wood. But as he was about to give it the first blow, he heard a little voice say imploringly, "Do not strike me too hard!"

Imagine good Master Cherry's astonishment! With the ax still raised in his hand he turned his eyes all around the room trying to discover where the little voice could possibly have come from. But he saw nobody!

"It is all my imagination," he said finally, laughing and scratching his wig. And raising the ax, he struck the piece of wood a tremendous blow.

"Oh! Oh! You have hurt me," cried the same faraway little voice. Master Cherry grew dumb. His eyes almost popped out of his head, and he shook all over. When he could speak he stuttered and trembled.

"Where on earth can that little voice have come from? There's no one here but me. Is it possible this piece of wood can have learned to cry like a child? I cannot believe it. Yet, might someone be hidden in it? If so, the worse for him. I'll soon settle him." And he seized the piece of wood and threw it against the wall as hard as he could.

He listened for the tiny voice to cry

and moan. For two minutes he stood with the wooden leg in his hand—nothing; five minutes—nothing; ten minutes —nothing.

"Oh, I see," he said trying to laugh bravely. "I surely must have imagined I heard the little voice. Well—to work once more!"

But just the same he was badly frightened, and he put away his ax. He tried to sing a gay song to give himself courage and he picked up his plane to make the piece of wood smooth.

He had scarcely begun when he heard the little voice cry laughingly, "Stop it! Oh stop it! You're tickling me all over!"

This time poor Master Cherry was so frightened, that he fell down as if he had been struck by lightning. Even the end of his nose, instead of being crimson, turned blue from fright.

In that very instant someone knocked loudly on the door. "Come in," said the carpenter getting to his feet.

A lively little old man named Geppetto walked into the shop.

"What brought you here, neighbor Geppetto?" asked Master Cherry, trying to calm himself.

"I have come to ask a favor of you," said Geppetto. "This morning an idea came to my head. I thought of making myself a beautiful wooden marionette— a wonderful one that would be able to dance, fence, and turn somersaults. With it I intend to travel all over the world, to earn my piece of bread and glass of wine."

"Well, then, neighbor Geppetto," said the carpenter, "what is the favor that you wish of me?"

"I want a piece of wood to make a marionette. Will you give it to me?"

Master Cherry was delighted and he immediately fetched the piece of wood that had frightened him so much. Thanking his friend for being so kind, Geppetto took the fine piece of wood and returned to his house.

Poor Geppetto lived in a small, badly lighted room. For furniture he had only a hard bed, a rickety chair, and a tumble-down table. He had no fire, but on one wall of the room was painted a picture of a fireplace full of burning logs. Over the fire was painted a pot full of something which kept boiling happily away, sending up clouds of what looked like real steam.

As soon as he reached home, Geppetto took his tools and began to cut and shape the wood into a marionette.

"What shall I name him?" he said to himself. "I think I'll call him Pinocchio. It is a name that should bring him luck."

After choosing the name for his marionette, Geppetto set seriously to work making the hair, the forehead, the eyes.

When the eyes were finished, imagine Geppetto's astonishment when he noticed that they moved and stared at him!

"Ugly wooden eyes, why do you stare so?" asked Geppetto. There was no answer.

After the eyes Geppetto went on and carved the nose. But as he carved, it began to grow. And it grew, and grew until it became so long, it seemed endless. Poor Geppetto kept cutting it, but the more he cut, the longer grew that impertinent nose. In despair he left it alone.

Next he made the mouth.

The mouth was not even finished when it began to laugh and make fun of him.

"Stop laughing!" said Geppetto angrily. But he might as well have spoken to the wall, for the mouth only stuck out its tongue at him. And though Geppetto was furious, he went on with his work rather than spoil it.

The hands were scarcely finished when Geppetto felt his wig snatched from his head.

"You young rascal!" said Geppetto indignantly. "You're not yet finished and you start out by being impudent to your old Papa. Very bad, my son, very bad!"

The legs and feet still had to be made. As soon as they were done, Geppetto felt a sharp kick on the tip of his nose.

"I deserve it!" he said to himself. "I should have thought of it sooner! Now it is too late!"

He took hold of the puppet under the arms and put him on the floor to teach him to walk.

When his legs were limbered up, Pinocchio started walking by himself and ran all round the room. He came to the open door, and with one leap he was out into the street. Away he ran!

Geppetto rushed after him but was not able to overtake the speeding Pinocchio.

"Catch him! Catch him!" Geppetto kept shouting. But the people in the streets, seeing a wooden puppet run-

ning like the wind, stood still to stare and laugh until they cried.

At last, by sheer luck, a policeman hearing the uproar caught the runaway by the nose as Pinocchio tried to scoot through his legs, and returned him to the perspiring Geppetto.

"We're going home at once," said Geppetto holding him firmly, "and as soon as we get there we'll settle our accounts."

Pinocchio, on hearing this, threw himself on the ground and would not take another step. Meanwhile a crowd began to gather around the two. "Poor puppet," said one man. "I'm not surprised he doesn't want to go home! Geppetto, that bad old man, will beat him!"

"Geppetto looks like a good man," said another, "but with boys he's a real tyrant. If we leave that poor marionette in his hands he may tear him to pieces!"

It ended in so much being said and done that the policeman at last set Pinocchio free and dragged Geppetto off to prison where he had to stay all night. As he was being led away the poor man sobbed out, "Ungrateful boy! To think how hard I worked to make you a well-behaved marionette!"

Meanwhile that imp, Pinocchio, finding himself free, ran off as fast as his legs could carry him.

On reaching Geppetto's home, he slipped into the room, locked the door, and threw himself on the floor, happy at his escape.

But his happiness lasted only a short time, for just then he heard someone saying, "Cri-cri-cri!"

"Who is calling me?" asked Pinocchio greatly frightened.

"I am!"

Pinocchio turned around and saw a large cricket crawling slowly up the wall.

"Tell me, Mr. Cricket, who are you?"

"I am the Talking Cricket, and I have been living in this room for more than one hundred years."

"Now, however, this room is mine," said the puppet, "so please go away at once."

"I will not go," answered the cricket, "until I have told you a great truth."

"Tell it then and hurry."

"Woe to boys who refuse to obey their parents and run away from home! They will never come to any good!"

"Sing away, cricket. I've made up my mind to run away tomorrow. I've no wish to go to school—I hate to study. It's much more fun to chase butterflies, or to climb trees."

"Poor little silly! You'll surely grow up a perfect donkey!"

"Hold your tongue, you ugly cricket," shouted Pinocchio.

"Poor Pinocchio! I'm sorry for you."

"Why?"

"Because you are a marionette, and what is worse, because you have a wooden head."

At these words Pinocchio jumped up in a rage, snatched a hammer from the bench, and threw it at the Talking Cricket.

Unfortunately it struck the cricket exactly on the head. With a last weak "cri-cri-cri" the cricket fell from the wall, dead!

After a while, with night coming on, Pinocchio curled up on the floor and went to sleep. It was daybreak when he woke up because someone was knocking at the door.

"Who is there?" he asked.

"It is I, Geppetto," answered the voice. "Open the door at once!" Rubbing his eyes and yawning, Pinocchio let him in.

"Dear Papa," said Pinocchio, sniffling as though his heart would break, "how glad I am to see you! I have terrible pains in my stomach and I know I shall die of hunger."

Hearing this, Geppetto, who had been in a towering rage at having had to spend the night in prison because of Pinocchio, felt his heart melt with pity for the marionette.

The kind man took three pears from his pocket and presented them to Pinocchio. "These pears were to be for my breakfast," he said, "but I'll give them to you willingly. Eat them and I hope they will do you good."

"To show you how grateful I am to you for what you have done for me," said Pinocchio after he had finished eating the pears, "I'll go to school now. But to go to school I shall need some clothes."

Geppetto did not have a penny in his pocket, so he made Pinocchio a jacket of flowered paper, a pair of shoes from the bark of a tree, and a cap from a bit of dough.

"By the way," said the marionette, "I shall still need something else to go to school. I must have a spelling book."

"To be sure," said Geppetto, puckering his brow thoughtfully. Suddenly he put on his old coat, full of darns and patches, and ran out of the house.

After a while he returned with the spelling book, but the old coat was gone. The poor man was in his shirt sleeves and the day was cold. When Pinocchio saw that the kind old man had sold his coat to get him a spelling book, he threw his arms around Geppetto's neck and kissed him again and again.

At last he started off to school, and he really did mean to be good. But as he walked along, sounds of music, as of a fife and drum, came from the town square.

"What can that music be? What a nuisance that I have to go to school! Otherwise . . . " Pinocchio struggled with his conscience.

"Today I'll go and hear the fifes and tomorrow I'll go to school," the young rascal decided finally, shrugging his shoulders.

Nearing the sound of the music he found himself in the middle of a square full of people, crowding around a gaily-painted building. From the talk around him he learned that the building was a Marionette Theater and that the play was about to begin. But he also learned that the price of admission was twopence. In desperation he struck a bargain with a nearby fellow who paid him twopence for his fine new spelling book.

And to think that poor Geppetto sat at home in his shirt sleeves, shivering

5

with cold, having sold his coat to buy
that little book for that ungrateful boy!

Quick as a flash Pinocchio disappeared into the Marionette Theater.
And then something happened that almost caused a riot.

On the stage Harlequin and Punchinello were as usual quarreling with
each other, threatening every moment
to come to blows, for that, as you must
know, was the play. The theater was
full of people who were laughing at the
antics of the marionettes.

Suddenly Harlequin stopped short
and pointing to someone far down the
theater exclaimed dramatically, "Look,
look! Am I dreaming or do I really see
Pinocchio?"

"It is indeed Pinocchio!" cried Punchinello, and all the other puppets joined
in, shouting in chorus.

"Pinocchio, come up here," cried
Harlequin. "Come throw yourself into
the arms of your wooden brothers!"

At such a loving invitation, Pinocchio
made three tremendous leaps that
landed him on the stage. It is impossible to describe the shrieks of joy, the
embraces, and the friendly greetings
that Pinocchio received from that excited company of puppets on the stage.

The sight was a moving one, but the
audience, seeing that the play had
stopped, became impatient and began
to yell, "The play, the play, we want
the play!"

The puppets paid no attention and
only made twice as much racket. They
were lifting Pinocchio up on their shoulders when out came the showman. He
was so very big and ugly that one look
at him was terrifying. His beard was

black as pitch and reached down to his feet and his mouth was as wide as an oven. He cracked a long whip made of snake-tails and cat-tails twisted together.

Instantly there was silence. One could almost hear a fly in the stillness. The puppets trembled like so many leaves.

"Why have you raised a disturbance in my theater?" the huge fellow asked Pinocchio in the voice of an ogre suffering with a cold.

"Believe me, honored sir, it was not my fault!"

"That is enough! Tonight we shall settle accounts!"

As soon as the play was over, the showman went into the kitchen where a fine leg of lamb was turning slowly on the spit in front of the fire. As there was not enough wood to finish roasting and browning it, he called Harlequin and Punchinello and said, "Bring that puppet here. It seems to me he is made of fine dry wood. I am sure that if he were thrown on the fire he would make a beautiful blaze for the roast."

Harlequin and Punchinello hesitated, but at a glance from the showman that made them shiver they obeyed. They returned to the kitchen carrying poor Pinocchio, who was wriggling and squirming like an eel and screaming desperately, "Papa, Papa, save me! I don't want to die! I don't want to die!"

Now the showman, Fire-Eater—for that was his name—was very ugly, but he was far from being as bad as he looked. In proof of this, when he saw poor Pinocchio struggling and screaming, he began to waver and then to weaken. After a little while he could control himself no longer and gave a loud sneeze.

"Ah," said Harlequin who had been weeping for Pinocchio, "you are saved."

For you must know that, instead of weeping when he felt sorry for anyone, Fire-Eater, the showman, always sneezed.

After a few more violent sneezes that fairly rocked the kitchen, Fire-Eater turned to the frightened puppet and said, "I am going to spare you. But something is due me for my trouble, too. My good dinner is spoiled. As you see, I have no more wood to finish roasting my mutton. So instead of burning you, I'll burn some other marionette. Hey, there! Officers!"

Two wooden policemen appeared, and the showman said in a harsh voice, "Take Harlequin, tie him, and throw him on the fire. I want my lamb well done!"

Think how poor Harlequin felt. His legs doubled up under him, and he fell on his face on the floor.

At this heartbreaking sight, Pinocchio threw himself at the fat showman's feet and wept bitterly.

"Have pity, Your Excellence!"

Upon hearing himself called by this title, the showman smiled proudly.

"Well, what do you want from me now, marionette?"

"I beg you to pardon my poor friend Harlequin."

"For him there can be no pardon, Pinocchio. I have spared you but I am hungry and my dinner must be cooked."

7

"In that case," cried Pinocchio proudly, "I know my duty. Come officers! Tie me up and throw me on those flames. It is not fair that poor Harlequin, my true friend, should die for me!"

These brave words, uttered in a loud voice, made all the other marionettes cry.

Little by little Fire-Eater's heart began to soften. At last he sneezed three or four times. Then he opened wide his arms and said to Pinocchio, "You are a good, brave boy! Come here and kiss me!"

Pinocchio scurried like a squirrel up the showman's long black beard and deposited a hearty kiss on the tip of his nose.

"The pardon is granted," said Fire-Eater. Then he added, sighing and shaking his head, "Tonight I shall have to eat my lamb half raw, but beware the next time . . . "

At the news of the pardon the puppets all ran to the stage, turned on all the lights, and danced and sang till dawn.

The next day Fire-Eater called Pinocchio aside and asked him about his father.

"My father is Geppetto, a woodcarver, and he earns so little that he never has a penny in his pockets. Just think! To buy me an A-B-C book for school, he had to sell the only coat he owned— and that was so patched it was a pity."

"Poor fellow! I feel sorry for him. Here, take these five gold pieces. Go, give them to him with my kindest regards."

Pinocchio, as may be easily imagined, thanked him a thousand times. He embraced all the puppets of the company, and beside himself with delight set out for home.

He had not gone far when he met a lame fox and a blind cat, walking together like two good friends. The lame fox leaned on the cat and the blind cat let the fox lead him along.

"Good day, Pinocchio," said the fox politely.

"How do you know my name?" asked the marionette.

"I know your father well. Only yesterday I saw him at the door of his house shivering with cold."

"Poor Papa! But soon he shall shiver no more."

"Why?"

"Well, if you know anything about it, you can see I have become rich. I have in my pocket five new gold pieces."

And he pulled out the gold pieces Fire-Eater had given him.

At the cheerful tinkle of gold, the fox unconsciously stretched out the paw that seemed to be crippled, and the cat opened wide his supposedly blind eyes. He closed them again so quickly that Pinocchio did not notice.

"What are you going to do with all that money, Pinocchio?" asked the lame fox eagerly.

"First of all," answered the marionette, "I'm going to buy my Papa a new coat made of gold and silver, with diamond buttons. And then I'll buy an A-B-C book for myself!"

"For yourself?"

"For myself. I want to go to school and study."

"Look at me," said the fox. "For the silly reason of wanting to study, I have lost a paw."

"Look at me," said the cat. "For the same foolish reason, I have lost the sight of both eyes."

Just then, a blackbird, perched on a fence near the road, called out sharp and clear, "Pinocchio, don't listen to bad advice. You'll be sorry if you do!"

Poor little blackbird! If he had only kept his words to himself! In a twinkling the cat had pounced on him and eaten him, feathers and all. He licked his lips and pretended again to be blind.

"Poor blackbird!" said Pinocchio to the cat. "Why did you treat him like that?"

"To teach him a lesson. Next time he will keep his words to himself."

They went on, walking and talking, when suddenly the fox halted and said to the marionette, "Do you want to double your money? Do you want one hundred, a thousand, two thousand gold pieces for your miserable five?"

"I should think so! But how?"

"It is easy enough. Instead of returning home you must go with us."

"And where will you take me?"

"To the City of Simple Simons."

Pinocchio thought a while and then said firmly, "No, I don't want to go. Home is near and Papa is waiting for me." He knew, too, that if he had not been a naughty boy the day before he would not have run into the danger he had been in.

"Well, then," said the fox, "go and so much the worse for you. Between today and tomorrow your five pieces would have become two thousand."

Pinocchio stood with his mouth open. "How could they have become so many?" he asked wonderingly.

"Oh," said the fox, "I will explain that to you at once. You must know that just outside the City of Simple Simons there is a sacred field called the Field of Miracles. In this field you dig a hole and in the hole you bury a gold piece. Then you cover it with earth and water it well. In the meanwhile, during the night, the gold pieces will grow and flower. In the morning when you return to the field you will find a beautiful shrub laden with two thousand five hundred gold pieces."

"Oh, how delightful!" exclaimed Pinocchio. "I will keep two thousand for myself and make you a present of the other five hundred."

"A gift for us?" cried the fox, pretending to be insulted. "Why of course not. We do not work for gain. We work only to enrich others."

"To enrich others," repeated the cat.

"What good people," thought Pinocchio. And forgetting his father, the new coat, the A-B-C book, and all the good things he meant to do, he went off with the fox and the cat.

They walked and walked and walked until at last, dead tired, they arrived toward evening at the Inn of the Red Lobster.

"Let us stop here a while" said the fox, "to eat a bite and rest for a few hours. At midnight we'll start out again, for at dawn we must be at the Field of Miracles."

They sat down at the table but the fox and the cat said they had no appetite. The poor cat was very weak and was able to eat only thirty-five white fish with tomato sauce, four portions of tripe, and asked only three times for butter and cheese to season it.

The fox, whose doctor had ordered him to be careful with his food, contented himself with a small hare dressed with a dozen young spring chickens. After the hare he finished with a dish made of partridges, rabbits, lizards, frogs, and other dainties. That was all. He couldn't eat another bite, he said.

Pinocchio, who thought continually of the Field of Miracles, and all the money he could make for his Papa, ordered bread and walnuts and left them on his plate.

After supper they went to bed. Pinocchio was so tired he fell asleep at once and began to dream. He was in the midst of a lovely dream about vines and trees covered with gold pieces and he was just reaching out to pick them when he was suddenly awakened by a thump! thump! thump! on the door.

It was the Innkeeper who had come to tell him that midnight had struck.

"Are my companions ready?" asked the puppet.

"Indeed, yes! They left two hours ago."

"Why in such a hurry?"

"Unfortunately the cat received a telegram saying his first-born was suffering from chilblains on the feet.

"Did they pay for supper?" asked Pinocchio.

"Oh, no!" said the Innkeeper, who was in league with the fox and the cat. "When they were traveling with a gentleman, they would not think of doing so."

"Too bad! That offense would have been more than pleasing to me," said Pinocchio, scratching his head. But he had to pay one of his gold pieces for the supper he had not eaten before he set out for the Field of Miracles, where the Innkeeper said the fox and the cat would meet him.

Outside the inn it was pitch dark and still. Not a leaf stirred. But as he walked along Pinocchio noticed a tiny insect glimmering on the trunk of a tree.

"Who are you?" asked Pinocchio.

"I am the ghost of the Talking Cricket," answered the little being in a faint voice sounding as if it came from a faraway world.

"I want to give you some advice. Go back and take the gold pieces to your poor father, who is weeping because you have not returned to him."

"I am determined to go on, for tomorrow my father will be a rich man. These four gold pieces will become two thousand."

"Don't listen to those who promise you wealth overnight, my boy. As a rule they are either fools or swindlers! Listen to me. Go home."

"But I want to go on!"

"The hour is late and the road dark and dangerous!"

"I want to go on."

"Remember, then, that boys who insist on having their own way sooner or later come to grief."

"Always the same stories. Goodnight, Cricket."

"Goodnight, Pinocchio. May Heaven preserve you from dangers and from assassins."

Then the Talking Cricket vanished as suddenly as a blown-out light, and the road was again plunged in darkness.

"Truly," said Pinocchio to himself, "everybody scolds us poor boys, and

warns us and gives us advice. I've never believed in assassins. I think they were invented to make boys afraid to go out at night!"

"Even if I were to meet them on the road, what of it? I'd just run up to them and say, 'Well, Signori, what do you want? Remember you can't fool with me! Run along and mind your business.'"

Pinocchio thought he heard a slight rustle among the leaves behind him.

He turned to look and there in the darkness he saw two evil-looking figures wearing charcoal sacks. The two figures leaped toward him as softly as if they were ghosts.

Not knowing where to hide his gold pieces, he stuck all four of them under his tongue for safe-keeping. Then he tried to escape. But he had not gone a step, when he felt his arms grasped and heard two horrible deep voices say to him: "Your money or your life!"

On account of the money in his mouth, Pinocchio could only bow and make signs. He tried to make out who had seized him, but he could see only two dim figures wrapped in sacks, their eyes peering through holes in the sacks.

"Deliver up your money, or you are dead!" said the taller of the two.

"And after we have killed you, we will also kill your father."

"No, no, not my father!" cried Pinocchio wild with terror. But as he screamed the gold pieces tinkled in his mouth.

"Ah, you rascal! So that's your game. You have the money hidden under your tongue. Out with it!"

They tried to force Pinocchio's mouth open but could not. Then the smaller of the two assassins drew out an ugly knife and tried to pry Pinocchio's mouth open with it. But Pinocchio, as quick as lightning, sank his teeth deep into the assassin's hand, bit it off and spat it out. Imagine his surprise when he found it was not a hand at all, but a cat's paw!

Encouraged by his victory, Pinocchio pulled himself away, jumped the hedge, and fled swiftly across the fields, followed by the assassins at full speed. They raced for miles and when Pinocchio could run no more, he climbed to the top of a tall pine tree where the assassins could not follow him.

But they were not to be beaten by so little. They gathered a bundle of wood, piled it up beneath the tree, and set fire to it. In a moment the pine was aflame like a candle in the wind. Not wishing to end his days like a roasted pigeon, Pinocchio made a tremendous leap, and away he went across the fields with the assassins close behind him as before.

Dawn was breaking when, without any warning whatsoever, Pinocchio found his path barred by a deep pool full of water the color of muddy coffee clear across it. The assassins jumped too, but not having measured their distance —splash!!!—they fell right into the middle of the pool. Pinocchio, who heard the splash and felt it too, cried out, laughing but never stopping in his race, "A fine bath to you, gentlemen assassins!"

He thought they must surely be drowned and turned his head to see. But there they were, still following him, though their black sacks were drenched and dripping with water.

As he ran, the marionette felt more and more certain that he would have to give himself up into the hands of his pursuers. Suddenly he saw a little cottage gleaming white as snow among the trees of the forest.

"If I have enough breath left to reach that little house, I may be saved," he said to himself. And he darted through the woods, the assassins still after him.

At last, after a desperate race, he arrived, tired and out of breath at the door of the cottage. He knocked. No one answered.

In despair, Pinocchio began to kick and bang against the door. At the noise, a window opened and a lovely maiden looked out. She had azure blue hair and a face as white as a waxen image.

In a voice that seemed to come from another world, she whispered, "No one lives in this house. Everyone is dead." Then she disappeared and the window closed without a sound.

Suddenly Pinocchio felt himself seized by the collar and two powerful hands grasped him by the neck. The voices of the two assassins growled threateningly, "Now we have you!" The marionette trembled so hard that the joints of his legs rattled and the coins tinkled under his tongue.

"Will you open your mouth now, or not?" the assassins demanded. "Ah! You do not answer? Very well, this time you shall open it."

And again the two tried to remove the gold pieces from Pinocchio's mouth; but to no avail.

"I see what we must do," said one of them. "There is nothing left to do now but to hang him."

"To hang him," repeated the other.

They tied Pinocchio's arms, passed a noose round his throat, and then hung him to the branch of a giant oak tree.

Satisfied with their work, they sat on the grass waiting for Pinocchio to give his last gasp. But at the end of three hours the marionette was as alive as ever.

Losing patience, the assassins called to him mockingly, "Goodby till tomorrow. When we return please be polite enough to be quite dead." With these words they went.

Little by little, as he swung there,

the puppet's eyes began to grow dim. Hardly conscious of what he was saying, he murmured to himself: "Oh, Papa, Papa! If only you were here!" And he closed his eyes, feeling his end had come.

As poor Pinocchio seemed more dead than alive, the beautiful maiden with the blue hair once again looked at him out of her window. Filled with pity at the sight of the poor little fellow being knocked helplessly about by the wind, she clapped her hands sharply together three times.

At the signal, a large falcon came and settled on the window ledge.

"What do you command, my charming fairy?" asked the falcon, bending his neck in deep reverence (for it must be known that, after all, the Lovely Maiden with Azure Hair was a very kind fairy who had lived, for more than a thousand years, near the forest)

"Do you see that marionette hanging from the limb of that giant oak tree?"

"I see him," answered the falcon.

"Very well. I want him brought here," commanded the fairy.

In a few moments the poor little marionette was gently carried into a dainty room with mother-of-pearl walls and put to bed. The fairy, bending over him, touched Pinocchio's forehead and saw he had a high fever. She therefore dissolved a white powder in half a glass of water and offered it to him.

"Drink this," she said lovingly, "and in a few days you'll be well."

Pinocchio looked at the glass, made a

13

face, and whiningly asked, "Is it sweet or bitter?"

"It is bitter, but it is good for you."

"If it's bitter, I don't want it."

"Drink it and I'll give you a lump of sugar to take the bitter taste from your mouth."

"I want the sugar first, then I'll drink the bitter water."

"Do you promise?"

"Yes."

The fairy gave him the sugar and Pinocchio, after chewing and swallowing it in a twinkling, said, "If only sugar were medicine, I'd take it every day."

"Now keep your promise and drink these few drops," said the fairy. "They'll be good for you."

Pinocchio took the glass and stuck his nose into it.

"It's too bitter, much too bitter! I can't drink it."

"How do you know, when you haven't tasted it?"

"I can imagine it. I smell it. I want another lump of sugar, then I'll drink it."

The fairy, with all the patience of a good mother, gave him more sugar and again handed him the glass.

The marionette made more wry faces and found more excuses for not drinking the water with the medicine in it—the feather pillow on his feet bothered him—the door was half open, and others beside.

Then he burst out crying, "I won't drink this awful water, I won't, I won't, I won't!"

"My boy, you'll be sorry."

"I don't care."

"But you are so sick."

"I don't care."

"In a few hours the fever will take you far away to another world."

"I don't care. I'd rather die than drink that awful medicine."

Just then the door of the room flew open and in came four rabbits as black as ink, carrying a little bier on their shoulders.

"What do you want with me?" cried Pinocchio sitting up in bed in a great fright.

"We have come to take you," said the biggest rabbit.

"To take me? But I am not yet dead!"

"No, not yet; but you have only a few minutes to live since you have refused the medicine that would have cured you."

"Oh, my fairy," the marionette cried out, "give me that glass! Quick please! I don't want to die! No, no, not yet— not yet!" And grasping the glass, he swallowed the medicine at one gulp.

"Well," said the four rabbits, "this time we have made the trip for nothing." And turning on their heels, they marched solemnly out of the room, muttering and grumbling between their teeth.

In a twinkling, Pinocchio felt fine. With one leap he was out of bed and into his clothes, for puppets have the privilege of being seldom ill and of being cured very quickly.

The fairy, seeing him run and jump around the room gay as a bird on the wing, said to him, "My medicine was

14

good for you, after all, wasn't it?"

"Good indeed! It has given me new life. Next time I won't have to be begged so hard. I'll remember those black rabbits!"

"Now come here and tell me how it happened that you were attacked by assassins."

Tearfully Pinocchio recounted his whole fantastic tale.

"Where are the gold pieces now?" the fairy asked.

"I lost them," answered Pinocchio. But he was telling a lie for he had them in his pocket.

He had scarcely told the lie when his nose, long though it was, became at least two inches longer.

"And where did you lose them?"

"In the woods."

At this second lie, his nose grew a few more inches.

"Have no fear," said the fairy. "Everything that is lost in the woods is always found."

"Ah, now I remember," replied the marionette, becoming more and more confused. "I didn't lose them. I swallowed them when I drank the medicine."

At this third lie, his nose became longer than ever, so long that he could not even turn around. If he turned to the right, he knocked it against the bed or into the windowpanes. If he turned to the left, he struck the wall or the door. If he raised it a bit, he almost put the fairy's eyes out.

The fairy looked at him and laughed.

"Why are you laughing?" Pinocchio asked her, worried now at the sight of his growing nose.

"I am laughing at the lies you are telling. Lies, my dear boy, are of two sorts. There are lies with short legs and lies with long noses. Yours, just now, happen to have long noses."

Pinocchio, not knowing where to hide his shame, tried to run out of the room, but his nose had grown so much that he could not get it out of the door.

To teach him a lesson, the fairy let Pinocchio cry and roar for a while over the plight of his silly nose. No matter how he tried, it would not go through the door. But when she thought he might have learned his lesson, and would stop telling lies, she began to feel sorry for him; so she clapped her hands together.

In a few moments a thousand woodpeckers flew in through the window and settled themselves on Pinocchio's nose. They pecked and pecked so hard at that enormous nose that soon it was reduced to its normal size.

"How good you are, my fairy," said Pinocchio drying his eyes, "and how much I love you!"

"I love you, too," answered the fairy, "and I want you to stay here with me."

"I'd love to stay, but what about my poor father?"

"I have thought of that. Your father has been sent for and he will be here tonight."

"Really?" shouted Pinocchio joyfully. "Then with your consent, I should like to go and meet him. I can't wait to kiss that dear old man who has suffered so much for my sake."

"Go then," said the fairy. "But be careful not to lose your way. Take the wood path and you'll surely meet him."

Pinocchio set out, and as soon as he found himself in the wood, he ran like a hare. But when he reached the great oak tree he stopped, for he thought he heard a rustle in the bushes. He was right. There stood the fox and the cat, the two traveling companions he had eaten with at the Inn of the Red Lobster.

"Why, here is our dear Pinocchio!" cried the fox embracing him. "We have been looking high and low for you. How did you happen here?"

"How did *you* happen here?" repeated the cat.

"It is a long story," said Pinocchio. "Let me tell it to you. The other night, when you left me alone at the Inn, I met the assassins on the road—"

"The assassins? Oh, my poor friend! And what did they want?"

"They wanted my gold pieces."

"Rascals!" said the fox.

"The worst sort of rascals!" added the cat.

"But I began to run," continued Pinocchio, "and they ran after me, until they overtook me and hanged me to the limb of that oak."

Pinocchio pointed to the giant oak near by.

"Could anything be worse?" said the fox.

"What an awful world to live in! Where shall we find a safe place for respectable people like ourselves?"

As the fox was talking, Pinocchio noticed that the cat carried his right paw in a sling.

"What happened to your paw?" asked Pinocchio.

The cat tried to answer, but he became so terribly twisted and confused in his speech that the fox had to help him out.

"My friend is too modest to answer. I'll answer for him. About an hour ago, we met an old wolf on the road. He was half starved and begged for help. Having nothing to give him, what do you think my friend did out of kindness of his heart? With his teeth he bit off the paw of his front foot and threw it at that poor beast, so that he might have something to eat."

As he spoke, the fox wiped away a tear.

Pinocchio, almost in tears himself, whispered in the cat's ear, "If all the cats were like you, how lucky the mice would be!"

"And now," said the fox, "what are you doing here?"

"I am waiting for my father, who will be here soon."

"And your gold pieces?"

"I have them in my pocket, all but the one I spent at the Inn of the Red Lobster."

"To think that those four gold pieces might become two thousand! Why don't you listen to me? Why don't you sow them in the Field of Miracles?"

"Today it is impossible. I'll go with you some other time."

"Another day will be too late," said the fox.

"Why?"

"Because that field has been bought by a very rich man, and today is the last day that it will be open to the public. After tomorrow no one will be allowed to bury money there."

"How far is this Field of Miracles?"

"Only two miles away. Will you come with us? We'll be there in half an hour. You can sow the money, and after a few minutes you will gather your two thousand coins and return home rich. Are you coming?"

Pinocchio thought of the good fairy, of old Geppetto, and of the warnings of the Talking Cricket; so he hesitated a little before answering. Then he ended by doing what all boys do when they have no heart and no sense: he shrugged his shoulders and said to the fox and the cat, "Let us go! I will come with you."

They walked and walked for a half a day at least and at last they came to the town called the City of Simple Simons. As soon as they entered the town, Pinocchio noticed that all the streets were filled with hairless dogs yawning with hunger, sheared sheep trembling with cold, cocks whose combs had been cut, large butterflies unable to use their wings because they had sold all their lovely colors, peacocks without tails and ashamed to show themselves, and pheasants grieving for their bright feathers of gold and silver now lost to them forever.

Through this starving crowd of paupers and beggars, a lordly carriage would pass now and then. Within it sat either a fox, a hawk, or a vulture.

The three companions crossed this miserable town, and on the other side they came to a lonely field, which looked more or less like any other field.

"Here we are," said the fox to Pinocchio. "Dig a hole here and put your gold pieces into it."

The marionette obeyed. He dug the hole, put the four gold pieces into it, and covered them up very carefully.

"Now," said the fox, "go to that nearby brook, bring back a pail of water, and sprinkle it over the spot."

Pinocchio followed the directions closely, but, as he had no pail, he pulled off his shoe, filled it with water, and sprinkled the earth which covered the gold. Then he asked, "Is there anything else to be done?"

"Nothing else," answered the fox. "Now we can go. Return in about twenty minutes and you will find the shrub already grown and the branches filled with gold pieces."

Pinocchio, beside himself with joy, thanked his benefactors a thousand times and promised the fox and the cat beautiful presents.

"We wish for no presents," answered the two rogues. "It is enough for us that we have helped you to become rich with little or no trouble. For this we are as happy as kings."

With that they said goodby to Pinocchio, and wishing him good luck, went on their way. Meanwhile Pinocchio walked impatiently to and fro and finally turned his nose toward the

ter above his head. Looking up, he saw a large parrot on a tree, busily preening its feathers.

"What are you laughing at?" Pinocchio asked.

"I am laughing because when I preened my feathers I tickled myself under the wings."

The marionette did not answer. He walked to the brook, filled his shoe with water, and once more sprinkled the ground. He was interrupted by mocking laughter from the parrot.

"Once for all," shouted Pinocchio in a rage, "may I know, Mr. Parrot, what amuses you so?"

"I am laughing at those fools who believe everything they hear and who allow themselves to be caught so easily in the traps people set for them."

Field of Miracles.

As he walked with hurried steps, his heart beat in an excited tick tock, tick tock, just as if it were a wall clock, and his busy brain kept thinking, "Suppose I should find five thousand gold pieces, or ten thousand, or a hundred thousand? I'll build myself a beautiful palace, that has a thousand stables filled with wooden horses for me to play with, a cellar overflowing with lemonade and ice cream soda, and a library of candies, cakes, fruits, and cookies."

While thus delighting in his fancies, he came to the Field of Miracles. There he stopped to see if there was a vine filled with gold coins in sight. But he saw nothing! He took a few steps forward, and still nothing! He ran up to the spot where he had dug the hole and buried the gold pieces. Again nothing!

And there he stood staring at the spot when he heard a hearty burst of laugh-

"Do you, perhaps, mean me?"

"I certainly do mean you, poor Pinocchio—you who are such a little silly as to believe that gold can be sown and gathered in the fields just like beans or squash. I have learned from sad experience that to come by money honestly one must work and earn it with hand or brain."

"I don't know what you're talking about," said Pinocchio who was beginning to tremble with fear.

"Too bad! I'll explain myself better," said the parrot. "While you were out of sight the fox and the cat returned here, dug up the four gold pieces you had buried, and fled like the wind."

Pinocchio stared at the parrot with his mouth wide open. He would not believe the parrot's words, and began to dig away furiously at the earth. He dug and dug until he had made a huge hole, but no money was there.

In desperation, he ran to the city and went straight to the courthouse to report the robbery to the magistrate.

The judge was a large old gorilla with a flowing beard covering his chest. Standing before him, Pinocchio told his pitiful tale. He gave the names and descriptions of the two knaves who had robbed him and begged for justice.

The judge listened patiently. He became very much interested in the story and he almost wept. When the marionette had no more to say, the judge rang a bell.

At the sound, two large mastiff dogs appeared, dressed in police uniforms.

Pointing to Pinocchio, the judge said solemnly, "This poor simpleton has been robbed. Take him, therefore, and throw him into prison."

The marionette, on hearing this sentence passed upon him, was thoroughly stunned. He tried to protest, but the two officers stopped his mouth and hustled him away to jail.

There he had to remain for four long weary months. And if it had not been for a very lucky chance, he probably would have had to stay even longer.

For it happened that the young emperor who ruled over the City of Simple Simons had won a splendid victory over his enemies. To celebrate, he had ordered great public rejoicings with displays of fireworks, and commanded that all the prisons should be opened and all the prisoners freed.

"If the others go, I go too," said Pinocchio to the jailer.

"Not you," answered the jailer. "You do not belong to the fortunate class—"

"I beg your pardon," interrupted Pinocchio. "I, too, am a criminal."

"In that case you also are free," said the jailer. Taking off his cap, he bowed low and opened the door of the prison. Pinocchio ran out and away, and you may be sure that he never gave the place a backward look.

—*Abridged excerpt*

Out in the Fields with God

By Elizabeth Barrett Browning

The little cares that fretted me,
    I lost them yesterday
Among the fields, above the sea,
    Among the winds at play,
Among the lowing of the herds,
    The rustling of the trees,
Among the singing of the birds,
    The humming of the bees.

The foolish fears of what may pass,
    I cast them all away
Among the clover-scented grass,
    Among the new-mown hay,
Among the rustling of the corn,
    Where drowsy poppies nod,
Where ill thoughts die and good are born—
    Out in the fields with God.

Flower in the Crannied Wall

By Alfred Tennyson

Flower in the crannied wall,
I pluck you out of the crannies,
I hold you here, root and all, in my hand,
Little flower—but if I could understand
What you are, root and all, and all in all,
I should know what God and man is.

My Garden

By Thomas Edward Brown

A garden is a lovesome thing, God wot!
    Rose plot,
    Fringed pool,
Ferned grot—
    The veriest school
    Of peace; and yet the fool
Contends that God is not.
Not God! in gardens when the eve is cool?
    Nay, but I have a sign;
    'Tis very sure God walks in mine.

Heidi at the Alm-Uncle's Hut

From HEIDI

By Johanna Spyri

When we tell you that HEIDI is a book about the beauty of the Swiss Alps, about a little girl's feelings of joy in life and of prayer and thanksgiving to God, about an embittered old man and some skittish mountain goats and a goatherd boy and an invalid girl and a mean old governess—when we have said all this, all of it true, we have still not explained the enormous popularity of Johanna Spyri's HEIDI.

Three generations of children have read this book—originally written in German—and probably no other story for children has been so dearly loved by so many. Why? It must be because Heidi herself finds so much joy in life and because she is so kind and patient and loving to others that our hearts go out to her in love and sympathy.

Any child who has ever read HEIDI will feel at home in Switzerland. If you ever go there, you will find yourself listening for goat-bells, looking for the frisky goats, and hoping to find, on the mountains rosy with sunset, the lovely little girl who was Heidi.

UP THE MOUNTAIN TO THE ALM-UNCLE'S HUT

FROM the old and pleasantly situated village of Mayenfeld, a footpath winds through green and shady meadows to the foot of the mountains, which on this side look down from their stern and lofty heights upon the valley below. The land grows gradually wilder as the path ascends, and the climber has not gone far before he begins to inhale the fragrance of the short grass and sturdy mountain plants, for the way is steep and leads directly up to the summits above.

On a clear sunny morning in June two figures might be seen climbing the narrow mountain path. One was a tall strong-looking young woman named Dete, the other a little girl called Heidi whom Dete was leading by the hand. Heidi's cheeks were so aglow with heat that the crimson color could be seen even through the dark, sun-burned skin. And this was hardly to be wondered at, for in spite of the hot June

sun the child was clothed as if to keep off the bitterest frost. She did not look more than five years old, if as much, but what her natural figure was like, it would have been hard to say, for she had on apparently two, if not three dresses, one above the other, and over these a thick red woollen shawl wound round about her, so that the little body presented a shapeless appearance. With her small feet shod in thick nailed mountain shoes, the child slowly and laboriously plodded her way up in the heat.

The two must have left the valley a good hour's walk behind them, when they came to the village known as Dorfli, which is situated half-way up the mountain. Here the wayfarers met with greetings from all sides, some calling to them from windows, some from open doors, others from outside, for the young woman was now in her old home. She did not, however, pause in her walk to respond to her friends' welcoming cries and questions, but passed on without stopping for a moment until she reached the last of the scattered houses of the hamlet. Here a voice called to her, "Wait a moment, Dete. If you are going up higher, I will come with you."

Dete stood still, and Heidi immediately let go her hand and seated herself on the ground.

"Are you tired, Heidi?" asked her companion.

"No, I am hot," answered the child.

"We shall soon get to the top now. If you walk bravely on a little longer, and take good long steps, we shall be there in another hour," said Dete in an encouraging voice.

They were now joined by a stout, good-natured-looking woman. "And where are you off with the child?" she asked Dete. "I suppose it is the child your sister left?"

"Yes," answered Dete. "I am taking her to her grandfather's. He lives up on the Alm where she must stay."

"Up there with that man they call the Alm-Uncle! You must be out of your senses, Dete! How can you think of such a thing! The old man, however, will soon send you and the child back home again!"

"He cannot very well do that, seeing that he is her grandfather. He must do something for her. I have had the charge of the child till now, and I can tell you, I am not going to give up the chance that has just come to me of getting a good job. It is for the grandfather now to do his duty by her."

"That would all be very well if he were like other people," said Dete's friend, Barbel. "But you know what he is like. And what can he do with a child, especially with one so young? The child cannot possibly live with him. But where are you thinking of going yourself?"

"To Frankfurt, where a good job awaits me," answered Dete.

"I should very much like to know," continued Barbel, "what the old man has on his conscience that he looks as he does and lives up there on the mountain like a hermit, hardly ever allowing himself to be seen. All kinds of things are said about him." Barbel put her arm through Dete's in a confidential sort of way, and said, "I know I can find out the real truth from you, and the meaning of these tales that are afloat about him. I believe you know the whole story. Now do just tell me what is wrong with the old man."

"How can I possibly tell you about him? I am only twenty-six and he is at least seventy. So you can hardly expect me to know much about his youth."

Dete stopped for a moment and looked back to make sure that Heidi was in sight. But the child was nowhere to be seen, and must have turned aside from following her companions some time before, while these were too occupied with their conversation to notice it. Dete looked around her in all directions. The footpath wound a little here and there, but could still be seen along its whole length nearly to Dorfli. No one, however, was visible upon it at this moment.

"I see where she is," exclaimed Barbel, "look over there!" and she pointed to a spot far away from the footpath. "She is climbing up that slope with the goatherd and his goats. I wonder why he is so late to-day bringing them up. Now do tell me more, Dete, about the Alm-Uncle."

"Well," Dete went on. "I *do* know that the old man has nothing now beyond his two goats, and his hut, though he was once owner of a large farm. But at that time nothing could please him but to play the grand gentleman and go driving about the country and mixing with bad company, strangers that nobody knew. He gambled away the whole of his property. Having nothing now left to him but his bad name, he disappeared. Nothing more was heard of him for twelve or fifteen years. At the end of that time he reappeared, bringing with him a young boy, his son, whom he tried to place with some of his people. Every door, however, was shut in his face, for no one wished to have any more to do with him. He could not have been entirely without money, for he apprenticed his son, Tobias, to a carpenter. Tobias was a steady lad, and kindly received by everyone in Dorfli. The old man was, however, still looked upon with suspicion. It was even rumored that he had killed a man in some brawl. We, however, did not refuse to acknowledge our relationship with him, my great-grandmother on my mother's side having been sister to his grandmother. So we called him Uncle and since he went to live on the mountainside he has been called by the name of Alm-Uncle."

"And what happened to Tobias?" asked Barbel, who was listening with deep interest.

"Tobias was taught his trade in Mels, and when he had served his apprenticeship he came back to Dorfli and married my sister, Adelaide. They had always been fond of one another, and they got on very well together after they were married. But their happiness did not last long. Tobias died only two years after their marriage. A beam fell on him as he was working, and killed him on the spot. My sister was so overcome with horror and grief that she fell into a fever from which she never recovered. And so two months after Tobias had been carried to the grave, his wife followed him.

"Their sad fate was the talk of everybody and the general opinion was that it was a punishment which the Uncle had deserved for the godless life he had led. All at once we heard that he had gone to live up the Alm and did not intend ever to come down again."

"And are you going to give this child over to such a man?" asked Barbel, in a voice of reproach.

"What do you mean?" retorted Dete. "I have done my duty by the child. What would you have me do with her now? I certainly cannot take a child of five with me to Frankfurt. But where are you going yourself, Barbel? We are now half-way up the Alm."

"We have just reached the place I wanted," answered Barbel: "I have something to say to the goatherd's wife, who does some spinning for me in the winter. So good-bye, Dete, and good luck to you!"

Dete shook hands with her friend and remained standing while Barbel went toward a small, dark brown hut, which stood a few steps away from the path in a hollow that afforded it some protection from the wind. The hut was situated half-way up the Alm Mountain from Dorfli, and it was so broken down and dilapidated that it must have been very unsafe to live in. When the stormy south wind came sweeping over the mountain, everything inside it, doors and windows, shook and rattled, and all the rotten old beams creaked and trembled. On such days as this, had the goatherd's dwelling been standing above on the exposed mountainside, it could not have escaped being blown straight down into the valley without a moment's warning.

Here lived Peter, the eleven-year-old boy, who every morning went down the mountainside to the village of Dorfli, to fetch his goats and drive them up to the mountain, where they would be free to browse till evening on the delicious mountain plants.

Then Peter, with his light-footed animals, would go running and leaping down the mountain again till he reached Dorfli, and there he would give a shrill whistle through his fingers, whereupon all the owners of the goats would come out to fetch home the animals that belonged to them. It was generally the small boys and girls who ran in answer to Peter's whistle for they were not afraid of the gentle goats, and this was the only hour of the day, through all the summer months, that Peter had any opportunity of seeing his young friends, since the rest of his time was spent alone with the goats.

Peter had a mother and a blind grandmother at home, it is true, but he was always obliged to start off very early in the morning, and only got home late in the evening from Dorfli, for he always stayed as long as he could talking and playing with the other children. He had just time enough at home to swallow down his bread and milk in the morning and again in the evening to get through a similar meal, lie down in bed, and go to sleep. His father, who had been also known as the goatherd, having earned his living as such when younger, had been accidentally killed while cutting wood some years before. His mother, whose real name was Brigitta, was always called the goatherd's wife, for the sake of old association, while the blind grandmother was just "Grandmother" to all the old and young in the neighborhood.

Dete had been standing for a good ten minutes looking about her in every direction for some sign of the children and the goats. Not a glimpse of them, however, was to be seen, so she climbed to a higher spot to get a fuller view of the mountain as it sloped beneath her to the valley. With ever increasing anxiety she continued to scan the surrounding slopes. Meanwhile the children were climbing up by a far and roundabout way, for Peter knew many spots where all kinds of good food, in the shape of shrubs and plants, grew for his goats, and he was in the habit of leading his flock aside from the beaten track. Heidi, exhausted with the heat and weight of her thick armor of clothes, panted and struggled after him at first with some difficulty. She said nothing, but her eyes kept watching first Peter, as he sprang nimbly hither and thither on his bare feet, clad only in his short light breeches, and then the slim-legged goats that went leaping over rocks and shrubs and up the steep places with even greater ease.

Heidi all at once sat down on the ground, and as fast as her little fingers could move, began pulling off her shoes and stockings. This done she rose, unwound the hot red shawl and threw it away, and then proceeded to undo her frock. It was off in a second, but there was still another to unfasten, for Dete had put the Sunday frock on over the everyday one, to save the trouble of carrying it. Quick as lightning the everyday frock followed the other, and now the child stood up, clad only in her light short-sleeved under garment, stretching out her little bare arms with glee. She put all her clothes together in a tidy little heap, and then went jumping and climbing up after Peter and the goats as nimbly as any of the party.

Peter had taken no heed of what Heidi was about when she stayed behind, but when she ran up to him in her new attire, his face broke into a grin, which grew broader still as he looked back and saw the small heap of clothes lying on the ground. He said nothing, however. The child, able now to move at her ease, began to enter into conversation with Peter, who had many questions to answer, for his companion wanted to know how many goats he had, where he was going with them, and what he had to do when he arrived there.

At last, after some time, they and the goats approached the hut and came within view of Dete. Hardly had she caught sight of them climbing up toward her when she shrieked, "Heidi, what have you been doing! What a sight you have made of yourself! And where are your two frocks and the red wrapper? And the new shoes I bought, and the new stockings I knitted for you—everything gone! Not a thing left! What can you have been thinking of, Heidi; where are all your clothes?"

The child quietly pointed to a spot below on the mountainside and answered, "Down there."

Dete, following the direction of her finger,

could just distinguish something lying on the ground, with a spot of red on the top of it which she had no doubt was the woollen wrapper.

"You good-for-nothing little thing!" exclaimed Dete angrily, "what could have put it into your head to do like that? What made you undress yourself? What do you mean by it?"

"I don't want the clothes," said the child, not showing any sign of repentance.

"You wretched, thoughtless child! Have you no sense in you at all?" continued Dete. "Who is going all that way down to fetch them? It's a good half-hour's walk! Peter, you go off and fetch them for me as quickly as you can, and don't stand there gaping at me, as if you were rooted to the ground!"

"I am already past my time," answered Peter slowly, without moving from the spot where he had been standing with his hands in his pockets, listening to Dete's outburst of anger.

"Well, you won't get far if you only keep on standing there with your eyes staring out of your head," was Dete's cross reply. "But see, you shall have something nice," and she held out a bright new piece of money to him that sparkled in the sun.

Peter was immediately up and off down the steep mountainside, taking the shortest cut, and in an amazingly short space of time he was back again.

Dete was obliged to give him a word of praise as she handed him the promised money. Peter promptly thrust it into his pocket and his face beamed with delight, for it was not often that he was the happy possessor of such riches.

"You can carry the things up for me as far as the grandfather's, as you are going the same way," went on Dete, who was preparing to continue her climb up the mountainside.

Peter willingly undertook to do this, and followed after her on his bare feet, with his left arm round the bundle and the right swinging his goatherd's stick, while Heidi and the goats went skipping and jumping joyfully beside him.

After a climb of more than three-quarters of an hour they reached the top of Alm mountain. The Alm-Uncle's hut stood on a projection of the rock, exposed to the winds, but where every ray of sun could rest upon it, and a full view could be had of the valley beneath. Behind the hut stood three old fir trees, with long, thick, branches. Beyond these rose a further wall of mountain, the lower heights still overgrown with beautiful grass and plants.

Against the hut, on the side toward the valley, the old man had put a seat. Here he was sitting, his pipe in his mouth and his hands on his knees, quietly looking out, when the children, the goats, and Dete suddenly clambered into view. Heidi was at the top first. She went straight up to the old man, put out her hand, and said, "Good-evening, Grandfather."

"Well, well, what is the meaning of this?" he asked gruffly, as he gave the child an abrupt shake of the hand, and gazed long and scrutinizingly at her from under his bushy eyebrows. Heidi stared steadily back at him without winking, for the grandfather, with his long beard and thick gray eyebrows that grew together over his nose and looked just like a bush, had such a remarkable appearance that Heidi could not take her eyes off him.

Meanwhile Dete had come up, with Peter who stood still to see what would happen.

"I wish you good day," said Dete, as she walked toward the old man, "and I have brought you Tobias' and Adelaide's child. You will probably not recognize her, as you have not seen her since she was a year old."

"And what has the child to do with me up here?" asked the old man curtly. "You there," he then called out to Peter, "be off with your goats. You are none too early as it is; and take mine with you."

Peter obeyed promptly and ran off, for the old man had given him a look that made him feel that he did not want to stay any longer.

"The child is here to remain with you," Dete answered. "I have, I think, done my duty by her for these four years, and now it is time for you to do yours."

"That's it, is it?" said the old man, as he looked at her with a flash of his eye. "And when the child begins to fret and whine after you, as is the way with these unreasonable little beings, what am I to do with her then?"

"That's your affair," retorted Dete. "I know I had to put up with her without complaint when she was left on my hands as an infant, and with enough to do as it was for my mother and self. Now I have to go and look after my own earnings, and you are the child's nearest relative. If you cannot arrange to keep her, do whatever you like with her. But you will have to answer for her if anything should happen to her, though you hardly need, I should think, add to the burden already on your conscience."

Now Dete was not quite easy in her own conscience about what she was doing; feeling hot and irritable, she had said more

27

than she intended. At her last words, Uncle rose from his seat. He looked at her in a way that made her draw back a step or two, then flinging out his arm, he said to her in a commanding voice. "Hurry and get back to where you came from and do not let me see your face again around here!"

Dete did not wait to be told twice. "Goodbye to you then, and to you too, Heidi," she called, as she turned quickly away and started to go down the mountain.

AT HOME WITH GRANDFATHER

As soon as Dete had gone, the old man went back to his bench, and there he remained seated, staring at the ground without uttering a sound, while thick curls of smoke floated up from his pipe. Heidi, meanwhile, was enjoying herself in her new surroundings. She looked about until she found a shed, built against the hut, where the goats were kept; she peeped in, and saw it was empty. She continued her search and soon came to the fir trees behind the hut. A strong breeze was blowing through them, and there was a rushing and roaring in their topmost branches. Heidi stood still and listened. The sound growing fainter, she went on again, to the farther corner of the hut, and so round to where her grandfather was sitting. Seeing that he was in exactly the same position as when she left him, she went and placed herself in front of the old man, and putting her hands behind her back, stood and gazed at him.

Her grandfather looked up, and seeing the child standing motionless before him he asked, "What are you going to do now?"

"I want to see what you have inside the house," said Heidi.

"Come then!" And her grandfather rose and went before her toward the hut.

"Bring your bundle of clothes in with you," he told her.

"I shan't want them any more," was her prompt answer.

The old man turned and looked searchingly at the child, whose dark eyes were sparkling in expectation of what she was going to see inside. "She is certainly not stupid," he murmured to himself. "And why shall you not want them any more?" he asked aloud.

"Because I want to go about like the goats with their thin light legs."

"Well, you can do so if you like," said her grandfather. "But bring the things in; we must put them in the cupboard."

Heidi did as she was told. The old man now opened the door and Heidi stepped inside after him. She found herself in a good-sized room, which covered the whole ground floor of the hut. There were a table and a chair and in one corner stood the grandfather's bed. In another was the hearth with a large kettle hanging above it; and on the other side was a large door in the wall— this was the cupboard. The grandfather opened it. Inside were his clothes, some hanging up, others, a couple of shirts, and some socks and handkerchiefs, lying on a shelf. On a second shelf were some plates and cups and glasses, and on a higher one still, a round loaf, smoked meat, and cheese, for everything that the grandfather needed for his food and clothing was kept in this cupboard.

As soon as the cupboard was opened, Heidi ran quickly forward and thrust in her bundle of clothes, as far behind her grandfather's things as possible, so that they might not easily be found again. She then looked carefully round the room, and asked, "Where am I to sleep, Grandfather?"

"Wherever you like," he answered.

Heidi was delighted. She began to examine all the nooks and corners to find out where it would be pleasantest to sleep. In the corner near her grandfather's bed she saw a short ladder against the wall. Heidi climbed up the ladder and found herself in the hayloft. There lay a large heap of fresh sweet-smelling hay, and through a round window in the wall there was a far-stretching and splendid view over the valley.

"Here's where I would like to sleep, Grandfather," she called down to him. "It's lovely up here. Come up and see."

"Oh, I know all about it," he called up in answer.

"I am getting the bed ready now," Heidi called down again, as she went busily to and fro at her work, "but I shall want you to bring me up a sheet."

"All right," said her grandfather, and he went to the cupboard. After rummaging about inside for a few minutes he drew out a long, coarse piece of cloth, which was all he had for a sheet. He carried it up to the loft, where he found Heidi had already made quite a nice bed. She had put an extra heap of hay at one end for a pillow, and had arranged it so that, when she was in bed, she would be able to see comfortably out through the round window.

"That is fine," said her grandfather. "Now we must put on the sheet, but wait a moment first." He went and fetched another large bundle of hay to make the bed thicker, so that the child should not feel the hard floor under her and said, "There, now bring it here."

Heidi had got hold of the sheet, but it was almost too heavy for her to carry. This was a good thing, however, as the close thick cloth would prevent the sharp stalks of the hay from pricking her. The two together now spread the sheet over the bed, and where it was too long or too wide, Heidi quickly tucked it in under the hay. It looked now as tidy and comfortable a bed as you could wish for, and Heidi stood gazing thoughtfully at her handiwork.

"We have forgotten one thing more, Grandfather," she said after a short silence.

"What's that?" he asked.

"A quilt. When you get into bed, you have to creep in between the sheet and the quilt."

"Oh, that's the way, is it? But suppose I have not got a quilt?" said the old man.

"Well, never mind, Grandfather," said Heidi in a consoling tone of voice, "I can take some more hay to put over me," and she was turning quickly to fetch another armful from the heap, when her grandfather stopped her. "Wait a moment," he said, and he climbed down the ladder again and went toward his bed. He returned to the loft with a large, thick sack, made of flax, which he threw down, exclaiming, "There, that is better than hay, isn't it?"

Heidi began tugging away at the sack with all her little might, in her efforts to get it smooth and straight, but her small hands were not fitted for so heavy a job. Her grandfather came to her aid, and when they had got it tidily spread over the bed, it all looked so nice and warm and comfortable that Heidi stood gazing at it in delight. "That is a splendid quilt," she said, "and the bed looks lovely altogether! I wish it were night, so that I might get right in it."

"I think we might have something to eat first," said her grandfather. "What do you think?"

Heidi in the excitement of bed-making had forgotten everything else. But now she felt terribly hungry, for she had had nothing to eat since the piece of bread and little cup of thin coffee that had been her breakfast early that morning before starting on her long, hot journey. So she answered quickly, "Yes, I think so too."

"Let us go down then, as we both think alike," said the old man, and he followed the child down the ladder. Then he went up to the hearth, pushed the big kettle aside, and drew forward the little one that was hanging on the chain. And then, sitting on the round-topped, three-legged stool before the fire, he blew it up into a clear bright flame. The kettle soon began to boil. Meanwhile the old man held a large piece of cheese on a long iron fork over the fire, turning it round and round till it was toasted a nice golden yellow. Heidi watched all that was going on with eager curiosity. Suddenly some new idea came to her, for she turned and ran to the cupboard, and then began going busily back and forth. Presently the Grandfather came to the table with a jug and the cheese, and there he saw it already tidily laid with the round loaf of bread and two plates and two knives each in its right place. Heidi had noticed that morning all that there was in the cupboard, and she knew which things would be wanted.

"Ah, that's right," said her grandfather. "I am glad you have some ideas of your own." And as he spoke he laid the toasted cheese on the bread. "But there is still something missing."

Heidi looked at the jug that was steaming away invitingly, and ran quickly back to the cupboard. At first she could only see a small bowl left on the shelf, but a moment later she caught sight of two glasses farther back, and she quickly returned with these and the bowl and put them down on the table.

"Good, I see you know how to set about things. But where are you going to sit?" Her grandfather himself was sitting on the only chair in the room. Heidi flew to the hearth, and dragging the three-legged stool up to the table, sat down.

"Well, you have managed to find a seat for yourself, I see, only rather a low one I am afraid," said her grandfather. "But you would not be tall enough to reach the table even if you sat in my chair. Now it is time to have something to eat, so come along."

With that he stood up, filled the bowl with milk, and placing it on the chair, pushed it in front of Heidi on her little three-legged stool, so that she now had a table to herself. Then he brought her a large slice of bread and a piece of the golden cheese, and told her to eat. After that he went and sat down on the corner of the table and began his own meal. Heidi lifted the bowl with both hands and drank without stopping for she was very thirsty after her long hot journey. Then she drew a deep breath and put down the bowl.

"Was the milk nice?" asked her grandfather.

"I never drank such good milk before," answered Heidi.

"Then you must have some more," said the old man and he filled her bowl again to the brim and set it before the child. Heidi was now hungrily beginning her bread, having first spread it with the cheese, which was soft as butter after having been toasted. The two together tasted delicious, and the child looked the picture of content as she sat eating.

When they had finished eating, grandfather went outside to put the goat shed in order, and Heidi watched with interest while he first swept it out, and then put fresh straw for the goats to sleep upon. Then he went to the little woodshed, and there he cut some long round sticks, and a small round board. In this he bored some holes and stuck the sticks into them, and there, as if made by magic, was a three-legged stool just like her grandfather's, only higher. Heidi stood and looked at it, speechless with astonishment.

"What do you think that is?" asked her grandfather.

"It's my stool, I know, because it is such a high one; and it was made all in a minute," said the child.

"She understands what she sees, her eyes are in the right place," remarked her grandfather to himself. Then he went round the hut, knocking in a nail here and there. Heidi followed him step by step, her eyes attentively taking in all he did, and everything he did interested her.

And so the time passed happily on till evening. Then the wind began to roar louder than ever through the old fir trees. Heidi listened with delight to the sound, and it filled her heart so full of gladness that she skipped and danced round the old trees joyously. Her grandfather stood and watched her from the shed.

Suddenly they heard a shrill whistle. Heidi paused in her dancing, and her grandfather came out. Down from the heights above, the goats came springing one after another, with Peter in their midst. Heidi sprang forward with a cry of joy and rushed among the flock, greeting first one and then another of her friends, for she had met them earlier that day. As they neared the hut the goats stood still, and then two of the beautiful slender animals, one white and one brown, ran straight to the old man and began licking his hands, for he was holding a little salt which he always had ready for his goats on their return home.

Peter disappeared with the remainder of his flock. Heidi tenderly stroked the two goats in turn, running first to one side of them and then the other, and jumping about in her glee at the pretty little animals.

"Are they ours, Grandfather? Are they both ours? Are you going to put them in the shed? Will they always stay with us?"

Heidi's questions came tumbling out one after the other, so that her grandfather had only time to answer each of them with "Yes, yes." When the goats had finished licking up the salt her grandfather told her to go and fetch her bowl and the bread.

Heidi obeyed and was soon back again. Her grandfather milked the white goat and filled her basin, and then breaking off a piece of bread, "Now eat your supper," he said, "and then go up to bed. Cousin Dete left another little bundle for you with a nightgown and other small things in it, which you will find at the bottom of the cupboard if you want them. I must go up and shut up the goats, so be off and sleep well."

"Good night, Grandfather! Good night. What are their names, Grandfather?" she called.

"The white one is named Little Swan, and the brown one Little Bear," answered the grandfather.

"Good night, Little Swan. Good night, Little Bear!" she called again at the top of her voice, for they were already inside the shed. Then she sat down on the seat and began to eat and drink, but the wind was so strong that it almost blew her away; so she hurried to finish her supper and then went indoors and climbed up to her bed, where she was soon lying as sweetly and soundly asleep as any young princess on her couch of silk.

Not long after, and while it was still twilight, her grandfather also went to bed, for he was up every morning at sunrise, and the sun came climbing up over the mountains at a very early hour during these summer months. The wind blew with such force during the night that the hut trembled and the old beams groaned and creaked. It came howling and wailing down the chimney like voices of those in pain, and raged with such fury among the old fir trees that here and there a branch was snapped and fell.

In the middle of the night the old man got up. "The child will be frightened," he murmured half aloud. He mounted the ladder and went and stood by Heidi's bed.

Outside the moon was struggling with the fast driving clouds, which at one moment left it clear and shining, and the next swept over it, and all again was dark. Just now the moonlight was falling through the round window straight onto Heidi's bed. She lay under the heavy quilt, her cheeks rosy with sleep, her head peacefully resting on her little round arm, and with a happy expression on her face as if dreaming of something pleasant. The old man stood looking down at her until the moon again disappeared behind the clouds and he could see no more. Then he went back to bed.

OUT WITH THE GOATS

Heidi was awakened early the next morning by a loud whistle. The sun was shining through the round window and falling in golden rays on her bed and on the large heap of hay. As she opened her eyes everything in the loft seemed gleaming with gold. She looked around her in astonishment and could not imagine for a while where she was. But she soon heard her grandfather's deep voice outside, and then Heidi recalled how she had come away from her former home and was now on the mountain with her grandfather.

She felt very happy as she remembered all the many new things that she had seen the day before and which she would see again that day, and above all she thought with delight of the two goats. Heidi jumped out of bed and dressed quickly. Then she climbed down the ladder and ran outside the hut.

There stood Peter with his flock of goats, and grandfather was just bringing his two out of the shed to join the others. Heidi ran forward to wish good morning to him and the goats.

"Do you want to go with them to the mountain?" asked her grandfather. Heidi jumped for joy.

"But you must first wash and make yourself tidy. The sun that shines so brightly overhead will laugh at you for being dirty. See, I have everything ready for you," and her grandfather pointed to a large tub full of water, which stood in the sun before the door.

Heidi ran to it and began splashing and rubbing till she quite glistened with cleanliness. Her grandfather meanwhile went inside the hut, calling to Peter to follow him and bring in his wallet. Peter obeyed with astonishment, and laid down the little bag which held his meager dinner.

"Open it," said the old man, and inside it he put a large piece of bread and an equally large piece of cheese, which made Peter open his eyes, for each was twice the size of the two portions which he had for his own dinner.

"There, now there is only a little milk to add," continued Heidi's grandfather. "You must milk two bowlfuls for her when she has her dinner, for she is going with you and will remain with you till you return this evening. Take care she does not fall over any of the rocks!"

Heidi now came running in. "Will the sun laugh at me now, Grandfather?" she asked anxiously. Her grandfather had left a coarse towel hanging up for her near the tub, and with this she had so thoroughly scrubbed her face, arms and neck, for fear of the sun, that as she stood there she was as red as a lobster. He gave a little laugh.

"No, there is nothing for him to laugh at now," he assured her. "But I tell you what— when you come home this evening, you will have to get right into the tub, like a fish, for if you run about like the goats, you will get your feet dirty. Now you can be off."

They started joyfully for the mountain. During the night the wind had blown away all the clouds; the dark blue sky was spreading overhead, and in its midst was the bright sun shining down on the green slopes of the mountain, where the flowers opened their little blue and yellow cups.

Heidi went running hither and thither, shouting with delight, for here were whole patches of delicate red primroses, and there the blue gleam of the lovely gentian. Enchanted with all this waving of brightly-colored flowers, Heidi forgot even Peter and the goats. She ran on in front and then off to the side, tempted first one way and then the other, as she caught sight of some bright spot of glowing red or yellow. And all the while she was plucking whole handfuls of the flowers which she put into her little apron,

for she wanted to take them all home and stick them in the hay, so that she might make her bedroom look just like the meadows outside.

Peter had to be very alert, and his round eyes, which did not move too quickly, had more work than they could well manage, for the goats were as lively as Heidi. They ran in all directions, and Peter had to follow, whistling and calling and swinging his stick to get all the runaways together again.

"Where have you got to now, Heidi?" he called out somewhat crossly.

"Here," she called. Peter could see no one, for Heidi was seated on the ground at the foot of a small hill thickly overgrown with sweet-smelling prunella. The air filled with its fragrance, and Heidi thought she had never smelt anything so delicious. She sat surrounded by the flowers, drawing in deep breaths.

"Come along here!" called Peter again. "You are not to fall over the rocks. Your grandfather gave orders that you were not to do so."

"Where are the rocks?" asked Heidi. But she did not move from her seat, for the scent of the flowers seemed sweeter to her with every breath of wind.

"Up above, right up above. We have a long way to go yet, so come along! And on the topmost peak of all the old bird of prey sits and croaks."

That did it. Heidi immediately sprang to her feet and ran up to Peter with her apron full of flowers.

"You have got enough now," said the boy as they began climbing up again together. "You will stay here forever if you go on picking, and if you gather all the flowers now there will be none for to-morrow."

This last argument seemed to convince

Heidi. Besides, her apron was already so full that there was hardly room for another flower, and it would never do to leave nothing to pick for another day. So she now kept close to Peter, and the goats also became more orderly, for they were beginning to smell the plants they loved that grew on the higher slopes and clambered up now without stopping.

The spot where Peter generally halted for his goats to pasture lay at the foot of the high rocks, which were covered for some distance up by bushes and fir trees, beyond which rose their bare and rugged summits. On one side of the mountain the rock was split into deep clefts, and the grandfather had reason to warn Peter of danger. Having climbed as far as the halting-place, Peter unslung his wallet and put it carefully in a little hollow of the ground, for he knew what the wind was like up there and did not want to see his precious belongings sent rolling down the mountain by a sudden gust. Then he threw himself at full length on the warm ground, for he was tired after all his climbing.

Heidi meanwhile had unfastened her apron and rolling it carefully round the flowers laid it beside Peter's wallet inside the hollow. She then sat down beside him and looked about her. The valley lay far below bathed in the morning sun. In front of her rose a broad snow-field, high against the dark blue sky, while to the left was a huge pile of rocks on either side of which a bare lofty peak, that seemed to pierce the blue, looked frowningly down upon her.

Heidi sat without moving, her eyes taking in the whole scene, and all around was a great stillness, broken only by soft light puffs of wind that swayed the light bells of the blue flowers and set them nodding merrily on their slender stems. Peter had fallen asleep after his fatigue and the goats were climbing about among the bushes overhead.

Heidi had never felt so happy in her life. She drank in the golden sunlight, the fresh air, the sweet smell of the flowers, and wished for nothing better than to stay there for ever. So the time went on, while to Heidi, who had so often looked up from the valley at the mountains above, these seemed now to have faces, and to be looking down at her like old friends.

Suddenly she heard a loud harsh cry overhead, and lifting her eyes she saw a bird, larger than any she had ever seen before, with great, spreading wings, wheeling round and round in wide circles, and uttering a piercing croaking kind of sound above her.

"Peter, Peter, wake up!" called out Heidi. "See, the great bird is there—look, look!"

Peter got up on hearing her call, and together they sat and watched the bird, which rose higher and higher in the blue air till it disappeared behind the gray mountain tops.

"Where has he gone?" asked Heidi, who had followed the bird's movements with intense interest.

"Home to his nest," said Peter.

"Is his home right up there? Oh, how nice to be up so high! Why does he make that noise?"

"Because he can't help it," explained Peter.

"Let us climb up there and see where his nest is," said Heidi.

"Oh! Oh! Oh!" exclaimed Peter, in disapproval. "Why, even the goats cannot climb as high as that. Besides didn't your grandfather say that you must be careful not to fall over the rocks?"

Peter now began whistling and calling so loudly that Heidi could not think what was happening. But the goats evidently understood his voice, for one after the other they came springing down the rocks until they were all assembled on the green plateau, some continuing to nibble at the juicy stems, others skipping about here and there or pushing at each other with their horns for pastime.

Heidi jumped up and ran in and out among them, for it was new to her to see the goats playing together like this and her delight was beyond words as she joined in their frolics. Meanwhile Peter had taken the wallet out of the hollow and placed the pieces of bread and cheese on the ground in the shape of a square, the larger two on Heidi's side and the smaller on his own, for he knew exactly which were hers and which his. Then he took the little bowl and milked some delicious fresh milk into it from the white goat, and afterward set the bowl in the middle of the square. Now he called Heidi to come, but she was so excited and amused at the lively capers of her new playfellows that she saw and heard nothing else. But Peter shouted till the very rocks above echoed his voice, and at last Heidi appeared, and when she saw the inviting meal spread out upon the ground she skipped for joy.

"Stop jumping about; it is time for dinner," said Peter. "Sit down now and begin."

Heidi sat down. "Is the milk for me?" she asked, giving another look of delight at the beautifully arranged square with the bowl as a chief ornament in the center.

"Yes," replied Peter, "and the two large pieces of bread and cheese are yours also, and when you have drunk up that milk you are to have another bowlful from the white goat, and then it will be my turn."

"And which do you get your milk from?"

inquired Heidi.

"From my own goat, the piebald one. But go on now with your dinner," said Peter.

Heidi now took up the bowl and drank her milk, and as soon as she had put it down empty, Peter rose and filled it again for her. Then she broke off a piece of her bread and held out the remainder, which was still larger than Peter's own piece, together with the whole big slice of cheese, to her companion, saying, "You can have that. I have plenty."

Peter looked at Heidi, unable to speak for astonishment, for never in all his life had he had enough to have said and done anything like that. He waited a moment, for he could not believe that Heidi was in earnest. But she kept on holding out the bread and cheese, and as Peter still did not take it, she laid it down on his knees. He saw then that she really meant it. He seized the food, nodded his thanks and ate the best meal he had ever had since he had been a goatherd. Heidi still continued to watch the goats. "Tell me all their names," she said.

Peter knew these by heart. So he began telling Heidi the name of each goat in turn as he pointed it out to her. Heidi listened with great attention, and it was not long before she herself could distinguish the goats from one another and could call each by name. Every goat had its own peculiarities which could not easily be mistaken. One had only to watch them closely, and this Heidi did. There was the great Turk with his big horns, who was always wanting to butt the others, so that most of them ran away when they saw him coming and would have nothing to do with their rough companion. Only Greenfinch, the slender nimble little goat, was brave enough to face him, and would make a rush at him, three or four

times in succession, with such swiftness and
skill that the great Turk often stood quite
astounded, not venturing to attack her
again, for Greenfinch was fronting him, prepared for more warlike action, and her horns
were sharp.

Then there was little White Snowflake,
who bleated in such a plaintive and be-
seeching manner that Heidi already had
several times run to it and taken its head in
her hands to comfort it. Just at this moment
the pleading young cry was heard again,
and Heidi jumped up running and, putting
her arms around the little creature's neck,
asked in sympathetic voice, "What is it, little Snowflake? Why do you cry so?" The
goat pressed closer to Heidi in a confiding
way and left off bleating.

Peter called out from where he was sitting
—for he had not yet finished his bread and
cheese, "She cries like that because the old
goat is not with her. She was sold at Mayenfeld the day before yesterday, and so she
will not come up the mountain any more."

"Who is the old goat?" asked Heidi.

"Why, her mother, of course," was the
answer.

"Where is her grandmother?" called
Heidi again.

"She has none."

"And the grandfather?"

"She has none."

"Oh, you poor little Snowflake!" exclaimed Heidi, clasping the animal gently
to her. "Don't cry like that any more. I
shall come up here with you every day, so

36

that you will not be alone any more, and if you want anything you have only to come to me."

The young animal rubbed its head contentedly against Heidi's shoulder, and stopped bleating. Peter now having finished his meal joined Heidi and the goats. Heidi by this time had found out a great many things about them. She had decided that by far the handsomest and best-behaved of the goats were the two belonging to her grandfather. They carried themselves with a certain air of distinction and generally went their own way, and as to the great Turk, they treated him with scorn.

The goats were now beginning to climb the rocks again. Each was seeking for the plants it liked in its own fashion. Some jumped over everything they met till they found what they wanted. Others went more carefully and cropped all the nice leaves by the way. The Turk now and then still gave the others a poke with his horns. Little Swan and Little Bear clambered lightly up and never failed to find the best bushes. Then they would stand gracefully poised on their pretty legs, delicately nibbling at the leaves. Heidi stood with her hands behind her back, carefully noting all they did.

"Peter," she said to the boy who had again thrown himself down on the ground, "the prettiest of all the goats are Little Swan and Little Bear."

"Yes, I know they are," was the answer. "Your grandfather brushes them down and washes them and gives them salt, and he has the nicest shed for them."

All of a sudden Peter leaped to his feet and ran hastily after the goats. Heidi followed him as fast as she could, for she was too eager to know what had happened to stay behind. Peter dashed through the middle of the flock toward that side of the mountain where the rocks were very steep and bare, and where any thoughtless goat, if it went too near, might fall over and break all its legs. He had caught sight of the inquisitive Greenfinch taking leaps in that direction, and he was only just in time, for the animal had already sprung to the edge of the cliff. All Peter could do was to throw himself down and seize one of her hind legs. Greenfinch, thus taken by surprise, began bleating furiously, angry at being held so fast and prevented from continuing her voyage of discovery. She struggled to get loose, and tried so hard to leap forward that Peter shouted to Heidi to come and help him, for he could not get up and was afraid of pulling out the goat's leg altogether.

Heidi had already run up and she saw at once the danger both Peter and the animal were in. She quickly gathered a bunch of sweet-smelling leaves, and holding them under Greenfinch's nose, she said coaxingly, "Come, come, Greenfinch, you must not be naughty! See, you might fall down there and break your leg, and that would give you dreadful pain!"

The young animal turned quickly and began contentedly eating the leaves out of Heidi's hand. Meanwhile Peter got onto his feet again and took hold of Greenfinch by the band around her neck from which her bell was hung. Heidi, taking hold of her in the same way on the other side, helped lead the wanderer back to the rest of the flock that was grazing peacefully. Peter, now that he had his goat in safety, lifted his stick to give her a good beating as punishment. Greenfinch, seeing what was coming shrank back in fear. But Heidi cried out, "No, no, Peter, you must not strike her. See how frightened she is!"

"She deserves it," growled Peter, and again lifted his stick. Then Heidi flung herself against him and cried indignantly, "You have no right to touch her, it will hurt her. Let her alone!"

Peter looked with surprise at the commanding little figure whose dark eyes were flashing, and reluctantly he let his stick drop. "Well, I will let her off if you will give me some more of your cheese to-morrow," he said, for he was determined to have something to make up to him for his fright.

"You shall have it all, tomorrow and every day. I do not want it," replied Heidi, giving ready consent to his demand. "And I will give you bread as well, as large a piece as you had today. But then you must promise never to beat Greenfinch, or Snowflake, or any of the goats."

"All right," said Peter. He now let go of Greenfinch, who joyfully sprang to join her companions.

The day had crept on to its close, and now the sun was on the point of sinking behind the high mountains. Heidi was again sitting on the ground, silently gazing at the blue bell-shaped flowers, as they glistened in the evening sun. A golden light lay on the grass and flowers, and the rocks above were beginning to shine and glow.

All at once she sprang to her feet, "Peter! Peter! Everything is on fire! All the rocks are burning, and the great snow mountain and the sky! Oh, the beautiful fiery snow! Stand up, Peter! See, the fire has reached the great bird's nest! Look at the rocks! Look at the fir trees! Everything, everything is on fire!"

"It is always like that," said Peter calmly, peeling the bark from his stick. "But it is not really fire."

"What is it then?" cried Heidi, as she ran backwards and forwards to look first on one side and then on the other, for she felt she could not have enough of such a beautiful sight. "What is it, Peter, what is it?" she repeated.

"It gets like that of itself," explained Peter.

"Look, look!" cried Heidi in fresh excitement. "Now they have turned all rose color! Look at that one with the high pointed rocks! Oh, how beautiful! Look at the crimson snow! And up there on the rocks there are ever so many roses! Oh, now they are turning gray! Oh! Oh! Now all the color has died away! It's all gone, Peter." And Heidi sat down on the ground looking as disappointed as if everything had really come to an end.

"It will be just the same tomorrow," said Peter. "Get up, we must go home now." He whistled to his goats and together they all started on their homeward way.

"Is it like that every day? Shall we see it every day when we bring the goats up here?" asked Heidi, as she clambered down the mountain at Peter's side. She waited eagerly for his answer, hoping he would tell her it was so.

"It is like that most days," he replied.

"But will it be like that tomorrow for certain?" Heidi persisted.

"Yes, yes, tomorrow for certain," Peter assured her.

Heidi now felt quite happy again, and her little brain was so full of new impressions and new thoughts that she did not speak any more until they had reached the hut. Her grandfather was sitting under the fir trees, where he had also put up a seat, waiting as usual for his goats which returned down the mountain on this side.

Heidi ran up to him followed by the white and brown goats, for they knew their own master and stall. Peter called out after her, "Come with me again tomorrow! Good night!" He was anxious for more than one reason that Heidi should go with him the next day.

Heidi ran back quickly and gave Peter her hand, promising to go with him. Then, making her way through the goats, she once more clasped Snowflake round the neck, saying in a gentle soothing voice, "Sleep well, Snowflake, and remember that I shall be with you again tomorrow, so you must not bleat so sadly any more."

Snowflake gave her a friendly and grateful look, and then went leaping joyfully after the other goats.

Heidi returned to the fir trees. "O Grandfather," she cried, even before she had come up to him, "it was so beautiful. The fire, and the roses on the rocks, and the blue and yellow flowers, and look what I have brought you!" And opening the apron that held her flowers she shook them all out at her grandfather's feet. But the poor flowers, how changed they were! Heidi hardly knew them again. They looked like dried bits of hay, not a single little flower cup stood open. "O Grandfather, what is the matter with them?" exclaimed Heidi in shocked surprise. "They were not like that this morning, why do they look so now?"

"They like to stand out there in the sun and not to be shut up in an apron," said her grandfather.

"Then I will never gather any more. But, Grandfather, why did the great bird go on croaking so?" she continued eagerly.

"Go along now and get into your bath while I go and get some milk. When we are together at supper I will tell you all about it."

Heidi obeyed, and when later she was sitting on her high stool before her milk bowl with her grandfather beside her, she repeated her question, "Why does the great bird go on croaking and screaming down at us, Grandfather?"

"He is mocking at the people who live down below in the villages, because they all go huddling and gossiping together. He calls out, 'If you would separate and each go your own way and come up here and live on a height as I do, it would be better for you!' " There was almost a wild tone in the old man's voice as he spoke, so that Heidi seemed to hear the croaking of the bird again even more distinctly.

"So you enjoyed being out with the goats?" her grandfather asked in a gentle tone, looking at little Heidi with a smile.

Then Heidi gave him an account of the whole day, and of how delightful it had all been, and she particularly described the fire that had burst out everywhere in the evening. And then nothing would do but that her grandfather must tell how it came, for Peter knew nothing about it.

Her grandfather explained that it was the sun that did it. "When he says good night to the mountains he throws his most beautiful colors over them, so that they may not forget him before he comes again in the morning."

Heidi was delighted with this explanation, and could hardly bear to wait for another day to come so that she might once more climb up with the goats and see the sun bid good night to the mountains. But she had to go to bed first, and all night she slept soundly on her bed of hay, dreaming of nothing but shining mountains with red roses all over them, with happy little Snowflake leaping in and out.

A VISIT TO GRANDMOTHER

The next morning the sun came out early as bright as ever, and then Peter appeared with the goats, and again the two children climbed up together to the high meadows, and so it went on day after day till Heidi, passing her life thus among the grass and flowers, was burned brown with the sun, and grew so strong and healthy that nothing ever ailed her. She was happy too, and lived from day to day as free and lighthearted as the little birds that make their home among the green forest trees.

Then the autumn came, and the wind blew louder and stronger, and her grandfather would say sometimes, "Today you must stay at home, Heidi. A sudden gust of wind would blow a little thing like you over the rocks into the valley below in a moment."

Whenever Peter heard that he had to go alone he looked very unhappy, for he saw nothing but mishaps of all kinds ahead, and did not know how he could bear the long dull day without Heidi. Then, too, there was the good meal he would miss, and, besides that, the goats on these days were so naughty and obstinate that he had twice the usual trouble with them, for they had grown so accustomed to Heidi's presence that they would run in every direction and refuse to go on unless she was with them.

Heidi was never unhappy, for wherever she was she found something to interest or amuse her. She liked best, it is true, to go out with Peter up to the flowers and the great bird, where there was much to be seen, and so many experiences to go through among the goats with their different characters. But she also found her grandfather's hammering and sawing and carpentering very enjoyable, and if it happened to be the day when the large round goat's milk cheese was made she loved watching her grandfather, as with sleeves rolled back he stirred the great caldron with his bare arms.

The thing which attracted her most, however, was the waving and roaring of the three old fir trees on these windy days. She would often run away from whatever she might be doing to listen to them, for nothing seemed so strange and wonderful to her as the deep mysterious sound in the tops of the trees. She would stand underneath them and look up, unable to tear herself away, looking and listening while they bowed and swayed and roared as the mighty wind rushed through them.

There was no longer now the warm bright sun that had shone all through the summer, so Heidi went to the cupboard and got out her shoes and stockings and dress. It was growing colder every day, and when Heidi stood under the fir trees the wind blew through her as if she were a thin little leaf. But still she felt she could not stay indoors when she heard the branches waving.

Then it grew very cold, and Peter would come up early in the morning blowing on his fingers to keep them warm. But he soon stopped coming, for one night there was a heavy fall of snow and the next morning the whole mountain was covered with it, and not a single green leaf even was to be seen anywhere upon it.

There was no Peter that day, and Heidi stood at the little window looking out in wonderment, for the snow was beginning again, and the thick flakes kept falling till the snow was up to the window, and still they continued to fall, and the snow grew higher, so that at last the window could not be opened, and she and her grandfather were shut up fast within the hut. Heidi thought this was great fun and ran from one window to the other to see what would happen next. If the snow was going to cover up the whole hut, they would have to light a lamp although it was broad daylight.

But things did not get as bad as that, and the next day it stopped snowing. Grandfather went out and shovelled away the snow round the house, and threw it into such great piles that they looked like mountains standing on either side of the hut. And now the windows and door could be opened.

As Heidi and her grandfather were sitting one afternoon on their three-legged stools before the fire, there came a great thump at the door followed by several others, and then the door opened. It was Peter, who had made all that noise knocking the snow off his shoes. He was still white all over with it, for he had had to fight his way through deep snowdrifts, and large lumps of snow that had frozen upon him still clung to his clothes. He had been determined, however, not to be beaten and to climb up to the hut, for it was a week now since he had seen Heidi.

"Good evening," he said as he came in. Then he went and placed himself as near the fire as he could, without saying another word, but his whole face was beaming with pleasure at finding himself there. Heidi looked on in astonishment, for in the warmth Peter was beginning to thaw all over, so that he had the appearance of a trickling waterfall.

"Well, General, and how goes it with you?" said the grandfather. "Now that you have lost your army you will have to turn to your pen and pencil."

"Why must he turn to his pen and pen-

cil?" asked Heidi, full of curiosity.

"During the winter he must go to school," explained her grandfather, "and learn how to read and write. It's a bit hard, although useful afterward. Am I not right, General?"

"Yes, indeed," agreed Peter.

Heidi's interest was now thoroughly awakened. She had so many questions to ask Peter about all that was to be done and seen and heard at school, and the conversation took so long that Peter had time to get quite dry. Peter always had great difficulty in putting his thoughts into words, and he found his share of the talk doubly difficult today. For by the time he had an answer ready to one of Heidi's questions, she had already asked him two or three more.

The grandfather sat without speaking during this conversation. Only now and then a twitch of amusement at the corners of his mouth showed that he was listening.

"Well, now, General, you have been under fire for some time and must want some refreshment. Come and join us," he said at last, and as he spoke he went to fetch the supper out of the cupboard, as Heidi pushed the stools to the table. There was also now a bench fastened against the wall, for as he was no longer alone the grandfather had put up benches of various kinds here and there, long enough to hold two persons, for Heidi had a way of always keeping close to her grandfather whether he was walking, sitting or standing. So there was comfortable space for all three, and Peter opened his round eyes very wide when he saw what a large piece of meat the old man gave him on his thick slice of bread. It was a long time since Peter had had anything so good to eat.

As soon as the pleasant meal was over Peter began to get ready to go home, for it was already growing dark. He had said his "good night" and his thanks, and was just going out, when he turned and said, "I shall come again next Sunday, and my grandmother sent word that she would like you to come and see her one day."

It was quite a new idea to Heidi that she should go and pay anybody a visit, and she could not get it out of her head. The first thing she said to her grandfather the next day was, "I must go down to see Peter's grandmother today."

"The snow is too deep," answered her grandfather, trying to put her off. But Heidi had made up her mind to go, since the grandmother had sent her that message. She stuck to her intention and not a day passed but what in the course of it she said five or six times to her grandfather, "I must certainly go today. The grandmother will be waiting for me."

On the fourth day, when the ground crackled with frost and the whole vast field of snow was hard as ice, Heidi was sitting on her high stool at dinner with the bright sun shining in upon her through the window, when she again repeated her little speech, "I must certainly go down to see Peter's grandmother today, or else I shall keep her waiting too long."

Her grandfather rose from the table, climbed up to the hay loft, brought down the thick sack that was Heidi's quilt, and said, "Come along then!"

The child skipped out gleefully after him into the glittering world of snow. The old fir trees were standing now quite silent, their branches covered with the white snow, and they looked so lovely as they glittered and sparkled in the sunlight that Heidi jumped for joy at the sight and kept on calling out, "Come here, come here, Grand-

father! The fir trees are all silver and gold!"

Her grandfather had gone into the shed and he now came out dragging a large hand sleigh along with him. Inside it was a low seat, and the sleigh could be pushed forward and guided by the feet of the one who sat upon it with the help of a pole that was fastened to the side. After he had been taken round the fir trees by Heidi that he might see their beauty from all sides, he got into the sleigh and lifted the child onto his lap. Then he wrapped her up in the quilt so that she would be nice and warm, and put his left arm closely round her, for it was necessary to hold her tight during the journey. He now grasped the pole with his right hand and gave the sleigh a push forward with his two feet. The sleigh shot down the mountainside so swiftly that Heidi thought they were flying through the air like a bird, and shouted aloud with delight.

Suddenly they came to a standstill, and there they were at Peter's hut. Her grandfather lifted her out and unwrapped her. "There you are! Now go in, and when it begins to grow dark you must start on your way home again." Then he left her and went up the mountain pulling his sleigh after him.

Heidi opened the door of the hut and stepped into a tiny kitchen that looked very dark, with a fireplace and a few dishes on a wooden shelf. She opened another door, and found herself in another small room, for the place was not a herdsman's hut like her grandfather's, with one large room on the ground floor and a hayloft above, but a very old cottage, where everything was narrow and poor and shabby. A table was close to the door, and as Heidi stepped in she saw a woman sitting at it, putting a patch on a jacket which Heidi recognized at once as Peter's. In the corner sat a blind old woman, bent with age, spinning. Heidi was quite sure this was Peter's grandmother, so she went up to the spinning-wheel and said, "Good day, Grandmother, I have come at last. Did you think I was a long time coming?"

The old woman raised her head and felt for the hand that the child held out to her, and when she had found it, she passed her own over it thoughtfully for a few seconds, and then said, "Are you the child who lives with the Alm-Uncle? Are you Heidi?"

"Yes, yes," answered Heidi, "I have just come down in the sleigh with Grandfather."

"Is it possible? Why, your hands are quite warm!" And then she said to Peter's mother, "Brigitta, did he come himself with the child?"

Peter's mother had left her work and risen from the table and now stood looking at Heidi with curiosity. "I do not know, Mother, whether he came himself."

But Heidi looked steadily at the woman and said, "It was indeed my grandfather who wrapped me up in my bedcover and brought me down in the sleigh."

"There was some truth then perhaps in what Peter used to tell us of him during the summer," said grandmother. "But who would ever have believed that such a thing was possible? I did not think the child would live three weeks up there. What is she like, Brigitta?"

"She has her mother's slenderness of figure, but her eyes are dark and her hair is curly like her father's and the old man's."

Heidi meanwhile had not been idle. She had looked around the room and examined everything there was to be seen. All of a sudden she exclaimed, "Grandmother, one of your shutters is flapping backward and forward. Grandfather could put a nail in and make it all right in a minute. It may break one of the panes some day. Look, how it keeps on banging!"

"Ah, dear child," said the old woman, "I am not able to see it, but I can hear that and many other things besides the shutter. Everything about the place rattles and creaks when the wind is blowing, and it gets inside through all the cracks and holes. The house is going to pieces, and in the night I often lie awake thinking that the whole place will give way and fall and kill us. And there is no one to mend anything for us, for Peter does not understand such work."

"But why can't you see, Grandmother, that the shutter is loose? Look, there it goes again; see, that one there!" And Heidi pointed to the particular shutter.

"Alas, child, it is not only that I cannot see—I can see nothing, nothing," said the grandmother mournfully.

"But suppose I run out and open the shutter so that you have more light, you can see then, Grandmother?"

"No, not even then! No one can give light to my eyes."

"But if you were to go outside among all the white snow, then surely you would find it light. Just come with me, Grandmother, and I will show you." Heidi took hold of the old woman's hand to lead her along, for she was beginning to feel quite distressed at the thought of her being without light.

"Let me be, dear child. It is always dark for me now."

"But surely not in summer, Grandmother," said Heidi, more and more anxious to find some way out of the trouble. "When the hot sun is shining down again, and the mountains all turn on fire, and the

yellow flowers shine like gold, then won't it be bright and beautiful for you again?"

"Ah, child, I shall never see the mountains on fire or the yellow flowers. It will never be light for me again on earth."

At these words Heidi began to weep aloud. In her distress she kept sobbing, "Who can make it light for you again? Isn't there anyone who can do it?"

The grandmother now tried to comfort the child, but it was not easy to quiet her. Heidi hardly ever cried, but when she did she could not get over her trouble for a long while.

The grandmother tried to soothe the little girl. At last she said, "Come here, dear Heidi, come and let me tell you something. You cannot think how glad one is to hear a kind word when one can no longer see, and it is such a pleasure to me to listen to you talk. So come and sit beside me and tell me something. Tell me what you do up there, and how your grandfather occupies himself. I knew him very well in old days; but for many years now I have heard nothing of him, except through Peter, who never says much."

This was a new and happy idea to Heidi. She quickly dried her tears and said in a comforting voice, "Wait, Grandmother, till I have told Grandfather everything. He will make it light for you again, I am sure, and will do something so that the house will not fall. He will put everything in good order for you."

The grandmother was silent. Heidi began to tell of her life with her grandfather, and of the days she spent on the mountain with the goats. Then she went on to tell of what she did now during the winter; and of how her grandfather was able to make all sorts of things, benches and stools, and mangers where the hay was put for Little Swan and Little Bear, besides a new large water-tub for her to bathe in and a new milk bowl and spoon. Heidi grew livelier as she described all the beautiful things her grandfather made so magically out of pieces of wood.

The grandmother listened with the greatest attention, only from time to time addressing her daughter, "Do you hear that, Brigitta? Do you hear what she is saying about her grandfather?"

The conversation was interrupted by a heavy thump on the door, and in marched Peter, who stood stock still, opening his eyes with astonishment when he caught sight of Heidi. Then he beamed as she called out, "Good evening, Peter."

"What, is the boy back from school already?" asked his grandmother in surprise. "I have not known an afternoon to pass so quickly as this one for years. How is the reading getting on, Peter?"

"Just the same," was Peter's answer.

The old woman gave a little sigh, "Ah, well," she said, "I hoped you would have something different to tell me by this time. You will be twelve years old in February."

"What was it you hoped he would have to tell you?" asked Heidi.

"I mean that he ought to have learned to read a bit by now," replied the grandmother. "Up there on the shelf is an old prayer book, with beautiful songs in it. I have not heard them for a long time and cannot remember them now. I hoped Peter would soon learn enough to be able to read one of them to me sometimes. But he finds it too difficult."

"I must light the lamp. It is getting too dark to see," said Peter's mother, who was still busy mending his jacket. "I feel too as if the afternoon had gone I hardly know how."

Heidi jumped up from her low chair, and holding out her hand, said, "Good night, Grandmother. If it is getting dark, I must go home at once." Then bidding good-bye to Peter and his mother she went toward the door.

But the grandmother called out anxiously, "Wait, wait, Heidi, you must not go alone. Peter must go with you. Take care that the child does not fall, Peter, and don't let her stand still or she might get frost-bitten. Has she something warm to put round her neck?"

Heidi called back, "I am sure I shall not be cold." And she ran outside so quickly that Peter could hardly follow her.

The grandmother, still anxious, called out to her daughter, "Run after her, Brigitta. The child will be frozen to death on such a night. Take my shawl. Run quickly!"

Brigitta ran out. But the children had taken only a few steps when they saw Heidi's grandfather coming down to meet them, and in another minute his long strides had brought him to their side.

"That's right, Heidi, you kept your word," he said. Then wrapping the quilt firmly round her he lifted her in his arms and strode off with her up the mountains. Brigitta was just in time to see him do this, and she went back to the hut with Peter and told the grandmother in great surprise what she had seen.

The old woman kept on saying, "God be thanked that he is good to the child, God be thanked! Will he let her come to me again, I wonder? The child has done me so much good. What a loving little heart she has!" And she continued to dwell with delight on the thought of the child until she went to bed. "If only she will come again!" she kept saying. "Now I have really something left in the world to take pleasure in."

Brigitta agreed with all her mother said, and Peter nodded his head in approval each time his grandmother spoke, saying, with a broad smile of satisfaction, "I told you so!"

Meanwhile Heidi was chattering away to her grandfather from inside her quilt. Her voice, however, could not reach him through the many thick folds of her wrap. They had no sooner reached home than Heidi said, "Grandfather, tomorrow we must take the hammer and the long nails and fasten the shutters at Peter's grandmother's and drive in a lot more nails in other places, for her house shakes and rattles all over."

"We must, must we? Who told you that?" asked her grandfather.

"Nobody told me, but I know it just the same," replied Heidi, "for when Peter's grandmother cannot sleep, she lies trembling for fear that any minute the house will fall down on their heads. And everything now is dark for the grandmother, and she does not think anyone can make it light for her again. But you can, of course, Grandfather. Think how dreadful it is for her to be always in the dark, and then to be frightened at what may happen. Tomorow we must go and help her. We will, won't we, Grandfather?"

The child was clinging to the old man and looking up at him trustfully. Her grandfather looked down at her for a while without speaking, and then said, "Yes, Heidi, we will do something to stop the rattling. At least we can do that. We will do it tomorrow."

The child went skipping round the room for joy, crying out, "We shall go tomorrow! We shall go tomorrow!"

Her grandfather kept his promise. On the following afternoon he brought the sleigh out again, and as on the previous day, he set Heidi down at the door of the grandmother's hut and said, "Go in now, and when it grows dark, come out again." Then he put the sack in the sleigh and went round the house.

Heidi had hardly opened the door when the grandmother called out from her corner, "It's the child again! Here she comes!" In her delight she let the thread drop from her fingers, and the wheel stood still as she stretched out both her hands in welcome. Heidi ran to her, and then quickly drew the little stool close up to the old woman, and seating herself upon it, began to talk.

All at once came the sound of heavy blows against the wall of the hut. The grandmother gave such a start that she nearly upset her spinning-wheel, and cried in a trembling voice, "Oh, heavens, now it has come! The house is going to fall upon us!"

But Heidi caught her by the arm, and said soothingly, "No, no, Grandmother, do not be frightened. It is only Grandfather with his hammer. He will make everything fast now, so that you won't have anything to be afraid of any more."

"Is it possible! Is it really possible! So the good God has not forgotten us!" exclaimed the grandmother. "Do you hear, Brigitta, what that noise is? Did you hear what the child says? Now, as I listen, I can tell it is a hammer. Go outside, Brigitta, and if it is Heidi's grandfather, tell him to come inside so that I can thank him."

Brigitta went outside and found the old

man fastening some heavy pieces of new wood along the wall. She stepped up to him and said, "Good evening. Mother and I have to thank you for doing us such a kind service, and she would like to tell you herself how grateful she is. I do not know who else would have done it for us. We shall not forget your kindness, for I am sure——"

"That will do," the old man interrupted. "I know what you think of me without your telling me. Go indoors again. I can find out for myself where the mending is needed."

Brigitta obeyed at once, for the old man had a way with him that made few people care to oppose him. He went on knocking with his hammer all round the house, and then climbed the narrow steps to the roof. There he hammered away until he had used up all the nails he had.

Meanwhile it had been growing dark, and he had hardly come down from the roof and dragged the sleigh out from behind the goat shed when Heidi appeared outside. He wrapped her up and took her in his arms as he had done the day before, for although he had to drag the sleigh up the mountain after him, he feared that if Heidi sat in it alone her wrappings might fall off and she would be nearly if not quite frozen. So he carried her warm and safe in his arms.

The winter went by. After many years of cheerless life, the blind grandmother had at last found something to make her happy. Her days were no longer passed in weariness and darkness, for now she always had something joyful to look forward to. She listened for the little tripping footsteps as soon as day broke, and when she heard the door open and knew Heidi was really there, she would call out, "God be praised! She has come again!"

Heidi would sit by her chattering and telling her everything she knew in such a pleasant way that the grandmother never noticed how the time went by, and never asked Brigitta, as she used to, "Isn't the day done yet?" Now, whenever the child closed the door behind her on leaving she would say, "How short the afternoon has seemed; don't you think so, Brigitta?"

"And Brigitta would answer, "I do indeed; it seems as if I had only just cleared away the mid-day meal."

And the grandmother would continue, "Pray God the child is not taken from me, and that her grandfather continues to let her come! Does she look well Brigitta?"

And Brigitta would answer, "She looks as bright and rosy as an apple."

Heidi had grown very fond of the old grandmother too, and when at last she knew for certain that no one could make it light for the old woman again, the child was very sad. But the grandmother told her again that she felt the darkness much less when Heidi was with her, and so every fine winter's day the child came traveling down in her sleigh. Her grandfather always took her, never raising any objection. Indeed he always carried the hammer and other things down in the sleigh with him, and he spent many an afternoon making the goatherd's cottage sound and tight. It no longer groaned and rattled the whole night through, and the grandmother, who for many winters had not been able to sleep in peace as she did now, said she should never forget what the old man had done.

"And now I can thank you for all you have done for me," she said to Heidi. "May God reward you! May God reward you!"

—*Abridged excerpt*

The Height
of the Ridiculous

By Oliver Wendell Holmes

I wrote some lines once on a time
  In wondrous merry mood,
And thought, as usual, men would say
  They were exceeding good.

They were so queer, so very queer,
  I laughed as I would die,
Albeit, in the general way,
  A sober man am I.

I called my servant and he came;
  How kind it was of him
To mind a slender man like me,
  He of the mighty limb.

"These to the printer," I exclaimed,
  And, in my humorous way,
I added (as a trifling jest),
  "There'll be the devil to pay."

He took the paper, and I watched
  And saw him peep within.
At the first line he read, his face
  Was all upon the grin

He read the next; the grin grew broad
  And shot from ear to ear.
He read the third; a chuckling noise
  I now began to hear.

The fourth; he broke into a roar.
  The fifth; his waistband split.
The sixth; he burst five buttons off
  And tumbled in a fit.

Ten days and nights, with sleepless eye,
  I watched that wretched man,
And since, I never dare to write
  As funny as I can.

Dorothy's Travels to the Land of Oz

From THE WIZARD OF OZ

By L. Frank Baum

THE WIZARD OF OZ, an entirely different kind of fairy tale from the old-fashioned tales of Grimm and Andersen, is a modern story written for modern children—a funny fairy tale The action takes place not in some European neverland but right in the heart of America.

Dorothy, the heroine, is as American as the Fourth of July, but her adventures, after she is blown away by a Kansas cyclone, are fantastic indeed—really quite beyond imagination.

Not only Dorothy and her little dog Toto but the Tin Woodman, the Scarecrow, the Cowardly Lion, and all the other odd people she meets on her way to the Emerald City, to say nothing of the great Wizard of Oz himself, are among the most beloved characters in all children's literature. As the author himself says of his book, "it was written solely to please children of today. Wonderment and joy are retained but the heartaches and nightmares are left out." You can read part of the story here.

THE CYCLONE

DOROTHY lived in the midst of the great Kansas prairies, with Uncle Henry, who was a farmer, and Aunt Em, who was the farmer's wife. Their house was small, for the lumber to build it had to be carried by wagon many miles. There were four walls, a floor and a roof, which made one room; and this room contained a rusty-looking cooking stove, a cupboard for the dishes, a table, three or four chairs, and the beds. Uncle Henry and Aunt Em had a big bed in one corner and Dorothy a little bed in another corner. There was no garret at all, and no cellar—except a small hole, dug in the ground, called a cyclone cellar, where the family could go in case one of those great whirlwinds arose, mighty enough to crush any building in its path. It was reached by a trap door in the middle of the floor, from which a ladder led down into the small, dark hole.

When Dorothy stood in the doorway and looked around, she could see nothing but the great gray prairie on every side. Not a tree nor a house broke the broad sweep of flat country that reached to the edge of the sky in all directions. The sun had baked the plowed land into a gray mass, with little cracks running through it. Even the grass was not green, for the sun had burned the tops of the long blades until they were the same gray color to be seen everywhere. Once the house had been painted, but the sun blistered the paint and the rains washed it away, and now the house was as dull and gray as everything else.

When Aunt Em came there to live she was a young pretty wife. The sun and wind had changed her, too. They had taken the sparkle from her eyes and left them a sober gray; they had taken the red from her cheeks and lips, and they were gray also. She was thin and gaunt, and never smiled now. When Dorothy, who was an orphan, first came to her, Aunt Em had been so startled by the child's laughter that she would scream and press her hand upon her heart whenever Dorothy's merry voice reached her ears; and she still looked at the little girl with wonder that she could find anything to laugh at.

Uncle Henry never laughed. He worked hard from morning till night and did not know what joy was. He was gray also, from his long beard to his rough boots, and he looked stern and solemn, and rarely spoke.

It was Toto that made Dorothy laugh, and saved her from growing as gray as her other surroundings. Toto was not gray; he was a little black dog, with long silky hair and small black eyes that twinkled merrily on either side of his funny, wee nose. Toto played all day long, and Dorothy played with him, and loved him dearly.

Today, however, they were not playing. Uncle Henry sat upon the doorstep and looked anxiously at the sky, which was even grayer than usual. Dorothy stood in the door with Toto in her arms, and looked at the sky too. Aunt Em was washing the dishes.

From the far north they heard a low wail of the wind, and Uncle Henry and Dorothy could see where the long grass bowed in waves before the coming storm. There now came a sharp whistling in the air from the south, and as they turned their eyes that way they saw ripples in the grass coming from that direction also.

Suddenly Uncle Henry stood up.

"There's a cyclone coming, Em," he called to his wife. "I'll go look after the stock." Then he ran toward the sheds where the cows and horses were kept.

Aunt Em dropped her work and came to the door. One glance told her of the danger close at hand.

"Quick, Dorothy!" she screamed. "Run for the cellar!"

Toto jumped out of Dorothy's arms and hid under the bed, and the girl started to get him. Aunt Em, badly frightened, threw open the trap door in the floor and climbed down the ladder into the small, dark hole. Dorothy caught Toto at last, and started to follow her aunt. When she was halfway across the room there came a great shriek from the wind, and the house shook so hard that she lost her footing and sat down suddenly upon the floor.

A strange thing then happened.

The house whirled around two or three times and rose slowly through the air. Dorothy felt as if she were going up in a balloon.

The north and south winds met where the house stood, and made it the exact center of the cyclone. In the middle of a cyclone the air is generally still, but the great pressure of the wind on every side of the house raised it up higher and higher, until it was at the very top of the cyclone; and there it remained and was carried miles away as easily as you could carry a feather.

It was very dark, and the wind howled horribly around her, but Dorothy found she was riding quite easily. After the first few whirls around, and one other time when the house tipped badly, she felt as if she were being rocked gently, like a baby in a cradle.

Toto did not like it. He ran about the room, now here, now there, barking loudly; but Dorothy sat quite still on the floor and waited to see what would happen.

Once Toto got too near the open trap door, and fell in; and at first the little girl thought she had lost him. But soon she saw one of his ears sticking up through the hole, for the strong pressure of the air was keep-ing him up so that he could not fall. She crept to the hole, caught Toto by the ear, and dragged him into the room again, afterward closing the trap door so that no more accidents could happen.

Hour after hour passed away, and slowly Dorothy got over her fright; but she felt quite lonely, and the wind shrieked so loudly all about her that she nearly became deaf. At first she had wondered if she would be dashed to pieces when the house fell again; but as the hours passed and nothing terrible happened, she stopped worrying and resolved to wait calmly and see what the future would bring. At last she crawled over the swaying floor to her bed, and lay down upon it; and Toto followed and lay down beside her.

In spite of the swaying of the house and the wailing of the wind, Dorothy soon closed her eyes and fell fast asleep.

COUNCIL WITH THE MUNCHKINS

She was awakened by a shock, so sudden and severe that if Dorothy had not been lying on the soft bed she might have been hurt. As it was, the jar made her catch her breath and wonder what had happened; and Toto put his cold little nose into her face and whined dismally. Dorothy sat up and noticed that the house was not moving; nor was it dark, for the bright sunshine came in at the window, flooding the little room. She sprang from her bed and with Toto at her heels ran and opened the door.

The litle girl gave a cry of amazement and looked about her, her eyes growing bigger and bigger at the wonderful sights she saw.

The cyclone had set the house down, very gently—for a cyclone—in the midst of a country of marvelous beauty. There were lovely patches of greensward all about, with stately trees bearing rich and luscious fruits. Banks of gorgeous flowers were on every hand, and birds with rare and brilliant plumage sang and fluttered in the trees and bushes. A little way off was a small brook, rushing and sparkling along between green banks, and murmuring in a voice very grateful to a little girl who had lived so long on the dry, gray prairies.

While she stood looking eagerly at the strange and beautiful sights, she noticed coming toward her a group of the queerest people she had ever seen. They were not as big as the grown folk she had always been used to; but neither were they very small. In fact, they seeemed about as tall as Dorothy, who was a well-grown child for her age, although they were, so far as looks go, many years older.

Three were men and one a woman, and all were oddly dressed. They wore round hats that rose to a small point a foot above their heads, with little bells around the brims that tinkled sweetly as they moved. The hats of the men were blue; the little woman's hat was white, and she wore a white gown that hung in pleats from her shoulders; over it were sprinkled little stars that glistened in the sun like diamonds. The men were dressed in blue, of the same shade as their hats, and wore well-polished boots with a deep roll of blue at the tops. The men, Dorothy thought, were about as old as Uncle Henry, for two of them had beards. But the little woman was doubtless much older: her face was covered with wrinkles, her hair was nearly white, and she walked rather stiffly.

When these people drew near the house where Dorothy was standing in the doorway, they paused and whispered among themselves, as if afraid to come farther. But the little old woman walked up to Dorothy made a low bow and said, in a sweet voice:

"You are welcome, most noble Sorceress, to the land of the Munchkins. We are so grateful to you for having killed the Wicked Witch of the East, and for setting our people free from bondage."

Dorothy listened to this speech with wonder. What could the little woman possibly mean by calling her a sorceress, and saying she had killed the Wicked Witch of the East? Dorothy was an innocent, harmless little girl, who had been carried by a cyclone many miles from home; and she had never killed anything in all her life.

But the little woman evidently expected her to answer; so Dorothy said, with hesitation, "You are very kind; but there must be some mistake. I have not killed anything."

"Your house did, anyway," replied the little old woman, with a laugh, "and that is the same thing. See!" she continued, pointing to the corner of the house. "There are her two toes, still sticking out from under a block of wood."

Dorothy looked, and gave a little cry of fright. There, indeed, just under the corner of the great beam the house rested on, two feet were sticking out, shod in silver shoes with pointed toes.

"Oh, dear! Oh, dear!" cried Dorothy, clasping her hands together in dismay. "The house must have fallen on her. Whatever shall we do?"

"There is nothing to be done," said the little woman, calmly.

"But who was she?" asked Dorothy.

"She was the Wicked Witch of the East, as I said," answered the little woman. "She has held all the Munchkins in bondage for many years, making them slave for her night and day. Now they are all set free, and are grateful to you for the favor."

"Who are the Munchkins?" inquired Dorothy.

"They are the people who live in this land of the East, where the Wicked Witch ruled."

"Are you a Munchkin?" asked Dorothy.

"No, but I am their friend, although I live in the land of the North. When they saw the Witch of the East was dead the Munchkins sent a swift messenger to me, and I came at once. I am the Witch of the North."

"Oh, gracious!" cried Dorothy. "Are you a real witch?"

"Yes, indeed," answered the little woman. "But I am a good witch, and the people love me. I am not as powerful as the Wicked Witch was who ruled here, or I should have set the people free myself."

"But I thought all witches were wicked," said the girl, who was half frightened at facing a real witch.

"Oh, no, that is a great mistake. There were only four witches in all the Land of Oz, and two of them, those who live in the North and the South, are good witches. I know this is true, for I am one of them myself, and cannot be mistaken. Those who dwelt in the East and the West were, indeed, wicked witches; but now that you have killed one of them, there is but one Wicked Witch in all the Land of Oz—the one who lives in the West."

"But," said Dorothy, after a moment's thought, "Aunt Em has told me that the witches were all dead—years and years ago."

"Who is Aunt Em?" inquired the little old woman.

"She is my aunt who lives in Kansas, where I came from."

The Witch of the North seemed to think for a time, with her head bowed and her eyes upon the ground. Then she looked up and said, "I do not know where Kansas is, for I have never heard that country mentioned before. But tell me, is it a civilized country?"

"Oh, yes," replied Dorothy.

"Then that accounts for it. In the civilized countries I believe there are no witches left, nor wizards, nor sorceresses, nor magicians. But, you see, the Land of Oz has never been civilized, for we are cut off from all the rest of the world. Therefore we still have witches and wizards amongst us."

"Who are the wizards?" asked Dorothy.

"Oz himself is the Great Wizard," answered the Witch, sinking her voice to a whisper. "He is more powerful than all the rest of us together. He lives in the City of Emeralds."

Dorothy was going to ask another question, but just then the Munchkins, who had been standing silently by, gave a loud shout and pointed to the corner of the house where the Wicked Witch had been lying.

"What is it?" asked the little old woman, and looked, and began to laugh. The feet of the dead Witch had disappeared entirely and nothing was left but the silver shoes.

"She was so old," explained the Witch of the North, "that she dried up quickly in the sun. That is the end of her. But the silver shoes are yours, and you shall have them to wear." She reached down and picked up the shoes, and after shaking the dust out of them handed them to Dorothy.

"The Witch of the East was proud of those silver shoes," said one of the Munchkins, "and there is some charm connected with them; but what it is we never knew."

Dorothy carried the shoes into the house and placed them on the table. Then she came out again to the Munchkins and said:

"I am anxious to get back to my aunt and uncle, for I am sure they will worry about me. Can you help me find my way?"

The Munchkins and the Witch first looked at one another, and then at Dorothy, and then shook their heads.

"At the East, not far from here," said one, "there is a great desert, and none could live to cross it."

"It is the same at the South," said another, "for I have been there and seen it. The South is the country of the Quadlings."

"I am told," said the third man, "that it is the same at the West. And that country, where the Winkies live, is ruled by the Wicked Witch of the West, who would make you her slave if you passed her way."

"The North is my home," said the old lady, "and at its edge is the same great desert that surrounds this Land of Oz. I'm afraid, my dear, you will have to live with us."

Dorothy began to sob at this, for she felt lonely among all these strange people. Her tears seemed to grieve the kind-hearted Munchkins, for they immediately took out their handkerchiefs and began to weep also. As for the little old woman, she took off her cap and balanced the point on the end of her nose, while she counted "One, two, three" in a solemn voice. At once the cap changed to a slate, on which was written

in big, white chalk marks:

Let Dorothy Go to the City of Emeralds

The little old woman took the slate from her nose, and having read the words on it, asked, "Is your name Dorothy, my dear?"

"Yes," answered the child, looking up and drying her tears.

"Then you must go to the City of Emeralds. Perhaps Oz will help you."

"Where is this city?" asked Dorothy.

"It is exactly in the center of the country, and is ruled by Oz, the Great Wizard I told you of."

"Is he a good man?" inquired the girl anxiously.

"He is a good Wizard. Whether he is a man or not I cannot tell, for I have never seen him."

"How can I get there?" asked Dorothy.

"You must walk. It is a long journey, through a country that is sometimes pleasant and sometimes dark and terrible. However, I will use all the magic arts I know of to keep you from harm."

"Won't you go with me?" pleaded the girl, who had begun to look upon the little old woman as her only friend.

"No, I cannot do that," she replied, "but I will give you my kiss, and no one will dare injure a person who has been kissed by the Witch of the North."

She came close to Dorothy and kissed her gently on the forehead. Where her lips touched the girl they left a round, shining mark, as Dorothy found out soon after.

"The road to the City of Emeralds is paved with yellow brick," said the Witch, "so you cannot miss it. When you get to Oz do not be afraid of him, but tell your story and ask him to help you. Good-by.

The three Munchkins bowed low to her

and wished her a pleasant journey, after which they walked away through the trees. The Witch gave Dorothy a friendly little nod, whirled around on her left heel three times, and straightway disappeared, much to the surprise of little Toto, who barked after her loudly enough when she had gone, because he had been afraid even to growl while she stood by.

But Dorothy, knowing her to be a witch, had expected her to disappear in just that way, and was not surprised in the least.

DOROTHY SAVES THE SCARECROW

When Dorothy was left alone she began to feel hungry. So she went to the cupboard and cut herself some bread, which she spread with butter. She gave some to Toto, and taking a pail from the shelf she carried it down to the little brook and filled it with clear, sparkling water. Toto ran over to the trees and began to bark at the birds sitting there. Dorothy went to get him, and saw such delicious fruit hanging from the branches that she gathered some of it, finding it just what she wanted to help out her breakfast.

Then she went back to the house, and having helped herself and Toto to a good drink of the cool, clear water, she set about making ready for the journey to the City of Emeralds.

She took a little basket and filled it with bread from the cupboard, laying a white cloth over the top. Then she looked down at her feet and noticed how old and worn her shoes were.

"They surely will never do for a long journey, Toto," she said. And Toto looked up into her face with his little black eyes and wagged his tail to show he knew what she meant.

At that moment Dorothy saw lying on the table the silver shoes that had belonged to the Witch of the East.

"I wonder if they will fit me," she said to Toto. "They would be just the thing to take a long walk in, for they could not wear out."

She took off her old leather shoes and tried on the silver ones, which fitted her as well as if they had been made for her.

Finally she picked up her basket.

"Come along, Toto," she said. "We will go to the Emerald City and ask the great Oz how to get back to Kansas again."

She closed the door, locked it, and put the key carefully in the pocket of her dress. And so, with Toto trotting along soberly behind her, she started on her journey.

There were several roads near by, but it did not take her long to find the one paved with yellow brick. Within a short time she was walking briskly toward the Emerald City, her silver shoes tinkling merrily on the hard, yellow roadbed.

She was surprised, as she walked along, to see how pretty the country was about her. There were neat fences at the sides of the road, painted a dainty blue color, and beyond them were fields of grain and vegetables in abundance. Evidently the Munchkins were good farmers and able to raise large crops. Once in a while she would pass a house, and the people came out to look at her and bow low as she went by; for everyone knew she had been the means of destroying the Wicked Witch and setting them free from bondage. The houses of the Munchkins were odd-looking dwellings, for each was round, with a big dome for a roof. All were painted blue, for in this country of the East blue was the favorite color.

When she had gone several miles she thought she would stop to rest, and so climbed to the top of the fence beside the road and sat down. There was a great cornfield beyond the fence, and not far away she saw a Scarecrow, placed high on a pole to keep the birds from the ripe corn.

Dorothy leaned her chin upon her hand and gazed thoughtfully at the Scarecrow. Its head was a small sack stuffed with straw, with eyes, nose and mouth painted on it to represent a face. An old, pointed blue hat, that had belonged to some Munchkin, was perched on his head, and the rest of the figure was a blue suit of clothes, worn and faded, which had also been stuffed with straw. On the feet were some old boots with blue tops, such as every man wore in this country, and the figure was raised above the stalks of corn by means of the pole stuck up its back.

While Dorothy was looking earnestly into the queer, painted face of the Scarecrow, she was surprised to see one of the eyes slowly wink at her. She thought she must have been mistaken at first, for none of the scarecrows in Kansas ever wink; but presently the figure nodded its head to her in a friendly way. Then she climbed down from the fence and walked up to it, while Toto ran around the pole and barked.

"Good day," said the Scarecrow, in a rather husky voice.

"Did you speak?" asked the girl, in wonder.

"Certainly," answered the Scarecrow. "How do you do?"

"I'm pretty well, thank you," replied Dorothy, politely. "How do you do?"

"I'm not feeling well," said the Scare-

crow with a smile, "for it is very tedious being perched up here night and day to scare away crows."

"Can't you get down?" asked Dorothy.

"No, for this pole is stuck up my back. If you will please take away the pole I shall be greatly obliged to you."

Dorothy reached up both arms and lifted the figure off the pole, for being stuffed with straw, it was quite light.

"Thank you very much," said the Scarecrow, when he had been set down on the ground. "I feel like a new man."

Dorothy was puzzled at this, for it sounded queer to hear a stuffed man speak, and to see him bow and walk along beside her.

"Who are you?" asked the Scarecrow when he had stretched himself and yawned. "And where are you going?"

"My name is Dorothy," said the girl, "and I am going to the Emerald City, to ask the great Oz to send me back to Kansas."

"Where is the Emerald City?" he inquired. "And who is Oz?"

"Why, don't you know?" she returned, in surprise.

"No, indeed; I don't know anything. You see, I am stuffed, so I have no brains at all," he answered, sadly.

"Oh," said Dorothy, "I'm awfully sorry for you."

"Do you think," he asked, "if I go to the Emerald City with you, that Oz would give me some brains?"

"I cannot tell," she returned; "but you may come with me, if you like. If Oz will not give you any brains you will be no worse off than you are now."

"That is true," said the Scarecrow. "You see," he continued confidentially, "I don't mind my legs and arms and body being stuffed, because I cannot get hurt. If anyone treads on my toes or sticks a pin into me, it doesn't matter, for I can't feel it. But I do not want people to call me a fool, and if my head stays stuffed with straw instead of with brains, as yours is, how am I ever to know anything?"

"I understand how you feel," said the little girl, who was truly sorry for him. "If you will come with me I'll ask Oz to do all he can for you."

"Thank you," he answered gratefully.

They walked back to the road. Dorothy helped him over the fence, and they started along the path of yellow brick for the Emerald City.

Toto did not like this addition to the party, at first. He smelled around the stuffed man as if he suspected there might be a nest of rats in the straw, and he often growled in an unfriendly way at the Scarecrow.

"Don't mind Toto," said Dorothy, to her new friend. "He never bites."

"Oh, I'm not afraid," replied the Scarecrow. "He can't hurt the straw. Do let me carry that basket for you. I shall not mind it, for I can't get tired. I'll tell you a secret," he continued, as he walked along. "There is only one thing in the world I am afraid of."

"What is that?" asked Dorothy. "The Munchkin farmer who made you?"

"No," answered the scarecrow. "It's a lighted match."

THE ROAD THROUGH THE FOREST

At noon they sat down by the roadside, near a little brook, and Dorothy opened her basket and got out some bread. She offered a piece to the Scarecrow, but he refused.

"I am never hungry," he said; "and it is a lucky thing I am not. For my mouth is only painted, and if I should cut a hole in it so I could eat, the straw I am stuffed with would come out, and that would spoil the shape of my head."

Dorothy saw at once that this was true, so she only nodded and went on eating her bread.

"Won't you tell me a story, while we are resting?" she asked.

The Scarecrow looked at Dorothy reproachfully, and answered.

"My life has been so short that I really know nothing whatever. I was only made day before yesterday. What happened in the world before that time is all unknown to me. Luckily, when the farmer made my head, one of the first things he did was to paint my ears, so that I heard what was going on. There was another Munchkin with him, and the first thing I heard was the farmer saying, 'How do you like those ears?'

" 'They aren't straight,' answered the other.

" 'Never mind,' said the farmer. 'They are ears just the same,' which was true enough.

" 'Now I'll make the eyes,' said the farmer. So he painted my right eye, and as soon as it was finished I found myself looking at him and at everything around me with a great deal of curiosity, for this was my first glimpse of the world.

" 'That's a rather pretty eye,' remarked the Munchkin who was watching the farmer. 'Blue paint is just the color for eyes.'

" 'I think I'll make the other a little bigger,' said the farmer; and when the second eye was done I could see much better than before. Then he made my nose and my mouth; but I did not speak, because at that time I didn't know what a mouth was for. I had the fun of watching them make my body and my arms and legs; and when they fastened on my head, at last, I felt very proud, for I thought I was just as good a man as anyone.

" 'This fellow will scare the crows fast enough,' said the farmer. 'He looks just like a man.'

" 'Why, he is a man,' said the other, and I quite agreed with him. The farmer carried me under his arm to the cornfield, and set me up on a tall stick, where you found me. He and his friend soon after walked away and left me alone.

"I did not like to be deserted this way; so I tried to walk after them, but my feet would not touch the ground, and I was forced to stay on that pole. It was a lonely life to lead, for I had nothing to think of, having been made such a little while before. Many crows and other birds flew into the cornfield, but as soon as they saw me they flew away again, thinking I was a Munchkin; and this pleased me and made me feel that I was quite an important person. By and by an old crow flew near me, and after looking at me carefully he perched upon my shoulder and said:

" 'I wonder if that farmer thought to fool me in this clumsy manner. Any crow of sense could see that you are only stuffed with straw.' Then he hopped down at my feet and ate all the corn he wanted. The other birds, seeing he was not harmed by me, came to eat the corn too, so in a short time there was a great flock of them about me.

58

"I felt sad at this, for it showed I was not such a good Scarecrow after all; but the old crow comforted me, saying: 'If you only had brains in your head you would be as good a man as any of them, and a better man than some of them. Brains are the only things worth having in this world, no matter whether one is a crow or a man.'

"After the crows had gone I thought this over, and decided I would try hard to get some brains. By good luck, you came along and pulled me off the stake, and from what you say I am sure the great Oz will give me brains as soon as we get to the Emerald City."

"I hope so," said Dorothy, earnestly, "since you seem anxious to have them."

"Oh, yes; I am anxious," returned the Scarecrow. "It is such an uncomfortable feeling to know one is a fool."

"Well," said the girl, "let us go." And she handed the basket to the Scarecrow.

There were no fences at all by the road side now, and the land was rough and untilled. Toward evening they came to a great forest, where the trees grew so big and close together that their branches met over the road of yellow brick. It was almost dark under the trees, for the branches shut out the daylight; but the travelers did not stop, and went on into the forest.

"If this road goes in, it must come out," said the Scarecrow, "and as the Emerald City is at the other end of the road, we must go wherever it leads us."

"Anyone would know that," said Dorothy.

"Certainly; that is why I know it," returned the Scarecrow. "If it required brains to figure it out, I never should have said it."

After an hour or so the light faded away, and they found themselves stumbling along in the darkness. Dorothy could not see at all, but Toto could, for some dogs see very well in the dark; and the Scarecrow declared he could see as well as by day. So she took hold of his arm, and managed to get along fairly well.

"If you see any house, or any place where we can pass the night," she said, "you must tell me; for it is very uncomfortable walking in the dark."

Soon after the Scarecrow stopped.

"I see a little cottage at the right of us," he said, "built of logs and branches. Shall we go there?"

"Yes, indeed," answered the child. "I am tired out."

So the Scarecrow led her through the trees until they reached the cottage, and Dorothy entered and found a bed of dried leaves in one corner. She lay down at once, and with Toto beside her soon fell into a sound sleep. The Scarecrow, who was never tired, stood up in another corner and waited patiently until morning came.

THE RESCUE OF THE TIN WOODMAN

When Dorothy awoke the sun was shining through the trees and Toto had long been out chasing birds around her. There was the Scarecrow, still standing patiently in his corner, waiting for her.

"We must go and search for water," she said to him.

"Why do you want water?" he asked.

"To wash my face clean after the dust of the road, and to drink, so the dry bread will not stick in my throat."

"It must be inconvenient to be made of flesh," said the Scarecrow, thoughtfully, "for you must sleep, and eat and drink.

59

brick, she was startled to hear a deep groan near by.

"What was that?" she asked, timidly.

"I cannot imagine," replied the Scarecrow; "but we can go and see."

Just then another groan reached their ears, and the sound seemed to come from behind them. They turned and walked through the forest a few steps, when Dorothy discovered something shining in a ray of sunshine that fell between the trees. She ran to the place and then stopped short, with a cry of surprise.

One of the big trees had been partly chopped through, and standing beside it, with an uplifted ax in his hands was a man made entirely of tin. His head and arms and legs were jointed upon his body, but he stood perfectly motionless, as if he could not stir at all.

Dorothy looked at him in amazement, and so did the Scarecrow, while Toto barked sharply and made a snap at the tin legs, which hurt his teeth.

"Did you groan?" asked Dorothy.

"Yes," answered the tin man, "I did. I've been groaning for more than a year, and no one has ever heard me before or come to help me."

"What can I do for you?" she inquired softly, for she was moved by the sad voice in which the man spoke.

"Get an oilcan and oil my joints," he answered. "They are rusted so badly that I cannot move them at all; if I am well oiled I shall soon be all right again. You

However, you have brains, and it is worth a lot of bother to be able to think properly."

They left the cottage and walked through the trees until they found a little spring of clear water, where Dorothy drank and bathed and ate her breakfast. She saw there was not much left in the basket, and the girl was thankful the Scarecrow did not have to eat anything, for there was scarcely enough for herself and Toto for the day.

When she had finished her meal, and was about to go back to the road of yellow will find an oilcan on a shelf in my cottage."

Dorothy at once ran back to the cottage and found the oilcan, and then she returned and asked, anxiously, "Where are your joints?"

"Oil my neck, first," replied the Tin Woodman. So she oiled it, and as it was quite badly rusted the Scarecrow took hold of the tin head and moved it gently from side to side until it worked freely, and then the man could turn it himself.

"Now oil the joints in my arms," he said. And Dorothy oiled them and the Scarecrow bent them carefully until they were quite free from rust and as good as new.

The Tin Woodman gave a sigh of satisfaction and lowered his ax, which he leaned against the tree.

"This is a great comfort," he said. "I have been holding that ax in the air ever since I rusted, and I'm glad to be able to put it down at last. Now, if you will oil the joints of my legs, I shall be all right once more."

So they oiled his legs until he could move them freely; and he thanked them again and again for his release, for he seemed a very polite creature, and very grateful.

"I might have stood there always if you had not come along," he said; "so you have certainly saved my life. How did you happen to be here?"

"We are on our way to the Emerald City, to see the great Oz," she answered, "and we stopped at your cottage to pass the night."

"Why do you wish to see Oz?" he asked.

"I want him to send me back to Kansas; and the Scarecrow wants him to put a few brains into his head," she replied.

The Tin Woodman appeared to think deeply for a moment. Then he said:

"Do you suppose Oz could give me a heart?"

"Why, I guess so," Dorothy answered. "It would be as easy as to give the Scarecrow brains."

"True," the Tin Woodman returned. "So, if you will allow me to join your party, I will also go to the Emerald City and ask Oz to help me."

"Come along," said the Scarecrow heartily; and Dorothy added that she would be pleased to have his company. So the Tin Woodman shouldered his ax and they all passed through the forest until they came to the road that was paved with yellow brick.

The Tin Woodman had asked Dorothy to put the oilcan in her basket. "For," he said, "if I should get caught in the rain, and rust again, I would need the oilcan badly."

It was a bit of good luck to have their new comrade join the party, for soon after they had begun their journey again they came to a place where the trees and branches grew so thick over the road that the travelers could not pass. But the Tin Woodman set to work with his ax and chopped so well that soon he cleared a passage for the entire party.

Dorothy was thinking so earnestly as they walked along that she did not notice when the Scarecrow stumbled into a hole and rolled over to the side of the road. Indeed he was obliged to call to her to help him up again.

"Why didn't you walk around the hole?" asked the Tin Woodman.

"I don't know enough," replied the Scarecrow cheerfully. "My head is stuffed with straw, you know, and that is why I am going to Oz to ask him for some brains."

61

"Oh, I see," said the Tin Woodman. "But, after all, brains are not the best things in the world."

"Have you any?" inquired the Scarecrow.

"No, my head is quite empty," answered the Woodman; "but once I had brains, and a heart also; so, having tried them both, I should much rather have a heart."

"And why is that?" asked the Scarecrow.

"I will tell you my story, and then you will know."

So, while they were walking through the forest, the Tin Woodman told the following story:

"I was born the son of a woodman who chopped down trees in the forest and sold the wood for a living. When I grew up I too became a woodchopper, and after my father died I took care of my old mother as long as she lived. Then I made up my mind that instead of living alone I would marry, so that I might not become lonely.

"There was one of the Munchkin girls who was so beautiful that I soon grew to love her with all my heart. She, on her part, promised to marry me as soon as I could earn enough money to build a better house for her; so I set to work harder than ever. But the girl lived with an old woman who did not want her to marry anyone, for she was so lazy she wished the girl to remain with her and do the cooking and the housework. So the old woman went to the Wicked Witch of the East, and promised her two sheep and a cow if she would prevent the marriage. Thereupon the Wicked Witch enchanted my ax, and when I was chopping away at my best one day, for I was anxious to get the new house and my wife as soon as possible, the ax slipped all at once and cut off my left leg.

"This at first seemed a great misfortune, for I knew a one-legged man could not do very well as a woodchopper. So I went to a tinsmith and had him make me a new leg out of tin. The leg worked very well, once I was used to it; but my action angered the Wicked Witch of the East, for she had promised the old woman I should not marry the pretty Munchkin girl. When I began chopping again my ax slipped and cut off my right leg. Again I went to the tinner, and again he made me a leg out of tin. After this the enchanted ax cut off my arms, one after the other; but, nothing daunted, I had them replaced with tin ones. The Wicked Witch then made the ax slip and cut off my head, and at first I thought that was the end of me. But the tinner happened to come along, and he made me a new head of tin.

"I thought I had beaten the Wicked Witch then, and I worked harder than ever; but I little knew how cruel my enemy could be. She thought of a new way to kill my love for the beautiful Munchkin maiden, and made my ax slip again, so that it cut right through my body, splitting me into two halves. Once more the tinner came to my help and made me a body of tin, fastening my tin arms and legs and head to it, by means of joints, so that I could move around as well as ever. But, alas! I had no heart, so that I lost all my love for the Munchkin girl, and did not care whether I married her or not. I suppose she is still living with the old woman, waiting for me to come after her.

"My body shone so brightly in the sun that I felt very proud of it and it did not matter now if my ax slipped, for it could not cut me. There was only one danger—that my joints would rust; but I kept an oilcan in my cottage and took care to oil myself whenever I needed it. However, there came a day when I forgot to do this, and, being caught in a rainstorm, before I thought of the danger my joints had rusted, and I was left to stand in the woods until you came to help me. It was a terrible thing to undergo, but during the year I stood there I had time to think that the greatest loss I had known was the loss of my heart. While I was in love I was the happiest man on earth; but no one can love who has not a heart, and so I am resolved to ask Oz to give me one. If he does, I will go back to the Munchkin maiden and marry her."

Both Dorothy and the Scarecrow had been greatly interested in the story of the Tin Woodman, and now they knew why he was so anxious to get a new heart.

"All the same," said the Scarecrow, "I shall ask for brains instead of a heart; for a fool would not know what to do with a heart if he had one."

"I shall take the heart," returned the Tin Woodman; "for brains do not make one happy, and happiness is the best thing in the world."

Dorothy did not say anything, for she was puzzled to know which of her two friends was right.

THE COWARDLY LION

All this time Dorothy and her companions had been walking through the thick woods. The road was still paved with yellow bricks, but these were much covered by dried branches and dead leaves from the trees, and the walking was not at all good.

There were few birds in this part of the forest, for birds love the open country where there is plenty of sunshine; but now and then there came a deep growl from some wild animal hidden among the trees. These sounds made the little girl's heart beat fast, for she did not know what made them; but Toto knew, and he walked close to Dorothy's side, and did not even bark in return.

"How long will it be," the child asked of the Tin Woodman, "before we are out of the forest?"

"I cannot tell," was the answer, "for I have never been to the Emerald City. But my father went there once, when I was a boy, and he said it was a long journey through a dangerous country, although nearer to the city where Oz dwells the country is beautiful. But I am not afraid so long as I have my oilcan, and nothing can hurt the Scarecrow, while you bear upon your forehead the mark of the good Witch's kiss, and that will protect you from harm."

"But Toto!" said the girl anxiously. "What will protect him?"

"We must protect him ourselves, if he is in danger," replied the Tin Woodman.

Just as he spoke there came from the forest a terrible roar, and the next moment a great Lion bounded into the road. With one blow of his paw he sent the Scarecrow spinning over and over to the edge of the road, and then he struck at the Tin Woodman, with his sharp claws. But, to the Lion's surprise, he could make no impression on the tin, although the Woodman fell over in the road and lay still.

Little Toto, now that he had an enemy to face, ran barking toward the Lion, and the great beast had opened his mouth to bite the dog, when Dorothy, fearing Toto would be killed, and heedless of danger, rushed forward and slapped the Lion upon his nose as hard as she could, while she cried out:

"Don't you dare to bite Toto! You ought to be ashamed of yourself, a big beast like you, to bite a poor little dog!"

"I didn't bite him," said the Lion, as he rubbed his nose with his paw where Dorothy had hit it.

"No, but you tried to," she retorted. "You are nothing but a big coward."

"I know it," said the Lion, hanging his head in shame. "I've always known it. But how can I help it?"

"I don't know, I'm sure. To think of your striking a stuffed man, like the poor Scarecrow!"

"Is he stuffed?" asked the Lion in surprise, as he watched her pick up the Scarecrow and set him upon his feet, while she patted him into shape again.

"Of course he's stuffed," replied Dorothy, who was still angry.

"That's why he went over so easily," remarked the Lion. "It astonished me to see him whirl around so. Is the other one stuffed also?"

"No," said Dorothy, "he's made of tin." And she helped the Woodman up again.

"That's why he nearly blunted my claws," said the Lion. "When they scratched against the tin it made a cold shiver run down my back. What is that little animal you are so tender of?"

"He is my dog, Toto," answered Dorothy.

"Is he made of tin, or stuffed?" asked the Lion.

"Neither. He's a—a—a meat dog," said the girl.

"Oh! He's a curious animal, and seems remarkably small, now that I look at him. No one would think of biting such a little

thing except a coward like me," continued the Lion sadly.

"What makes you a coward?" asked Dorothy, looking at the great beast in wonder, for he was as big as a small horse.

"It's a mystery," replied the Lion. "I suppose I was born that way. All the other animals in the forest naturally expect me to be brave, for the Lion is everywhere thought to be the King of Beasts. I learned that if I roared very loudly every living thing was frightened and got out of my way. Whenever I've met a man I've been awfully scared; but I just roared at him, and he has always run away as fast as he could go. If the elephants and the tigers and the bears had ever tried to fight me, I should have run myself—I'm such a coward; but just as soon as they hear me roar they all try to get away from me, and of course I let them go."

"But that isn't right. The King of Beasts shouldn't be a coward," said the Scarecrow.

"I know it," returned the Lion, wiping a tear from his eye with the tip of his tail. "It is my great sorrow, and makes my life very unhappy. But whenever there is danger my heart begins to beat fast."

"Perhaps you have heart disease," said the Tin Woodman.

"It may be," said the Lion.

"If you have," continued the Tin Woodman, "you ought to be glad, for it proves you have a heart. For my part, I have no heart; so I cannot have heart disease."

"Perhaps," said the Lion thoughtfully, "if I had no heart I should not be a coward."

"Have you brains?" asked the Scarecrow.

"I suppose so. I've never looked to see," replied the Lion.

"I am going to the great Oz to ask him

to give me some," remarked the Scarecrow, "for my head is stuffed with straw."

"And I am going to ask him to give me a heart," said the Woodman.

"And I am going to ask him to send Toto and me back to Kansas," added Dorothy.

"Do you think Oz could give me courage?" asked the Cowardly Lion.

"Just as easily as he could give me brains," said the Scarecrow.

"Or give me a heart," said the Tin Woodman.

"Or send me back to Kansas," said Dorothy.

"Then, if you don't mind, I'll go with you," said the Lion, "for my life is simply unbearable without a bit of courage."

"You will be very welcome," answered Dorothy, "for you will help to keep away the other wild beasts. It seems to me they must be more cowardly than you are if they allow you to scare them so easily."

"They really are," said the Lion, "but that doesn't make me any braver, and as long as I know myself to be a coward I shall be unhappy."

So once more the little company set off upon the journey, the Lion walking with stately strides at Dorothy's side. Toto did not approve this new comrade at first, for he could not forget how nearly he had been crushed between the Lion's great jaws; but after a time he became more at ease, and presently Toto and the Cowardly Lion had grown to be good friends.

During the rest of that day there was no other adventure to mar the peace of their journey. Once, indeed, the Tin Woodman stepped upon a beetle that was crawling along the road, and killed the poor little thing. This made the Tin Woodman very unhappy, for he was always careful not to hurt any living creature; and as he walked along he wept several tears of sorrow and regret. These tears ran slowly down his face and over the hinges of his jaw, and there they rusted. When Dorothy presently asked him a question the Tin Woodman could not open his mouth, for his jaws were tightly rusted together. He became greatly frightened at this and made many motions to Dorothy to relieve him, but she could not understand. The Lion was also puzzled to know what was wrong. But the Scarecrow seized the oilcan from Dorothy's basket and oiled the Woodman's jaws, so that after a few moments he could talk as well as before.

"This will serve me a lesson," said he, "to look where I step. For if I should kill another bug or beetle I should surely cry again, and crying rusts my jaws so that I cannot speak."

Thereafter he walked very carefully, with his eyes on the road, and when he saw a tiny ant toiling by he would step over it, so as not to harm it. The Tin Woodman knew very well he had no heart, and therefore he took great care never to be cruel or unkind to anything.

"You people with hearts," he said, "have something to guide you, and need never do wrong; but I have no heart, and so I must be very careful. When Oz gives me a heart of course I needn't mind so much."

THE DEADLY POPPY FIELD

After a while they came upon a broad river, flowing swiftly just before them. On the other side of the water they could see the road of yellow brick running through a beautiful country, with green meadows dotted with bright flowers and all the road bordered with trees hanging full of delicious fruits. They were greatly pleased to see this delightful country before them.

They walked along listening to the singing of the bright-colored birds and looking at the lovely flowers which now became so thick that the ground was carpeted with them. There were big yellow and white and blue and purple blossoms, besides great clusters of scarlet poppies, which were so brilliant in color they almost dazzled Dorothy's eyes.

"Aren't they beautiful?" the girl asked, as she breathed in the spicy scent of the flowers.

"I suppose so," answered the Scarecrow. "When I have brains I shall probably like them better."

"If I only had a heart I should love them," added the Tin Woodman.

"I always did like flowers," said the Lion; "they seem so helpless and frail. But there are none in the forest so bright as these."

They now came upon more and more of the big scarlet poppies, and fewer and fewer of the other flowers; and soon they found themselves in the midst of a great meadow of poppies. Now it is well known that when there are many of these flowers together their odor is so powerful that anyone who breathes it falls asleep, and if the sleeper is not carried away from the scent of the flowers he sleeps on and on forever. But Dorothy did not know this, nor could she get away from the bright red flowers that were everywhere about; so presently her eyes grew heavy and she felt she must sit down to rest and to sleep.

But the Tin Woodman would not let her do this.

"We must hurry and get back to the road of yellow brick before dark," he said; and the Scarecrow agreed with him. So they kept walking until Dorothy could stand no longer. Her eyes closed in spite of herself

and she forgot where she was and fell among the poppies, fast asleep.

"What shall we do?" asked the Tin Woodman.

"If we leave her here she will die," said the Lion. "The smell of the flowers is killing us all. I myself can scarcely keep my eyes open and the dog is asleep already."

It was true; Toto had fallen down beside his little mistress. But the Scarecrow and the Tin Woodman, not being made of flesh, were not troubled by the scent of the flowers.

"Run fast," said the Scarecrow to the Lion, "and get out of this deadly flower bed as soon as you can. We will bring the little girl with us, but if you should fall asleep you are too big to be carried."

So the Lion aroused himself and bounded forward as fast as he could go. In a moment he was out of sight.

"Let us make a chair with our hands, and carry her," said the Scarecrow. So they picked up Toto and put the dog in Dorothy's lap, and then they made a chair with their hands for the seat and their arms for the arms and carried the sleeping girl between them through the flowers.

On and on they walked, and it seemed that the great carpet of deadly flowers that surrounded them would never end. They followed the bend of the river, and at last came upon their friend the Lion, lying fast asleep among the poppies. The flowers had been too strong for the huge beast and he had given up, at last, and fallen only a short distance from the end of the poppy bed, where the sweet grass spread in beautiful green fields before them.

"We can do nothing for him," said the Tin Woodman, sadly; "for he is much too heavy to lift. We must leave him here to sleep on forever, and perhaps he will dream that he has found courage at last."

"I'm sorry," said the Scarecrow. "The Lion was a very good comrade for one so cowardly. But let us go on."

They carried the sleeping girl to a pretty spot beside the river, far enough from the poppy field to prevent her breathing any more of the poison of the flowers, and here they laid her gently on the soft grass and waited for the fresh breeze to waken her.

THE QUEEN OF THE FIELD MICE

"We cannot be far from the road of yellow brick now," remarked the Scarecrow, as he stood beside the girl, "for we have come nearly as far as the river carried us away."

The Tin Woodman was about to reply when he heard a low growl, and turning his head (which worked beautifully on hinges) he saw a strange beast come bounding over the grass toward them. It was, indeed, a great, yellow Wildcat, and the Woodman thought it must be chasing something, for its ears were lying close to its head and its mouth was wide open, showing two rows of ugly teeth, while its red eyes glowed like balls of fire. As it came nearer the Tin Woodman saw that running before the beast was a little gray field mouse, and although he had no heart he know it was wrong for the Wildcat to try to kill such a pretty, harmless creature.

So the Woodman raised his ax, and as the Wildcat ran by he gave it a quick blow that cut the beast's head clean off from its body, and it rolled over at his feet in two pieces.

The field mouse, now that it was freed from its enemy, stopped short; and coming slowly up to the Woodman it said, in a squeaky little voice:

"Oh, thank you! Thank you ever so much for saving my life."

"Don't speak of it, I beg of you," replied the Woodman. "I have no heart, you know, so I am careful to help all those who may need a friend, even if it happens to be only a mouse."

"Only a mouse!" cried the little animal, indignantly. "Why, I am a Queen—the Queen of all the field mice!"

"Oh, indeed," said the Woodman, making a bow.

"Therefore you have done a great deed, as well as a brave one, in saving my life," added the Queen.

At that moment several mice were seen running up as fast as their little legs could carry them, and when they saw their Queen they exclaimed:

"Oh, your Majesty, we thought you would be killed! How did you manage to escape the great Wildcat?" and they all bowed so low to the little Queen that they almost stood upon their heads.

"This funny Tin Man," she answered, "killed the Wildcat and saved my life. So hereafter you must all serve him, and obey his slightest wish."

"We will!" cried all the mice, in a shrill chorus. And then they scampered in all directions, for Toto had awakened from his sleep, and seeing all these mice around him he gave one bark of delight and jumped right into the middle of the group. Toto had always loved to chase mice when he lived in Kansas, and he saw no harm in it.

But the Tin Woodman caught the dog in his arms and held him tight, while he called to the mice: "Come back! Come back! Toto shall not hurt you."

At this the Queen of the Mice stuck her head out from underneath a clump of grass and asked, in a timid voice, "Are you sure he will not bite us?"

"I will not let him," said the Woodman; "so do not be afraid."

One by one the mice came creeping back, and Toto did not bark again, although he tried to get out of the Woodman's arms, and would have bitten him had he not known very well he was made of tin. Finally one of the biggest mice spoke.

"Is there anything we can do," it asked, "to repay you for saving the life of our Queen?"

"Nothing that I know of," answered the Woodman; but the Scarecrow, who had been trying to think, but could not because his head was stuffed with straw, said, quickly, "Oh, yes; you can save our friend, the Cowardly Lion, who is asleep in the poppy bed."

"A Lion!" cried the little Queen. "Why, he would eat us all up."

"Oh, no," declared the Scarecrow; "this Lion is a coward."

"Really?" asked the Mouse.

"He says so himself," answered the Scarecrow, "and he would never hurt anyone who is our friend. If you will help us to save him I promise that he shall treat you all with kindness."

"Very well," said the Queen, "we will trust you. But what shall we do?"

"Are there many of these mice which call you Queen and are willing to obey you?"

"Oh, yes; there are thousands," she replied.

"Then send for them all to come here as soon as possible, and let each one bring a long piece of string."

The Queen turned to the mice that attended her and told them to go at once and get all her people. As soon as they heard her orders they ran away in every direction as fast as possible.

"Now," said the Scarecrow to the Tin Woodman, "you must go to those trees by the riverside and make a truck that will carry the Lion."

So the Woodman went at once to the trees and began to work; and he soon made a truck out of the limbs of trees, from which he chopped away all the leaves and branches. He fastened it together with wooden pegs and made the four wheels out of short pieces of a big tree-trunk. So fast and so well did he work that by the time the mice began to arrive the truck was all ready for them.

They came from all directions, and there were thousands of them: big and little mice and middle-sized mice; and each one brought a piece of string in his mouth. It was about this time that Dorothy woke from her long sleep and opened her eyes. She was greatly astonished to find herself lying upon the grass, with thousands of mice standing around and looking at her timidly. But the Scarecrow told her about everything, and turning to the dignified little Mouse, he said:

"Permit me to introduce to you her Majesty, the Queen."

Dorothy nodded gravely and the Queen made a curtsy, after which she became quite friendly with the little girl.

The Scarecrow and the Woodman now began to fasten the mice to the truck, using the strings they had brought. One end of a string was tied around the neck of each mouse and the other end to the truck. Of course the truck was a thousand times bigger than any of the mice who were to draw it; but when all the mice had been harnessed they were able to pull it quite easily. Even the Scarecrow and the Tin Woodman could sit on it, and were drawn swiftly by their queer little horses to the place where the Lion lay asleep.

After a great deal of hard work, for the Lion was heavy, they managed to get him up on the truck. Then the Queen hurriedly gave her people the order to start, for she feared if the mice stayed among the poppies too long they also would fall asleep.

At first the little creatures, many though they were, could hardly stir the heavily loaded truck; but the Woodman and the Scarecrow both pushed from behind, and they got along better. Soon they rolled the Lion out of the poppy bed to the green fields, where he could breathe the sweet, fresh air again, instead of the poisonous scent of the flowers.

Dorothy came to meet them and thanked the little mice warmly for saving her companion from death. She had grown so fond of the big Lion she was glad he had been rescued.

Then the mice were unharnessed from the truck and scampered away through the grass to their homes. The Queen of the Mice was the last to leave.

"If ever you need us again," she said, "come out into the field and call, and we shall hear you and come to your assistance. Good-by!"

"Good-by!" they all answered, and away the Queen ran, while Dorothy held Toto tightly lest he should run after her and frighten her.

After this they sat down beside the Lion until he should awaken; and the Scarecrow brought Dorothy some fruit from a tree near by, which she ate for her dinner.

It was some time before the Cowardly Lion awakened, for he had lain among the poppies a long while, breathing in their deadly fragrance; but when he did open his eyes and roll off the truck he was very glad to find himself still alive.

"I ran as fast as I could," he said, sitting down and yawning; "but the flowers were too strong for me. How did you get me out?"

Then they told him of the field mice, and how they had generously saved him from death; and the Cowardly Lion laughed and said:

"I have always thought myself very big and terrible; yet such little things as flowers came near to killing me, and such small animals as mice have saved my life. How strange it all is! But, comrades, what shall we do now?"

"We must journey on until we find the road of yellow brick again," said Dorothy; "and then we can keep on to the Emerald City."

So, the Lion being fully refreshed, and feeling quite himself again, they all started upon the journey, greatly enjoying the walk through the soft, fresh grass; and it was not long before they reached the road of yellow brick and turned again toward the Emerald City where the great Oz dwelt.

—Abridged excerpt

The Mountain and the Squirrel

By Ralph Waldo Emerson

The mountain and the squirrel
Had a quarrel,
And the former called the latter "little prig."
Bun replied,
"You are doubtless very big;
But all sorts of things and weather
Must be taken in together
To make up a year,
And a sphere.
And I think it no disgrace
To occupy my place.
If I'm not so large as you,
You are not so small as I,
And not half so spry.
I'll not deny you make
A very pretty squirrel track.
Talents differ; all is well and wisely put:
If I cannot carry forests on my back,
Neither can you crack a nut."

Toby Tyler and Mr. Stubbs

From TOBY TYLER *or* TEN WEEKS WITH A CIRCUS

By James Otis

TOBY TYLER or TEN WEEKS WITH A CIRCUS, is still a favorite with boys and girls for it is the story of a real boy and a true picture of his experiences with circus life. It was written by James Otis Kaler, who wrote under the name of James Otis, and it was first published in 1880.

Toby has run away from his Uncle Dan'l's farm and its dull chores to find fun and excitement in the tinsel and tanbark of a traveling circus. There he meets strange people and strange animals. There, too, he is harshly treated by cruel Mr. Lord who has put him to work at his candy counter. It is when he meets Mr. Stubbs, the monkey, that life becomes more bearable for Toby. You will find out why when you read the story.

"NOW, then, lazy bones," was Mr. Lord's warning cry as Toby came out of the tent, "if you've fooled away enough of your time, you can come here an' tend shop for me while I go to supper. You crammed yourself this noon, an' it'll teach you a good lesson to make you go without anything to eat tonight. It'll make you move round more lively in future."

Instead of becoming accustomed to such treatment as he was receiving from his employers, Toby's heart grew more tender with each brutal word, and this last punishment—that of losing his supper—caused the poor boy more sorrow than blows would. Mr. Lord started for the hotel as he concluded his cruel speech, and poor little Toby, going behind the counter, leaned his head upon the rough boards and cried as if his heart would break.

All the fancied brightness and pleasure of a circus life had vanished, and in its place was the bitterness of remorse that he had repaid Uncle Daniel's kindness by the ingratitude of running away. Toby thought that if he could only nestle his head on the pillows of his little bed in that rough room at Uncle Daniel's, he would be the happiest and best boy, in the future, in all the great wide world.

While he was still sobbing, he heard a voice close at his elbow and, looking up, saw the thinnest man he had ever seen in all his life. The man had flesh-colored tights on. A spangled red velvet garment that was neither pants (because there were no legs to it) nor a coat (because it did not come above his waist) made up the remainder of his costume.

Because he was so wonderfully thin, because of the costume he wore, and because of a highly colored painting which was hanging in front of one of the small tents, Toby knew that the Living Skeleton was before him. His big brown eyes opened all the wider as he gazed at him.

"What is the matter, little fellow?" asked the man in a kindly tone. "What makes you cry so? Has Job Lord been up to his old tricks again?"

"I don't know what his old tricks are." And Toby sobbed, the tears coming again because of the sympathy which this man's voice expressed for him, "but I know that he's a mean, ugly thing—that's what I know. An' if I could only get back to Uncle Dan'l, there hain't elephants enough in all the circuses in the world to pull me away again."

"Oh, you ran away from home, did you?"

"Yes, I did," sobbed Toby, "an' there hain't any boy in any Sunday-school book that ever I read that was half so sorry he'd been bad as I am. It's awful, an' now I can't have any supper, 'cause I stopped to talk with Mr. Stubbs."

"Is Mr. Stubbs one of your friends?" asked the Skeleton as he seated himself in Mr. Lord's own private chair.

"Yes, he is, an' he's the only one in this whole circus who 'pears to be sorry for me. You'd better not let Mr. Lord see you sittin' in that chair or he'll raise a row."

"Job won't raise any row with me," said the Skeleton. "But who is this Mr. Stubbs? I don't seem to know anybody by that name."

"I don't think that is his name. I only call him so, 'cause he looks so much like a feller I know who is named Stubbs."

This satisfied the Skeleton that this Mr. Stubbs must be someone attached to the show, and he asked, "Has Job Lord been whipping you?"

"No. Ben, the driver on the wagon where I ride, told him not to do that again; but he hain't going to let me have any supper, 'cause I was so slow about my work— though I wasn't slow. I only talked to Mr. Stubbs when there wasn't anybody round his cage."

"Sam! Sam! Sam-u-el!"

This name, which was shouted twice in a quick loud voice and the third time in a slow manner, ending almost in a screech, did not come from either Toby or the Skeleton, but from an enormously large woman, in a gaudy blue-and-black dress, cut very short and with low neck and an apology for sleeves, who had just come out from the tent whereon the picture of the Living Skeleton hung.

"Samuel," she screamed again, "come inside this minute, or you'll catch your death o' cold, an' I shall have you wheezin' around with the phthisic all night. Come in, Sam-u-el."

"That's her," said the Skeleton to Toby, as he pointed his thumb in the direction of the fat woman, but paying no attention to the outcry she was making. "That's my wife, Lilly, an' she's the Fat Woman of the show. She's always yellin' after me that way the minute I get out for a little fresh air, an' she's always sayin' just the same thing. Bless you, I never have the phthisic, but *she* does awful. I s'pose 'cause she's so large, she can't feel all over her, an' she thinks it's me that has it."

"Is — is all that — is that your wife?" stammered Toby, in astonishment, as he looked at the enormously fat woman who stood in the tent door and then at the wonderfully thin man who sat beside him.

"Yes, that's her," said the Skeleton. "She weighs pretty nigh four hundred, though of course the show cards says it's over six hundred, an' she earns almost as much money as I do. Of course she can't get so much, for skeletons is much scarcer than fat folks. But we make a pretty good thing travelin' together."

"Sam-u-el!" again came the cry from the Fat Woman. "Are you never coming in?"

"Not yet, my angel," said the Skeleton, placidly, as he crossed one thin leg over the other and looked calmly at her. "Come here an' see Job's new boy."

"Your carelessness is wearin' me away so that I sha'n't be worth five dollars a week to any circus," she said, impatiently, at the same time coming toward the candy stand

73

as rapidly as her very great size would admit.

"This is my wife Lilly—Mrs. Treat," said the Skeleton, with a proud wave of his hand, as he rose from his seat and gazed admiringly at her. "This is my flower—my queen, Mr.—Mr.—"

"Tyler," said Toby, supplying the name which the Skeleton—or Mr. Treat, as Toby now learned his name was—did not know, "Tyler is my name—Toby Tyler."

"Why, what a little chap you are!" said Mrs. Treat, paying no attention to the awkward little bend of the head which Toby intended for a bow. "How small he is, Samuel!"

"Yes," said the Skeleton. He looked Toby over from head to foot, as if he were mentally trying to calculate exactly how many inches high he was. "He is small; but he's got all the world before him to grow in, an' if he only eats enough— There, that reminds me. Job isn't going to give him any supper, because he didn't work hard enough."

"He won't, won't he?" exclaimed the large lady, savagely. "Some day I shall just give him a good shakin'-up, that's what I'll do. I get all out of patience with that man's ugliness."

"An' she'll do just what she says," said the Skeleton to Toby, with an admiring shake of the head. "That woman hain't afraid of anybody, an' I wouldn't be a bit surprised if she did give Job Lord a pretty rough time."

Toby thought, as he looked at her, that she was large enough to give 'most anyone a pretty rough time, but he did not venture to say so. While he was looking first at her and then at her very thin husband, the Skeleton told his wife the little that he had learned regarding the boy's history; and when he had finished, she waddled away toward her tent.

"Great woman that," said the Skeleton, as he saw her disappear within the tent.

"Yes," said Toby. "She's the greatest I ever saw."

"I mean that she's got a great head. You'll see how much she cares for what Job says."

"If I was as big as her," said Toby, with just a shade of envy in his voice, "I wouldn't be afraid of anybody."

"It hain't so much the size," said the Skeleton. "I can scare that woman almost to death when I feel like it."

Toby looked for a moment at Mr. Treat's thin legs and arms and then he said, warningly, " I wouldn't feel like it very often if I was you, Mr. Treat, 'cause she might break some of your bones if you didn't happen to scare her enough."

"Don't fear for me, my boy—don't fear for me. You'll see how I manage her if you stay with the circus long enough. Now, I often—"

If Mr. Treat was about to confide a family secret to Toby, it was fated that he should not hear it then, for Mrs. Treat had just come out of her tent, carrying in her hands a large tin plate piled high with a miscellaneous assortment of pie, cake, bread, and meat.

She placed this in front of Toby, and as she did so, she handed him two pictures.

"There, little Toby Tyler," she said, "there's something for you to eat, if Mr. Job Lord and his precious partner did say you shouldn't have any supper; an' I've brought you a picture of Samuel an' me.

We sell 'em for ten cents apiece, but I'm going to give them to you, because I like the looks of you."

Toby was quite overcome with the presents and seemed at a loss how to thank her for them. He attempted to speak but could not get the words out at first. Then he said, as he put the two photographs in the same pocket with his money, "You're awful good to me, an' when I get to be a man, I'll give you lots of things. I wasn't so very hungry, if I am such a big eater, but I did want something."

"Bless your dear little heart, and you *shall* have something to eat," said the Fat Woman, as she seized Toby, squeezed him close up to her, and kissed his freckled face as kindly as if it had been as fair and white as possible. "You shall eat all you want to; an' if you get the stomach-ache, as Samuel does sometimes when he's been eatin' too much, I'll give you some catnip tea out of the same dipper that I give him his. He's a great eater, Samuel is," she added, in a burst of confidence, "an' it's a wonder to me what he does with it all sometimes."

"Is he?" exclaimed Toby, quickly. "How funny that is, for I'm an awful eater. Why, Uncle Dan'l used to say that I ate twice as much as I ought to, an' it never made me any bigger. I wonder what's the reason?"

"I declare I don't know," said the Fat Woman, thoughtfully, "an' I've wondered at it time an' time again. Some folks is made that way, an' some folks is made different. Now, I don't eat enough to keep a chicken alive, an' yet I grow fatter an' fatter every day. Don't I, Samuel?"

"Indeed you do, my love," said the Skeleton, with a world of pride in his voice, "but you mustn't feel bad about it, for every

pound you gain makes you worth just so much more to the show."

"Oh, I wasn't worryin', I was only wonderin'. But we must go, Samuel, for the poor child won't eat a bit while we are here. After you've eaten what there is there, bring the plate in to me," she said to Toby, as she took her lean husband by the arm and walked him off toward their own tent.

Toby gazed after them a moment, and then he commenced a vigorous attack upon the eatables which had been so kindly given him. Of the food which he had taken from the dinner table he had eaten some while he was in the tent, and after that he had entirely forgotten that he had any in his pocket. Therefore, at the time that Mrs. Treat had brought him such a liberal supply he was really very hungry.

He succeeded in eating nearly all the food which had been brought to him, and the very small quantity which remained he readily found room for in his pockets. Then he washed the plate nicely, and seeing no one in sight, he thought he could leave the booth long enough to return the plate.

He ran with it quickly into the tent occupied by the Fat Woman and handed it to her, with a profusion of thanks for her kindness.

"Did you eat it all?" she asked.

"Well," hesitated Toby, "there was three doughnuts an' a piece of pie left over, an' I put them in my pocket. If you don't care, I'll eat them some time tonight."

"You shall eat it whenever you want to, an' any time you get hungry again, you come right to me."

"Thank you, ma'am. I must go now, for I left the store all alone."

"Run, then; an' if Job Lord abuses you,

just let me know it, an' I'll keep him from cuttin' up any monkeyshines."

Toby hardly heard the end of her sentence, so great was his haste to get back to the booth. And just as he emerged from the tent on a quick run, he received a blow on the ear which sent him sprawling in the dust, and he heard Mr. Job Lord's angry voice as it said, "So, just the moment my back is turned, you leave the stand to take care of itself, do you, an' run around tryin' to plot some mischief against me, eh?" And the brute kicked the boy twice with his heavy boot.

"Please don't kick me again!" pleaded Toby. "I wasn't gone but a minute, an' I wasn't doing anything bad."

"You're lying now, an' you know it, you young cub!" exclaimed the angry man as he advanced to kick the boy again. "I'll let you know who you've got to deal with when you get hold of me!"

"And I'll let you know who you've got to deal with when you get hold of me!" said a woman's voice, and, just as Mr. Lord raised his foot to kick the boy again, the Fat Woman seized him by the collar, jerked him back over one of the tent ropes, and left him quite as knocked out as he had left Toby.

"Now, Job Lord," said the angry woman, as she towered above the thoroughly enraged but thoroughly frightened man, "I want you to understand that you can't knock and beat this boy while I'm around. I've seen enough of your capers, an' I'm going to put a stop to them. That boy wasn't in this tent more than two minutes, an' he attends to his work better than anyone you have ever had, so see that you treat him decent. Get up," she said to Toby,

who had not dared to rise from the ground, "and if he tries to strike you again, come to me."

Toby scrambled to his feet and ran to the booth in time to attend to one or two customers who had just come up. He could see from out the corner of his eye that Mr. Lord had arisen to his feet also and was engaged in an angry conversation with Mrs. Treat, the result of which he very much feared would be another and a worse whipping for him.

But in this he was mistaken, for Mr. Lord, after the conversation was ended, came toward the booth and began to attend to his business without speaking one word to Toby. When his partner, Mr. Jacobs, returned from his supper, Mr. Lord took him by the arm and walked him out toward the rear of the tents. Toby was very positive that he was to be the subject of their conversation, which made him not a little uneasy.

It was nearly time for the performance to begin when Mr. Lord returned. He had nothing to say to Toby, save to tell him to go into the tent and begin his work there. The boy was only too glad to escape so easily, and he went to his work as if he were entering upon some pleasure.

When he met Mr. Jacobs, that gentleman spoke to him very sharply about being late and seemed to think it no excuse at all that he had just been relieved from the outside work by Mr. Lord.

But the boy really surprised him by his way of selling goods, though he was very careful not to say anything about it. Toby's private hoard of money was increased that evening, by ninety cents, and he began to look upon himself as almost a rich man.

When the performance was nearly over,

Mr. Jacobs called to him to help in packing up; and by the time the last spectator had left the tent, the worldly possessions of Messrs. Lord and Jacobs were ready for removal, and Toby was allowed to do as he had a mind to, as long as he was careful to be on hand when Old Ben was ready to start.

Toby thought that he would have time to pay a visit to his friends, the Skeleton and the Fat Woman, and to that end started toward the place where their tent had been standing. But to his sorrow he found that it was already being taken down, and he had only time to thank Mrs. Treat and to

press the fleshless hand of her shadowy husband as they entered their wagon to drive away.

He was disappointed, for he had hoped to be able to speak with his new-made friends a few moments before the weary night's ride commenced; but, failing in that, he went hastily back to the monkey's cage.

Old Ben was there, getting things ready for a start, but the wooden sides of the cage had not been put up and Toby had no difficulty in calling the aged monkey, whom he had named Mr. Stubbs, up to the bars. He held one of the Fat Woman's doughnuts in his hand and said, as he passed it though to the animal, "I thought perhaps you might be hungry, Mr. Stubbs, and this is some of what the Skeleton's wife gave me. I hain't got very much time to talk with you now, but the first chance I can get away tomorrow, an' when there hain't anybody 'round, I want to tell you something."

The monkey had taken the doughnut in his handlike paws and was tearing it to pieces, eating small portions of it very rapidly.

"Don't hurry yourself," said Toby, warningly, "for Uncle Dan'l always told me the worst thing a feller could do was to eat fast. If you want any more before we start, just put your hand through the little hole up near the seat, and I'll give you all you want."

From the look on his face Toby confidently believed the monkey was about to make some reply, but just then Ben shut up the sides, separating Toby and Mr. Stubbs, and the order was given to start.

Toby clambered up on to the high seat, Ben followed him, and in another instant the team was moving along slowly down the dusty road, preceded and followed by the many wagons, with their tiny, swinging lights.

"Well," said Ben, when he had got his team well under way and felt that he could indulge in a little conversation, "how did you get along today?"

Toby related all of his movements and gave the driver a faithful account of all that had happened to him, concluding his story by saying, "That was one of Mrs. Treat's doughnuts that I just gave to Mr. Stubbs."

"To whom?" asked Ben, in surprise.

"To Mr. Stubbs—the old fellow here in the cart, you know, that's been so good to me."

Toby heard a sort of gurgling sound, saw the driver's body sway back and forth in a trembling way, and was just becoming thoroughly alarmed, when he thought of the previous night and understood that Ben was only laughing in his own peculiar way.

"How did you know his name was Stubbs?" asked Ben, after he had recovered his breath.

"Oh, I don't know that that is his real name," was the quick reply. "I only call him that because he looks so much like a feller with that name that I knew at home. He don't seem to mind because I call him Stubbs."

Ben looked at Toby earnestly for a moment, acting all the time as if he wanted to laugh again, but didn't dare to, for fear he might burst a blood vessel; and then he said, as he patted him on the shoulder, "Well, you are the queerest little fish I ever saw in all my travels. You seem to think that monkey knows all you say to him."

"I'm sure he does," said Toby, positively. "He don't say anything right out to me, but he knows everything I tell him. Do you suppose he could talk if he tried to?"

"Look here, Mr. Toby Tyler," and Ben turned half around in his seat and looked Toby full in the face so as to give more emphasis to his words, "are you heathen enough to think that that monkey could talk if he wanted to?"

"I know I hain't a heathen," said Toby, thoughtfully, "for if I had been, some of the missionaries would have found me out a good while ago. But I never saw anybody like this old Mr. Stubbs before, an' I thought he could talk if he wanted to, just as the Living Skeleton does, or his wife. Anyhow, Mr. Stubbs winks at me; an' how could he do that if he didn't know what I've been sayin' to him?"

"Look here, my son," said Ben, in a fatherly fashion, "monkeys hain't anything but beasts, an' they don't know how to talk any more than they know what you say to 'em."

"Didn't you ever hear any of them speak a word?"

"Never. I've been in a circus, man an' boy, nigh on to forty years, an' I never seen nothin' in a monkey more'n any other beast, except their awful mischiefness."

"Well," said Toby, still unconvinced, "I believe Mr. Stubbs knows what I say to him, anyway."

"Now don't be foolish, Toby," pleaded Ben. "You can't show me one thing that a monkey ever did because you told him to."

Just at that moment, Toby felt someone pulling at the back of his coat. Looking round, he saw a little brown hand reaching through the bars of the air hole of the cage, tugging away at his coat.

"There!" he said, triumphantly, to Ben. "Look there! I told Mr. Stubbs if he wanted anything more to eat, to tell me, an' I would give it to him. Now you can see for yourself that he's come for it." Toby took a doughnut from his pocket and put it into the tiny hand, which was immediately withdrawn. "Now what do you think of Mr. Stubbs knowing what I say to him?"

"They often stick their paws up through there," said Ben, in a matter-of-fact tone. "I've had 'em pull my coat in the night till they made me as nervous as ever any old woman was. You see, Toby, my boy, mon-

keys is monkeys; an' you mustn't go to gettin' the idea that they're anything else, for it's a mistake. You think this old monkey in here knows what you say? Why, that's just the cuteness of the old fellow. He watches you to see if he can't do just as you do, an' that's all there is about it."

Toby was more than half convinced that Ben was putting the matter in its proper light, and he would have believed all that had been said if, just at that moment, he had not seen that brown hand reaching through the hole to clutch him again by the coat.

The action seemed so natural, so like a hungry boy who gropes in the dark pantry for something to eat, that it would have taken more arguments than Ben had at his disposal to persuade Toby that his Mr. Stubbs could not understand all that was said to him. Toby put another doughnut in the outstretched hand and then sat silently, as if in a brown study over some difficult problem.

For some time the ride was continued in silence. Ben was going through all the motions of whistling without uttering a sound —a favorite amusement of his—and Toby's thoughts were far away.

Toby's thoughtfulness had made him sleepy, and his eyes were almost closed in slumber, when he was startled by a crashing sound, was conscious of a feeling of being hurled from his seat by some great force, and then he lay senseless by the side of the road, while the wagon became a perfect wreck, from out of which a small army of monkeys was escaping.

Ben's experienced ear had told him at the first crash that his wagon was breaking down. So, without having time to warn

79

Toby of his peril, he had leaped clear of the wreck, keeping his horses under perfect control, thus averting more trouble. It was the breaking of one of the axles which Toby had heard just before he was thrown from his seat and when the body of the wagon came down upon the hard road.

The monkeys, thus suddenly released from confinement, had scampered off in every direction, and by a singular chance, Toby's aged friend started for the woods in such a direction as to bring him directly before the boy's insensible form.

The monkey, on coming up to Toby, stopped, urged by the well-known curiosity of its race, and began to examine the boy's person carefully, prying into pockets and trying to open the boy's half-closed eyelids.

Fortunately for Toby, he had fallen upon a mud bank and was only stunned for the moment, having received no serious bruises. The attentions bestowed upon him by the monkey served the purpose of bringing him to his senses; and, after he had looked around him in the gray light of the coming morning, it would have taken far more of a philosopher than Old Ben to persuade the boy that monkeys did not possess reasoning faculties.

The monkey was busy at Toby's ears, nose, and mouth, as monkeys will do when they get an opportunity, and the expression of its face was as grave as possible. Toby firmly believed that the monkey's face showed sorrow at his fall, and imagined that his attentions were for the purpose of learning whether he had been injured or not.

"Don't worry, Mr. Stubbs," said Toby, anxious to reassure his friend, as he sat upright and looked about him. "I didn't get hurt any; but I would like to know how I got 'way over here."

It really seemed as if the monkey was pleased to know that his little friend was not hurt, for he seated himself on his haunches, and his face expressed the liveliest pleasure that Toby was well again—or at least that was how the boy interpreted the look.

By this time the news of the accident had been shouted ahead from one team to the other, and all hands were hurrying to the scene for the purpose of rendering aid. As Toby saw them coming, he also saw a number of small forms, looking something like diminutive men, hurrying past him, and for the first time he understood how it was that the aged monkey was at liberty, and knew that those little dusky forms were the other occupants of the cage escaping to the woods.

"See there, Mr. Stubbs! See there!" he exclaimed, pointing toward the fugitives, "they're all going off into the woods! What shall we do?"

The sight of the runaways seemed to excite the old monkey quite as much as it did the boy. He sprang to his feet, chattering in the most excited way, screamed two or three times, as if he were calling them back, and then started off in vigorous pursuit.

"Now he's gone, too!" said Toby, disconsolately, believing that the old fellow had run away from him. "I didn't think Mr. Stubbs would treat me this way!"

The boy tried to rise to his feet, but his head whirled so, and he felt so dizzy and sick from the effects of his fall, that he was obliged to sit down again. Meanwhile the crowd around the wagon paid no attention to him, and he lay there quietly enough, until he heard the hateful voice of Mr. Lord

80

asking if his boy were hurt.

The sound of his voice affected Toby very much as the chills and fever affect a sufferer, and he shook so with fear and his heart beat so loudly, that he thought Mr. Lord must know where he was by the sound. Seeing, however, that his employer did not come directly toward him, the thought flashed upon his mind that now would be a good chance to run away, and he acted upon it at once. He rolled himself over in the mud until he reached a low growth of fir trees that skirted the road. Beneath their friendly shade, he arose to his feet and walked swiftly toward the woods, following the direction the monkeys had taken.

He no longer felt dizzy and sick. The fear of Mr. Lord had dispelled all that, and he felt strong and active again.

He had walked rapidly for some distance and was nearly beyond the sound of the voices in the road, when he was startled by seeing quite a procession of figures emerge from the trees and come directly toward him.

He could not understand the meaning of this strange company, and it so frightened him that he attempted to hide behind a tree, in the hope that they might pass without seeing him. But a strange, shrill chattering came from the foremost of the group, and in an instant Toby came out of his hiding-place.

He had recognized the peculiar sound as that of the old monkey who had left him a few moments before, and he knew now what he did not know then, owing to the darkness. The newcomers were the monkeys that had escaped from the cage and had been overtaken and compelled to come back by the old monkey, who seemed to have

the most perfect control over them.

The old fellow was leading the band, and all were linked "hand in hand" with each other, which gave the whole crowd a most comical appearance as they came up to Toby, half hopping, half walking upright, and all chattering and screaming like a crowd of children out for a holiday.

Toby stepped toward the noisy crowd, held out his hand gravely to the old monkey, and said, in tones of heartfelt sorrow, "I felt awful bad because I thought you had gone off an' left me, when you only went off to find the other fellows. You're awful good, Mr. Stubbs, an' now, instead of runnin' away, as I was goin' to do, we'll all go back together."

The old monkey grasped Toby's extended hand with his disengaged paw and, clinging firmly to it, the whole crowd followed in unbroken line, chattering and scolding at the most furious rate, while every now and then, Mr. Stubbs would look back and scream out something.

It was really a comical sight, but Toby seemed to think it the most natural thing in the world that they should follow him in this manner, and he chattered to the old monkey quite as fast as any of the others were doing.

Toby told him very gravely all he knew about the accident, explained why it was that he conceived the idea of running away, and he really believed that Mr. Stubbs understood every word he was saying.

Very shortly after Toby had started to run away, the owner of the circus drove up to the scene of disaster; and, after seeing that the wagon was being rapidly fixed up so that it could be hauled to the next town, he ordered that a search should be made

for the monkeys. It was very important that they should be captured at once, and he seemed to think more of the loss of the animals than of the damage done to the wagon.

While the men were forming plans to search for the truants, so that in the case of a capture they could let each other know, the noise made by Toby and his party was heard, and the men stood still to learn what it meant.

The entire party burst into shouts of laughter as Toby and his companions walked into the circle of light formed by the glare of the lanterns. The merriment was by no means abated at Toby's serious behavior. The wagon was now standing upright, with the door open, and Toby therefore led his companions directly to it, gravely motioning them to enter.

The old monkey, instead of obeying,

stepped back to Toby's side and screamed to the others in such a manner that they all entered the cage, leaving him on the outside with the boy.

Toby motioned him to get in, too, but he clung to his hand and scolded so furiously that it was apparent he had no idea of leaving his boy companion. One of the men stepped up and was about to force him into the wagon, when the owner ordered him to stop

"What boy is that?" he asked.

"Job Lord's new boy," said someone in the crowd.

The man asked Toby how it was that he had succeeded in capturing all the runaways, and he answered, "Mr. Stubbs an' I are good friends, an' when he saw the others runnin' away, he just stopped 'em an' brought 'em back to me. I wish you'd let Mr. Stubbs ride with me. We like each other a good deal."

"You can do just what you please with Mr. Stubbs, as you call him. I expected to lose half the monkeys in that cage, and you have brought back every one. That monkey shall be yours, and you may put him in the cage whenever you want to or take him with you, just as you choose, for he belongs entirely to you."

Toby's joy knew no bounds. He put his arm around the monkey's neck, and the monkey clung firmly to him, until even Job Lord was touched at the evidence of affection between the two.

While the wagon was being repaired, Toby and the monkey stood hand in hand watching the work go on, while those in the cage scolded and raved because they had been induced to return to captivity. After a while the old monkey seated himself on Toby's arm and cuddled up to him, uttering now and then a contented sort of little squeak as the boy talked to him.

That night Mr. Stubbs slept in Toby's arms, in the band wagon, and both boy and monkey appeared very well contented with their lot, which a short time previous had seemed so hard.

When Toby awakened to his second day's work with the circus, his monkey friend was seated by his side, gravely exploring his pockets, and all the boy's treasures were being spread out on the floor of the wagon by his side. Toby reproved him for this breach of confidence, but Mr. Stubbs was more in the mood for sport than for grave conversation. The more Toby talked, the more mischievous he became, until at length the boy gathered up his little store of treasures, took the monkey by the paw, and walked him toward the cage from which he had escaped on the previous night.

"Now, Mr. Stubbs," said Toby, speaking in an injured tone, "you must go in here and stay till I have more time to fool with you."

He opened the door of the cage, but the monkey struggled as well as he was able, and Toby was obliged to exert all his strength to put him in.

When once the door was fastened upon him, Toby tried to impress upon the monkey's mind the importance of being more sedate, and he was convinced that the words had sunk deep into Mr. Stubb's heart, for, by the time he had finished, the old monkey was seated in the corner of the cage, looking up from under his shaggy eyebrows in the most reproachful manner possible.

Toby felt sorry that he had spoken so harshly and was about to make amends, when Mr. Lord's gruff voice recalled him to the fact that his time was not his own. He therefore commenced his day's work, but with a lighter heart than he had had for a long time.

As far as his relations with other members of the company were concerned, Toby now stood in a much better position than before. Those who had witnessed the scene told the others how Toby had led in the monkeys, and nearly every member of the company had a kind word for the little fellow whose head could hardly be seen above the counter of Messrs. Lord and Jacobs's booth.

Three Things to Remember

By William Blake

A robin redbreast in a cage
Puts all Heaven in a rage.

A skylark wounded on the wing
Doth make a cherub cease to sing.

He who shall hurt the little wren
Shall never be beloved by men.

Be Like the Bird

By Victor Hugo

Be like the bird who,
Halting in his flight
On limb too slight,
Feels it give way beneath him,
Yet sings
Knowing he has wings.

Adventures of Black Beauty

By Anna Sewell

If you love horses and like to read sad stories about them, you will probably love BLACK BEAUTY. It is about a gentle carriage horse who tells her own story of the hardships and cruelties she had to suffer in her long and varied career.

Of course no such horse as Black Beauty ever really existed, and even if horses could think and talk, no horse of today would think and talk in the lady-like way Black Beauty did. Yet when the book first came out, in 1877, it did a great deal of good. It called people's attention to the many brutalities horses had to bear at the hands of cruel or thoughtless masters. Most of these are now things of the past, and for their abolition we may indeed have this heartbreaking book, and its author Anna Sewell, to thank.

Children who live only in the realistic present may find BLACK BEAUTY too sentimental or too old-fashioned for their taste. Those who are capable of suffering with a sadly mistreated horse will cry over it and love it. For them let us say, in closing, that the book has a happy ending with Black Beauty living in clover ever after.

MY EARLY HOME

THE first place I can remember well was a pleasant meadow with a pond of clear water in it. Some shady trees leaned over it, and rushes and water lilies grew at the deep end. Over the hedge on one side we looked into a plowed field, and on the other we looked over a gate at our master's house, which stood by the roadside. At the top of the meadow was a grove of fir trees, and at the bottom a running brook, overhung by a steep bank.

While I was young I lived on my mother's milk, as I was not yet old enough to eat grass. In the daytime I ran by her side, and at night I lay down close by her. When it was hot, we used to stand by the pond in the shade of the trees, and when it was cold, we had a warm shed near the grove.

As soon as I could eat grass, my mother went to work in the daytime, and came back in the evening.

There were six young colts in the meadow besides me. They were older than I was; some were nearly as large as grown-up horses. I used to run with them, and had great fun. We used to gallop all together round the field, as hard as we could go. Sometimes the play was rough, for they would frequently bite and kick, as well as gallop.

One day, when there was a good deal of kicking, my mother whinnied to me to come to her, and then she said, "I want you to pay attention to what I am going to say to you. The colts who live here are cart-horse colts, and of course they have not learned manners. You have been well-bred and well-born. Your father has a great name in these parts, and your grandfather won the cup two years at the Newmarket races. Your grandmother had the sweetest temper of any horse I ever knew, and I think you have never seen me kick or bite. I hope you will grow up gentle and good, and never learn bad ways. Do your work with a good will, lift your feet up well when you trot, and never bite or kick even in play."

I have never forgotten my mother's advice; I knew she was a wise horse, and our master thought a great deal of her. Her name was Duchess, but he called her Pet.

Our master was a good kind man. He gave us good food, good lodging, and kind words. We were all fond of him, and my mother loved him very much. When she saw him at the gate, she would neigh with joy, and trot up to him. He would pat and stroke her and say, "Well, old Pet, and how is your little Darkie?"

I was a dull black, so he called me Darkie. Then he would give me a piece of bread, and sometimes he brought a carrot for my mother. All the horses would come to him, but I think we were his favorites. My mother always took him to town on a market day in a light gig.

We had a plowboy, Dick, who sometimes

86

came into our field to pluck blackberries from the hedge. When he had eaten all he wanted, he would have what *he* called fun with the colts, throwing stones and sticks at them to make them gallop.

We did not much mind him, for we could gallop off; but sometimes a stone would hit us. One day he was at this game, and did not know that the master was in the next field. But he was, watching what was going on. Over the hedge he jumped in a snap, and catching Dick by the arm, he gave him such a box on the ear as made him roar with pain and surprise. As soon as we saw the master, we trotted up nearer to see what went on.

"Bad boy!" he said. "Bad boy to chase the colts! This is not the first time, nor the second, but it shall be the last. There— take your money and go home. I shall not want you on my farm again."

So we never saw Dick any more. Old Daniel, the man who looked after the horses, was just as gentle as our master; so we were well off.

THE HUNT

Before I was two years old, something happened that I have never forgotten. It was early in the spring. There had been a little frost in the night, and a light mist still hung over the woods and meadows. We colts were feeding at the lower part of the field when we heard, far in the distance, what sounded like the cry of dogs.

The oldest of the colts raised his head, pricked his ears, and said, "There are the hounds!"

He then cantered off, followed by the rest of us, to the upper part of the field, where we could look over the hedge and see several fields beyond. My mother and an old riding horse of our master's were also standing near, and seemed to know all about it.

"They have found a hare," said my mother, "and if they come this way we shall see the hunt."

Soon the dogs were all tearing down the field of young wheat next to ours. I never heard such a noise as they made. They did not bark, nor howl, nor whine, but kept on a "Yo! yo, o, o! Yo! yo, o, o!" at the top of their voices. After them came a number of men on horseback, all galloping as fast as they could.

The old horses snorted and looked eagerly after them. We young colts wanted to be galloping with them, but they were soon away into the fields lower down. Here it seemed as if they had come to a stand. The dogs left off barking and ran about every way with their noses to the ground.

"They have lost the scent," said the old horse. "Perhaps the hare will get off."

"What hare?" I said.

"Oh, I don't know *what* hare. Likely enough it may be one of our own hares out of the woods. Any hare they can find will do for the dogs and men to run after."

Before long the dogs began their "Yo, yo, o, o!" again, and back they came all together at full speed, making straight for our meadow at the part where the high bank and hedge overhang the brook.

"Now we shall see the hare," said my mother. And just then a hare, wild with fright, rushed by and made for the woods.

On came the dogs. They burst over the bank, leaped the stream, and came dashing across the field, followed by the huntsmen. Six or eight men leaped their horses clean over, close upon the dogs. The hare tried to get through the fence. It was too thick, and she turned sharp around to make for the road. But it was too late; the dogs were upon her with their wild cries. We heard one shriek and that was the end of her. One of the huntsmen rode up and whipped off the dogs, who would soon have torn her to pieces. He held her up by the leg, torn and bleeding, and all the gentlemen seemed well pleased.

As for me, I was so astonished that I did not at first see what was going on by the brook. When I did look, there as a sad sight. Two fine horses were down. One was struggling in the stream, the other groaning on the grass. One of the riders was getting out of the water, covered with mud. The other lay quite still.

"His neck is broken," said my mother.

"And serves him right, too," said one of the colts. I thought the same, but my mother did not join with us.

"Well, no," she said, "you must not say that. But though I am an old horse, and have seen and heard a great deal, I never yet could make out why men are so fond of this sport. They often hurt themselves, often spoil good horses, and tear up the fields, and all for a hare, or a fox, or a stag, that they could get more easily some other way. However, we are only horses, and we don't know."

While my mother was saying this, we stood and looked on. Many of the riders had gone to the young man. My master, who had been watching what was going on, was the first to raise him. His head fell back and his arms hung down, and everyone looked very serious. There was no noise now. Even the dogs were quiet and seemed to know that something was wrong.

They carried him to our master's house.

I heard afterwards that it was young George Gordon, the Squire's only son, a fine tall young man, and the pride of his family.

They were now riding in all directions— to the doctor's, to the farrier's, and to Squire Gordon's, to let him know about his son.

When the farrier looked at the black horse that lay groaning on the grass, he felt him all over, and shook his head. One of his legs was broken.

Then someone ran to our master's house and came back with a gun. Presently there was a loud bang and a dreadful shriek, and then all was still. The black horse moved no more.

My mother seemed much troubled; she said she had known that horse for years, and that his name was Rob Roy. He was a good horse, and there was no vice in him. She never would go to that part of the field afterwards.

Not many days after, we heard the church bell tolling for a long time, and looking over the gate, we saw a long strange coach covered with black cloth and drawn by black horses; after that came another and another and another, and all were black, while the bell kept tolling, tolling. They were carrying young Gordon to the churchyard to bury him. He would never ride again. What they did with Rob Roy I never knew. But all this sorrow was for one little hare.

A STORMY DAY

One day late in the autumn my master had a long journey to go on business. I was put into the dog-cart, and John, the coachman, went with his master. I always liked to go in the dog-cart, it was so light, and the high wheels ran along so pleasantly. There had been a great deal of rain, and now the wind was high and blew the dry leaves in a shower.

We went along merrily till we came to the toll bar and the low wooden bridge. The river banks were rather high, and the bridge went across just level, so that in the middle, when the river was full, the water would be nearly up to the woodwork and planks. But as there were good substantial rails on each side, people did not mind it.

The man at the gate said the river was rising fast, and he feared it would be a bad night. Many of the meadows were under water, and in one low part of the road the water was halfway up to my knees. But the bottom was good, and master drove gently, so it was no matter.

When we got to the town, the master's business engaged him a long time, and we did not start for home till rather late in the afternoon. The wind was then much higher, and I heard the master say to John he had never been out in such a storm; and so I thought, as we went along the skirts of a wood, where the great branches were swaying about like twigs, and the rushing sound was terrible.

"I wish we were well out of this wood," said my master.

"Yes, sir," said John. "It would be rather awkward if one of these branches came down."

The words were scarcely out of his mouth when there was a groan, and a crack, and a splitting sound. Crashing down among the other trees came an oak, torn up by the roots, and it fell right across the road just before us. I will never say I was not frightened, for I was. I stopped still, and trembled. Of course I did not turn around or run away; I was not brought up to that. John jumped out, and was at my head in a moment.

"What's to be done now?" said my master.

"Well, sir, we can't drive over that tree, nor yet get around it. There will be nothing for it but to go back to the four crossways, and that will be a good six miles before we get to the wooden bridge again. It will make us late, but the horse is fresh."

So back we went and by the crossroads, but by the time we got back to the bridge it was nearly dark. We could just see that the water was over the middle of it; but as that happened sometimes when the floods were out, master did not stop.

We were going along at a good pace, but the moment my feet touched the first part of the bridge, I felt sure there was something wrong, and I made a dead stop.

"Go on, Beauty," said my master, and he gave me a touch of the whip. But I dared not stir. He gave me a sharp cut. I jumped, but I dared not go forward.

"There's something wrong, sir," said John, and he sprang out of the dog-cart, and came to my head and looked all about. He tried to lead me forward. "Come on, Beauty, what's the matter?"

Of course I could not tell him, but I knew very well that the bridge was not safe.

Just then a man at the toll-gate on the other side ran out of the house, tossing a torch about like one mad.

"Hello! Stop!" he cried.

"What's the matter?" shouted my master.

"The bridge is broken in the middle, and part of it is carried away. If you come on you'll be in the river."

"You Beauty!" said John, and took my bridle and gently turned me round to the right-hand road by the river side.

"Thank God!" said my master.

The sun had set. The wind seemed to have lulled off after that furious blast which tore up the tree. It grew darker and darker, stiller and stiller. I trotted quietly along, the wheels hardly making a sound on the soft road. For a good while neither master nor John spoke, and then master began in a serious voice.

I could not understand much of what they said, but I found they thought that if I had gone on as the master had wanted me to, most likely the bridge would have given way under us, and as the current was flowing very strongly, and there was no light and no help at hand, it was more than likely we should all have been drowned. Master said God had given men reason, by which they could find out things for themselves. But He had given animals knowledge, which did not depend on reason, and which was much more perfect in its way, and by which they had often saved the lives of men.

At last we came to the park gates, and found the gardener looking for us, fearing some accident had happened.

We saw a light at the hall door and at the upper windows, and as we came up mistress ran out, saying to master, "Are you really safe, my dear? Oh! I have been so anxious, fancying all sorts of things. Have you had no accident?"

"No, my dear; but if your Black Beauty had not been wiser than we were, we should all have been carried down the river at the wooden bridge."

I heard no more, as they went into the house, and John took me to the stable. Oh, what a good supper he gave me that night, a good bran mash and some crushed beans with my oats, and such a thick bed of straw! And I was glad of it, for I was really tired.

THE DEVIL'S TRADEMARK

One day when John and I had been out on some business of my master's, and were returning gently on a long, straight road, at some distance we saw a boy trying to leap a pony over a gate. The pony would not take the leap, and the boy cut him with the whip, but he only turned off on one side. He whipped him again, but the pony turned off on the other side. Then the boy got off and gave him a good hard thrashing, and knocked him about the head. Then he got up again and tried to make him leap the gate, kicking him all the time shamefully. But still the pony refused.

When we were nearly at the spot, the pony put down his head and threw up his heels and sent the boy neatly over into a broad quickset hedge. Then with the rein dangling from his head he set off home at a full gallop. John laughed out quite loud. "Served him right," he said.

"Oh, oh, oh!" cried the boy as he struggled about among the thorns, "I say, come and help me out "

"I think you are quite in the right place," said John, "and maybe a little scratching will teach you not to leap a pony over a gate that is too high for him," and with that John rode off.

"It may be," said he to himself, "that young fellow is a liar as well as a cruel one. We'll just go home by Farmer Bushby's, Beauty, and then if anybody wants to know, you and I can tell 'em." So we turned off to the right and soon came up to the stack yard, and within sight of the house. The farmer was hurrying out into the road, and his wife was standing at the gate, looking very frightened.

"Have you seen my boy?" said Mr.

Bushby, as we came up. "He went out an hour ago on my black pony, and the creature is just come back without a rider."

" I should think, sir," said John, "he had better be without a rider, unless he can be ridden properly."

"What do you mean?" asked the farmer.

"Well, sir, I saw your son whipping and kicking that good little pony shamefully, because he would not leap a gate that was too high for him. The pony behaved well, sir, and showed no vice; but at last he just threw up his heels, and tipped the young gentleman into the thorn hedge. He wanted me to help him out; but I hope you will excuse me, sir, I did not feel inclined to do so. There are no bones broken, sir, only a few scratches. I love horses, and it riles me to see them badly used. It is a bad plan to aggravate an animal till he uses his heels. The first time is not always the last."

During this time the mother began to cry, "Oh my poor Bill, I must go and meet him."

"You had better go into the house, wife," said the farmer. "Bill needs a lesson about this, and I must see that he gets it. This is not the first time, nor the second, that he has ill-used that pony, and I shall stop it. I am much obliged to you, John Manly."

So we went on, Jonn chuckling all the way home; then he told the groom about it, who laughed and said:

"Served him right. I knew that boy at school. He took great airs on himself. He used to swagger about and bully the little boys. Of course we would not have any of that nonsense.

"I well remember one day, just before afternoon school, I found him at a large window catching flies and pulling off their wings. He did not see me, and I gave him a box on the ears that laid him sprawling on the floor. He roared and bellowed in such a style, the boys rushed in from the playground, and the master ran in from the road to see who was being murdered.

"Of course, I said what I had done, and why. Then I showed the master the flies, some crushed and some crawling helpless, and I showed him the wings on the window sill.

"I never saw him so angry. Then he talked to all the boys very seriously about cruelty, and said how cowardly it was to hurt the weak and the helpless. But what stuck in my mind was this: he said that if we saw anyone who took pleasure in cruelty we might know he belonged to the devil. On the other hand, people who loved their neighbors, and were kind to man and beast, belonged to God."

And John replied, "Your master never taught a truer thing."

THE FIRE

One evening a traveler's horse was brought in by the second groom, and while he was cleaning him a young man with a pipe in his mouth lounged into the stable to gossip.

"I say, Dick Towler," said the groom, "just run up the ladder into the loft and put some hay down into this horse's rack, will you? Only lay down your pipe."

"All right," said the other, and went up through the trapdoor. I heard him step across the floor overhead and put down the hay. James Howard, the groom, came in to look at us the last thing, and then the door was locked.

I cannot say how long I had slept, or what time in the night it was, but I woke up feeling very uncomfortable, though I hardly knew why. I got up. The air seemed all thick and choking. I heard one of the other horses coughing, and another one seemed very restless. It was quite dark, and I could see nothing, but the stable seemed full of smoke.

The trapdoor had been left open, and I thought it was the place it came through. I listened, and heard a soft rushing sort of noise and a low crackling and snapping. I did not know what it was, but there was something in the sound so strange that it made me tremble all over. The other horses were now all awake. Some were pulling at their halters, others were stamping.

At last I heard steps outside, and the groom who had put up the traveler's horse burst into the stable with a lantern. He began to untie the horses and tried to lead them out. But he seemed in such a hurry and so frightened himself that he frightened me still more.

The first horse would not go with him. He tried the second and the third, and they, too, would not stir. He came up to me next and tried to drag me out of the stall by force.

Of course that was no use. He tried us all by turns, and then left. No doubt we were very foolish, but danger seemed to be all around, and there was nobody we knew to trust in, and all was strange and uncertain.

The fresh air that had come in through the open door made it easier to breathe, but the rushing sound overhead grew louder, and as I loooked upward, through the bars of my empty rack, I saw a red light flickering on the wall. Then I heard a cry of "Fire!" outside, and the old groom quietly and quickly came in. He got one horse out, and went to another, but the flames were playing around the trapdoor, and the roaring overhead was dreadful.

The next thing I heard was James's voice, quiet and cheery, saying "Come, my beauties, it is time for us to be off. So wake up and come along."

I stood nearest the door, so he came to

me first, patting me as he came in. "Come, Beauty, on with your bridle, my boy. We will soon be out of this smother."

He put the bridle on me in no time. Then he took the scarf off his neck and tied it lightly over my eyes, and patting and coaxing, he led me out of the stable. Safe in the yard, he slipped the scarf off my eyes and shouted, "Here, somebody! Take this horse while I go back for the other."

A tall, broad man took me, and James darted back in the stable. I set up a shrill whinny as I saw him go.

There was much confusion in the yard while the horses were being got out of other stables, and the carriages and gigs were being pulled out of houses and sheds, lest the flames should spread farther. On the other side of the yard windows were thrown up, and the people were shouting all sorts of things. But I kept my eye fixed on the stable door, where the smoke poured out thick, and I could see flashes of red light. Presently I heard above all the stir and din a loud clear voice, which I knew was master's: "James Howard! James Howard! Are you there?"

There was no answer, but I heard a crash of something falling in the stable, and the next moment I gave a loud joyful neigh, for I saw James coming through the smoke leading another horse with him. She was coughing violently, and he was not able to speak.

"My brave lad!" said master, laying his hand on his shoulder. "Are you hurt?"

James shook his head, for he could not yet speak.

"Ay," said the big man who held me, "he is a brave lad, and no mistake."

"And now," said master, "when you have got your breath, James, we'll get out of this as quickly as we can."

We were moving toward the entry, when from the market place there came a sound of galloping feet and loud, rumbling wheels.

"'Tis the fire engine!" shouted two or three voices. "Stand back, make way!" And clattering and thundering over the stones, two horses dashed into the yard with the heavy engine behind them. The firemen leaped to the ground. There was no need to ask where the fire was— it was rolling up in a great blaze from the roof.

We got out as fast as we could into the broad, quiet market place. The stars were shining, and, except for the noise behind us, all was still.

Master led the way to a large hotel on the other side, and as soon as the groom came he said, "James, I must now hasten to your mistress. I trust the horses entirely to you. Order whatever you think is needed." And with that he was gone. The master did not run, but I never saw mortal man walk so fast as he did.

There was a dreadful sound before we got into our stalls. The shrieks of those poor horses left burning in the stable! It was very terrible and made me feel very badly. We were taken in and well done by.

The next morning the master came to see how we were and to speak to James. I did not hear much, for the groom was rubbing me down, but I could see that James looked very happy, and I thought the master was proud of him. Our mistress had been so much alarmed in the night that the journey was put off till the afternoon. So James had the morning on hand, and went first to the inn to see about our harness and the carriage, and then to hear more about the fire.

When he came back we heard him tell the other groom about it.

At first no one could guess how the fire had been caused, but at last a man said he saw Dick Towler go into the stable with a pipe in his mouth, and when he came out he did not have one. But he got himself another. Then the under-groom said he had asked Dick to go up the ladder to put down some hay, but told him to lay down his pipe first.

Dick denied taking the pipe with him, but no one believed him. I remember our John Manly's rule never to allow a pipe in the stable, and I thought it ought to be the rule everywhere.

James said the roof and floor had all fallen in, and that only the black walls were standing. The two poor horses that could not be got out were buried under the burned rafters and tiles.

GOING FOR THE DOCTOR

One night, I had eaten my hay and was lying down in my straw fast asleep, when I was suddenly roused by the stable bell ringing very loudly. I heard the door of John's house open, and his feet running up to the Hall. He was back again in no time. He unlocked the stable door, and came in, calling out, "Wake up, Beauty! You must go fast now, if ever you did."

Almost before I could think he had got the saddle on my back and the bridle on my head. He just ran around for his coat, and then took me at a quick trot up to the Hall door. The Squire stood there, with a lamp in his hand.

"Now, John," he said, "ride for your life —that is, for your mistress's life; there is not a moment to lose. Give this note to Dr. White. Give your horse a rest at the inn, and be back as soon as you can."

John said, "Yes, sir," and was on my back in a minute. The gardener who lived at the lodge had heard the bell ring, and was ready with the gate open, and away we went through the park, and through the village, and down the hill till we came to the toll-gate. John called very loud and thumped upon the door. The man was soon out and flung open the gate.

"Now," said John, "keep the gate open for the doctor; here's the money," and off we went again.

There was before us a long piece of level road by the riverside. John said to me, "Now, Beauty, do your best."

I did. I needed no whip nor spur, and for two miles I galloped as fast as I could lay my feet to the ground. I don't believe that my old grandfather, who won the race at Newmarket, could have gone faster. When we came to the bridge, John pulled me up a little and patted my neck. "Well done, Beauty, good old fellow," he said. He would have let me go slower, but my spirit was up, and I was off again as fast as before.

The air was frosty, the moon was bright; it was very pleasant. We came through a village, then through a dark wood, then up-hill, then downhill. After an eight miles' run we came to the town and into the market place. It was all quite still except the clatter of my feet on the stones—everybody was asleep.

The church clock struck three as we drew up at Dr. White's door. John rang the bell twice, and then knocked at the door like thunder. A window was thrown up, and Dr. White put his head out and said, "What do you want?"

"Mrs. Gordon is very ill, sir. Master wants you to come at once. He thinks she will die if you cannot get there. Here is a note."

"Wait," he said. "I will come."

He shut the window and was soon at the door.

"The worst of it is," he said, "my horse has been out all day and is quite done up. My son has just taken the other. What is to be done? Can I have your horse?"

"He has come at a gallop nearly all the way, sir, and I was to give him a rest here; but I think my master would not be against it, if you think fit, sir."

"All right," he said. "I will soon be ready."

John stood by me and stroked my neck. I was very hot. The doctor came out with his riding whip.

"You need not take that, sir," said John. "Black Beauty will go till he drops. Take care of him, sir, if you can. I should not like any harm to come to him."

"No, no, John," said the doctor, "I hope not." In a minute we had left John far behind.

I will not tell about our way back. The doctor was a heavier man than John, and

95

not so good a rider. But I did my very best. The man at the toll-gate had it open. When we came to the hill, the doctor drew me up. "Now, my good fellow," he said, "take some breath."

I was nearly spent, but that breathing helped me on, and soon we were in the park.

A groom named Joe was at the lodge gate; master at the Hall door. The doctor went into the house with him, and Joe led me to the stable.

I was glad to get home. My legs shook under me, and I could only stand and pant. I had not a dry hair on my body; the water ran down my legs, and I steamed all over.

Joe rubbed my legs and my chest, but he did not put warm cloth on me. He thought I was so hot I should not like it. Then he gave me a pailful of water to drink. It was cold and good, and I drank it all. Then he gave me some hay and some corn, and, thinking he had done right, he went away.

Soon I began to shake and tremble, and turned deadly cold. My legs ached, my loins ached, and my chest ached. I felt sore all over. Oh! how I wished for my warm, thick cloth as I stood and trembled. I wished for John, but he had eight miles to walk, so I lay down in my straw and tried to go to sleep.

After a long while I heard him at the door. I gave a low moan, for I was in great pain. He was at my side in a moment, stooping down by me. I could not tell him how I felt, but he seemed to know. He covered me up with two or three warm cloths, and then ran to the house for some hot water. He made me some warm gruel, which I drank, and then I think I went to sleep.

John seemed to be very much put out. I heard him say to himself over and over again, "Stupid boy, stupid boy! No cloth put on, and I dare say the water was cold, too."

I was now very ill. A strong inflammation had attacked my lungs, and I could not draw my breath without pain. John nursed me night and day. He would get up two or three times in the night. My master, too, often came to see me.

"My poor Beauty," he said one day, "my good horse, you saved your mistress's life, Beauty; yes, you saved her life."

I was very glad to hear that, for it seems the doctor had said if we had been a little later it would have been too late.

I do not know how long I was ill. Mr. Bond, the horse doctor, came every day.

The other horses had been moved into the other stables, so that I might be quiet, for the fever had made me very quick of hearing. Any little noise seemed quite loud and I could tell everyone's footstep going to and from the house. I knew all that was going on. One night John had to give me a draft. Tom Green came in to help him.

For a while both men sat silent, and then Tom said in a low voice, "I wish, John, you'd say a bit of a kind word to Joe. The boy is quite broken-hearted; he can't eat his meals, and he can't smile. He says he knows it was all his fault, and he says if Beauty dies, no one will ever speak to him again. It goes to my heart to hear him. I think you might give him just a word."

After a short pause, John said slowly, "You must not be too hard on me, Tom. I know he *meant* no harm; I know he is not a bad boy. But you see I am sore myself. That horse is the pride of my heart, to say nothing of his being such a favorite with the master and mistress. To think that his life may be flung away in this manner is more than I can bear. But if you think I am hard on the boy, I will try to give him a good word tomorrow—that is, if Beauty is better."

"Well, John, thank you. I knew you did not wish to be too hard, and I am glad you see it was only ignorance."

John's voice almost startled me as he answered, "Only ignorance! How can you talk about *only* ignorance? Don't you know that it is the worst thing in the world, next to wickedness? And which does the most mischief Heaven only knows."

I heard no more of this conversation, for the medicine sent me to sleep, and in the morning I felt much better.

When I came to know more of the world I often thought of John's words and of how true they are!

What is Good?

By John Boyle O'Reilly

"What is the real good?"
I asked in musing mood.
Order, said the law court;
Knowledge, said the school;
Truth, said the wise man;
Pleasure, said the fool;
Love, said the maiden;
Beauty, said the page;
Freedom, said the dreamer;
Home, said the sage;
Fame, said the soldier;
Equity, the seer—

Spake my heart full sadly,
"The answer is not here."

Then within my bosom
Softly this I heard:
"Each heart holds the secret;
Kindness is the word."

Canticle of the Sun

By St. Francis of Assisi

FROM THE TRANSLATION OF MATTHEW ARNOLD

O MOST high, Almighty God,
    to Thee belong praise, glory, honor, and all blessing!
Praised be my Lord with all His creatures;
    and specially our Brother, the Sun,
        who brings us the day, and who brings us the light;
        fair is he, and shining with a very great splendor.
Praised be my Lord for our Sister, the Moon, and for the stars
    which He has set clear and lovely in heaven.
Praised be my Lord for our Brother, the Wind,
    and for air and cloud, calms and all weather,
    by the which Thou upholdest life in all creatures.
Praised be my Lord for our Sister, Water,
    who is very serviceable unto us, and humble, and precious, and clean.
Praised be my Lord for our Brother, Fire,
    through whom Thou givest us light in the darkness;
    and he is bright, and pleasant, and very mighty, and strong.
Praised be my Lord for our Mother, the Earth,
    which doth sustain us and keep us,
    and bringeth forth fruits and flowers of many colors and grass . . .
Praise ye, and bless ye the Lord,
    and give thanks unto Him,
    and serve Him with great humility.

Little Daylight

From AT THE BACK OF THE NORTH WIND

By George MacDonald

Once upon a time there was a little boy named Diamond. One night when he was in his bed in the hayloft, The North Wind came in and whisked him out into the night. She taught him many strange things and through her he had many fantastic and wonderful adventures.

But the strangest thing about this book, AT THE BACK OF THE NORTH WIND, is that Diamond's dream-life adventures are no more fantastic than the actual adventures he had in his real life.

This is a long book, taking Diamond through thirty-eight thrilling adventures. Diamond, in real life, is a very good little boy indeed, and he does many fine things for people, children and grown-ups alike, especially those who need help.

The mystery of the book concerns the fabulous land that lies at the back of the North Wind and the miraculous experience Diamond has there.

If you like stories about dream happenings, you will like AT THE BACK OF THE NORTH WIND by George MacDonald. You will find part of the book here.

NO HOUSE to be called a palace is in the least worthy of the name, unless it has a wood near it—very near it—the nearer the better. Not all around it—I don't mean that, for a palace ought to be open to the sun and the wind, and stand high and brave, with weathercocks glittering and flags flying; but on one side of every palace there must be a wood.

There was a very grand wood indeed beside the palace of the king who was going to be Daylight's father; such a grand wood, that nobody yet had ever got to the other end of it. Near the house it was kept very trim and nice, and it was free of brushwood for a long way in. But by degrees it got wild, and it grew wilder and wilder until some said wild beasts did what they liked there. The King and his courtiers often hunted, however, and this kept the wild beasts far away from the palace.

One glorious summer morning, when the wind and sun were out together, when the vanes were flashing and the flags frolicking against the blue sky, little Daylight made her appearance from somewhere—nobody could tell where. She was a beautiful baby, with such bright eyes that she might have come from the sun, only she showed such lively ways that she might equally well have come out of the wind.

There was great jubilation in the palace, for this was the first baby the Queen had had, and there is as much happiness over a new baby in a palace as in a cottage.

But there is one disadvantage of living near a wood: you do not know quite who your neighbors may be. Everybody knew there were several fairies, living within a few miles of the palace, who always had had something to do with each new baby that came; for fairies live so much longer than human mortals, that they can have business with a good many generations. The curious houses they lived in were well known also—one, a hollow oak; another, a

99

birch-tree, though nobody could ever find how that fairy made a house of it; another, a hut of growing trees intertwined, and patched up with turf and moss.

But there was another fairy who ha‹ lately come to the palace, and nobody even knew she was a fairy except the other fairies. A wicked old thing she was, always concealing her power, and being as disagreeable as she could, in order to tempt people to give her offense, that she might have the pleasure of taking vengeance upon them. The people about thought she was a witch, and those who knew her by sight were careful to avoid offending her. She lived in a mud house, in a swampy part of the forest.

In all history we find that fairies give their remarkable gifts to any child of sufficient importance in their eyes, always at the christening. Now this we can understand. because it is an ancient custom amongst human beings as well; and it is not hard to explain why wicked fairies should choose the same time to do unkind things; but it is difficult to understand how they should be *able* to do them, for you would fancy all wicked creatures would be powerless on such an occasion. But I never knew of any interference on the part of the wicked fairy that did not turn out a good thing in the end.

Of course all the known fairies were invited to Daylight's christening. But the King and Queen never thought of inviting an old witch. For the fairies have their power by nature; whereas a witch gets her power by wickedness. The good fairies, knowing the danger, provided as well as they could against accidents from her quarter. But they could neither render her powerless, nor could they arrange their gifts in reference to

hers beforehand, for they could not tell what those might be.

Of course the old hag was there without being asked. Not to be asked was just what she wanted, that she might have a sort of reason for doing what she wished to do. For somehow even the wickedest of creatures likes a pretext for doing the wrong thing.

Five fairies had one after the other given the child good gifts, and the fifth had just stepped back to her place in the surrounding splendor of ladies and gentlemen, when, mumbling a laugh between her toothless gums, the wicked fairy hobbled out into the middle of the circle, and at the moment when the Archbishop was handing the baby to the lady at the head of the nursery department of state affairs, addressed him thus, giving a bite or two to every word before she could part with it:

"Please your Grace, I'm very deaf. Would your Grace mind repeating the Princess's name?"

"With pleasure, my good woman," said the Archbishop, stooping to shout in her ear. "The infant's name is little Daylight."

"And little daylight it shall be," cried the fairy, in the tone of a dry axle, "and little good shall any of her gifts do her. For I bestow upon her the gift of sleeping all day long, whether she will or not. Ha, ha! He, he! Hi, hi!"

Then out started the sixth fairy. The others had arranged that she should come after the wicked one, to undo as much as she might.

"If she sleep all day," said the sixth good fairy, "she shall, at least, wake all night."

"A nice prospect for her mother and me!" thought the poor King; for they loved her far too much to give her up to nurses, especially at night, as most Kings and Queens do—and are sorry for it afterwards.

"You spoke before I had done," said the wicked fairy. "That's against the law. It gives me another chance. I hadn't done laughing. I had only got to Hi, hi! and I had to go through Ho, ho! and Hu, hu! So I decree that if she wakes all night she shall wax and wane with its mistress, the moon. And what that may mean I hope her royal parents will live to see. Ho, ho! Hu, hu!"

But out stepped another fairy, for they had been wise enough to keep two in reserve.

"Until," said the seventh fairy, "a Prince comes who shall kiss her without knowing it."

The wicked fairy made a horrid noise like an angry cat, and hobbled away. She could not pretend that she had not finished her speech this time, for she had laughed Ho, ho! and Hu, hu!

"I don't know what that means," said the poor King to the seventh fairy.

"Don't be afraid. The meaning will come with the thing itself," said she.

The assembly broke up, miserable enough —the Queen, at least, prepared for a good many sleepless nights, and the lady at the head of the nursery department anything

101

but comfortable in the prospect before her, for of course the Queen could not do it all. As for the King, he made up his mind, with what courage he could summon, to meet the demands of the case, but wondered whether he could require the First Lord of the Treasury to take a share in the burden laid upon him.

I will not attempt to describe what they had to go through at first. But at last the household settled into a regular system—a very irregular one in some respects. For at certain seasons the palace rang all night with bursts of laughter from little Daylight, whose heart the old fairy's curse could not reach. She was Daylight still, only a little in the wrong place, for she always dropped asleep at the first hint of dawn in the east. But her merriment was short. When the moon was at the full, she was in glorious spirits, and as beautiful as it was possible for a child of her age to be. But when the moon waned and finally disappeared, she faded too until she was wan and withered like the poorest sickliest child.

Then the night was quiet as the day, for the little creature lay in her gorgeous cradle, night and day, with hardly a motion, and indeed without even a moan, like one dead. At first they often thought she *was* dead, but at last they got used to it, and only consulted the almanac to find the moment when she would begin to revive, which, of course, was with the first appearance of the silver thread of the crescent moon. Then she would move her lips, and they would give her a little nourishment; and she would grow better and better until for a few days she was splendidly well. When well, she was always merriest out in the moonlight; but even when near her worst, she seemed

better when, in warm summer nights, they carried her cradle out into the light of the waning moon. Then in her sleep she would smile the faintest, most pitiful smile.

For a long time very few people ever saw her awake. But as she grew older she became such a favorite that about the palace there were always some who would contrive to keep awake at night, to be near her.

But she soon began to take every chance of getting away from her nurses and enjoying her moonlight alone. And thus things went on until she was nearly seventeen years old. Her father and mother had by that time got so used to the odd state of things that they had ceased to wonder at them. They made all their arrangements with reference to the state of the Princess Daylight. But it did not seem possible that any Prince would ever find her and deliver her from her spell.

As she grew older she had grown more and more beautiful, with the sunniest hair and the loveliest eyes of heavenly blue, brilliant and profound as the sky of a June day. But so much more painful and sad was the change in her when it came on. The more beautiful she was in the full moon, the more withered and worn did she become as the moon waned.

At the time at which my story has now arrived, when the moon was small or gone, she looked like an old woman exhausted with suffering. This was the more painful in that her appearance was unnatural; for her hair and eyes did not change. Her wan face was both drawn and wrinkled, and had an eager hungry look. Her skinny hands moved as if wishing to lay hold of something, but unable. Her shoulders were bent forward, her chest went in, and she stooped as if she were eighty years old. At last she had to be put to bed, and there await the flow of the tide of life with the return of the new moon. But she grew to dislike being seen, still more being touched by any hands, during this season.

One lovely summer evening, when the moon lay all but gone on the horizon, she vanished from her attendants, and it was only after searching for her a long time in great terror, that they found her fast asleep in the forest, at the foot of a silver birch, and carried her home.

A little way from the palace there was a great open glade, covered with the greenest and softest grass. This was her favorite haunt, for here the full moon shone free and glorious, while through a vista in the trees she could generally see more or less of the dying moon as it crossed the opening. Here she had a little rustic house built for her, and here she mostly resided. None of the court might go there without leave, and she was very much at liberty there. Whether the good fairies had anything to do with it or not I cannot tell, but at last she got into the way of retreating further into the wood every night as the moon waned, so that sometimes they had great trouble in finding her. She was always very angry if she discovered that they were watching her. One night they thought they had lost her altogether. It was morning before they found her. Feeble as she was, she had wandered into a thicket a long way from the glade, and there she lay—fast asleep, of course.

Although the fame of her beauty and sweetness had gone abroad, yet everybody knew she was under a bad spell so no King in the neighborhood had any desire to have her for a daughter-in-law.

About this time, in a neighboring kingdom, in consequence of the wickedness of the nobles, an insurrection took place upon the death of the old King, the greater part of the nobility was massacred, and the young Prince had to flee for his life, disguised like a peasant. For some time, until he got out of the country, he suffered much from hunger and fatigue. But when he got into the country ruled by the Princess's father, and had no longer any fear of being recognized, he fared better, for the people were kind.

He did not abandon his disguise, however. One reason was that he had no other clothes to put on, and another that he had very little money, and did not know where to get any more. There was no good telling everybody he met that he was a Prince, for he felt that a Prince ought to be able to get on like other people, else his rank only made a fool of him. He had read of Princes setting out upon adventure; and here he was in similar case, only without having had a choice in the matter. He would go on, and see what would come of it.

For a day or two he had been walking through the palace-wood, and had had next to nothing to eat, when he came upon the strangest little house, inhabited by a very nice, tidy, motherly old woman. She was one of little Daylight's good fairies. The moment she saw him she knew who he was and what would happen. But she did not have the power to interfere with the orderly march of events.

She received the young man with the kindness she would have shown to any other traveller, and gave him bread and milk, which he thought the most delicious food he had ever tasted, wondering that they did

not have it for dinner at the palace sometimes.

The motherly old woman invited him to stay all night. When he awoke he was amazed to find how well and strong he felt. She would not take any of the money he offered, but begged him, if he found occasion to remain in the neighborhood, to return.

"Thank you much, good mother," answered the Prince, "but there is little chance of that. The sooner I get out of this wood the better."

The Prince turned and walked away. The fairy stood at the door of her little house looking after him till the trees hid him.

Then she said "At last!" and went in.

The Prince wandered and wandered, and got nowhere. The sun sank and went out of sight, and he seemed no nearer the end of the wood than ever. He sat down on a fallen tree, ate a bit of bread the old woman had given him, and waited for the moon. Up she came, slow and slow, but of a good size, pretty nearly round indeed; whereupon, greatly refreshed with his piece of bread, he got up and went—he knew not whither.

After walking a considerable distance, he thought he was coming to the outside of the forest. But when he reached what he thought the last of it, he found himself on the edge of a great open space in it, covered with grass. The moon shone very bright, and he thought he had never seen a more lovely spot.

All at once he spied something in the middle of the grass. What could it be? It moved; it came nearer. Was it a human creature, gliding across—a girl dressed in white, gleaming in the moonshine? She came nearer and nearer. He crept behind a tree and watched, wondering. It must be some strange being of the wood—a nymph whom the moonlight and the warm dusky air had enticed from her tree. But when she came close to where he stood, he no longer doubted she was human—for he had caught sight of her sunny hair, and her clear blue eyes, and the loveliest face and form that he had ever seen.

All at once she began singing like a nightingale, and dancing to her own music, with her eyes ever turned toward the moon. She passed close to where he stood, dancing on by the edge of the trees and away in a great circle towards the other side, until he could see but a spot of white in the yellowish green of the moonlit grass. But when he feared it would vanish quite, the spot grew, and became a figure once more. She approached him again, singing and dancing, and waving her arms over her head, until she had completed the circle. She stood just opposite his tree, ceased her song, dropped her arms, and broke out into a long clear laugh, musical as a brook. Then, as if tired, she threw herself on the grass, and lay gazing at the moon. The Prince was almost afraid to breathe lest he should startle her, and she should vanish from his sight. As to venturing near her, that never came into his head.

She had lain for a long hour or longer, when the Prince began again to think she was but a vision of his own fancy. Or was she a spirit of the wood, after all? If so, he too would haunt the wood, glad to have lost kingdom and everything for the hope of being near her. He would build himself a hut in the forest, and there he would live for the pure chance of seeing her again. On nights like this at least she would come out and bask in the moonlight, and make his soul blessed.

But as he hoped and dreamed, the lovely girl sprang to her feet, turned her face full to the moon, and began singing in an exquisite voice. She looked more beautiful than ever. Again she began dancing to her own music, and danced away into the distance, then returned. But although the Prince was watching as eagerly as before, what with fatigue and the strain of gazing, he fell asleep before she came near him. When he awoke it was broad daylight, and the Princess was nowhere to be seen.

He dared not leave the place. What if she should come the next night! He would gladly endure a day's hunger to see her again. He walked around the glade to see if he could discover any prints of her feet. But the grass was so short, and her steps had been so light, that she had not left a single trace behind her. He walked halfway around the wood without seeing anything to account for her presence.

Then he spied a lovely little house, with thatched roof and low eaves, surrounded by an exquisite garden, with doves and peacocks walking in it. Of course this must be where the gracious lady who loved the moonlight lived.

Forgetting his appearance, he walked towards the door, determined to make inquiries. But as he passed a little pond full

105

of gold and silver fishes, he caught sight of himself and turned to find the door to the kitchen. There he knocked, and asked for a piece of bread. The good-natured cook brought him in, and gave him an excellent breakfast, which the prince found none the worse for being served in the kitchen. While he ate, he talked with the cook, and learned that this was the favorite retreat of the Princess Daylight. But he learned nothing more, both because he was afraid of seeming inquisitive, and because the cook did not choose to be heard talking about her mistress to a peasant lad who had begged for his breakfast.

As he rose to take his leave, it occurred to him that he might not be so far from the old woman's cottage as he had thought, and he asked the cook whether she knew anything of such a place, describing it as well as he could.

She said she knew it well enough, adding with a smile, "It's there you're going, is it?"

"Yes, if it's not far off."

"It's not more than three miles. But mind what you are about, you know."

"Why do you say that?"

"If you're after any mischief, she'll make you repent it."

"The best thing that could happen under the circumstances," remarked the Prince.

"What do you mean by that?" asked the cook.

"Why, it stands to reason," answered the Prince, "that if you wish to do anything wrong, the best thing for you is to be made to repent of it."

"I see," said the cook. "Well, I think you may venture. She's a good old soul."

"Which way does it lie from here?" asked the Prince.

She gave him full instructions, and he left her with many thanks.

But the Prince did not go back to the cottage that day. He remained in the forest, amusing himself as best as he could, but waiting anxiously for the night, in the hope that the Princess would again appear. Nor was he disappointed for, directly the moon rose, he spied a glimmering shape far across the glade. As it drew nearer, he saw it was she indeed—not dressed in white as before but in pale blue like the sky, that made her look lovelier still. He thought it was that the blue suited her even better than the white. He did not know that she was really more beautiful because the moon was nearer the full.

The Prince feared for some time that she was not coming near his hiding-place; but the circles in her dance ever widened as the moon rose, until at last they embraced the whole glade, and she came still closer to the trees where he was hiding than she had come the night before. He was entranced with her loveliness, for it was indeed a marvellous thing. All night long he watched her, but dared not go near her. How beautiful she was! He watched the whole night long, and saw that as the moon went down she retreated in smaller and smaller circles, until at last he could see her no more.

Weary as he was, he set out for the old woman's cottage, where he arrived just in time for breakfast, which she shared with him. He then went to bed, and slept for many hours. When he awoke the sun was down and he departed in great anxiety lest he should lose a glimpse of the lovely vision.

But, whether it was by the evil-doing of the wicked fairy, or merely that it is one thing to go and another to return by the same road, he lost his way.

I shall not attempt to describe his misery when the moon rose, and he saw nothing but trees, trees, trees. She was high in the heavens before he reached the glade. Then indeed his troubles vanished, for there was the Princess dancing towards him, in a dress that shone like gold, and with shoes that glimmered through the grass like fireflies. She was even more beautiful than before. Like an embodied sunbeam she passed him, and danced away into the distance.

Before she returned in her circle, the clouds had begun to gather about the moon. The wind rose, the trees moaned, and their lighter branches leaned all one way before it. The Prince feared that the Princess would go in, and he should see her no more that night. But she came dancing on more jubilant than ever, her golden dress and her sunny hair streaming out upon the blast. She waved her arms towards the moon, and in the exuberance of her delight ordered the clouds away from her face. The Prince could hardly believe she was not a creature of the elements, after all.

By the time she had completed another circle, the clouds had gathered deep, and there were growlings of distant thunder. Just as she passed the tree where the young man stood, a flash of lightning blinded him for a moment. When he saw again, to his horror, the Princess lay on the ground. He darted to her, thinking she had been struck. But when she heard him coming, she was on her feet in a moment.

"What do you want?" she asked.

"I beg your pardon. I thought—the lightning—" said the Prince, hesitating.

"There's nothing the matter," said the Princess, waving him off rather haughtily.

The poor Prince turned and walked towards the wood.

"Come back," said Daylight. "I like you. You do what you are told."

He stood before her waiting.

"Can you tell me what the sun is like?" she asked.

"Why, everybody knows that," he answered.

"That's the very thing: I'm not everybody. I've never seen the sun."

"Then no one can tell you. You can't know what it's like till you do see it."

"I think you must be a Prince," said the Princess.

"Do I look like one?" said the Prince.

"I can't quite say that."

"Then why do you think so?"

"Because you both do what you are told and speak the truth. Is the sun so very bright?"

"As bright as the lightning."

"But it doesn't go out like that, does it?"

"Oh, no. It shines like the moon, rise and sets like the moon, is much the same shape as the moon, only so bright that you can't look at it for a moment."

"But I *would* look at it," said the Princess.

"But you couldn't," said the Prince.

"But I could," said the Princess.

"Why don't you, then?"

"Because I can't."

"Why can't you?"

"Because I can't wake. And I never shall wake until—"

Here she hid her face in her hands, turned away, and walked in the slowest, stateliest manner towards the house.

The Prince followed her at a little distance, but she turned and made a haughty gesture.

He waited a long time, but as she did not come near him again, and as the night

had now cleared, he set off at last for the old woman's cottage. It was long past midnight when he reached it, and to his surprise, the old woman was paring potatoes at the door. Fairies are fond of doing odd things at odd times. The night is always their day. So it is with all who have fairy blood in them.

"Why, what are you doing there, this time of the night, mother?" said the Prince, for that was the kind way in which any young man in his country would address a very old woman.

"Getting your supper ready," she answered.

"Oh, I don't want any supper," said the Prince.

"Ah, you've seen Daylight," said she.

"I've seen a Princess who never saw daylight," said the Prince.

"Do you like her?" asked the fairy.

"Oh!" said the Prince. "More than you would believe, mother."

"A fairy can believe anything that ever was or ever could be," said the old woman.

"Then are you a fairy?" asked the Prince.

"Yes," said she.

"Then what do you do for things *not* to believe?" asked the Prince.

"There's plenty of them—everything that never was and never could be."

"Plenty, I grant you," said the Prince. "But do you believe there could be a Princess who never saw the daylight?"

This the Prince said, not that he doubted the Princess, but that he wanted the fairy to tell him more. She was too old a fairy, however, to be caught so easily.

"Of all people, fairies must not tell secrets," she told him. "Besides, she's a Princess."

"Well, I'll tell *you* a secret. I'm a Prince."

"I know that."

"How do you know it?"

"By the curl of the third eyelash on your left eyelid."

"Which corner do you count from?"

"That's a secret."

"Another secret? Well, since I am a Prince, there can be no harm in your telling me about a Princess."

But he could get nothing more out of the fairy, and had to go to bed unanswered, which was something of a trial.

Now wicked fairies will not be bound by the law which the good fairies obey, and this always seems to give the bad the advantage over the good, for they use means to gain their ends which the others will not. But what they do never succeeds. In the end it brings about the very thing they are trying to prevent. So you see that somehow, for all their cleverness, wicked fairies are dreadfully stupid.

The Prince had so far stolen a march upon the wicked fairy in that she did not know he was in the neighborhood until after he had seen the Princess, those three times. When she found it out she consoled herself by deciding that the Princess must be far too proud and too modest for any young man to venture even to speak to her before he had seen her six times at least. But there was even less danger than the wicked fairy thought; for, however much the Princess might desire to be set free, she was dreadfully afraid of the wrong Prince. Now, however, the fairy was going to do all she could.

She so contrived it, by her deceitful spells, that the next night the Prince could not find his way to the glade. The poor Prince wandered about the forest till daylight, and then fell fast asleep. The same thing occurred for seven following days, during which he could not find the good fairy's cottage.

After the third quarter of the moon, however, the bad fairy thought she might be at ease about the affair for a fortnight at least, for she knew there was no chance of the Prince wishing to kiss the Princess during that period.

The first day of the fourth quarter he did find the cottage, and the next day he found the glade. For nearly another week he haunted it. But the Princess never came. I have little doubt she *was* on the farther edge of it some part of every night, but at this period she always wore black, and, there being little or no light, the Prince never saw her. Nor would he have known her if he had seen her. How could he have taken the worn decrepit creature she was now for the glorious Princess Daylight?

At last, one night when there was no moon at all, he ventured near the house. There he heard voices talking, although it was past midnight. It turned out that her women were in considerable uneasiness, because the one whose turn it was to watch the Princess had fallen asleep and had not seen which way she went, and this was a night when she would probably wander very far into a part of the forest of which the Prince knew nothing. When he understood from what they said that she had disappeared, and that she must have gone somewhere in the said direction, he plunged at once into the wood to see if he could find her. For hours he roamed with nothing to guide him but the vague notion of a circle which on one side bordered on the house, for so much had he picked up from the talk he had overheard.

It was getting towards the dawn, but as

yet there was no streak of light in the sky, when he came to a great birch tree, and sat down, weary, at the foot of it.

While he sat—very miserable, you may be sure—full of fear for the Princess, and wondering how her attendants could take it so quietly, he thought it would not be a bad plan to light a fire, which if she were anywhere near, would attract her. This he managed with a tinder-box, which the good fairy had given him. It was just beginning to blaze up, when he heard a moan, which seemed to come from the other side of the tree. He sprang to his feet, but his heart throbbed so that he had to lean for a moment against the tree before he could move.

When he got around, there lay a human form in a little dark heap on the earth. There was light enough from his fire to show that it was not the Princess. He lifted it in his arms, hardly heavier than a child, and carried it to the flame. The face was that of an old woman, but it had a fearfully strange look. A black hood concealed her hair, and her eyes were closed. He laid her down as comfortably as he could, chafed her hands, and put a little cordial from a bottle, also the gift of the fairy, into her mouth. He took off his coat and wrapped it about her as best he could.

In a little while she opened her eyes and looked at him—so pitifully! The tears rose and flowed from her grey wrinkled cheeks, but she said never a word. She closed her eyes again, but the tears kept on flowing, and her whole appearance was so utterly pitiful that the Prince was near crying too.

He begged her to tell him what was the matter, promising to do all he could to help her. But still she did not speak. He thought she was dying, and took her in his arms again to carry her to the Princess's house, where he thought the good-natured cook might be able to do something for her. When he lifted her, the tears flowed yet faster, and she gave such a sad moan that it went to his very heart.

"Poor old mother!" he said, and he kissed her on the withered lips.

She started. And what eyes they were that opened upon him! But he did not see them, for it was still very dark, and he had enough to do to make his way through the trees towards the house.

Just as he approached the door, feeling more tired than he could have imagined possible—she was such a little thin old thing—she began to move. She became so restless that, unable to carry her a moment longer, he thought to lay her on the grass. But she stood upright on her feet. Her hood had dropped, and her hair fell about her. The first gleam of the morning was caught on her face. That face was bright as the never-aging Dawn, and her eyes were lovely as the sky of darkest blue.

The Prince recoiled in over-mastering wonder. It was Daylight herself whom he had brought from the forest!

He fell at her feet, nor dared to look up until she laid her hand upon his head. He rose then.

"You kissed me when I was an old woman. So I kiss you when I am a young Princess," murmured Daylight, and added to his joy, "Is that the sun coming?"

Christmas with Queen Bess

From MASTER SKYLARK

By John Bennett

Master Skylark, as Nick Attwood is called, is a Stratford boy of Shakespeare's time—a boy with a wonderful voice who runs away from home and falls in with a company of strolling players. They take him to London where he is enrolled in a boys' choir school conducted by a famous musician and teacher, Master Gyles.

In its delightful portrayal of Elizabethan England, MASTER SKYLARK captures and holds you through many incidents both tender and gay, vigorous and sad. It is crowded with characters (among them the Queen herself and Will Shakespeare) who bring to life the spirit of England's glorious days.

In the chapter reprinted here, Nick Attwood, homesick and longing for his mother and his native Stratford, takes part, with others of the choir, in a Christmas Masque at the Queen's palace. The excitement and tension of the boy actors and singers, as well as the colorful details of the presentation, are so skillfully brought out that they may well inspire you to read the whole book.

CHRISTMAS morning came and went as if on swallow-wings, in a gale of royal merriment. Four hundred sat down to dinner that day in Greenwich halls, and all the palace streamed with banners and green garlands.

Within the courtyard two hundred horses neighed and stamped around a water-fountain playing in a bowl of ice and evergreen. Grooms and pages, hostlers and dames, went hurry-scurrying to and fro. Cooks, bakers, and scullions steamed about, leaving hot mouth-watering streaks of fragrance in the air. Bluff men-at-arms went whistling here and there; and serving-maids with rosy cheeks ran breathlessly up and down the winding stairways.

The palace stirred like a mighty boiling pot, for the hour of the revelries was come.

Over the beech-wood and far across the black heath the wind trembled with the boom of the castle bell. Within the walls of the palace its clang was muffled by a sound of voices that rose and fell like the wind upon the sea.

The ambassadors of Venice and France were there, with their courtly trains. The Lord High Constable of England had come to sit below the Queen. The earls, too, of Southampton, Montgomery, Pembroke, and Huntington were there; and William Cecil, Lord Burleigh, the Queen's High Treasurer, to smooth his care-lined forehead with a Yule-tide jest.

Up from the entry ports came shouts of "Room! Room! Room for my Lord Strange! Room for the Duke of Devonshire!" And about the outer gates there was a tumult like the cheering of a great crowd.

The palace corridors were lined with guards. Gentlemen pensioners under arms went flashing to and fro. Now and then through the inner throng some handsome page with windblown hair and rainbow-colored cloak, pushed to the great door, calling: "Way, sirs, way for my Lord—way for my Lady of Alderstone!" And one by one, or in blithe groups, the courtiers, clad in silks and satins, velvets, jewels, and lace of gold, came up through the lofty folding-doors to their places in the hall.

Where the Usher of the Black Rod stood, and the gentlemen of the chamber came and went with golden chains about their necks, there was bowing and scraping without stint, and reverent civility. Men that were wise and noble were passing by, men that were handsome and brave. Ladies sweet as a summer day, and as fair to see as spring, laughed by their sides and chatted behind their fans, or daintily nibbled comfits, lacking anything to say.

The windows were all curtained in, making a night-time in midday. And from the walls and galleries flaring links and great bouquets of candles threw an eddying flood of yellow light across the stirring scene. From clump to clump of banner-staves and burnished arms, spiked above the wainscot, garlands of red-berried holly, spruce, and mistletoe were twined across the tapestry, till all the room was bound about with a chain of living green.

There were sweet odors floating through the air, and hazy threads of fragrant smoke from perfumes burning in rich braziers. Under foot was the crisp, clean rustle of new rushes.

From time to time, above the hum of voices, came the sound of music from a room beyond—cornets and flutes, fifes, lutes, and harps with an organ exquisitely played, and voices singing to it. From behind the players' curtain, swaying slowly in its rings at the back of the stage, came a murmur of whispering childish voices, now high in eager questioning, now low, rehearsing some doubtful fragment of a song.

Behind the curtain it was dark—not total darkness, but twilight. A dull glow came down overhead from the lights in the hall outside, and faint yellow bars went up and down the dusk from crevices in the screen. The boys stood here and there in nervous groups. Now and then a sharp complaint was heard when an impatient lad would not stand still to be dressed.

Master Gyles went to and fro, twisting the manuscript of the Revel in his hands, and pausing kindly to pat some faltering lad upon the back. Nick and Colley were peeping by turns through a hole in the screen at the throng in the audience-chamber.

They could see a confusion of fans, jewels, and faces, and now and again could hear a burst of subdued laughter over the steadily increasing buzz of voices. Then from the gallery above, all at once there came a murmur of instruments tuning together. A voice in the corridor was heard calling, "Way here, way here!" in masterful tones.

The tall folding-doors at the side of the hall swung wide, and eight dapper pages white and gold came in with the Master of Revels. After them came fifty ladies and noblemen clad in white and gold, and a guard of gentlemen pensioners with glittering halberds.

There was a sharp rustle. Every head in the audience-chamber bowed low. Nick's heart gave a jump—for the Queen was was there.

She came with an air that was at once serious and royal, bearing herself haughtily, yet with a certain grace and sprightliness that became her very well. She was quite tall and well made, and her quickly changing face was long and fair, though wrinkled and no longer young. Her complexion was clear and of an olive hue. Her nose was a little hooked; her firm lips were thin; and her small black eyes though keen and bright, were pleasant and merry. Her hair was a coppery red, and false. In her ears hung two great pearls. There was a fine small crown studded with diamonds upon her head, a necklace of exceeding fine gold and jewels about her neck. She was attired in a white silk gown bordered with pearls the size of beans, and over it she wore a mantle of black silk, shot with silver threads. Her ruff was vast, her farthingale vaster; and her train, which was very long, was borne by a marchioness who made more ado about it than Elizabeth did of ruling her realm.

"The Queen!" gasped Colley.

"Dost think I did na know it?" answered Nick, his heart beginning to beat a tattoo as he stared through the peep-hole in the screen.

He saw the great folk bowing like a gardenful of flowers in a storm. In its midst Elizabeth erect, speaking to those about her in a lively and good-humored way, addressed all the foreigners according to their tongue — in French, Italian, Spanish, Dutch. But hers was funny Dutch, and while she spoke she smiled and made a joke of it in Latin, at which they all laughed heartily, whether they understood what it meant or not. Then, with her ladies-in-waiting, she passed to a dais near the stage, and stood a moment, stately, fair, and proud, while all her nobles made obeisance. Then she sat and gave a signal for the players to begin.

"Rafe Fullerton!" the prompter whispered shrilly. And out from behind the screen slipped Rafe, the smallest of them all, and down the stage to speak the foreword of the piece. He was frightened, and his voice shook as he spoke, but every one was smiling, so he took new heart.

"It is a masque of Summer-time and Spring," said he, "wherein both claim to be best-loved, and have their say of wit and humor, and each her part of songs and dances suited to her time, the sprightly nimble jig for Spring, the slow stately peacock dance, for Summer-time. And win who may, fair Summer-time or merry Spring, the winner is but that beside our Queen!" — with which he snapped his fingers in the faces of them all—"God save Queen Bess!"

At that the Queen's eyes twinkled, and she nodded, highly pleased, so that everyone clapped mightily.

The play soon ran its course amid great laughter and applause. Spring won. The English ever loved her best, and the quick-paced jig took their fancy too. "Up and be doing!" was its tune, and it gave one a chance to cut fine capers with his heels.

Then the stage stood empty and the music stopped.

At this strange end a whisper of surprise ran through the hall. The Queen tapped with the inner side of her rings upon the broad arm of her chair. From the look on her face she was whetting her tongue. But before she could speak, Nick and Colley, dressed as a farmer boy and girl, with a garland of house-grown flowers about them, came down the stage hand in hand, bowing.

The audience-chamber grew very still. *This* was something new. Nick felt a swallowing in his throat, and Colley's hand winced in his grip. There was no sound but a silky rustling in the room.

Then suddenly the boys behind the players' curtain laughed together, not loud, but such a jolly little laugh that all the people smiled to hear it. After the laughter came a hush.

Then the pipes overhead made a merry sound as of shepherds piping on oaten straws in new grass where there are daisies; and there was a little elfish laughter of clarinets, and a fluttering among the cool flutes like spring wind blowing through crisp young leaves in April. The harps began to pulse and throb with a soft cadence like raindrops falling into a clear pool where brown leaves lie upon the bottom and bubbles float above green stones and smooth white pebbles. Nick lifted up his head and sang.

It was a happy little song of the coming and the triumph of the spring. The words were all forgotten long ago. They were not much: enough to serve the turn, no more. But the notes to which they went were like barn swallows twittering under the eaves, goldfinches clinking in purple weeds beside old roads, and robins singing in common gardens at dawn. And wherever Nick's voice ran Colley's followed, the pipes laughing after them a note or two below; while the flutes kept gurgling softly to themselves as a hill brook gurgles through the woods, and the harps ran gently up and down like rain among the daffodils.

One voice called, the other answered. There were echo-like refrains. And as they sang Nick's heart grew full. He cared not a stiver for the crowd, the golden palace, or the great folk there. He listened only for Colley's voice coming up lovingly after his own and running away when he followed it down, like a lad and a lass through the bloom of the May. And Colley was singing as if his heart would leap out of his mouth. They sang till they came to the end and the skylark's song.

There Colley ceased, and Nick went singing on alone, heeding nought but the song that was in his throat.

The Queen's fan dropped from her hand upon the floor. No one saw it or picked it up. The Venetian ambassador scarcely breathed.

Nick came down the stage, his hands before him, lifted as if he saw the very lark he followed with his song—up, up, up into the sun. His cheeks were flushed and his eyes were wet, though his voice was a song and a laugh in one.

Then they were gone behind the curtain, into the shadow and the twilight there, Colley with his arms about Nick's neck, not quite laughing, not quite sobbing. The manuscript of the Revel lay torn in two upon the floor, and Master Gyles had a foot upon each piece.

In the hall beyond the curtain was a silence that was deeper than a hush, a stillness rising from the hearts of men.

Then Elizabeth turned in the chair where she sat. Her eyes were as bright as a blaze. And out of the sides of her eyes she looked at the Venetian ambassador. He was sitting far out on the edge of his chair, his lips parted.

Queen Elizabeth laughed to herself. "It is a good song, Signor," said she, and those about her started at the sound of her voice. *"Chi tace confessa*—it is so! There are no songs like English songs—there is no spring like an English spring — there is no land like England, *my* England!" She clapped her hands. "I will speak with those lads," said she.

Straightway certain pages ran through the press and came behind the curtain where Nick and Colley stood together, still trembling with the music not yet gone out of them. The pages brought the boys through the hall to where the Queen sat, everyone whispering, "Look!" as they passed.

On the dais they knelt together, bowing

side by side. Elizabeth, with a kindly smile, leaning a little forward, raised them with her slender hand. "Stand, dear lads," said she, heartily. "Be lifted up by thine own singing, as our hearts have been uplifted by thy song. And name me the price of that same song—'twas sweeter than the sweetest song we had ever heard before."

"Or ever shall hear again," said the Venetian ambassador, under his breath, rubbing his forehead as if just wakening out of a dream.

"Come," said Elizabeth, tapping Colley's cheek with her fan, "what wilt thou have of me, fair maid?"

Colley turned red, then very pale. "That I may stay in the palace forever and sing for your Majesty," said he. His fingers shivered in Nick's.

"Now that is right prettily asked," cried Elizabeth, and was well pleased. "Thou shalt indeed stay for a singing page in our household—a voice and a face like thine are merry things upon a rainy Monday. And thou, Master Lark," said she, fanning the hair back from Nick's forehead with her perfumed fan, "thou that comest up out of the field with a song like the angels sing— what wilt thou have: that thou mayst sing in our choir and play on the lute for us?"

Nick looked up at the torches on the wall, drawing a deep long breath. When he looked down again his eyes were dazzled and he could not see the Queen.

"What wilt thou have?" he heard her ask.

"Let me go home," said he.

There were red and green spots in the air. He tried to count them, since he could see nothing else, and everything was very still. But they all ran into one purple spot which came and went like a firefly's glow, and in the middle of the purple spot he saw the Queen's face coming and going.

"Surely, boy, that is an ill-considered speech," said she, "or thou dost deem us very poor, or most exceeding stingy!"

Nick hung his head, for the walls seemed tapestried with staring eyes.

"Or else this home of thine must be a very famous place," continued the Queen.

The maids of honour tittered. Further off somebody laughed. Nick looked up, and squared his shoulders.

It is hard to be a stranger in a palace, young, country-bred, and laughed at all at once. But down in Nick Attwood's heart was a stubborn streak that all the flattery on earth could not cajole nor ridicule efface. He might be simple, shy, and slow. But what he loved he loved: that much he knew. When they laughed at him for loving home they seemed to mock not him, but home—and *that* touched the fighting-spot.

"I would rather be there than here," said he.

The Queen's face flushed. "Thou art more curt than courteous," said she. "It is not good enough for thee here?"

"I could na live in such a place."

The Queen's eyes snapped. "In such a place? Tell me, art thou so choice? These others find no fault with the life."

"Then they are born to it," said Nick, "or they could abide no more than I—they would na fit."

"Haw, haw!" said the Lord High Constable.

The Queen shot one quick glance at him. "Old pegs have been made to fit new holes before today," said she, "and the trick can be done again."

The Constable smothered the rest of that laugh in his hand.

"But come, boy," the Queen went on,

":speak up! What hath put thee out with our best-beloved palace?"

"There is na one thing likes me here. I can na bide in a place so fine, for there's not so much as a corner in it feels like home. I could na sleep in the bed last night."

"What, how? We commanded good beds!" exclaimed Elizabeth angrily, for the Venetian ambassador was smiling in his beard. "This shall be seen to."

"Oh, it *was* a good bed—a very good bed indeed, your Majesty!" cried Nick. "But the feather mattress puffed up like a cloud, and almost smothered me; and it was so soft and so hot that it gave me a fever."

Elizabeth leaned back in her chair and laughed. The Lord High Constable hastily finished the laugh that he had hidden in his hand. Everybody laughed.

"Upon my word," said the Queen, "it is an odd skylark cannot sleep in feathers! What didst thou do, forsooth?"

"I slept in the coverlet on the floor," said Nick. "It was na hurt—I dusted the place well—and I slept like a top."

"Now, verily," laughed Elizabeth, "if it be floors that thou dost desire, we have acres to spare. Thou shalt have thy pick of the lot. Come, we are ill used to begging people to be favored. Thou'lt stay?"

Nick shook his head.

"*Ma foi!*" exclaimed the Queen, "it is a queer fancy makes a face at such a pleasant dwelling! What is it sticks in thy throat?"

Nick stood silent. What was there to say? If he came here he never would see Stratford town again. *This* was no abiding-place for him. They would not even let him go to the fountain himself to draw water with which to wash. They fetched it for him in a silver ewer and a copper basin, with towels and a flask of perfume!

Elizabeth was tapping with her fan. "Thou art bedazzled like," she said." Think twice—preferment does not gooseberry on the hedge-row every day. This is a rare chance. Consider well. Come, thou wilt accept?"

Nick slowly shook his head.

"Go then, if thou wilt go!" said she. And as she spoke she shrugged her shoulders, ill-pleased, and turning toward Colley, took him by the hand and drew him closer to her, smiling at his guise. "Thy comrade hath more wit," she said.

"He hath no mother," Nick said quietly, loosing his hold at last on Colley's hand. "I would rather have my mother than his wit."

Elizabeth turned sharply back. Her keen eyes were sparkling, yet soft.

"Thou art no fool," said she.

A little murmur went through the room.

She sat a moment, silent, studying his face. "Or if thou art, upon my word I like the breed. It is a stubborn dog; but Hold-fast is his name. Ay, sirs," she said, and sat up very straight, looking into the faces of her court, "Brag is a good dog, but Hold-fast is better. A lad who loves his mother thus makes a man who loveth his native land—and it's no bad streak in the blood. Master Skylark, thou shalt have thy wish. To London thou shalt go this very night."

"I do na live in London," Nick began.

"What matters the place?" said she. "Live wheresoever thine heart doth please. Thou mayst kiss our hand."

She held her hand out, bright with jewels. He knelt and kissed it as if it were all a doing in a dream, or in some unlikely story he had read. But for a long while after, he could smell the perfume from her slender fingers on his lips.

Then a page standing by him touched

his arm as he arose, and, bowing backward from the throne, came with him to the curtain and the rest. Old Master Gyles was standing there apart. It was too dark to see his face, but he laid his hand upon Nick's head. "Thy cake is burned to a coal," said he.

Hark, Hark! The Lark

By William Shakespeare

Hark, hark! the lark at heaven's gate sings,
    And Phoebus 'gins arise,
His steeds to water at those springs
    On chaliced flowers that lies;
And winking Mary-buds begin
    To ope their golden eyes:
With every thing that pretty is,
    My lady sweet, arise:
      Arise, arise.

Who is Silvia?

By William Shakespeare

Who is Silvia? What is she,
    That all our swains commend her?
Holy, fair, and wise is she;
    The heaven such grace did lend her,
That she might admired be.

Is she kind as she is fair?
    For beauty lives with kindness.
Love doth to her eyes repair,
    To help him of his blindness,
And, being helped, inhabits there.

Then to Silvia let us sing,
    That Silvia is excelling;
She excels each mortal thing
    Upon the dull earth dwelling:
To her let us garlands bring.

Lassie Come-Home

By Eric Knight

LASSIE COME HOME, originally a short story, is here in full for your reading enjoyment. It was written in this century, and it is about a magnificent thoroughbred collie, Lassie, who all but gives up her life for the boy she loves so dearly.

Lassie's story is a very sad one. Many children, and grown-ups too, have cried as they read of the heartbreaking hardships Lassie suffered. They have held their breath with the suspense of not knowing whether Lassie is going to be able to make the long trip home after escaping from the Duke's Scottish hunting lodge four hundred miles away. But they have rejoiced when they found that the dog and the boy are united at last.

Eric Knight understood both boys and dogs so well that when he wrote this story he knew it would have to have a happy ending, and it has.

THE dog had met the boy by the school gate for five years. Now she couldn't understand that times were changed and she wasn't supposed to be there any more. But the boy knew.

So when he opened the door of the cottage, he spoke before he entered, "Mother," he said, "Lassie's come home again."

He waited a moment, as if in hope of something. But the man and woman inside the cottage did not speak. "Come in, Lassie," the boy said.

He held open the door, and the tricolor collie walked in obediently. Going head down, as a collie does when it knows something is wrong, it went to the rug and lay down before the hearth, a black-white-and-gold aristocrat. The man, sitting on a low stool by the fireside, kept his eyes turned away. The woman went to the sink and busied herself there.

"She were waiting at school for me, just like always," the boy went on. He spoke fast, as if racing against time. "She must ha' got away again. I thought, happen this time, we might just—"

"No!" the woman exploded.

The boy's carelessness dropped. His voice rose in pleading.

"But this time, mother! Just this time. We could hide her. They wouldn't ever know."

"Dogs, dogs, dogs!" the woman cried. The words poured from her as if the boy's pleading had been a signal gun for her own anger.

"I'm sick o' hearing about tykes around this house. Well, she's sold and gone and done with, so the quicker she's taken back the better. Now get her back quick, or first thing you know we'll have Hynes round here again. Mr. Hynes!"

Her voice sharpened in imitation of the Cockney accent of the south. "Hi know you Yorkshiremen and yer come-'ome dogs. Training yer dogs to come 'ome so's yer can sell 'em hover and hover again.

"Well, she's sold, so ye can take her out o' my house and home to them as bought her!"

The boy's bottom lip crept out stubbornly, and there was silence in the cottage. Then the dog lifted its head and nudged the man's hand, as a dog will when asking for patting. But the man drew away and stared silently into the fire.

The boy tried again, with the ceaseless guile of a child, his voice coaxing.

"Look, feyther, she wants thee to bid her welcome. Aye, she's that glad to be home. Happen they don't tak' good care on her up there? Look, her coat's a bit poorly, don't ye think? A bit o' linseed strained through her drinking water—that's what I'd gi' her."

Still looking in the fire, the man nodded. But the woman, as if perceiving the boy's new attack, sniffed.

"Aye, tha wouldn't be a Carraclough if tha didn't know more about tykes nor breaking eggs wi' a stick. Nor a Yorkshireman. My goodness, it seems to me sometimes that chaps in this village thinks more on their tykes nor they do o' their own flesh and blood. They'll sit by their firesides and let their own bairns starve so long as t' dog gets fed."

The man stirred, suddenly, but the boy cut in quickly.

"But she does look thin. Look, truly — they're not feeding her right. Just look!"

"Aye," the woman chattered. "I wouldn't put it past Hynes to steal t' best part o' t' dog meat for himself. And Lassie always was a strong eater."

"She's fair thin now," the boy said.

Almost unwillingly the man and woman looked at the dog for the first time.

"My gum, she is off a bit," the woman said. Then she caught herself. "Ma goodness, I suppose I'll have to fix her a bit o' summat. She can do wi' it. But soon as she's fed, back she goes. And never another dog I'll have in my house. Never another. Cooking and nursing for 'em, and as much

trouble to bring up as a bairn!"

So, grumbling and chatting as a village woman will, she moved about, warming a pan of food for the dog. The man and boy watched the collie eat. When it was done, the boy took from the mantelpiece a folded cloth and a brush, and began prettying the collie's coat. The man watched for several minutes, and then could stand it no longer.

"Here," he said.

He took the cloth and brush from the boy and began working expertly on the dog, rubbing the rich, deep coat, then brushing the snowy whiteness of the full ruff and the apron, bringing out the heavy leggings on the forelegs. He lost himself in his work, and the boy sat on the rug, watching contentedly. The woman stood it as long as she could.

"Now will ye please tak' that tyke out o' here?"

The man flared in anger.

"Well, ye wouldn't have me tak' her back looking like a mucky Monday wash, wouldta?"

He bent again, and began fluffing out the collie's petticoats.

"Joe!" the woman pleaded. "Will ye tak' her out o' here? Hynes'll be nosing round afore ye know it. And I won't have that man in my house. Wearing his hat inside, and going on like he's the duke himself — him and his leggings!"

"All right, lass."

"And this time, Joe, tak' young Joe wi' ye."

"What for?"

"Well, let's get the business done and over with. It's him that Lassie runs away for. She comes for young Joe. So if he went wi' thee, and told her to stay, happen she'd

120

be content and not run away no more, and then we'd have a little peace and quiet in the home—though heaven knows there's not much hope o' that these days, things being like they are." The woman's voice trailed away, as if she would soon cry in weariness.

The man rose. "Come, Joe," he said. "Get thy cap."

The Duke of Rudling walked along the gravel paths of his place with his grand-daughter, Philippa. Philippa was a bright

and knowing young woman, allegedly the only member of the duke's family he could address in unspotted language. For it was also alleged that the duke was the most irascible, vile-tempered old man in the three Ridings of Yorkshire.

"Country going to pot!" the duke roared, stabbing at the walk with his great black-thorn stick. "When I was a young man! Hah! Women today not as pretty. Horses today not as fast. As for dogs—ye don't see dogs today like—"

Just then the duke and Philippa came round a clump of rhododendrons and saw a man, a boy and a dog.

"Ah," said the duke, in admiration. Then

his brow knotted. "Damme, Carraclough! What're ye doing with my dog?"

He shouted it quite as if the others were in the next county, for it was also the opinion of the Duke of Rudling that people were not nearly so keen of hearing as they used to be when he was a young man.

"It's Lassie," Carraclough said. "She runned away again and I brought her back."

Carraclough lifted his cap, and poked the boy to do the same, not in any servile gesture, but to show that they were as well brought up as the rest.

"Damme, ran away again!" the duke roared. "And I told that utter nincompoop Hynes to—where is he? Hynes! Hynes! Damme, Hynes, what're ye hiding for?"

"Coming, your lordship!" sounded a voice, far away behind the shrubberies. And soon Hynes appeared, a sharp-faced man in check coat, riding breeches, and the cloth leggings that grooms wear.

"Take this dog," roared the duke, "and pen her up! And damme, if she breaks out again, I'll—I'll—"

The duke waved his great stick threateningly, and then, without so much as a thank you or kiss the back of my hand to Joe Carraclough, he went stamping and muttering away.

"I'll pen her up," Hynes muttered, when the duke was gone. "And if she ever gets awye agyne, I'll—"

He made as if to grab the dog, but Joe Carraclough's hobnailed boot trod heavily on Hynes' foot.

"I brought my lad wi' me to bid her to stay, so we'll pen her up this time. Eigh—sorry! I didn't see I were on thy foot. Come, Joe, lad."

They walked down the crunching gravel

path, along by the neat kennel buildings. When Lassie was behind the closed door, she raced into the high wire run where she could see them as they went. She pressed close against the wire, waiting.

The boy stood close, too, his fingers through the meshes touching the dog's nose.

"Go on, lad," his father ordered. "Bid her stay!"

The boy looked around, as if for help that he did not find. He swallowed, and then spoke, low and quickly.

"Stay here, Lassie, and don't come home no more," he said. "And don't come to school for me no more. Because I don't want to see ye no more. 'Cause tha's a bad dog, and we don't love thee no more, and we don't want thee. So stay there forever and leave us be, and don't never come home no more."

Then he turned, and because it was hard to see the path plainly, he stumbled. But his father, who was holding his head very high as they walked away from Hynes, shook him savagely, and snapped roughly: "Look where tha's going!"

Then the boy trotted beside his father. He was thinking that he'd never be able to understand why grownups sometimes were so bad-tempered with you, just when you needed them most.

After that, there were days and days that passed, and the dog did not come to the school gate any more. So then it was not like old times. There were so many things that were not like old times.

The boy was thinking that as he came wearily up the path and opened the cottage door and heard his father's voice, tense with anger: ". . . walk my feet off. If tha thinks I like—"

Then they heard his opening of the door and the voice stopped and the cottage was silent.

That's how it was now, the boy thought. They stopped talking in front of you. And this, somehow, was too much for him to bear.

He closed the door, ran out into the night, and onto the moor, that great flat expanse of land where all the people of that village walked in lonesomeness when life and its troubles seemed past bearing.

A long while later, his father's voice cut through the darkness.

"What's tha doing out here, Joe lad?"

"Walking."

"Aye."

They went on together, aimlessly, each following his own thoughts. And they both thought about the dog that had been sold.

"Tha maun't think we're hard on thee, Joe," the man said at last. "It's just that a chap's got to be honest. There's that to it. Sometimes, when a chap doesn't have much he clings right hard to what he's got. And honest is honest, and there's no two ways about it.

"Why, look, Joe. Seventeen year I worked in that Clarabelle Pit till she shut down, and a good collier too. Seventeen year! And butties I've had by the dozen, and never a man of 'em can ever say that Joe Carraclough kept what wasn't his, nor spoke what wasn't true. Not a man in his Riding can ever call a Carraclough mishonest.

"And when ye've sold a man summat, and ye've taken his brass, and ye've spent it—well, then done's done. That's all. And ye've got to stand by that."

"But Lassie was—"

"Now, Joe! Ye can't alter it, ever. It's

done—and happen it's for t' best. No two ways, Joe, she were getting hard to feed. Why, ye wouldn't want Lassie to be going around getting peaked and pined, like some chaps around here keep their tykes. And if ye're fond of her, then just think on it that now she's got lots to eat, and a private kennel, and a good run to herself, and living like a veritable princess, she is. Ain't that best for her?"

"We wouldn't pine her. We've always got lots to eat."

The man blew out his breath, angrily, "Eigh, Joe, nowt pleases thee. Well then, tha might as well have it. Tha'll never see Lassie no more. She run home once too often, so the duke's taken her wi' him up to his place in Scotland, and there she'll stay. So it's good-by and good luck to her, and she'll never come home no more, she won't. Now, I weren't off to tell thee, but there it is, so put it in thy pipe and smoke it, and let's never say a word about it no more—especially in front of thy mother."

The boy stumbled on in the darkness. Then the man halted.

"We ought to be getting back, lad. We left thy mother alone."

He turned the boy about, and then went on, but as if he were talking to himself.

"Tha sees, Joe, women's not like men. They have to stay home and manage best they can, and just spend the time in wishing. And when things don't go right, well, they have to take it out in talk and give a man hell. But it don't mean nowt, really, so tha shouldn't mind when thy mother talks hard.

"Ye just got to learn to be patient and let 'em talk, and just let it go up t' chimney wi' th' smoke."

123

Then they were quiet, until, over the rise, they saw the lights on the village. Then the boy spoke: "How far away is Scotland, feyther?"

"Nay, lad, it's a long, long road."

"But how far, feyther?"

"I don't know — but it's a longer road than thee or me'll ever walk. Now, lad. Don't fret no more, and try to be a man— and don't plague thy mother no more, wilta?"

Joe Carraclough was right. It is a long road, as they say in the North, from Yorkshire to Scotland. Much too far for a man to walk — or a boy. And though the boy often thought of it, he remembered his father's words on the moor, and he put the thought behind him.

But there is another way of looking at it; and that's the distance from Scotland to Yorkshire. And that is just as far as from Yorkshire to Scotland. A matter of about four hundred miles, it would be, from the Duke of Rudling's place far up in the Highlands, to the village of Holdersby. That would be for a man, who could go fairly straight.

To an animal, how much farther would it be? For a dog can study no maps, read no signposts, ask no directions. It could only go blindly, by instinct, knowing that it must keep on to the south, to the south. It would wander and err, quest and quarter, run into firths and lochs that would send it side-tracking and back-tracking before it could go again on its way—south.

A thousand miles, it would be, going that way—a thousand miles over strange terrain.

There would be moors to cross and burns to swim. And then those great, long lochs that stretch almost from one side of that dour land to another would bar the way and send a dog questing a hundred miles before it could find a crossing that would allow it to go south.

And, too, there would be rivers to cross, wide rivers like the Forth and the Clyde, the Tweed and the Tyne, where one must go miles to find bridges. And the bridges would be in towns. And in the towns there would be officials—like the one in Lanarkshire. In all his life he had never let a captured dog get away—except one. That was a gaunt, snarling collie that whirled on him right in the pound itself, and fought and twisted loose to race away down the city street—going south.

But there are also kind people, too; ones knowing and understanding in the ways of dogs. There was an old couple in Durham who found a dog lying exhausted in a ditch one night—lying there with its head to the south. They took that dog into their cottage and warmed it and fed it and nursed it. And because it seemed an understanding, wise dog, they kept it in their home, hoping it would learn to be content. But, as it grew stronger, every afternoon toward four o'clock it would go to the door and whine, and then begin pacing back and forth between the door and the window, back and forth as the animals do in their cages at the zoo.

They tried every wile and every kindness to make it bide with them, but finally, when the dog began to refuse food, the old people knew what they must do. Because they understood dogs, they opened the door one afternoon and they watched a collie go, not down the road to the right, or to the left, but straight across a field toward

124

the south; going steadily at a trot, as if it knew it still had a long, long road to travel.

Ah, a thousand miles of tor and brae, of shire and moor, of path and road and plowland, of river and stream and burn and brook and beck, of snow and rain and fog and sun, is a long way, even for a human being. But it would seem too far—much, much too far—for any dog to travel blindly and win through.

And yet—and yet—who shall say why, when so many weeks had passed that hope against hope was dying, a boy coming out of school, out of the cloakroom that always smelled of damp wool drying, across the concrete play yard with the black, waxed slides, should turn his eyes to a spot by the school gate from force of five years of habit, and see there a dog?

Not a dog, this one, that lifted glad ears above a proud, slim head with its black-and-gold mask; but a dog that lay weakly, trying to lift a head that would no longer

lift, trying to wag a tail that was torn and blotched and matted with dirt and burrs, and managing to do nothing much except to whine in a weak, happy, crying way as a boy on his knees threw arms about it, and hands touched it that had not touched it for many a day.

Then who shall picture the urgency of a boy, running, awkwardly, with a great dog in his arms running through the village, past the empty mill, past the Labor Exchange, where the men looked up from their deep ponderings on life and the dole? Or who shall describe the high tones of a voice—a boy's voice, calling as he runs up a path: "Mother! Oh, Mother! Lassie's come home! Lassie's come home!"

Nor does anyone who ever owned a dog need to be told the sound a man makes as he bends over a dog that has been his for many years; nor how a woman moves quickly, preparing food—which might be the family's condensed milk stirred into warm water; nor how the jowl of a dog is lifted so that raw egg and brandy, bought with precious pence, should be spooned in; nor how bleeding pads are bandaged, tenderly.

That was one day. There was another day when the woman in the cottage sighed with pleasure, for a dog lifted itself to its feet for the first time to stand over a bowl of oatmeal, putting its head down and lapping again and again while its pinched flanks quivered.

And there was another day when the boy realized that, even now, the dog was not to be his again. So the cottage rang again with protests and cries, and a woman shrilling: "Is there never to be no more peace in my house and home?" Long after he was in bed that night the boy heard the rise and fall of the woman's voice, and the steady, reiterative tone of the man's. It went on long after he was asleep.

In the morning the man spoke, not looking at the boy, saying the words as if he had long rehearsed them.

"Thy mother and me have decided upon it that Lassie shall stay here till she's better. Anyhow, nobody could nurse her better than us. But the day that t' duke comes back, then back she goes, too. For she belongs to him, and that's honest, too. Now tha has her for a while, so be content."

In childhood, "for a while" is such a great stretch of days when seen from one end. It is a terribly short time seen from the other.

The boy knew how short it was that morning as he went to school and saw a motorcar driven by a young woman. And in the car was a gray-thatched, terrible old man, who waved a cane and shouted: "Hi! Hi, there! Damme, lad! You there! Hi!"

Then it was no use running, for the car could go faster than you, and soon it was beside you and the man was saying: "Damme, Philippa, will you make this smelling thing stand still a moment? Hi, lad!"

"Yes, sir."

"You're What's-'is-Name's lad, aren't you?"

"Ma feyther's Joe Carraclough."

"I know. I know. Is he home now?"

"No, sir. He's away to Allerby. A mate spoke for him at the pit and he's gone to see if there's a chance."

"When'll he be back?"

"I don't know. I think about tea."

"Eh, yes. Well, yes. I'll drop around about fivish to see that father of yours. Something important."

It was hard to pretend to listen to lessons. There was only waiting for noon. Then the boy ran home.

"Mother! T' duke is back and he's coming to take Lassie away."

"Eigh, drat my buttons. Never no peace in this house. Is tha sure?"

"Aye. He stopped me. He said tell feyther he'll be round at five. Can't we hide her? Oh, mother."

"Nay, thy feyther—"

"Won't you beg him? Please, please. Beg feyther to—"

"Young Joe, now it's no use. So stop thy teasing! Thy feyther'll not lie. That much

I'll give him. Come good, come bad, he'll not lie."

"But just this once, mother. Please beg him, just this once. Just one lie wouldn't hurt. I'll make it up to him. I will. When I'm growed up, I'll get a job. I'll make money. I'll buy him things—and you, too. I'll buy you both anything you want if you'll only—"

For the first time in his trouble the boy became a child, and the mother, looking over, saw the tears that ran openly down his contorted face. She turned her face to the fire, and there was a pause. Then she spoke.

"Joe, tha mustn't," she said softly. "Tha must learn never to want nothing in life like that. It don't do, lad. Tha mustn't want things bad, like tha wants Lassie."

The boy shook his clenched fists in impatience.

"It ain't that, mother. Ye don't understand. Don't ye see—it ain't me that wants her. It's her that wants us! Tha's wha made her come all them miles. It's her that wants us, so terrible bad!"

The woman turned and stared. It was as if, in that moment, she were seeing this child, this boy, this son of her own, for the first time in many years. She turned her head down toward the table. It was surrender.

"Come and eat, then," she said. "I'll talk to him. I will that, all right. I feel sure he won't lie. But I'll talk to him, all right. I'll talk to Mr. Joe Carraclough. I will indeed."

At five that afternoon, the Duke of Rudling, fuming and muttering, got out of a car at a cottage gate to find a boy barring his way. This was a boy who stood, stubbornly, saying fiercely: "Away wi' thee! Thy tyke's net here!"

"Damme, Philippa, th' lad's touched," the Duke said. "He is. He's touched."

Scowling and thumping his stick, the old duke advanced until the boy gave way, backing down the path out of the reach of the waving blackthorn stick.

"Thy tyke's net here," the boy protested.

"What's he saying?" the girl asked.

"Says my dog isn't here. Damme, you going deaf? I'm supposed to be deaf, and I hear him plainly enough. Now, ma lad, what tyke o' mine's net here?"

As he turned to the boy, the duke spoke in broadest Yorkshire, as he did always to the people of the cottages — a habit which the Duchess of Rudling, and many more members of the duke's family, deplored.

"Coom, coom, ma lad. Whet tyke's net here?"

"No tyke o' thine. Us hasn't got it." The words began running faster and faster as the boy backed away from the fearful old man who advanced. "No tyke could have done it. No tyke can come all them miles. It isn't Lassie. It's another one that looks like her. It isn't Lassie!"

"Why, bless ma heart and sowl," the duke puffed. "Where's thy father, ma lad?"

The door behind the boy opened, and a woman's voice spoke.

"If it's Joe Carraclough ye want, he's out in the shed — and been there shut up half the afternoon."

"What's this lad talking about—a dog of mine being here?"

"Nay," the woman snapped quickly. "He didn't say a tyke o' thine was here. He said it wasn't here."

"Well, what dog o' mine isn't here, then?"

The woman swallowed, and looked about as if for help. The duke stood, peering from under his jutting eyebrows. Her answer, truth or lie, was never spoken, for then they heard the rattle of a door opening, and a man making a pursing sound with his lips, as he will when he wants a dog to follow, and then Joe Carraclough's voice said, "This is t' only tyke us has here. Does it look like any dog that belongs to thee?"

With his mouth opening to cry one last protest, the boy turned. And his mouth stayed open. For there he saw his father, Joe Carraclough, the collie fancier, standing with a dog at his heels—a dog that sat at his left heel patiently, as any well-trained dog should do—as Lassie used to do. But this dog was not Lassie. In fact, it was ridiculous to think of it at the same moment as you thought of Lassie.

For where Lassie's skull was aristocratic and slim, this dog's head was clumsy and rough. Where Lassie's ears stood in twin-lapped symmetry, this dog had one ear draggling and the other standing up Alsatian fashion in a way to give any collie breeder the cold shivers. Where Lassie's coat was rich tawny gold, this dog's coat had ugly patches of black; and where Lassie's apron was a billowing stretch of snow-white, this dog had puddles of off-color blue-merle mixture. Besides, Lassie had four white paws, and this one had one paw white, two dirty-brown, and and one almost black.

That is the dog they all looked at as Joe Carraclough stood there, having told no lie, having only asked a question. They all stood, waiting the duke's verdict.

But the duke said nothing. He only walked forward, slowly, as if he were seeing a dream. He bent beside the collie, look-

ing with eyes that were as knowing about dogs as any Yorkshireman alive. And those eyes did not waste themselves upon twisted ears, or blotched marking, or rough head. Instead they were looking at a paw that the duke lifted, looking at the underside of the paw, staring intently at five black pads,

128

crossed and recrossed with the scars where thorns had lacerated, and stones had torn.

For a long time the duke stared, and when he got up he did not speak in Yorkshire accents any more. He spoke as a gentleman should, and he said: "Joe Carraclough. I never owned this dog. 'Pon my soul, she's never belonged to me. Never!"

Then he turned and went stumping down the path, thumping his cane and saying: "Bless my soul. Four hundred miles! Damme, wouldn't ha' believed it. Damme—five hundred miles!"

He was at the gate when his granddaughter whispered to him fiercely.

"Of course," he cried. "Mind your own business. Exactly what I came for. Talking about dogs made me forget. Carraclough! Carraclough! What're ye hiding for?"

"I'm still here, sir."

"Ah, there you are. You working?"

"Eigh, now. Working," Joe said. That's the best he could manage.

"Yes, working, working!" The duke fumed.

"Well, now—" Joe began.

Then Mrs. Carraclough came to his rescue, as a good housewife in Yorkshire will.

"Why, Joe's got three or four things that he's been considering," she said, with proper display of pride. "But he hasn't quite said yes or no to any of them yet."

"Then say no, quick," the old man puffed. "Had to sack Hynes. Didn't know a dog from a drunken filly. Should ha' known all along no damn Londoner could handle dogs fit for Yorkshire taste. How much, Carraclough?"

"Well, now," Joe began.

"Seven pounds a week, and worth every penny," Mrs. Carraclough chipped in.

"Five," roared the duke—who, after all, was a Yorkshireman, and couldn't help being a bit sharp about things that pertained to money.

"Six," said Mrs. Carraclough.

"Five pound ten," bargained the duke, cannily.

"Done," said Mrs. Carraclough, who would have been willing to settle for three pounds in the first place. "But, o' course, us gets the cottage too."

"All right," puffed the duke. "Five pounds ten and the cottage. Begin Monday. But—on one condition. Carraclough, you can live on my land, but I won't have that thick-skulled, screw-lugged, gay-tailed eyesore of a misshapen mongrel on my property. Now never let me see her again. You'll get rid of her?"

He waited, and Joe fumbled for words. But it was the boy who answered, happily, gaily: "Oh, no, sir. She'll be waiting at school for me most o' the time. And, anyway, in a day or so we'll have her fixed up and coped up so's ye'd never, never recognize her."

"I don't doubt that," puffed the duke, as he went to the car. "I don't doubt ye could do just exactly that."

It was a long time afterward, in the car, that the girl said: "Don't sit there like a lion on the Nelson column. And I thought you were supposed to be a hard man."

"Fiddlesticks, m'dear. I'm a ruthless realist. For five years I've sworn I'd have that dog by hook or crook, and now, egad, at last I've got her."

"Pooh! You had to buy the man before you could get his dog."

"Well, perhaps that's not the worst part of the bargain."

129

Abou Ben Adhem

By Leigh Hunt

Abou Ben Adhem (may his tribe increase!)
Awoke one night from a deep dream of peace,
And saw, within the moonlight in his room,
Making it rich, and like a lily in bloom,
An Angel writing in a book of gold.
Exceeding peace had made Ben Adhem bold,
And to the Presence in the room he said,
"What writest thou?" The Vision raised its head,
And with a look made of all sweet accord
Answered, "The names of those who love the Lord."
"And is mine one?" said Abou. "Nay, not so,"
Replied the Angel. Abou spoke more low
But cheerily still, and said, "I pray thee, then,
Write me as one that loves his fellow men."

The Angel wrote, and vanished. The next night
It came again with a great wakening light,
And showed the names whom love of God had blessed,
And lo! Ben Adhem's name led all the rest!

The King of the Golden River

By John Ruskin

Here is a fairy tale for you that has all the terror and mystery of a legend of long ago. As you will see when you read it, this is an exciting tale of gold and greed and revenge. The characters get into the most dangerous and terrifying situations, but in the end, you will be glad to learn, the good ones are rewarded and the bad ones meet the horrible fate they deserve.

In a way, THE KING OF THE GOLDEN RIVER is a Cinderella story, only here the characters are young men instead of women. It is a dramatic story written by an author, John Ruskin, whose other stories are much more grown-up than this one and not nearly so exciting.

IN A secluded and mountainous part of Styria there was, in an olden time, a valley of the most surprising fertility. It was surrounded by steep mountains, always covered with snow, and from which torrents came down in cataracts. One of these fell westward so that when the sun had set, and all below was darkness, his beams still shone upon this waterfall, and it looked like a shower of gold. It was therefore called by the people of the neighborhood the Golden River.

Strangely, none of the streams fell into the valley itself. But the clouds rested so softly in the hollow of the hills that, when all the country round was burned up, there was still rain in the little valley. Its crops were so rich that it was a marvel to everyone who beheld it, and it was commonly called Treasure Valley.

The whole of this little valley belonged to three brothers named Schwartz, Hans, and Gluck. Schwartz and Hans, the elder, were ugly men, with overhanging eyebrows and small dull eyes. They lived by farming the Treasure Valley, and very good farmers they were. But they worked their servants without wages, till they would not work

any more; and then quarreled with them, and turned them out of doors without paying them.

It would have been very odd if, with such a farm and such a system of farming, they hadn't got very rich; and very rich they *did* get. They generally managed to keep their grain till it was very dear, and then sell it for twice its value. They had heaps of gold lying about on their floors, yet they had never been known to give so much as a penny or a crust of bread to the poor. They never went to church, and were so cruel and grinding that all those with whom they had any dealings called them the "Black Brothers."

Gluck was completely different, in both appearance and character, from his brothers. He was about twelve years old, fair, blue-eyed, and kind. He did not agree with his brothers, or rather, they did not agree with him. He was usually made to be the turnspit when there was anything to roast, which was not often. At other times he cleaned the shoes, the floors, and sometimes the plates, getting what was left on them for encouragement, and blows for education.

Things went on in this manner for a long

time. At last came a very wet summer, and everything went wrong in the country around. The haystacks were floated bodily down to the sea by floods; the vines were cut to pieces by hail; the crops were killed by a blight. Only in Treasure Valley, as usual, all was safe. As it had rained when there was rain nowhere else, so it had sun when there was sun nowhere else. Everybody came to buy food at the farm, and went away angry at the "Black Brothers," who asked what they liked and got it except from the poor people, who could not pay and several of whom starved to death at their very door.

It was drawing toward winter, and very cold weather, when one day the two elder brothers went out. They left Gluck to mind the roast with their usual warning that he was to let nobody in, and give nothing out. Gluck sat down quite close to the fire, for it was raining hard, and he turned and turned the roast so that it grew nice and brown.

"What a pity," thought Gluck, "my brothers never ask anybody to dinner! When they have such a nice piece of mutton as this, and nobody else has so much as a piece of dry bread, it would do them good to have somebody to eat it with them."

Just as he spoke there came a double knock at the house door, more like a puff than a knock.

"It must be the wind," said Gluck.

No, it wasn't the wind. It came again, and Gluck went to the window, and put his head out to see who it was.

It was the most extraordinary-looking little gentleman he had ever seen in his life. He had a very large nose, slightly brass-colored; his cheeks were round and red, his eyes twinkled merrily through long silky eyelashes, and his hair, of a curious mixed pepper-and-salt color, hung far over his shoulders. He was about four feet tall and wore a pointed cap of nearly the same height, with a black feather some three feet long. Over his curious long-tailed coat he wore an enormous black, glossy-looking cloak, which must have been very much too long in calm weather, as the wind, whistling round the old house, carried it clear out from his shoulders to about four times his own length.

The old gentleman, having knocked again, turned round to look after his fly-away cloak. In so doing he caught sight of Gluck's head in the window.

"Hello!" said the little gentleman, "I'm wet; let me in."

"I beg pardon, sir," said Gluck; "I'm very sorry, but I really can't."

"Can't what?" said the old gentleman.

"I can't let you in—I can't indeed. My brothers would beat me to death. What do you want, sir?"

"Want?" said the old gentleman. "I want fire and shelter. Let me in; I want to warm myself."

By this time, Gluck's head had been so long out of the window that he began to feel it was really cold; and when he turned and saw the fire rustling and roaring and throwing long bright tongues up the chimney, his heart melted that it should be burning away for nothing.

"He does look very wet," thought little Gluck. "I'll just let him in for a quarter of an hour."

The door opened, and as the little gentleman walked in, a gust of wind made the old chimneys totter.

"That's a good boy," he said. "Never mind your brothers; I'll talk to them."

"Please, sir, don't," said Gluck. "You can't stay till they come; they'd kill me."

"Dear me," said the old gentleman, "how long may I stay?"

"Only till the mutton's done, sir," replied Gluck, "and it's very brown."

Then the old gentleman sat down, with the top of his cap up the chimney, for it was much too high for the roof.

"You'll soon dry there, sir," said Gluck, and he sat down to turn the mutton.

But the old gentleman did *not* dry. He went on dripping, and the fire sputtered and began to look very black. Never was such a cloak; every fold in it ran like a gutter.

"I beg pardon, sir," said Gluck at last, "mayn't I take your cloak?"

"No, thank you," said the old gentleman.

"Your cap, sir?"

"I'm all right, thank you," said the old man gruffly.

"But—sir—I'm very sorry," said Gluck, hesitatingly; "but—really, sir—you're putting the fire out."

"It'll take longer then to do the mutton," said the visitor.

Gluck, very much puzzled by the behavior of his guest, turned away for another five minutes.

"That mutton looks very nice," said the old gentleman. "Can't you give me a little bit?"

"Impossible, sir," said Gluck.

Said the old gentleman, "I've had nothing to eat yesterday, nor to-day. They surely couldn't miss a bit from the knuckle!"

He spoke in so melancholy a tone that it melted Gluck's heart. "They promised me one slice to-day, sir," said he. "I can give you that, but no more."

"That's a good boy," said the old gentleman again.

Then Gluck warmed a plate and sharpened a knife. "I don't care if I do get beaten," thought he. Just as he had cut a large slice out of the mutton, there came a tremendous rap at the door. Gluck fitted the slice into the mutton again, and ran to the door.

"Why did you keep us waiting in the rain?" said Schwartz, as he walked in, throwing his umbrella at Gluck.

"Ay! why indeed, you little vagabond?" said Hans, giving him a box on the ear, as he followed his brother into the kitchen.

"Bless my soul!" said Schwartz when he opened the door.

"Amen," said the little gentleman, who had taken off his cap and was standing in

the middle of the kitchen, bowing.

"Who's that?" said Schwartz, catching up a rolling-pin, and turning to Gluck with a fierce frown.

"I don't know, brother," said Gluck, in terror.

"How did he get in?" roared Schwartz.

"My dear brother," said Gluck, "he was so *very* wet!"

The rolling-pin was descending on Gluck's head, but the old gentleman held out his cap, on which it crashed. Oddly the rolling-pin no sooner touched the cap, than it flew out of Schwartz's hand, spinning like a straw in a high wind, and fell into the far corner.

"Who are you, sir?" demanded Schwartz.

"What's your business?" snarled Hans.

"I'm a poor old man, sir," said the little gentleman, "and I saw your fire through the window, and begged shelter."

"Have the goodness to walk out again," said Schwartz. "We've enough water here without making this a drying-house."

"It is a cold day to turn an old man out, sir. Look at my gray hairs." "Ay!" said Hans, "they are enough to keep you warm. Go!"

"I'm very, very hungry, sir. Couldn't you spare me a bit of bread before I go?"

"Bread, indeed!" said Schwartz. "Do you suppose we've nothing to do but give it to such fellows as you?"

"Why don't you sell your feather?" said Hans sneeringly.

"Be off!" said Schwartz.

"Off and be hanged!" cried Hans, seizing him by the collar. But he had no sooner touched the old gentleman's collar than away he went after the rolling-pin, spinning round and round, till he fell into the corner on the top of it.

Then Schwartz ran at the old gentleman to turn him out; but he also had hardly touched him when away he went after Hans and the rolling-pin, and hit his head against the wall as he tumbled into the corner. And so there they lay, all three.

Then the old gentleman spun himself round and continued to spin until his cloak was all wound about him. Then he clapped his cap on his head and said with perfect coolness: "Gentlemen, I wish you good morning. At twelve o'clock tonight I'll call again. That visit is the last I shall ever pay you."

"If ever I catch you here again . . ." muttered Schwartz coming out of the corner. But before he could finish his sentence, the old gentleman had shut the house-door behind him with a bang, and past the window drove a wreath of ragged cloud, that whirled down the valley in all manner of shapes, turning over and over in the air, and melting away at last in a gush of rain.

"A pretty business, Gluck!" said Schwartz. "Dish the mutton. Bless me, it has been cut!"

"You promised me one slice, brother," said Gluck.

"Oh, and you were cutting it hot, I suppose, and going to catch all the gravy. It'll be long before I promise you such a thing again. Leave the room!"

Gluck left. The brothers ate as much as they could, locked the rest away, and got very drunk after dinner.

Such a night as it was! Howling wind and rustling rain without stop. The brothers had just sense enough to close the shutters, and double-bar the door, before they went to bed.

As the clock struck twelve, they were both awakened by a crash. Their door burst open with a violence that shook the house from top to bottom.

"What's that?" cried Schwartz, starting up in his bed.

"Only I," said the little gentleman.

The two brothers sat up and stared into the darkness. The roof was off, the room was full of water, and in the misty moonlight they could see an enormous foam globe spinning round and bobbing up and down like a cork. On it sat the little old gentleman.

"Sorry to inconvenience you," he said ironically. "I'm afraid your beds are dampish. Perhaps you had better go to your brother's room. I've left the ceiling on there."

They rushed into Gluck's room, wet through, and in an agony of terror.

Dawn came at last, and the two brothers looked out on a scene of desolation. The floods had swept away trees, crops, and cattle, and left a waste. The two brothers crept, shivering and horror-struck, into the kitchen. Grain, money, everything was gone, and there was left only a small white card

on the kitchen table. On it were engraved the words:

SOUTHWEST WIND, ESQUIRE

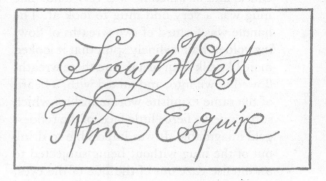

II

Southwest Wind, Esquire, was as good as his word. He entered Treasure Valley no more; and, what was worse, he had so much influence with his relatives, the West Winds, that they all took the same line of conduct. So no rain fell in the valley from one year's end to another. What had once been the richest soil in the kingdom became a desert, and the brothers abandoned their home in despair. Their money was gone, and they had nothing left but some curious, old-fashioned pieces of gold plate, the last of their wealth. They had to earn money somehow.

"Suppose we turn goldsmiths," said Schwartz to Hans, as they journeyed toward the city. "It is a good knave's trade: we can put a great deal of copper into the gold, without anyone's finding out."

So they hired a furnace and turned goldsmiths. But people did not approve of the coppered gold; and the elder two brothers, when they sold anything, left Gluck to mind the furnace, and spent the money in the ale-house. So they melted all their gold, without making money enough to buy more, and had nothing left but one large drinking-mug which an uncle had given to little Gluck, and of which he was very fond. The mug was a very odd mug to look at. The handle was formed of two wreaths of flowing golden hair so finely spun that it looked more like silk than metal, and these wreaths flowed down into, and mixed with, a beard of the same exquisite workmanship, which surrounded a fierce little face, of the reddest gold imaginable. It was impossible to drink out of the mug without being subjected to an intense gaze out of the side of the eyes; and Schwartz said positively that once he had seen them wink!

When Hans and Schwartz decided to melt down the mug it half broke little Gluck's heart. But his brothers laughed at him, tossed the mug into the melting-pot, and staggered to the ale-house, leaving him, as usual, to pour the gold into bars when it was ready.

When they were gone, Gluck took a farewell look at the mug. The hair was all gone; nothing remained but the eyes. Gluck sauntered to the window, and sat down to catch the air.

Now, this window commanded a view of the range of mountains which overhung Treasure Valley, and especially of the peak from which fell the Golden River. It was the close of day, and Gluck saw the mountain-tops all crimson and purple with the sunset; and the river fell in a waving column of pure gold with the double arch of a broad rainbow across it.

"Ah!" said Gluck aloud, "if that river were really all gold, what a nice thing it would be!"

"No, it wouldn't, Gluck," said a clear voice at his ear.

"Bless me, what's that?" exclaimed Gluck, jumping up. He looked around the room and under the table, but there was nobody there. He sat down again, and he couldn't help thinking that it would be very convenient if the river were really gold.

"Not at all, my boy," said the same voice.

"Bless me!" said Gluck, "what *is* that?" He looked into all the corners and cupboards, then began thinking there was someone behind him when the same voice struck again on his ear.

It was singing now very merrily—no words, only a soft melody, something like that of a kettle on the boil. Gluck looked out. No, it was certainly in the house, in that very room, coming in quicker time and clearer notes every moment, "Lala-lira-la." All at once Gluck thought it sounded louder near the furnace. Then it seemed to be coming not only out of the furnace but out of the pot. He uncovered it, and ran back in a great fright, for the pot was certainly singing! In a minute or two, the singing stopped and a clear voice said:

"Hello!"

Gluck made no answer.

"Hello, Gluck, my boy!" said the pot again.

Gluck summoned all his energies, walked straight up to the pot, drew it out of the furnace, looked in, and saw from beneath the gold the red nose and the sharp eyes of his old friend of the mug.

"Come, Gluck, my boy," said the voice, "I'm all right; pour me out."

But Gluck was too astonished to do anything.

"Pour me out, I say," said the voice.

By a violent effort, Gluck took hold of the

136

pot, to pour out the gold. But instead of a liquid stream, out came a little golden dwarf, about a foot and a half high.

He was dressed in a wonderful coat of spun gold, and over this brilliant coat his hair and beard fell half-way to the ground, in waving curls, so beautifully soft that Gluck could hardly tell where they ended; they seemed to melt into air. The features of the face, however, were rather coarse, and slightly coppery in complexion.

After a moment the dwarf turned his small, sharp eyes full on Gluck, and stared at him deliberately for a minute or two.

"No, it wouldn't, Gluck, my boy," said the little man.

"Wouldn't it, sir?" said Gluck, very mildly indeed.

"No," said the dwarf. "No, it wouldn't." And with that he pulled his cap hard over his brows, and took two turns up and down the room. This gave Gluck time to collect his thoughts and as his curiosity overcame his amazement, he asked hesitatingly, "Were you my mug?"

"Listen!" said the little man. "I am the King of what you mortals call the Golden River. The shape you saw me in was owing to the malice of a stronger King, from whose

enchantments you have just freed me. From what I have seen of you, and your conduct to your wicked brothers, I am willing to serve you. Therefore attend to what I tell you. Whoever shall climb to the top of that mountain and shall cast into the stream at its source three drops of holy water, for him, and for him only, the river shall turn to gold. But no one failing in his first try can succeed in a second, and if anyone shall cast unholy water into the river, he will become a black stone."

So saying, the King of the Golden River turned away, and deliberately walked into the hottest flame of the furnace. His figure became red, white, transparent, dazzling—and disappeared. The King of the Golden River had evaporated.

III

The King of the Golden River had hardly disappeared before Hans and Schwartz came in. When they discovered their last piece of plate was gone, they beat Gluck steadily for a quarter of an hour; after which they asked him what he had to say for himself. Gluck told them his story, which they did not believe. So they beat him again, and went to bed. In the morning, however, the steadiness with which he stuck to his story almost convinced them; and after wrangling a long time on the knotty question as to which of them should try for his fortune first, the brothers drew their swords and began fighting. The noise alarmed the neighbors, who sent for the police.

Hans hid himself; but Schwartz was taken before a judge, fined for breaking the peace, and was thrown into prison until his fine was paid.

When Hans heard this, he was delighted,

and determined to set out immediately for the Golden River. How to get the holy water was the question, for the priest would not give it to so abandoned a character. So Hans went to vespers for the first time in his life, stole a cupful, and returned home in triumph.

Next morning he got up before the sun rose, put the holy water into a strong flask, and some meat in a basket, and set off for the mountains.

On his way out of town, he had to pass the prison, and as he looked in at the windows whom should he see but Schwartz himself.

"Good morning, brother," said Hans. "Have you any message for the King of the Golden River?"

Schwartz gnashed his teeth with rage, and shook the bars with all his strength; but Hans only laughed at him, shouldered his basket, shook the bottle of holy water in Schwartz's face, and marched off in high spirits.

It was, indeed, a morning that might have made anyone happy, even with no Golden River to seek for. Lines of dewy mist lay stretched along the valley, out of which rose the giant mountains. Far beyond, pure and changeless, slept, in the blue sky, the peaks of the eternal snow.

The Golden River was now nearly in shadow, all but the uppermost jets of spray, which rose like slow smoke and floated away in fine wreaths upon the morning wind.

On the river and on this alone, Hans's eyes and thoughts were fixed. Forgetting the distance he had to go, he set off at a rate which wearied him before he had climbed the first range of hills. He was, moreover, surprised to find that a large glacier, or ice field, of whose existence he had not known,

lay between him and the Golden River. He entered on it with the boldness of a good climber, yet he thought he had never crossed so strange or so dangerous a glacier in his life. The ice, broken into thousands of confused shapes, was very slippery; and out of all its chasms came wild sounds of gushing water. Myriads of shadows and curious lights played and floated about, dazzling the traveler's eyes, while his head became giddy with the constant rush and roar of waters. The ice crashed and yawned at his feet. Tottering spires nodded around him, and fell thundering across his path. He was exhausted and shuddering when he leaped the last chasm and flung himself on the firm grassy mountainside.

His way now lay straight up a ridge of bare red rocks, without a blade of grass to ease the foot, or an overhanging cliff to give an inch of shade from the south sun. It was past noon, and the rays beat upon the steep path. Intense thirst was soon added to

Hans's great weariness. Glance after glance he cast on the flask of water at his belt. "Three drops are enough," he told himself at last. "I may, at least, cool my lips with it."

He opened the flask, and was raising it to his lips when his eye fell on a small dog which appeared to be dying from thirst. Its tongue was out, its jaws dry, and a swarm of black ants were crawling about its lips and throat. Its eye moved to the flask Hans held in his hand. Hans raised it, drank,

spurned the animal with his foot, and passed on. And he did not know how it was, but he thought that a strange shadow had suddenly come across the blue sky.

The path became steeper and more rugged and the high hill air, instead of refreshing him, seemed to throw his blood into a fever. The noise of the little waterfalls sounded like mockery in his ears; they were all distant, and his thirst increased every moment.

Another hour passed, and he again looked at the flask. It was half empty, but there was much more than three drops in it. He stopped to open it, and as he did so, he saw a fair child, stretched nearly lifeless on the rock, her breast heaving with thirst, her eyes closed, lips parched and burning. Hans eyed her deliberately, drank, and passed on. And a dark gray cloud came over the sun and sent long shadows creeping along the mountain-sides.

Hans struggled on. The sun was sinking, but the evening seemed to bring no coolness. The dead air pressed upon him, but the goal was near. He saw the Golden River springing from the hillside, scarcely five hundred feet above him.

At this instant a faint cry fell on his ear. He turned, and saw a gray-haired old man lying on the rocks. His eyes were sunk, his features deadly pale. He stretched his arms to Hans, and cried feebly, "Water! I am dying."

"I have none," replied Hans and he strode over the body and went on. A flash of blue lightning shaped like a sword rose out of the east, shook three times over the whole heaven, and left it dark. The sun was setting; it plunged toward the horizon like a red-hot ball.

Hans stood at the brink of the Golden River. Its waves were filled with the red glory of the sunset. Their sound came mightier and mightier. His brain grew giddy. Shuddering, he hurled the flask into the center of the torrent. As he did so, an icy chill shot through him. He staggered, shrieked, and fell. And the moaning of the river rose wildly into the night as it gushed over *THE BLACK STONE*.

IV

Poor little Gluck waited anxiously alone in the house for Hans's return, but Hans did not come. When he got up in the morning there was no bread in the house, nor any money; so Gluck hired himself to another goldsmith, and he worked so hard that he soon got enough money to pay his brother's fine; and he went and gave it to Schwartz, who was now let out of prison. Then Schwartz was pleased, and said he should have some of the gold of the river; but Gluck only begged that he go and see what had become of Hans.

Now when Schwartz had heard that Hans had stolen the holy water, he realized the King of the Golden River would not be pleased. He determined to manage matters better. As soon as Schwartz was free he took some more of Gluck's money and went to a bad priest, who readily gave him some holy water for it. Then Schwartz was sure it was quite all right. So the next day Schwartz got up before the sun rose, and took some bread and wine in a basket, and put his holy water in a flask, and set off for the mountains. Like his brother, he was much surprised at the sight of the glacier, and had difficulty in crossing it, even after leaving his basket behind him. As he climbed the steep rock path, thirst came upon him, as it had upon his brother, and he lifted his flask to his lips to drink. Then he saw the fair child lying on the rocks, and she cried to him, and moaned for water.

"Water, indeed!" said Schwartz. "I haven't half enough for myself," and passed on. And as he went he thought the sunbeams grew dim, and he saw a low bank of black cloud rise out of the west; and when he had climbed for another hour thirst overcame him again.

Then he saw the old man lying before him on the path, and heard him cry out for water.

"Water, indeed!" said Schwartz. "I haven't half enough for myself." And on he went.

Then again the light seemed to fade from before his eyes, and he looked up, and, behold, a mist the color of blood had come over the sun.

Then Schwartz climbed for another hour, and again his thirst returned; and, as he lifted his flask to his lips, he thought he saw his brother Hans lie exhausted on the path before him, stretching his arms to him, and crying for water.

"Ha, ha," laughed Schwartz, "are you there? Water, indeed! do you suppose I carried it all the way here for *you?*" And he strode over the figure. When he had gone a few yards, he looked back, but the figure was not there.

A sudden horror came over Schwartz, but his greed for gold was stronger than his fear, and he rushed on. The bank of black cloud rose higher, and out of it came bursts of lightning. When Schwartz stood by the brink of the Golden River, its waves were black like thunder-clouds, but their foam was like fire. He cast the flask into the stream, and, as he did so, the earth gave way beneath him, and the waters closed over him. And the moaning of the river rose wildly into the night, as it gushed over *THE TWO BLACK STONES.*

V

When Gluck found that Schwartz did not come back, he did not know what to do. He had no money, and he had to hire himself again to the goldsmith, who worked him very hard, and gave him very little. After a month or two, Gluck made up his mind to go and try his fortune with the Golden River. So he went to the priest, and the priest gave him some holy water as soon as he asked for it. Then Gluck took some bread in his basket, and the bottle of water, and set off very early for the mountains.

If the glacier had made his two brothers weary, it was twenty times worse for him, who was neither so strong nor so practised on the mountains. He had several bad falls, lost his basket and bread, and was very much frightened at the strange noises under the ice. He lay a long time to rest on the grass, after he had got over, and began to climb the hill in the hottest part of the day. When he had climbed for an hour, he got thirsty, and was going to drink, when he saw a feeble old man coming down the path, leaning on a staff.

"My son," said the old man, "I am faint with thirst. Please give me some water."

Gluck saw that he was pale and weary, and gave him the water. "Only please don't drink it all," said Gluck. But the old man drank a great deal, and gave him back the bottle nearly empty. Then he bade him goodspeed, and Gluck went on again merrily. The path became easier to his feet, and two or three blades of grass appeared upon it, and some grasshoppers began to sing on the bank beside it.

Then Gluck went on for another hour, and he grew so thirsty that he thought he should *have* to drink. But, as he raised the flask, he saw a little child panting by the roadside, and she cried out for water.

Gluck struggled with himself and determined to bear the thirst a little longer; and he put the bottle to the child's lips, and she drank it all but a few drops. Then she smiled at him and ran down the hill. Gluck looked after her till she became as small as a little star. And then there were all kinds of sweet flowers growing on the rocks. Crimson and purple butterflies darted here and there, and the sky sent down such pure light that Gluck had never felt so happy in his life.

Yet, when he had climbed for another hour, his thirst became almost more than he could bear. But there were only five or six drops left in his bottle, and he could not drink those.

As he was hanging the flask to his belt again, he saw a little dog lying on the rocks gasping for breath. And Gluck stopped and looked at it, and then at the Golden River, not five hundred yards away. He thought of the dwarf's words, that no one could succeed except in his first attempt. But the dog whined, and Gluck stopped again.

"Poor beastie," said Gluck, "it'll be dead when I come down again, if I don't help

141

So saying the dwarf stooped and plucked a lily that grew at his feet. On its white leaves hung three drops of clear dew, and the dwarf shook them into the flask which Gluck held in his hand. "Cast these into the river," he said, "and descend on the other side of the mountains into Treasure Valley and so goodspeed."

As he spoke, the figure of the dwarf became like a shadow. The colors of his robe formed themselves into a mist of dewy light. The colors grew faint, the mist rose into the air; the dwarf had evaporated.

Gluck climbed to the brink of the Golden River, and its waves were as clear as crystal. And when he cast the three drops of dew into the stream, there opened a small whirlpool, into which the waters descended with a musical noise.

Gluck stood watching it for a time, and he was very much disappointed because the river was not turned into gold. Then he obeyed his friend, the dwarf, and went down toward Treasure Valley; and, as he went, he thought he heard a noise of water working its way under the ground. And when he came in sight of Treasure Valley, behold, a river like the Golden River was springing from a new cleft of the rocks, and was flowing among the dry heaps of red sand!

And as Gluck gazed, fresh grass sprang beside the new streams. Young flowers opened suddenly along the river sides, as stars leap out in twilight; and thickets of myrtle and tendrils of vine cast lengthening shadows over the valley as they grew. And thus Treasure Valley became a garden again, and the inheritance which had been lost by cruelty was regained by love.

Gluck went and dwelt in the valley, and the poor were never driven from his door; so that his barns became full of grain, and

it." And he opened the flask and poured all the water into the dog's mouth.

The dog sprang up and stood on its hind legs. Its tail disappeared, its ears became long, silky, golden; its nose became very red, its eyes became very twinkling. In three seconds the dog was gone, and before Gluck stood the King of the Golden River.

"Thank you," said the dwarf. "But why didn't you come before instead of sending me those wicked brothers of yours to pour unholy water into my stream?"

"Why," said Gluck, "they got the water out of the church font."

"Very probably," replied the dwarf, sternly, "but when water has been refused to the cry of the weary and dying, it becomes unholy, though it had been blessed by every saint in heaven."

his house full of treasure. And, for him, the river had, according to the dwarf's promise, become a River of Gold.

And to this day the people who live there point out the place where the holy dew was cast into the stream, and trace the course of the Golden River until it comes out in Treasure Valley. And at the top of the cataract of the Golden River are still to be seen two black stones, around which the waters howl mournfully every day at sunset; and these stones are still called by the people of the Valley *THE BLACK BROTHERS*. —*Abridged*

The Pied Piper of Hamelin

By Robert Browning

Hamelin Town's in Brunswick
By famous Hanover city;
The river Weser, deep and wide,
Washes it walls on the southern side;
A pleasanter spot you never spied.

But when begins my ditty,
Almost five hundred years ago,
To see the townsfolk suffer so
From vermin was a pity.
Rats!
They fought the dogs, and killed the cats,
And bit the babies in the cradles,
And ate the cheeses out of the vats,
And licked the soup from the cook's own
    ladles,
Split open the kegs of salted sprats,
Made nests inside men's Sunday hats,
And even spoiled the women's chats
By drowning out their speaking
With shrieking and squeaking
In fifty different sharps and flats.

At last the people in a body
To the Town Hall came flocking.
"Tis clear," cried they, "our Mayor's a
    noddy;
And as for our Corporation—shocking
To think that we buy gowns lined with
    ermine
For dolts that can't or won't determine
What's best to rid us of our vermin!
Rouse up sirs! Give your brains a racking
To find the remedy we're lacking,
Or, sure as fate, we'll send you packing!"
At this the Mayor and Corporation
Quaked with a mighty consternation.

An hour they sat in council,
At length the Mayor broke silence.
"For a guilder I'd my ermine gown sell;
I wish I were a mile hence!

It's easy to bid one rack one's brain—
I'm sure my poor head aches again,
I've scratched it so, and all in vain.
Oh for a trap, a trap, a trap!"
Just as he said this, what should hap
At the chamber door but a gentle tap?
"Bless us," cried the Mayor, "what's that?"

(With the Corporation as he sat,
Looking little though wondrous fat;
Nor brighter was his eye, nor moister,
Than a too-long-opened oyster,
Save when at noon his pauch grew mutinous
For a plate of turtle green and glutinous).
"Only a scraping of shoes on the mat?
Anything like the sound of a rat
Makes my heart go pit-a-pat!"

"Come in!" the Mayor cried, looking bigger:
And in did come the strangest figure.
His queer long coat from heel to head
Was half of yellow and half of red;
And he himself was tall and thin,
With sharp blue eyes, each like a pin,
And light loose hair, yet swarthy skin,
No tuft on cheek nor beard on chin,
But lips where smiles went out and in.
There was no guessing his kith and kin!
And nobody could enough admire
The tall man and his quaint attire.

Quoth one: "It's as my great grandsire,
Starting up at the Trump of Doom's tone,
Had walked this way from his painted
    tombstone."

He advanced to the council-table:
And, "Please, your honors," said he,
    "I'm able,
By means of a secret charm, to draw
All creatures living beneath the sun,

That creep or swim or fly or run
After me as you never saw!
And I chiefly use my charm
On creatures that do people harm:
The mole, the toad, the newt, the viper;
And people call me the Pied Piper."

(And here they noticed round his neck
A scarf of red and yellow stripe,
To match his coat of the selfsame check;
And at the scarf's end hung a pipe;
And his fingers, they noticed, were ever
    straying
As if impatient to be playing
Upon this pipe, as low it dangled
Over his vesture so old-fangled).

"Yet," said he, "poor piper as I am,
In Tartary I freed the Cham
Last June from his huge swarms of gnats;
I eased in Asia the Nizam

145

Of a monstrous brood of vampire bats;
And, as for what your brain bewilders,
If I can rid your town of rats
Will you give me a thousand guilders?"

"One? Fifty thousand!" was the exclamation
Of the astonished Mayor and Corporation.

Into the street the Piper stepped,
Smiling first a little smile,
As if he knew what magic slept
In his quiet pipe the while;
Then, like a musical adept,
To blow the pipe his lips he wrinkled,
And green and blue his sharp eyes twinkled
Like a candle-flame where salt is sprinkled;
And ere three shrill notes the pipe had
        uttered,
You heard as if an army muttered;
And the muttering grew to a grumbling;
And the grumbling grew to a mighty
        rumbling;
And out of the houses the rats came
        tumbling.
Great rats, small rats, lean rats, brawny rats,
Brown rats, black rats, gray rats, tawny rats,
Grave old plodders, gay young friskers,
Fathers, mothers, uncles, cousins,
Cocking tails and pricking whiskers,
Families by tens and dozens,
Brothers, sisters, husbands, wives
Followed the Piper for their lives.

From street to street he piped advancing,
And step by step they followed dancing,

Until they came to the river Weser
Wherein all plunged and perished
—Save one, who, stout as Julius Caesar,
Swam across and lived to carry
(As he the manuscript he cherished)
To Rat-land home his commentary,
Which was, "At the first shrill notes of the
        pipe,
I heard a sound as of scraping tripe,
And putting apples, wondrous ripe,
Into a cider press's gripe;
And a moving away of pickle-tub boards,
And a leaving ajar of conserve cupboards,
And a drawing the corks of train-oil flasks,
And a breaking the hoops of butter casks;
And it seemed as if a voice
(Sweeter far than by harp or by psaltery
Is breathed) called out, "Oh, rats, rejoice!
The world is grown to one vast dry-saltery!
So munch on, crunch on, take your
        nuncheon,
Breakfast, supper, dinner, luncheon!
And just as a bulky sugar puncheon,
All ready staved, like a great sun shone
Glorious scarce an inch before me,
Just as methought it said, Come, bore me!
—I found the Weser rolling o'er me."

You should have heard the Hamelin people
Ringing the bells till they rocked the steeple.
"Go," cried the Mayor, "and get long poles!
Poke out the nests and block up the holes!
Consult with carpenters and builders,
And leave in our town not even a trace
Of the rats!"—when suddenly up the face

Of the Piper perked in the market place,
With a, "First, if you please, my thousand
    guilders!"

A thousand guilders! The Mayor looked
    blue;
So did the Corporation too.
To pay this sum to a wandering fellow
With a gipsy coat of red and yellow!
"Beside quoth the Mayor, with knowing
    wink,
"Our business was done at the river's
    brink;
We saw with our eyes the vermin sink,
And what's dead can't come to life, I think.
So, friend, we're not the folks to shrink
From the duty of giving you something to
    drink,
And a matter of money to put in your poke,
But, as for the guilders, what we spoke
Of them, as you very well know, was in
    joke.
Besides, our losses have made us thrifty;
A thousand guilders! Come, take fifty!"

The Piper's face fell, and he cried,
"No trifling! I can't wait beside!
I've promised to visit by dinnertime
Bagdad, and accepted the prime
Of the Head Cook's pottage, all he's rich in,
For having left in the Caliph's kitchen,
Of a nest of scorpions no survivor.
With him I proved no bargain-driver,
With you, don't think I'll bate a stiver!
And folks who put me in a passion
May find me pipe to another fashion."

"How?" cried the Mayor, "d'ye think I'll
    brook
Being worse treated than a Cook?
Insulted by a lazy ribald

With idle pipe and vesture piebald?
You threaten us, fellow? Do your worst,
Blow your pipe there till you burst!"

Once more he stepped into the street,
And to his lips again
Laid his long pipe of smooth straight cane;
And ere he blew three notes (such sweet
Soft notes as yet musician's cunning
Never gave the enraptured air),
There was a rustling that seemed like a
    bustling
Of merry crowds justling, at pitching and
    hustling,
Small feet were pattering, wood shoes
    clattering,
Little hands clapping, and little tongues
    chattering,
And, like fowls in a farmyard when barley
    is scattering,
Out came the children running.
All the little boys and girls,
With rosy cheeks and flaxen curls,
And sparkling eyes and teeth like pearls,
Tripping and skipping, ran merrily after
The wonderful music with shouting and
    laughter.

The Mayor was dumb, and the Council
    stood
As if they were changed into blocks of
    wood,
Unable to move a step, or cry
To the children merrily skipping by
And could only follow with the eye
That joyous crowd at the Piper's back.

And now the Mayor was on the rack,
And the wretched Council's bosoms beat,
As the Piper turned from the High Street
To where the Weser rolled its waters

147

Right in the way of their sons and
    daughters!
However, he turned from South to West,
And to Koppelberg Hill his steps addressed,
And after him the children pressed;
Great was the joy in every breast.

"He never can cross that mighty top!
He's forced to let the piping drop
And we shall see our children stop!"
When lo! as they reached the mountain's
    side,
A wondrous portal opened wide,
As if a cavern was suddenly hollowed;
And the Piper advanced and the children
    followed,
And when all were in to the very last,
The door in the mountain-side shut fast.

Did I say all? No! one was lame,
And could not dance the whole of the way;
And in after years, if you would blame
His sadness, he was used to say:
"It's dull in our town since my playmates
    left;
I can't forget that I'm bereft

Of all the pleasant sights they see,
Which the Piper also promised me;
For he led us, he said, to a joyous land,
Joining the town and just at hand,
Where waters gushed and fruit trees grew,
And flowers put forth a fairer hue,
And everything was strange and new.
The sparrows were brighter than peacocks
    here,
And their dogs outran our fallow deer,
And honey-bees had lost their stings;
And horses were born with eagle's wings;
And just as I became assured
My lame foot would be speedily cured,
The music stopped, and I stood still,
And found myself outside the hill,
Left alone against my will,
To go now limping as before,
And never hear of that country more!"

Alas, alas for Hamelin!
There came into many a burgher's pate
A text which says that Heaven's Gate
Opes to the rich at as easy rate
As the needle's eye takes a camel in!

The Mayor sent East, West, North and
    South,
To offer the Piper, by word of mouth,
Wherever it was men's lot to find him,
Silver and gold to his heart's content,
If he would return the way he went,
And bring the children all behind him.

But when they saw 'twas a lost endeavor,
And Piper and dancers were gone forever,
They made a decree that lawyers never
Should think their records dated duly

If, after the day of the month and year,
These words did not as well appear:
"And so long after what happened here
On the twenty-second of July,
Thirteen hundred and seventy-six."
And the better in memory to fix
The place of the children's last retreat,
They called it the Pied Piper's Street
Where anyone playing on pipe or tabor
Was sure for the future to lose his labor.
Nor suffered they hostelry or tavern
To shock with mirth a street so solemn;
But opposite the place of the cavern
They wrote the story on a column,
And on the great church window painted
The same, to make the world acquainted
How their children were stolen away,
And there it stands to this very day.

And I must not omit to say
That in Transylvania there's a tribe
Of alien people who ascribe
The outlandish ways and dress,
On which their neighbors lay such stress,
To their fathers and mothers having risen
Out of some subterraneous prison,
Into which they were trepanned
Long ago in a mighty band
Out of Hamelin town in Brunswick land,
But how or why they don't understand.

So, Willy, let you and me be wipers
Of scores out with all men especially
    pipers;
And, whether they pipe us free from rats or
    from mice,
If we've promised them aught, let us keep
    our promise.

                      —Abridged

Sea Fever

By John Masefield

I must go down to the seas again, to the lonely sea and the sky,
And all I ask is a tall ship and a star to steer her by,
And the wheel's kick and the wind's song and the white sail's shaking,
And a gray mist on the sea's face and a gray dawn breaking.

I must go down to the seas again, for the call of the running tide
Is a wild call and a clear call that may not be denied;
And all I ask is a windy day with the white clouds flying,
And the flung spray and the brown spume and the sea-gulls crying.

I must go down to the seas again, to the vagrant gypsy life,
To the gull's way and the whale's way, where the wind's like a whetted knife;
And all I ask is a merry yarn from a laughing fellow-rover,
And quiet sleep and a sweet dream when the long trick's over.

A Midsummer-Night's Dream

One of the TALES FROM SHAKESPEARE

By Charles Lamb

Charles and Mary Lamb were a brother and sister who loved Shakespeare. About a hundred and fifty years ago they retold twenty of his most popular plays in such a lively way that now we can all quickly and easily know the plots and the people Shakespeare wrote about.

It is wonderful how the Lambs have kept the spirit of the original in these Tales and how they have woven Shakespeare's own words into the retelling. By the way, these Tales give us the only retelling of a classic of English literature that is in itself a classic.

Take A MIDSUMMER NIGHT'S DREAM. It has a very complicated plot; yet the Lambs have unrolled it like a moving picture on a screen. It is a funny play where the King and Queen of the Fairies make the heroine see the ugly weaver Bottom as though he were a Fairy Prince.

THE TEMPEST is quite different. It is full of storms at sea and shipwrecks and wicked plots. And here you meet Ariel, the most famous sprite in literature, and that horrid villain Caliban, as well as a variety of other immortal characters.

After you have read LAMB'S TALES FROM SHAKESPEARE, you will get double pleasure from Shakespeare when you see his plays in the theater.

THERE was a law in the city of Athens which gave to its citizens the power of compelling their daughters to marry whomsoever they pleased. Upon a daughter's refusing to marry the man her father had chosen to be her husband, the father was empowered by this law to cause her to be put to death. But as fathers do not often desire the death of their own daughters, even when they happen to be a little difficult, this law was seldom or never put into execution.

There was, however, an old man, named Egeus, who actually did come before Theseus (at that time the reigning Duke of Athens) to complain that his daughter Hermia whom he had commanded to marry Demetrius, a young man of noble Athenian family, refused to obey him because she loved another young Athenian named Lysander.

Egeus demanded of Theseus that this cruel law be put in force against his daughter.

Hermia pleaded in excuse for her disobedience that Demetrius had formerly professed love for her dear friend Helena, and that Helena loved Demetrius to distraction. But this honorable reason which Hermia gave for not obeying her father's command did not move the stern Egeus.

Theseus, though a great and merciful Prince, had no power to alter the laws of his country. Therefore he could only give Hermia four days to consider it, and at the end of that time, if she still refused to marry Demetrius, she was to be put to death.

When Hermia was dismissed from the presence of the Duke, she went to her lover Lysander, and told him that she must either give him up and marry Demetrius, or lose her life in four days.

Lysander was stricken at hearing these

evil tidings. But he had an aunt who lived at some distance from Athens, and at the place where she lived the cruel law could not be put in force against Hermia (this law not extending beyond the boundaries of the city); so he proposed to Hermia that she should steal out of her father's house that night, and go with him to his aunt's house, where he would marry her. "I will meet you," said Lysander, "in the woods a few miles outside the city; in the delightful wood where we have so often walked with Helena in the pleasant month of May."

Hermia joyfuly agreed; and she told no one of her intended flight except her friend Helena. Helena (as maidens will do foolish things for love) decided to tell this to Demetrius, though she could hope no benefit from betraying her friend's secret but the poor pleasure of following her faithless lover to the wood; for she well knew that Demetrius would go thither in pursuit of Hermia.

The wood in which Lysander and Hermia were to meet was the favorite haunt of those little beings known by the name of Fairies.

Oberon and Titania, the King and Queen of the Fairies, with all their tiny train of followers, held their midnight revels in this wood.

Between this little King and Queen of

sprites there happened, at this time a sad disagreement. They never met by moonlight in the shady walks of this pleasant wood but they were quarreling, till all their fairy elves would creep into acorn-cups and hide themselves for fear.

The cause of this unhappy disagreement was Titania's refusing to give Oberon a little changeling boy whose mother had been Titania's friend. Upon her death the Fairy Queen stole the child from his nurse and brought him up in the woods.

The night on which the lovers were to meet in this wood, Titania, walking with some of her maids of honor, met Oberon attended by his train of courtiers.

"Ill met by moonlight, proud Titania," said the Fairy King.

The Queen replied, "What, jealous Oberon, is it you? Fairies, skip hence; I have forsworn his company."

"Tarry, rash fairy," said Oberon. "Am not I thy lord? Why does Titania cross her Oberon? Give me your little changeling boy to be my page."

"Set your heart at rest," answered the Queen. "Your whole fairy kingdom cannot buy the boy of me." She then left her lord in great anger.

"Well, go your way," said Oberon. "Before the morning dawns, I will torment you for this injury."

Oberon then sent for Puck, his favorite counselor.

Puck (or, as he was sometimes called, Robin Goodfellow) was a shrewd and knavish sprite who used to play comical pranks in the neighboring villages. Sometimes he got into the dairies and skimmed the milk. Sometimes he plunged his light and airy form into the butter-churn, and while he was dancing in the churn, the dairy-maid would labor in vain to change her cream into butter. And when a few good neighbors met to drink some comfortable ale together, Puck would jump into the bowl of ale in the likeness of a roasted crab; and when some old goody was going to drink, he would bob against her lips and spill the ale over her withered chin. Then afterwards when the same old dame was gravely seating herself to tell her neighbors a sad story, Puck would slip her three-legged stool from under her, and down toppled the poor old woman. And the old gossips would hold their sides and laugh at her.

"Come hither, Puck," said Oberon to this little merry wanderer of the night. "Fetch me the flower which maids call *Love in Idleness*. The juice of that little purple flower laid on the eyelids of those who sleep will make them, when they awake, fall in love with the first thing they see. Some of the juice of that flower I will drop on the eyelids of my Titania when she is asleep; and the first thing she looks upon when she opens her eyes she will fall in love with, even though it be a lion or a bear, a meddling monkey or a busy ape. And before I take this charm from her sight, which I can do with another charm I know of, I will make her give me that boy to be my page."

Puck, who loved mischief with all his heart, was highly diverted with this intended frolic of his master, and ran to seek the flower.

Meanwhile Oberon observed Demetrius and Helena entering the wood. He overheard Demetrius reproaching Helena for following him, and after many unkind words on his part, and gentle ones from Helena, reminding him of his former love for her, he left her, as he said, to the mercy of the wild beasts. But she ran after him as swiftly as she could.

The Fairy King, who was always friendly to true lovers, felt great compassion for Helena. So when Puck returned with the little purple flower, Oberon said to him, "Take a part of this flower. There has been a sweet Athenian lady here, who is in love with a disdainful youth. If you find him sleeping, drop some of the love-juice in his eyes, but do it when she is near him so that the first thing he sees when he awakes may be this lady. You will know the man by the Athenian garments he wears."

Puck promised to manage this matter very dexterously. And then Oberon went, unseen by Titania, to her bower, where she was preparing to go to rest.

So beautiful was the bower where she slept that Oberon described it later to Puck in the words of this song:

I know a bank where the wild thyme
    blows,
Where oxlips and the nodding violet
    grows,
Quite over-canopied with luscious wood-
    bine,
With sweet musk-roses and with eglantine.
There sleeps Titania some time of the
    night,
Lulled in these flowers with dances and
    delight.
And there the snake throws her enamelled
    skin,
Weed wide enough to wrap a fairy in.

Oberon found Titania giving orders to her fairies, what they were to do while she slept. "Some of you," she said, "must kill cankers in the musk-rose buds, and some wage war with the bats for their leathern wings, to make my small elves coats; and

some of you keep watch that the clamorous owl, that nightly hoots, come not near me. But first sing me to sleep." Then they began to sing this song:

You spotted snakes with double tongue,
Thorny hedgehogs, be not seen;
Newts and blind-worms do no wrong,
Come not near our Fairy Queen.
Philomel, with melody,
Sing in our sweet lullaby,
Lulla, lulla, lullaby; lulla lulla, lullaby;
Never harm, nor spell, nor charm,
Come our lovely lady nigh;
So good night with lullaby.

When the fairies had sung their Queen asleep with this lullaby, they left her to perform their various services. Oberon then softly drew near his Titania and dropped some of the love-juice on her eyelids, saying:

What thou seest when thou dost wake,
Do it for thy true love take.

But to return to Hermia: She made her escape out of her father's house that night to avoid the death she was doomed to for refusing to marry Demetrius. When she entered the wood, she found dear Lysander waiting to take her to his aunt's house. But before they had passed half through the wood, Hermia was very weary. Lysander was extremely careful of this dear lady, who had proved her affection for him even by hazarding her life for his sake, and he persuaded her to rest till morning on a bank of soft moss. Then lying down himself, they soon fell fast asleep.

Here they were found by Puck, who, seeing a handsome young man asleep, his clothes made in the Athenian fashion, and a pretty lady sleeping near him, concluded that this must be the Athenian maid and her disdainful lover whom Oberon had sent him to seek. Naturally enough, as they were alone together, he thought, she must be the first thing he would see when he awoke. So without more ado, he proceeded to pour some of the juice of the little purple flower into Lysander's eyes.

But it so fell out that Helena came that way, and, instead of Hermia, Helena was the first object Lysander beheld when he opened his eyes. And so powerful was the love-charm that all his love for Hermia vanished away, and Lysander fell in love with Helena.

Had he first seen Hermia when he awoke, the blunder Puck committed would have been of no consequence, for he could not love that faithful lady too well. But for poor Lysander to be forced by a fairy love-charm to forget his own true Hermia, and to run after another lady, and leave Hermia asleep quite alone in a wood at midnight, was a sad chance indeed.

Thus this misfortune happened. Helena, as has been before related, tried to keep pace with Demetrius when he ran away so rudely from her. But she could not continue this unequal race long, men being always better runners in a long race than ladies. Helena soon lost sight of Demetrius, and as she was wandering about, dejected and forlorn, she arrived at the place where Lysander was sleeping.

"Ah!" said Helena to herself. "This is Lysander lying on the ground. Is he dead or asleep?" Then, gently touching him, she said, "Good sir, if you are alive, awake."

Upon this Lysander opened his eyes, and (the love-charm beginning to work) immediately addressed Helena in terms of extravagant love and admiration, telling her she as much excelled Hermia in beauty as a dove does a raven, and that he would run through fire for her sweet sake, and many more such lover-like speeches.

Helena, knowing Lysander was her friend Hermia's lover, and that he was solemnly engaged to marry her, was in the utmost rage when she heard herself addressed in this manner, for she thought (as well she might) that Lysander was making a jest of her.

"Oh!" said she, "why was I born to be mocked and scorned by everyone? Is it not enough, young man, that I can never get a sweet look or a kind word from Demetrius, but *you,* too, must pretend in this disdainful manner to court me? I thought, Lysander, you were a lord of more true gentleness."

Saying these words in great anger, Helena ran away, and Lysander followed her, quite forgetful of his own Hermia, who was still asleep.

When Hermia awoke she was in a sad fright at finding herself alone. She wandered about the wood, not knowing what had become of Lysander or which way to seek for him.

In the meantime, Demetrius, not being able to find Hermia and his rival Lysander, and fatigued with his fruitless search, was observed by Oberon fast asleep.

Oberon had learnt by some questions he had asked of Puck, that he had applied the love-charm to the wrong person's eyes; and now, having found the person first intended, he touched the eyelids of the sleeping Demetrius with the love-juice. He instantly awoke, and the first thing he saw being Helena, he, as Lysander had done before, began to address love-speeches to her.

But just at that moment Lysander, followed by Hermia (for through Puck's unlucky mistake it was now become Hermia's turn to run after her lover), made his apperance, and then Lysander and Demetrius, both speaking together, made love to Helena, they being each one under the influence of the same potent charm.

The astonished Helena thought that Demetrius, Lysander, and her once dear friend Hermia, were all in a plot together to make a jest of her.

Hermia was as much surprised as Helena. She knew not why Lysander and Demetrius, who before loved her, were now become the lovers of Helena; and to Hermia the matter seemed to be no jest.

The ladies who before had always been the dearest of friends, now fell to high words together.

"Unkind Hermia," said Helena, "you have set Lysander on to vex me with mock praises; and your other lover, Demetrius, who used almost to spurn me with his foot, have you not bid him to call me goddess, nymph, rare, precious, and celestial? He would not speak thus to me, whom he hates, if you did not set him on to make a jest of me. Unkind Hermia, to join with men in scorning your poor friend! Have you forgot our friendship? How often, Hermia, have we two, sitting on one cushion, both singing one song, with our needles working the same flower, both on the same sample wrought; growing up together in fashion of a double cherry, scarcely seeming parted? Hermia, it is not friendly in you to join with men in scorning your poor friend."

"I am amazed at your passionate words," said Hermia. "I scorn you not; it seems you scorn me."

"Ay," returned Helena, "persevere, counterfeit serious looks, and make mouths

at me when I turn my back! If you had any pity, grace, or manners, you would not use me thus."

While Hermia and Helena were speaking these angry words to each other, Demetrius and Lysander left to fight each other in the wood for the love of Helena.

When they found the gentlemen had left them, the two maidens departed, and once more they wandered weary, in the wood, in search of their lovers.

As soon as they were gone, the Fairy King, who had been listening to their quarrels, said to Puck, "This is your negligence, Puck. Or did you do this wilfully?"

"Believe me, King," answered Puck, "it was a mistake. Did not you tell me I should know the man by his Athenian garments? However, I am not sorry this has happened, for I think their jangling makes excellent sport."

"You heard," said Oberon, "that Demetrius and Lysander are gone to seek a convenient place to fight in? I command you to overhang the night with a thick fog, and lead these quarrelsome lovers so astray in the dark that they shall not be able to find each other. Counterfeit each of their voices to the other, and with bitter taunts provoke them to follow you, while they think it is their rival's tongue they hear. See you do this till they are so weary they can go no farther. And when you find they are asleep, drop the juice of this other flower into Lysander's eyes and when he awakes he will forget his new love for Helena, and return to his old passion for Hermia. Then the two fair ladies may each one be happy with the man she loves, and they will think all that has passed a vexatious dream. About this quickly, Puck, and I will go and see what sweet love my Titania has found."

Titania was still sleeping. Oberon saw a clown near her, who had lost his way in the wood and was likewise asleep.

"This fellow," said Oberon, "shall be my Titania's true love." And he clapped an ass's head over the clown's so that it seemed to fit him as well as if it had grown upon his own shoulders. Though Oberon fixed the ass's head on very gently, it awakened the clown, and rising up, unconscious of what Oberon had done to him, he went towards the bower where Titania, the Fairy Queen, slept.

"Ah! what angel is that I see?" said Titania, opening her eyes, the juice of the little purple flower beginning to take effect. "Are you as wise as you are beautiful?"

"Why, mistress," said the foolish clown, "if I have wit enough to find the way out of this wood, I have enough to serve my turn."

"Out of the wood do not desire to go," said the enamored Queen. "I am a spirit of no common rate. I love you. Go with me, and I will give you fairies to attend upon you."

She then called four of her fairies; Pease-blossom, Cobweb, Moth, and Mustard-seed.

"Attend," said the Queen, "upon this sweet gentleman. Hop in his walks, and gambol in his sight. Feed him with grapes and apricots, and steal for him the honey-bags from the bees." And "Come, sit with me," said she to the clown, "and let me

157

play with your amiable hairy cheeks, my beautiful ass! Let me kiss your fair large ears, my gentle joy!"

"Where is Pease-blossom?" said the ass-headed clown, not much regarding the Fairy Queen's courtship, but very proud of his new attendants.

"Here, sir," said little Pease-blossom.

"Scratch my head," said the clown. "Where's Cobweb?"

"Here, sir," said Cobweb.

"Good Mr. Cobweb," said the foolish clown, "kill me the red bumble-bee on the top of that thistle yonder; and, good Mr. Cobweb, bring me the honey-bag. Do not fret yourself too much in the action, Mr. Cobweb, and take care the honey-bag break not. I should be sorry to have you over-flown with a honey-bag. Where is Mustard-seed?"

"Here, sir," said Mustard-seed. "What is your will?"

"Good Mr. Mustard-seed," said the clown, "help Mr. Pease-blossom to scratch. I must go to a barber's, Mr. Mustard-seed, for methinks I am marvellous hairy about the face."

"My sweet love," said the Queen, "what will you have to eat? I have a venturesome fairy who shall seek the squirrel's hoard, and fetch you some new nuts."

"I had rather have a handful of dried pease," said the clown, who with his ass's head had got an ass's appetite. "But, I pray, let none of your people disturb me, for I have a mind to sleep."

"Sleep, then," said the Queen, "and I will hold you in my arms. O how I love you! How I dote upon you!"

When the Fairy King saw the clown sleeping in the arms of his Queen, he ad-vanced within her sight and reproached her with having lavished her favors upon an ass.

This she could not deny, as the clown was then sleeping within her arms with his ass's head crowned by her with flowers.

When Oberon had teased her for some time, he again demanded the changeling-boy; and she, ashamed of being discovered by her lord with her new favorite, did not dare to refuse him.

Oberon, having thus obtained the little boy he had so long wished for to be his page, took pity on the disgraceful situation into which, by his merry contrivance, he had brought his Titania, and threw some of the juice of the other flower into her eyes. At that the Fairy Queen immediately re-covered her senses. She wondered at herself, saying how she now loathed the sight of the strange monster.

Oberon likewise took the ass's head from off the clown, and left him to finish his nap with his own fool's head upon his shoulders.

Oberon and his Titania being now per-fectly reconciled, he related to her the history of the lovers and their midnight quarrels; and she agreed to go with him and see the end of their adventures.

The Fairy King and Queen found the lovers and their fair ladies sleeping on a grass-plot, for Puck, to make amends for his former mistake, had contrived with the utmost diligence to bring them all to the same spot, unknown to each other; and he had carefully removed the charm from off the eyes of Lysander with the antidote the Fairy King gave to him.

Hermia first awoke, and finding her lost Lysander asleep so near her, looked at him and wondered at his strange inconstancy. Lysander presently opened his eyes. Seeing his dear Hermia, he recovered his reason, and with it his love for Hermia. They began to talk over the adventures of the night, doubting if these things had really happened, or if they had both been dreaming the same bewildering dream.

Helena and Demetrius were by this time awake; and a sweet sleep having quieted Helena's angry spirits, she listened with delight to the professions of love which Demetrius made to her, and which, to her surprise as well as pleasure, she saw were sincere.

These fair night-wandering ladies, now no longer rivals, became once more true friends. All the unkind words which had passed were forgiven, and they calmly consulted together what was best to be done in their present situation. It was soon agreed that as Demetrius had given up his pretensions to Hermia, he should endeavor to prevail upon her father to revoke the cruel sentence of death which had been passed against her.

Demetrius was preparing to return to Athens for this friendly purpose when they were surprised at the sight of Egeus, Hermia's father, who came to the wood in pursuit of his runaway daughter.

When Egeus understood that Demetrius would not now marry his daugher, he no longer opposed her marriage with Lysander, but gave his consent that they should be wedded on the fourth day from this time, being the same day on which Hermia had been condemned to lose her life. And on that same day Helena joyfully agreed to marry her beloved and now faithful Demetrius.

The Fairy King and Queen, who were invisible spectators of this reconciliation, and now saw the happy ending of the lovers' history brought about through the good offices of Oberon, resolved to celebrate the approaching nuptials with sports and revels throughout their fairy kingdom.

And now, if any judge this story of fairies and their pranks as incredible and strange, they have only to think that they have been asleep and dreaming, and that all these adventures were visions which they saw in their sleep. I hope none of my readers will be so unreasonble as to be offended with a pretty harmless Midsummer-Night's Dream.

—*Adapted*

Forbearance

By Ralph Waldo Emerson

Hast thou named all the birds without a
    gun?
Loved the wood-rose, and left it on its stalk?
At rich men's tables eaten bread and pulse?
Unarmed, faced danger with a heart of
    trust?

And loved so well a high behavior,
In man or maid, that thou from speech
    refrained,
Nobility more nobly to repay?

O, be my friend, and teach me to be thine!

The Tempest

One of the TALES FROM SHAKESPEARE

By Charles Lamb

THERE was a certain island in the sea, and the only people who lived on it were an old man, whose name was Prospero, and his beautiful daughter Miranda. She came to this island so young that she had no memory of having seen any other human face than her father's.

They lived in a cave or cell, made out of a rock. It was divided into several rooms, one of which Prospero called the study. There he kept his books, which chiefly treated of magic, and the knowledge of this art he found very useful to him; for this island had been enchanted by a witch called Sycorax, who had died there a short time before Prospero's arrival. By his knowledge of magic, Prospero had released many good spirits that Sycorax had imprisoned in the bodies of large trees because they had refused to execute her wicked commands. These gentle spirits were ever after obedient to the will of Prospero. Of these Ariel was the chief.

The lively little sprite Ariel had nothing mischievous in his nature, except that he took rather too much pleasure in tormenting an ugly monster called Caliban, for he owed him a grudge because he was the son of his old enemy Sycorax.

Prospero had found this Caliban in the woods, a strange misshapen thing, far less human in form than an ape. He took him home to his cell, and taught him to speak. Prospero would have been very kind to him, but the bad nature which Caliban in-herited from his mother Sycorax would not let him learn anything good or useful. Therefore he was employed like a slave, to fetch wood and do the hardest labor. And Ariel was in charge of making him do these services.

When Caliban was lazy and neglected his work, Ariel (who was invisible to all eyes but Prospero's) would come slyly and pinch him, and sometimes tumble him down in the mire. Then Ariel, in the likeness of an ape, would make mouths at him. Then swiftly changing his shape, in the likeness of a hedgehog, he would lie tumbling in Caliban's way, who feared the hedgehog's sharp quills would prick his bare feet. With a variety of such-like vexatious tricks, Ariel would often torment him whenever Caliban neglected the work which Prospero commanded him to do.

Having these powerful spirits obedient to his will, Prospero could command the winds and the waves of the sea. By his orders they raised a violent storm, and in the midst of it, struggling with the wild sea-waves that every moment threatend to swallow it up, he showed his daughter Miranda a fine large ship full of living beings like themselves.

"O my dear Father," said she, "if by your art you have raised this dreadful storm, have pity on their sad distress. See! The vessel will be dashed to pieces. Poor souls! They will all perish. If I had power, I would sink the sea beneath the earth rather than see the good ship destroyed with all the precious souls within her."

"Be not so amazed, daughter Miranda," said Prospero. "There is no harm done. I have so ordered it that no person in the ship shall receive any hurt. What I have done has been for your sake, my dear child. You are ignorant who you are, or where you come from, and you know no more of me but that I am your father, and live in this poor cave. Can you remember a time before you came to this cell? I think you cannot, for you were then not three years of age."

"Certainly I can," replied Miranda.

"By what?" asked Prospero. "By any other house or person? Tell me what you can remember, my child."

Miranda said, "It seems to me like the recollection of a dream. But had I not once four or five women who attended upon me?"

Prospero answered, "You had, and more. How is it that this still lives in your mind? Do you remember how you came here?"

"I remember nothing more," said Miranda.

"Twelve years ago," continued Prospero, "I was the Duke of Milan, and you were a Princess, and my only heir. I had a younger brother, whose name was Antonio, to whom I trusted everything; and as I was fond of retirement and deep study, I commonly left the mangement of my state affairs to your uncle, my false brother (for so indeed he proved). I, negelecting all worldly ends, buried among my books, did dedicate my whole time to the bettering of my mind.

My brother Antonio, being thus in possession of my power, began to think himself
the Duke indeed. The opportunity I gave
him of making himself popular among my
subjects awakened in his bad nature a proud
ambition to deprive me of my Dukedom.
This he soon accomplished with the aid of
the King of Naples, a powerful Prince, who
was my enemy."

"Wherefore," said Miranda, "did they
not destroy us?"

"My child," answered her father, "they
dared not, so dear was the love that my
people bore me. Antonio carried us on board
a ship, and when we were some leagues out
at sea, he forced us into a small boat, without either tackle, sail, or mast. There he
left us, as he thought, to perish. But a kind
lord of my court, one Gonzalo, who loved
me, had privately placed in the boat water,
provisions, apparel, and some books which
I prize above my dukedom."

"O my Father," said Miranda, "what a
trouble must I have been to you then!"

"No, my love," said Prospero. "You were
a little cherub that did preserve me. Your
innocent smiles made me bear up against
my misfortunes. Our food lasted till we
landed on this desert island. Since then my
chief delight has been in teaching you,
Miranda; and well have you profited by
my instructions."

"Heaven thank you, my dear Father,"
said Miranda. "Now pray tell me your reason for raising this sea-storm."

"Know then," said her father, "that this
storm has cast my enemies, the King of
Naples, and my cruel brother upon this
island."

Having so said, Prospero gently touched
his daughter with his magic wand to make
her fall fast asleep, for Ariel just then pre-

sented himself before his master to give an
account of the tempest and of how he had
disposed of the ship's company; and though
spirits like Ariel were always invisible to
Miranda, Prospero did not choose her to
hear him holding converse (as would seem
to her) with the empty air.

"Well, my brave spirit," said Prospero to
Ariel, "how have you performed your task?"

Ariel gave a lively description of the
storm, and of the terrors of the mariners. He
related how the King's son, Ferdinand, was
the first who leaped into the sea, and how
his father thought he saw his dear son
swallowed up by the waves and lost.

"But he is safe," said Ariel, "in a corner
of the isle, sitting with his arms folded, sadly
lamenting the loss of the King, his father,
whom he thinks to be drowned. Not a hair
of his head is injured, and his princely garments, though drenched in the sea-waves,
look fresher than before."

"That's my delicate Ariel," said Prospero.
"Bring him hither. My daughter must see
this young Prince. Where is the King, and
my brother?"

"I left them," answered Ariel, "searching for Ferdinand, whom they have little
hopes of finding, thinking they saw him
perish. Of the ship's crew not one is missing, though each one thinks himself the
only one saved. The ship, though invisible
to them, is safe in the harbor."

"Ariel," said Prospero, "thy charge is
faithfully performed; but there is more work
yet."

"*More* work?" exclaimed Ariel. "Let me
remind you, master, you have promised me
my liberty. I have done you worthy service,
told you no lies, made no mistakes, served
you without grudge or grumbling."

"How now!" said Prospero. "You do not

recollect what a torment I freed you from? Have you forgotten the wicked witch Sycorax, who with age and envy was almost bent double? Where was she born? Speak; tell me."

"Sir, in Algiers," said Ariel.

"O, was she so?" said Prospero. "I must recount what you have been, which I find you do not remember. This bad witch, Sycorax, for her terrible witchcrafts was banished from Algiers, and here left by the sailors. Because you were a spirit too delicate to execute her wicked commands, she shut you up in a tree, where I found you howling. This torment, remember, I did free you from."

"Pardon me, dear master," said Ariel, ashamed to seem ungrateful. "I will obey your commands."

"Do so," said Prospero, "and I will set you entirely free."

Prospero then told him what further he would have to do; and away went Ariel to where he had left Ferdinand, and found him still sitting on the grass in the same melancholy posture.

"O my young gentleman," said Ariel when he saw him, "I will soon move you. You must be brought, I find, for the Lady Miranda to have a sight of you. Come sir, follow me."

He then began singing,

Full fathom five thy father lies;
  Of his bones are coral made;
Those are pearls that were his eyes:
  Nothing of him that doth fade,
But doth suffer a sea-change
Into something rich and strange.
Sea-nymphs hourly ring his knell:
Hark! Now I hear them—Ding-dong, bell.

This strange news of his lost father soon roused the Prince. He followed in amazement the sound of Ariel's voice till it led him to Prospero and Miranda, who were sitting under the shade of a large tree. Now, Miranda had never seen a man before, except her own father.

"Miranda," said Prospero, "tell me what you are looking at yonder."

"O Father," said Miranda in a strange surprise, when she beheld the young man, "surely that is a spirit! How it looks about! Believe me, it is a beautiful creature. Is it not a spirit?"

"No, girl," answered her father. "It eats and sleeps and has senses such as we have. This young man you see was in the ship. He is somewhat altered by grief; otherwise you might call him a handsome person. He has lost his companions and is wandering about to find them."

Miranda, who thought all men had grave faces and gray beards like her father, was delighted with the appearance of this beautiful young Prince. And Ferdinand, seeing such a lovely lady in this desert place, thought that he must be on an enchanted island, and that Miranda was its goddess. As such he began to address her.

She timidly answered that she was no goddess, but a simple maid. She was going to give him an account of herself when Prospero interrupted her. He was well pleased to find they admired each other, for he plainly saw that they had fallen in love at first sight. But to test Ferdinand he resolved to throw some difficulties in their way. So he addressed the Prince with a stern air, telling him he came to the island as a spy, to take it from him who was the lord of it.

"Follow me," said Prospero. "I will tie

your neck and feet together. You shall drink sea-water. Shellfish, withered roots, and husks of acorns shall be your food."

"No," said Ferdinand. "I will resist such entertainment till I see a more powerful enemy." Ferdinand drew his sword; but Prospero, waving his magic wand, fixed him to the spot where he stood, so that he had no power to move.

Miranda hung upon her father, saying, "Why are you so ungentle? Have pity! This is the second man I ever saw, and to me he seems a true one."

"Silence!" said her father. "One word more will make me chide you, girl! You think there are no more such fine men, having seen only him and Caliban. I tell you, foolish girl, most men as far excel this one as he does Caliban." This he said to test his daughter.

But Miranda replied, "My affections are most humble. I have no wish to see a goodlier man."

"Come on, young man," said Prospero to the Prince. "You have no power to disobey me."

"I have not indeed, answered Ferdinand. Not knowing that it was by magic he was deprived of all power of resistance, he was astonished to find himself so strangely compelled to follow Prospero. Looking back on Miranda as long as he could see her, he said, as he went after Prospero into the cave, "My spirits are all bound up as if I were in a dream; but this man's threats would seem light to me if from my prison I might once a day behold this fair maid."

Prospero did not keep Ferdinand long within the cell. He soon brought out his prisoner and set him a severe task to perform, taking care to let his daughter know the hard labor he had imposed on him. Then, pretending to go into his study, he secretly watched them both.

Prospero had commanded Ferdinand to pile up some heavy logs of wood. Kings' sons being not much used to laborious work, Miranda soon after found him almost dying with fatigue. "Alas!" said she, "do not work so hard, my father is at his studies, safe for these three hours. Pray rest yourself."

"O my dear lady," said Ferdinand, "I must finish my task before I take my rest."

"If you will sit down," said Miranda, "I will carry your logs the while." But this Ferdinand would by no means agree to. Instead of a help Miranda became a hindrance, for they began a long conversation so that the business of log-carrying went on very slowly.

Prospero, who had given Ferdinand this task merely as a trial of his love, was not at his books as his daughter supposed, but was standing by them, invisible, to overhear what they said.

Ferdinand inquired her name, which she told, saying it was against her father's express command she did so.

Prospero only smiled at this first instance of his daughter's disobedience, for having by his magic art caused his daughter to fall in love so suddenly, he was not angry that she showed her love by forgetting to obey his commands. And he listened, well pleased, to a long speech of Ferdinand's professing to love her above all the ladies he ever saw.

In answer to his praises of her beauty, which he said exceeded all the women in the world, she replied, "I do not remember the face of any woman, nor have I seen any more men than my dear father and you, my good friend. But believe me, sir, I would not wish any companion in the world but you, nor can my imagination form any shape but yours that I could like. But I fear I talk to you too freely, and my father's precepts I forget."

At this Prospero smiled, and he nodded his head as much as to say, "This goes on exactly as I could wish. My girl will be Queen of Naples."

And then Ferdinand, in another fine long speech (for young Princes speak in courtly phrases), told the innocent Miranda he was heir to the crown of Naples, and that she should be his Queen.

"Ah!" said she, "I am a fool to weep at what I am glad of. I will answer you in plain and holy innocence. I will be your wife if you will marry me."

Prospero prevented Ferdinand's thanks by appearing visible before them.

"Fear nothing, my child," said he. "I have overheard and approve of all you have said. And, Ferdinand, if I have been too severe with you, I will make you rich amends by giving you my daughter. All your vexations were but trials of your love, and you have nobly stood the test. Now as my gift, which your true love has worthily purchased, take my daughter." Then, telling them that he had business which required his presence, he asked them to sit down and talk together till he returned. This command Miranda seemed not at all disposed to disobey.

When Prospero left them, he called the spirit Ariel, who quickly appeared before him, eager to relate what he had done with Prospero's brother and the King of Naples. Ariel said he had left them almost out of their senses with fear at the strange things he had caused them to see and hear.

When fatigued with wandering about, and famished for want of food, he had suddenly set before them a delicious banquet. Then, just as they were going to eat, he appeared visible before them in the shape of a harpy, a monster with wings, and the feast vanished away. To their utter amazement, this seeming harpy spoke to them, reminding them of their cruelty in driving Prospero from his dukedom, and leaving him and his infant daughter to perish in the sea. For this reason, he said, these terrors were sent to them.

The King of Naples and Antonio, the false brother, repented the injustice they had done to Prospero; and Ariel told his master he was certain their penitence was sincere, and that he, though a spirit, could not but pity them.

"Then bring them hither, Ariel," said Prospero. "If you, who are but a spirit, feel for their distress, shall not I, who am a human being like themselves, take pity on them? Bring them quickly, my dainty Ariel."

Ariel soon returned with the King, Antonio, and old Gonzalo, who had all followed him, wondering at the wild music he played in the air to draw them on to his master's presence. This Gonzalo was the same who had so kindly provided Prospero with books and provisions when his wicked brother left him, as he thought, to perish in an open boat in the sea.

Grief and terror had so stupefied their senses that they did not know Prospero. He introduced himself to the good old Gonzalo, calling him the preserver of his life; and then his brother and the King knew he was the injured Prospero.

Antonio, with tears and sad words of sorrow and true repentance, implored his brother's forgiveness. And the King expressed his sincere remorse for having assisted Antonio to depose his brother.

Prospero forgave them; and, upon their agreeing to restore his dukedom, he said to the King of Naples, "I have a gift for you too." And opening a door, he showed the King his son Ferdinand playing chess with Miranda.

Nothing could exceed the joy of the father and the son at this unexpected meeting, for they each thought the other drowned in the storm.

"O wonder!" said Miranda, "what noble creatures these are! It must surely be a brave world that has such people in it."

The King of Naples was almost as much astonished at the beauty and grace of the young Miranda as his son had been. "Who is this maid?" said he. "She seems the goddess that has parted us and brought us thus together."

"No, sir," answered Ferdinand, smiling to find his father had fallen into the same mistake that he had done when he first saw Miranda. "She is a mortal, but I chose her when I could not ask you, Father, for your consent, not thinking you were alive. She is the daughter of this Prospero, who is the famous Duke of Milan, of whose renown I have heard so much but never saw till now. From him I have received a new life. He has made himself a second father to me, giving me this dear lady."

"Then I must be _her_ father," said the King. "But how oddly will it sound, that I must ask my own child's forgiveness."

"No more of that," said Prospero. "Let us not remember our troubles past, since they so happily have ended." And then Prospero embraced his brother and again assured him of his forgiveness. He said that

a wise Providence had permitted him to be driven from his poor dukedom of Milan so that his daughter might inherit the crown of Naples, for by their meeting in this desert island it had happened that the King's son had loved Miranda.

These kind words which Prospero spoke, meaning to comfort his brother, so filled Antonio with shame and remorse that he wept and was unable to speak. And the kind old Gonzalo prayed for blessings on the young couple.

Prospero now told them that their ship was safe in the harbor, and the sailors all on board, and that he and his daughter would accompany them home the next morning. "In the meantime," he added, "partake of such refreshments as my poor cave affords. And for your evening's entertainment I will relate the history of my life from my first landing in this desert island."

He then called for Caliban to prepare some food and set the cave in order. The company were astonished at the uncouth and savage appearance of this ugly monster who, Prospero said, was the only attendant he had to wait on him.

Before Prospero left the island, he dismissed Ariel from his service, to the great joy of that lively little sprite who, though he had been a faithful servant to his master, was always longing to enjoy his freedom to wander uncontrolled in the air, like a wild bird, under green trees, among pleasant fruits and sweet-smelling flowers. "My quaint Ariel," said Prospero to the little sprite when he made him free, "I shall miss you; yet you shall have your freedom."

"Thank you, my dear master," said Ariel. "But let me attend your ship home with prosperous winds. Then, master, when I am free, how merrily I shall live!" Here

Ariel sang this pretty song:

Where the bee sucks, there suck I;
In a cowslip's bell I lie;
There I couch when owls do cry.
On the bat's back I do fly
After summer merrily.
Merrily, merrily, shall I live now
Under the blossom that hangs on the bough.

Prospero then buried deep in the earth his magical books and wand, for he was resolved never more to make use of the magic art. And having thus overcome his enemies, and being reconciled with his brother and the King of Naples, nothing now remained to complete his happiness but to revisit his native land, to take possession of his dukedom, and to witness the happy marriage of his daughter and Prince Ferdinand, which the King said should be celebrated with great splendor on their return to Naples. And there, after a pleasant voyage under the safe convoy of Ariel, they soon arrived.

—*Adapted.*

The First Christmas

From THE BIBLE
St. Luke 2:8-16

And there were in the same country shepherds abiding in the field, keeping watch over their flock by night.

And, lo, the angel of the Lord came upon them, and the glory of the Lord shone round about them: and they were sore afraid.

And the angel said unto them, Fear not; for, behold, I bring you good tidings of great joy, which shall be to all people,

For unto you is born this day in the city of David a Savior, which is Christ the Lord.

And this shall be a sign unto you: Ye shall find the Babe wrapped in swaddling clothes, lying in a manger.

And suddenly there was with the angel a multitude of the heavenly host praising God, and saying,

Glory to God in the highest, and on earth peace, good will toward men.

And it came to pass, as the angels were gone away from them into heaven, the shepherds said one to another, Let us now go even unto Bethlehem, and see this thing which is come to pass, which the Lord hath made known unto us.

And they came with haste, and found Mary, and Joseph, and the Babe lying in a manger.

Christmas at the Marches

From LITTLE WOMEN

By Louisa M. Alcott

LITTLE WOMEN, Louisa May Alcott's most popular book, opens with this story of Christmas at the Marches. The Marches are the Alcotts, of course. Jo is Louisa herself. Meg, Beth, and Amy are her sisters. "Marmee" is their mother.

It is undoubtedly because Louisa May wrote this book out of her own experiences that so many young people, girls especially, have laughed and cried over it ever since it was written almost a century ago. Perhaps, too, it is such a well-loved story because the Marches, poor and hard-working as they were, nevertheless felt themselves rich and happy in family feeling.

The book takes the "little women" (all but Beth) through childhood and young ladyhood, to parenthood. It makes us happy to know that in the end they are appreciated for their lives of courage and self-sacrifice and kindliness and love. Here is part of the story.

"CHRISTMAS won't be Christmas without any presents," grumbled Jo, lying on the rug.

"It's so dreadful to be poor!" sighed Meg, looking down at her old dress.

"I don't think it's fair for some girls to have plenty of pretty things, and other girls nothing at all," added little Amy, with an injured sniff.

"We've got father and mother and each other," said Beth contentedly, from her corner.

The four young faces on which the firelight shone brightened at the cheerful words, but darkened again as Jo said sadly, "We haven't got father, and shall not have him for a long time." She didn't say "perhaps never," but each silently added it, thinking of father far away, where the fighting was.

Nobody spoke for a minute; then Meg said in an altered tone: "You know the reason mother proposed not having any presents this Christmas was because it is going to be a hard winter for everyone; and she thinks we ought not to spend money for pleasure, when our men are suffering so in the army. We can't do much, but we can make our little sacrifices, and ought to do it gladly. But I am afraid I don't." Meg shook her head as she thought regretfully of all the pretty things she wanted.

"But I don't think the little we should spend would do any good. We've each got a dollar, and the army wouldn't be much helped by our giving that. I agree not to expect anything from mother or you, but I do want to buy 'Undine and Sintram' for myself; I've wanted it *so* long," said Jo, who was a bookworm.

"I have planned to spend mine in new music," said Beth, with a little sigh, which no one heard but the hearth brush and kettle holder.

"I shall get a nice box of Faber's drawing pencils; I really need them," said Amy decidedly.

"Mother didn't say anything about our money, and she won't wish us to give up everything. Let's each buy what we want, and have a little fun; I'm sure we work hard

169

enough to earn it," cried Jo, examining the heels of her shoes in a gentlemanly manner.

"I know *I* do—teaching those tiresome children nearly all day, when I'm longing to enjoy myself at home," began Meg, in the complaining tone again.

"You don't have half such a hard time as I do," said Jo. "How would you like to be shut up for hours with a nervous, fussy old lady, who keeps you trotting, is never satisfied, and worries you till you're ready to fly out of the window or cry?"

"It's naughty to fret; but I do think washing dishes and keeping things tidy is the worst work in the world. It makes me cross; and my hands get so stiff, I can't practice well at all." Beth looked at her rough hands with a sigh that anyone could hear that time.

"I don't believe any of you suffer as I do," cried Amy, "for you don't have to go to school with impertinent girls who plague you if you don't know your lessons, and laugh at your dresses, and label your father if he isn't rich, and insult you when your nose isn't nice."

"If you mean *libel*, I'd say so, and not talk about *labels,* as if papa was a pickle bottle," advised Jo, laughing.

"I know what I mean, and you needn't be *statirical* about it. It's proper to use good words, and improve your *vocabilary,*" returned Amy, with dignity.

"Don't peck at one another, children. Don't you wish we had the money papa lost when we were little, Jo? Dear me, how happy and good we'd be, if we had no worries!" said Meg, who could remember better times.

"You said, the other day, you thought we were a deal happier than the King chil-dren, for they were fighting and fretting all the time, in spite of their money."

"So I did, Beth. Well, I think we are; for, although we do have to work, we make fun for ourselves, and are a pretty jolly set, as Jo would say."

"Jo does use such slang words!" observed Amy, with a reproving look at the long figure stretched on the rug. Jo immediately sat up, put her hands in her pockets, and began to whistle.

"Don't Jo; it's so boyish!"

"That's why I do it."

"I detest rude, unladylike girls!"

"I hate affected, niminy-piminy chits!"

" 'Birds in their little nests agree,' " sang Beth, the peacemaker, with such a funny face that both sharp voices softened to a laugh, and the "pecking" ended for that time.

"Really, girls, you are both to be blamed," said Meg, beginning to lecture in her elder-sisterly fashion. "You are old enough to leave off boyish tricks, and to behave better, Josephine. It didn't matter so much when you were a little girl; but now you are so tall, and turn up your hair, you should remember that you are a young lady."

"I'm not! And if turning up my hair makes me one, I'll wear it in two tails till I'm twenty," cried Jo, pulling off her net, and shaking down a chestnut mane. "I hate to think I've got to grow up, and be Miss March, and wear long gowns, and look as prim as a China aster! It's bad enough to be a girl, anyway, when I like boys' games and work and manners! I can't get over my disappointment in not being a boy; and it's worse than ever now, for I'm dying to go and fight with Papa, and I can only stay at home and knit, like a poky old woman!" And Jo shook the blue army sock till the needles rattled like castanets, and her ball bounded across the room.

"Poor Jo! It's too bad, but it can't be helped; so you must try to be contented with making your name boyish, and playing brother to us girls," said Beth, stroking the rough head at her knee with a hand that all the dish-washing and dusting in the world could not make ungentle in its touch.

"As for you, Amy," continued Meg, "you are altogether too particular and prim. Your airs are funny now; but you'll grow up an affected little goose if you don't take care. I like your nice manners and refined ways of speaking, when you don't try to be elegant. But your absurd words are as bad as Jo's slang."

"If Jo is a tomboy and Amy a goose, what am I, please?" asked Beth, ready to share the lecture.

"You're a dear, and nothing else," answered Meg warmly. And no one contradicted her, for the "Mouse" was the pet of the family.

The four sisters, sat knitting away in the twilight, while the December snow fell quietly without, and the fire crackled cheerfully within. It was a comfortable old room, though the carpet was faded and the furniture very plain. A good picture or two hung on the walls, books filled the recesses, chrysanthemums and Christmas roses bloomed in the windows, and a pleasant atmosphere of home peace pervaded it.

Margaret, the eldest of the four, was sixteen, and very pretty, being plump and fair, with large eyes, plenty of soft brown hair, a sweet mouth, and white hands, of which she was rather vain.

Fifteen-year-old Jo was very tall, thin, and brown, and reminded one of a colt; for she never seemed to know what to do with her long legs, which were very much in her way. She had a decided mouth, a comical nose, and sharp, gray eyes, which appeared to see everything, and were by turns fierce, funny, or thoughtful. Her long, thick hair was her one beauty; but it was usually bundled into a net, to be out of her way. Round shoulders had Jo, big hands and feet, a flyaway look to her clothes, and the uncomfortable appearance of a girl who was rapidly shooting up into a woman, and didn't like it.

Elizabeth—or Beth, as everyone called her—was a rosy, smooth-haired, bright-eyed girl of thirteen, with a shy manner, a timid voice, and a peaceful expression, which was seldom disturbed. Her father called her "Little Tranquillity," and the name suited her excellently, for she seemed to live in a happy world of her own, only venturing out to meet the few whom she trusted and loved. Amy, though the youngest, was a most important person — in her own opinion at least. A regular snow-maiden, with blue eyes, and yellow hair curling on her shoulders, pale and slender, and always carrying herself like a young lady mindful of her manners.

The clock struck six; and, having swept up the hearth, Beth put a pair of slippers down to warm. Somehow the sight of the old shoes had a good effect upon the girls. Mother was coming, and everyone brightened to welcome her. Meg stopped lecturing, and lighted the lamp; Amy got out of the easy chair without being asked; and Jo forgot how tired she was as she sat up to hold the slippers nearer to the blaze.

"They are quite worn out. Marmee must have a new pair."

"I thought I'd get her some with my dollar," said Beth.

"No, I shall!" cried Amy.

"I'm the oldest," began Meg, but Jo cut in with a decided "I'm the man of the family now Papa is away, and *I* shall provide the slippers, for he told me to take special care of Mother while he was gone."

"I'll tell you what we'll do," said Beth. "Let's each get her something for Christmas, and not get anything for ourselves."

"That's like you, dear! What will we get?" exclaimed Jo.

Everyone thought soberly for a minute. Then Meg announced, as if the idea was suggested by the sight of her own pretty hands, "I shall give her a nice pair of gloves."

"Army shoes, best to be had," cried Jo.

"Some handkerchiefs, all hemmed," said Beth.

"I'll get a little bottle of cologne. She likes it, and it won't cost much, so I'll have some left to buy my pencils," added Amy.

"How will we give the things?" asked Meg.

"Put them on the table, and bring her in and see her open the bundles. Don't you remember how we used to do on our birthdays?" answered Jo.

"I used to be *so* frightened when it was my turn to sit in the big chair with the crown on, and see you all come marching round to give the presents, with a kiss. I liked the things and the kisses, but it was dreadful to have you sit looking at me while I opened the bundles," said Beth, who was toasting her face and the bread for tea at the same time.

"Let Marmee think we are getting things for ourselves, and then surprise her. We must go shopping tomorrow afternoon, Meg. There is so much to do about the play for Christmas night," said Jo, marching up and down with her hands behind her back and her nose in the air.

"I don't mean to act any more after this time. I'm getting too old for such things," observed Meg, who was as much a child as ever about "dressing-up" frolics.

"You won't stop, I know, as long as you can trail round in a white gown with your hair down, and wear gold-paper jewelry. You are the best actress we've got, and there'll be an end of everything if you quit the boards," said Jo. "We ought to rehearse tonight. Come here, Amy, and do the fainting scene, for you are as stiff as a poker in that."

"I can't help it. I never saw anyone faint, and I don't choose to make myself all black and blue, tumbling flat as you do. If I can go down easily, I'll drop. If I can't, I shall fall into a chair and be graceful. I don't care if Hugo does come at me with a pistol," returned Amy, who was not gifted with dramatic power, but was chosen because she was small enough to be borne out shrieking by the villain of the piece.

"Do it this way: Clasp your hands so, and stagger across the room, crying frantically, 'Roderigo! save me! save me!'" And away went Jo with a melodramatic scream which was truly thrilling.

Amy followed, but she poked her hands out stiffly before her, and jerked herself along as if she went by machinery. Her "Ow!" was more suggestive of pins being run into her than of fear and anguish.

Jo gave a despairing groan, and Meg laughed outright, while Beth let her bread burn as she watched the fun.

"It's no use! Do the best you can when the time comes, and if the audience laughs, don't blame me. Come on, Meg."

Then things went smoothly, for Don Pedro defied the world in a speech of two pages without a single break. Hagar, the witch, chanted an awful incantation over her kettleful of simmering toads, with weird effect. Roderigo rent his chains asunder manfully, and Hugo died in agonies of remorse and arsenic, with a wild "Ha! ha!"

"It's the best we've had yet," said Meg, as the dead villain sat up and rubbed his elbows.

"I don't see how you can write and act such splendid things, Jo. You're a regular Shakespeare!" exclaimed Beth, who firmly believed that her sisters were gifted with wonderful genius in all things.

"Not quite," replied Jo modestly. "I do think 'The Witch's Curse, an Operatic Tragedy,' is rather a nice thing; but I'd like to try Macbeth, if we only had a trap door for Banquo. I always wanted to do the killing part. 'Is that a dagger that I see before me?'" muttered Jo, rolling her eyes and clutching at the air, as she had seen a famous tragedian do.

"No, it's the toasting fork, with mother's shoe on it instead of the bread. Beth's stage-struck!" cried Meg, and the rehearsal ended

in a general burst of laughter.

"Glad to find you so merry, my girls," said a cheery voice at the door, and actors and audience turned to welcome a tall, motherly lady, with a "can-I-help-you" look about her which was truly delightful. She was not elegantly dressed, but a noble-looking woman, and the girls thought the gray cloak and unfashionable bonnet covered the most splendid Mother in the world.

"Well, dearies, how have you got on to-day? There was so much to do, getting the boxes ready to go tomorrow, that I didn't come home to dinner. Has anyone called, Beth? How is your cold, Meg? Jo, you look tired to death. Come and kiss me, baby."

While making these inquiries Mrs. March got her wet things off, her warm slippers on, and sitting down in the easy chair, drew Amy to her lap, preparing to enjoy the happiest hour of her busy day.

The girls flew about trying to make things comfortable, each in her own way. Meg arranged the tea table. Jo brought wood and set chairs, dropping, overturning, and clattering everything she touched. Beth trotted to and fro between parlor and kitchen, quiet and busy; while Amy gave directions to everyone, as she sat with her hands folded.

As they gathered about the table, Mrs. March said, with a particularly happy face, "I've got a treat for you after supper."

A quick, bright smile went round like a streak of sunshine. Beth clapped her hands, regardless of the biscuit she held, and Jo tossed up her napkin, crying, "A letter! a letter! Three cheers for Father!"

"Yes, a nice long letter. He is well, and thinks he shall get through the cold season better than we feared. He sends all sort of loving wishes for Christmas, and an especial message to you girls," said Mrs. March, patting her pockets as if she had a treasure there.

"Hurry and get done! Don't stop to quirk your little finger, and simper over your plate, Amy," cried Jo, choking in her tea, and dropping her bread, butter side down, on the carpet, in her haste to get at the treat.

Beth ate no more, but crept away, to sit in her shadowy corner and brood over the delight to come, till the others were ready.

"I think it was so splendid of Father to go as a chaplain when he was too old to be drafted, and not strong enough for a soldier," said Meg warmly.

"Don't I wish I could go as a drummer, or a nurse, so I could be near him and help him," exclaimed Jo, with a groan.

"It must be very disagreeable to be in a war and sleep in a tent, and eat all sorts of bad-tasting things, and drink out of a tin mug," sighed Amy.

"When will he come home, Marmee?" asked Beth, with a little quiver in her voice.

"Not for many months, dear, unless he is sick. He will stay and do his work faithfully as long as he can, and we won't ask for him back a minute sooner than he can be spared from this terrible war between the North and the South. Now come and hear the letter."

They all drew to the fire, Mother in the big chair with Beth at her feet, Meg and Amy perched on either arm of the chair, and Jo leaning on the back, where no one would see any sign of emotion if the letter should happen to be touching. Very few letters were written in those hard times that were not touching, especially those which fathers sent home. In this one little was said of the hardships endured, the dangers faced, or the homesickness conquered. It was a cheerful, hopeful letter, full of lively descriptions of camp life, marches, and military news. Only at the end did the writer's heart overflow with fatherly love and longing for the little girls at home.

"Give them all my dear love and a kiss. Tell them I think of them by day, pray for them by night, and find my best comfort in their affection at all times. A year seems very long to wait before I see them, but remind them that while we wait we may all work, so that these hard days need not be wasted. I know they will remember all I said to them, that they will be loving children to you, will do their duty faithfully, fight their enemies bravely, and conquer themselves so beautifully that when I come back to them I may be fonder and prouder than ever of my little women."

Everybody sniffed when they came to that part. Jo wasn't ashamed of the great tear that dropped off the end of her nose, and Amy never minded the rumpling of her curls as she hid her face on her Mother's shoulder and sobbed out. "I *am* a selfish girl! But I'll truly try to be better, so he mayn't be disappointed in me by and by."

"We all will!" cried Meg. "I think too much of my looks, and hate to work, but I won't any more, if I can help it."

"I'll try to be what he loves to call me, a 'little woman,' and not be rough and wild, but do my duty here instead of wanting to be somewhere else," said Jo, thinking that keeping her temper at home was a much harder task than facing a rebel or two down South.

Beth said nothing, but wiped away her tears with the blue army sock, and began to knit with all her might, losing no time in doing the duty that lay nearest her, while she resolved in her quiet little soul to be all that father hoped to find her when the year brought round the happy coming home.

Mrs. March broke the silence that followed Jo's words by saying in her cheery voice, "Do you remember how you used to play *Pilgrim's Progress* when you were little things? Nothing delighted you more than to have me tie my piece bags on your backs for burdens, give you hats and sticks and rolls of paper, and let you travel through the house from the cellar, which was the City of Destruction, up, up, to the house-top, where you had all the lovely things you could collect to make a Celestial City."

"What fun it was, especially going by the lions, fighting Apollyon, and passing through the Valley where the hob-goblins were!" said Jo.

"I liked the place where the bundles fell off and tumbled downstairs," said Meg.

"My favorite part was when we came out on the flat roof where our flowers and arbors and pretty things were, and all stood and sang for joy up there in the sunshine," said Beth, smiling, as if that pleasant moment had come back to her.

"I don't remember much about it, except that I was afraid of the cellar and the dark entry, and always liked the cake and milk we had up at the top. If I wasn't too old for such things, I'd rather like to play it over again," said Amy, who began to talk of renouncing childish things at the mature age of twelve.

"We never are too old for this, my dear, because it is a play we are all playing all the time in one way or another. Our bur-

175

dens are here, our road is before us, and the longing for goodness and happiness is the guide that leads us through many troubles and mistakes to the peace which is a true Celestial City. Now, my little pilgrims, suppose you begin again, not in play, but in earnest, and see how far on you can get before Father comes home."

"Really, Mother? Where are our bundles?" asked Amy, who was a very literal young lady.

"Each of you told what your burden was just now, except Beth. I rather think she hasn't got any," said Mother.

"Yes, I have. Mine is dishes and dusters, and envying girls with nice pianos, and being afraid of people."

Beth's bundle was such a funny one that everybody wanted to laugh; but nobody did, for it would have hurt her feelings very much.

"Let us do it," said Meg thoughtfully. "It is only another name for trying to be good, and the story may help us; for though we do want to be good, it's hard work, and we forget, and don't do our best."

"We were in the Slough of Despond tonight, and Mother came and pulled us out as Help did in the book. We ought to have our roll of directions, like Christian. What shall we do about that?" asked Jo, delighted with the fancy which lent a little romance to the very dull task of doing her duty.

"Look under your pillows Christmas morning, and you will find your guidebook," replied Mrs. March.

They talked over the new plan while old Hannah cleared the table. Then out came the four little workbaskets, and the needles flew as the girls made sheets for Aunt March. It was uninteresting sewing, but tonight no one grumbled. They adopted Jo's plan of dividing the long seams into four parts, and calling the quarters Europe, Asia, Africa, and America, and in that way got on capitally, especially when they talked about the different countries as they stitched their way through them.

At nine they stopped work, and sang, as usual, before they went to bed. No one but Beth could get much music out of the old piano; but she had a way of softly touching the yellow keys, and making a pleasant accompaniment to the simple songs. Meg had a voice like a flute, and she and her Mother led the little choir. Amy chirped like a cricket, and Jo wandered through the airs at her own sweet will, always coming out at the wrong place with a croak or a quaver.

They had always done this from the time they could lisp *"Crinkle, crinkle, 'ittle 'tar,"* and it had become a household custom, for the Mother was a born singer. The first sound in the morning was her voice, as she went about the house singing like a lark; and the last sound at night was the same cheery sound, for the girls never grew too old for the familiar lullaby.

A MERRY CHRISTMAS

JO WAS the first to wake in the gray dawn of Christmas morning. No stockings hung at the fireplace, and for a moment she felt as much disappointed as she did long ago when her little sock fell down because it was so crammed with goodies. Then she remembered her Mother's promise, and slipping her hand under her pillow, drew out a little crimson-covered book. She knew it very well, for it was that beautiful old story of the best life ever lived, and Jo felt that it was a true guide-book for any pilgrim going the long journey.

Jo woke Meg with a "Merry Christmas," and bade her see what was under her pillow. A green-covered book appeared, with the same picture inside, and a few words written by their Mother, which made their one present very precious in their eyes.

Presently Beth and Amy woke, to rummage and find their little books also—one dove-colored, the other blue. They all sat looking and talking while the east grew rosy with the coming day.

In spite of her small vanities, Margaret had a sweet and pious nature which unconsciously influenced her sisters, especially Jo, who loved her very tenderly, and obeyed her because her advice was so gently given.

"Girls," said Meg seriously, looking from the tumbled head beside her to the two little night-capped ones in the room beyond, "Mother wants us to read and love these books, and we must begin at once. We used to be faithful about it; but since Father went away, and all this war trouble unsettled us, we have neglected many things. You can do as you please; but *I* shall keep my book on the table here, and read a little every morning as soon as I wake, for I know it will do me good, and help me through the day."

Then she opened her new book and began to read. Jo put her arm around her, and, leaning cheek to cheek, read also, with the quiet expression so seldom seen on her restless face.

"How good Meg is! Come, Amy, let's do as they do. I'll help you with the hard words, and they'll explain things if we don't understand," whispered Beth, very much impressed by the pretty books and her sisters' example.

"I'm glad mine is blue," said Amy. And then the rooms were very still while the pages were softly turned, and the winter sunshine crept in to touch the bright heads and serious faces with a Christmas greeting.

"Where is Mother?" asked Meg, as she and Jo ran down to thank her for their gifts, half an hour later.

"Goodness only knows. Some poor creeter come a-beggin', and your Ma went straight off to see what was needed. There never *was* such a woman for givin' away vittles and drink, clothes and firin'," replied Hannah, who had lived with the family since Meg was born.

"She will be back soon, I think; so fry your cakes, and have everything ready," said Meg, looking over the presents which were collected in a basket and kept under the sofa, ready to be produced at the proper time. "Why, where is Amy's bottle of cologne?" she added, as the little flask did not appear.

"She took it out a minute ago, and went off with it to put a ribbon on it, or some such notion," replied Jo, dancing about the room to take the first stiffness off the new army slippers.

"How nice my handkerchiefs look, don't they? I marked them all myself," said Beth, looking proudly at the somewhat uneven letters which had cost her such labor.

"Bless the child! She's gone and put 'Mother' on them instead of 'M. March.' How funny!" cried Jo, taking up one.

"Isn't it right? I thought it was better to do it so, because Meg's initials are 'M. M.,' and I don't want anyone to use these but Marmee," said Beth, looking troubled.

"It's all right, dear, and a very pretty idea — quite sensible, too, for no one can ever mistake now. It will please her very much, I know," said Meg, with a frown for Jo and a smile for Beth.

"There's mother. Hide the basket, quick!" cried Jo, as a door slammed, and steps sounded in the hall.

Amy came in hastily, and looked rather abashed when she saw her sisters all waiting for her.

"Where have you been, and what are you hiding behind you?" asked Meg, surprised to see, by her hood and cloak, that lazy Amy had been out so early.

"Don't laugh at me, Jo! I didn't mean anyone should know till the time came. I only meant to change the little bottle for a big one, and I gave *all* my money to get it, and I'm truly trying not to be selfish any more."

As she spoke, Amy showed the handsome flask which replaced the cheap one; and looked so earnest and humble in her little effort to forget herself that Meg hugged her on the spot, and Jo pronounced her "a trump," while Beth ran to the window, and picked her finest rose to ornament the stately bottle.

"You see I felt ashamed of my present, after reading and talking about being good this morning. So I ran round the corner and changed it the minute I was up. I'm *so* glad, for mine is the handsomest now."

Another bang of the street door sent the basket under the sofa, and the girls to the table, eager for breakfast.

"Merry Christmas, Marmee! Many of them! Thank you for our books. We read some, and mean to every day," they cried, in chorus.

"Merry Christmas, little daughters! I'm glad you began at once, and hope you will keep on. But I want to say one word before we sit down. Not far away from here lies a poor woman, Mrs. Hummel, with a little newborn baby. Six children are huddled into one bed to keep from freezing, for they have no fire. There is nothing to eat over there; and the oldest boy came to tell me they were suffering hunger and cold. My girls, will you give them your breakfast as a Chrismas present?"

They were all unusually hungry, having waited nearly an hour, and for a minute no one spoke; but only for a minue, for Jo exclaimed impetuously, "I'm so glad you came before we began!"

"May I go and help carry the things to the poor little children?" asked Beth eagerly.

"*I* shall take the cream and the muffins," added Amy, heroically giving up the articles she most liked.

Meg was already covering the buckwheats, and piling the bread into one big plate.

"I thought you'd do it," said Mrs. March, smiling as if satisfied. "You all help me, and when we come back we will have bread and milk for breakfast, and make it up at dinner-time."

They were soon ready, and the procession set out. Fortunately it was early, and they went through back streets, so few people saw them, and no one laughed at the queer party.

A poor, bare, miserable room it was, with broken windows, no fire, ragged bedclothes, a sick Mother, wailing baby, and a group of pale, hungry children cuddled under one old quilt, trying to keep warm.

How the big eyes stared and the blue lips smiled as the girls went in!

"*Ach, mein Gott!* It is good angels come to us!" said the poor woman, crying for joy.

"Funny angels in hoods and mittens," said Jo, and set them laughing.

In a few minutes it really did seem as if kind spirits had been at work there. Hannah, who had carried wood, made a fire, and stopped up the broken panes with old hats and her own cloak. Mrs. March gave the mother tea and gruel, and comforted her with promises of help, while she dressed the little baby as tenderly as if it had been her own. The girls, meantime, spread the table, set the children round the fire, and fed them like so many hungry birds—laughing, talking, and trying to understand the funny broken English.

"*Das ist gut!*" "*Die Engel-kinder!*" cried the poor things, as they ate, and warmed their purple hands at the comfortable blaze.

The girls had never been called angel children before, and thought it very agreeable, especially Jo, who had been considered a "Sancho" ever since she was born. That was a very happy breakfast, though they didn't get any of it; and when they went away, leaving comfort behind, I think there were not in all the city four merrier people than the hungry little girls who gave away their breakfasts and contented them-

selves with bread and milk on Christmas morning.

"That's loving our neighbor better than ourselves, and I like it," said Meg, as they set out their presents, while their Mother was upstairs collecting clothes for the poor Hummels.

Not a very splendid show, but there was a great deal of love done up in the few little bundles; and the tall vase of red roses, white chrysanthemums, and trailing vines, which stood in the middle, gave quite an elegant air to the table.

"She coming! Strike up, Beth! Open the door, Amy! Three cheers for Marmee!" cried Jo, prancing about, while Meg went to conduct Mother to the seat of honor.

Beth played her gayest march, Amy threw open the door, and Meg acted as escort with great dignity. Mrs. March was both surprised and touched; and smiled with her eyes full as she examined her presents, and read the little notes which accompanied them. The slippers went on at once, a new handkerchief was slipped into her pocket, well scented with Amy's cologne, the rose was fastened to her bosom, and the nice gloves were pronounced a "perfect fit."

There was a good deal of laughing and kissing and explaining, in the simple loving fashion which makes these home festivals so pleasant at the time, so sweet to remember long afterward. Then they all fell to work.

The morning charities and ceremonies took so much time that the rest of the day was devoted to preparations for the evening festivities. Being still too young to go often to the theater, and not rich enough to afford any great outlay for private performances, the girls put their wits to work, and—ne-

cessity being the mother of invention—made whatever they needed. Very clever were some of their productions—pasteboard guitars, antique lamps made of old-fashioned butter boats covered with silver paper, gorgeous robes of old cotton, glittering with tin spangles from a pickle factory, and armor covered with the same useful diamond-shaped bits, left in sheets when the lids of tin preserve pots were cut out. The furniture was used to being turned topsy-turvy, and the big room was the scene of many revels.

No gentlemen were admitted; so Jo played male parts to her heart's content, and took immense satisfaction in a pair of russet-leather boots given her by a friend, who knew a lady who knew an actor. These boots, an old foil, and a slashed doublet once used by an artist for some picture, were Jo's chief treasures, and appeared on all occasions.

The smallness of the company made it necessary for the two principal actors to take several parts apiece. They certainly deserved credit for the hard work they did in learning three or four different parts, whisking in and out of various costumes, and managing the stage besides. It was excellent drill for their memories, a harmless amusement, and employed many hours which otherwise would have been idle, lonely, or spent in less profitable society.

On Christmas night, a dozen girls piled onto the bed which was the dress circle, and sat before the blue and yellow chintz curtains in a most flattering state of expectancy. There was a good deal of rustling and whispering behind the curtain, a trifle of lamp smoke, and an occasional giggle from Amy, who was apt to get hysterical in the excitement of the moment. Presently a bell sounded, the curtains flew apart, and the Operatic Tragedy began.

"A gloomy wood," according to the one playbill, was represented by a few shrubs in pots, green baize on the floor, and a cave in the distance. This cave was made with a clothes-horse for a roof, bureaus for walls; and in it was a small furnace in full blast, with a black pot on it, and an old witch bending over it. The stage was dark, and the glow of the furnace had a fine effect, especially as real steam issued from the kettle when the witch took off the cover.

A moment was allowed for the first thrill to subside. Then Hugo, the villain, stalked in with a clanking sword at his side, a slouched hat, black beard, mysterious cloak, and the boots. After pacing to and fro in much agitation, he struck his forehead, and burst out in a wild strain, singing of his hatred for Roderigo, his love for Zara, and his pleasing resolution to kill the one and win the other. The gruff tones of Hugo's voice, with an occasional shout when his feelings overcame him, were very impressive, and the audience applauded the moment he paused for breath. Bowing with the air of one accustomed to public praise, he stole to the cavern, and ordered Hagar to come forth with a commanding "What ho, minion! I need thee!"

Out came Meg, with gray horsehair hanging about her face, a red and black robe, a staff, and cabalistic signs upon her cloak. Hugo demanded a potion to make Zara adore him, and one to destroy Roderigo. Hagar, in a fine dramatic melody, promised both, and proceeded to call up the spirit who would bring the love philter:

> Hither, hither, from thy home,
> Airy sprite, I bid thee come!
> Born of roses, fed on dew,
> Charms and potions canst thou brew?
> Bring me here, with elfin speed,
> The fragrant philter which I need;
> Make it sweet and swift and strong,
> Spirit, answer now my song!

A soft strain of music sounded, and then at the back of the cave appeared a little figure in cloudy white, with glittering wings, golden hair, and a garland of roses on its head. Waving a wand, it sang:

> Hither I come,
> From my airy home,
> Afar in the silver moon.
> Take the magic spell,
> And use it well,
> Or its power will vanish soon!

Dropping a small, gilded bottle at the witch's feet, the spirit vanished. Another chant from Hagar produced another apparition—not a lovely one; for, with a bang, an ugly black imp appeared, and having croaked a reply, tossed a dark bottle at Hugo, and disappeared with a mocking laugh. Having warbled his thanks and put the potions in his boots, Hugo departed; and Hagar informed the audience that, as he had killed a few of her friends in times past, she has cursed him, and intends to thwart his plans, and be revenged on him. The curtain fell, and the audience reposed and ate candy while discussing the merits of the play.

A good deal of hammering went on before the curtain rose again; but when it became evident what a masterpiece of stage carpentering had been got up, no one murmured at the delay. It was truly superb! A tower rose to the ceiling. Halfway up ap-

181

peared a window, with a lamp burning at it, and behind the white curtain appeared Zara in a lovely blue and silver dress, waiting for Roderigo. He came in gorgeous array, with plumed cap, red cloak, chestnut lovelocks, a guitar, and the boots, of course. Kneeling at the foot of the tower, he sang a serenade in melting tones. Zara replied, and, after a musical dialogue, consented to fly.

Then came the grand effect of the play. Roderigo produced a rope ladder, with five steps to it, threw up one end, and invited Zara to descend. Timidly she crept from her lattice, put her hand on Roderigo's shoulder, and was about to leap gracefully down, when—"Alas! alas for Zara"—she forgot her train. It caught in the window; the tower tottered, leaned forward, fell with a crash, and buried the unhappy lovers in the ruins!

A universal shriek arose as the russet boots waved wildly from the wreck, and a golden head emerged, exclaiming, "I told you so! I told you so!"

With wonderful presence of mind, Don Pedro, the cruel sire, rushed in, dragged out his daughter with a hasty aside: "Don't laugh! Act as if it was all right!"

And, ordering Roderigo up, she banished him from the kingdom with wrath and scorn.

Though decidedly shaken by the fall of the tower upon him, Roderigo defied the old gentleman, and refused to stir. This dauntless example fired Zara. She also defied her sire, and he ordered them both to the deepest dungeons of the castle.

A stout little retainer came in with chains, and led them away, looking very much frightened, and evidently forgetting the

speech he ought to have made.

Act Three was the castle hall. Here Hagar appears, having come to free the lovers and finish Hugo. She hears him coming, and hides; sees him put the potions into two cups of wine, and bid the timid little servant "Bear them to the captives in their cells, and tell them I shall come anon."

The servant takes Hugo aside to tell him something, and Hagar changes the cups for two others which are harmless. Ferdinando, the "minion," carries them away, and Hagar puts back the cup which holds the poison meant for Roderigo.

Hugo, getting thirsty after a long warble, drinks it, loses his wits, and, after a good deal of clutching and stamping, falls flat and dies, while Hagar informs him what she has done in a song of exquisite power and melody.

This was a truly thrilling scene, though some persons might have thought that the sudden tumbling down of a quantity of long hair rather marred the effect of the villain's death. He was called before the curtain, and with great propriety appeared, leading Hagar, whose singing was considered more wonderful than all the rest of the performance put together.

Act Four displayed the despairing Roderigo on the point of stabbing himself, because he had been told that Zara has deserted him. Just as the dagger is at his heart, a lovely song is sung under his window, informing him that Zara is true, but in danger, and he can save her, if he will. A key is thrown in, which unlocks the door, and in a spasm of rapture he tears off his chains, and rushes away to find and rescue his lady-love.

Act Five opened with a stormy scene between Zara and Don Pedro. He wishes her to go into a convent, but she won't hear of it; and, after a touching appeal, is about to faint when Roderigo dashes in and demands her hand.

Don Pedro refuses, because he is not rich. They shout and gesticulate tremendously, but cannot agree, and Roderigo is about to bear away the exhausted Zara when the timid servant enters with a letter and a bag from Hagar, who has mysteriously disappeared. The letter informs the party that she bequeaths untold wealth to the young pair, and an awful doom to Don Pedro, if he doesn't make them happy.

The bag is opened, and several quarts of tin money shower down upon the stage, till it is quite glorified with the glitter.

This entirely softens the "stern sire." He consents without a murmur, all join in a joyful chorus, and the curtain falls upon the lovers kneeling to receive Don Pedro's blessing in attitudes of the most romantic grace.

Tumultuous applause followed, but received an unexpected check; for the cot bed, on which the "dress circle" was built, suddenly closed up, and extinguished the enthusiastic audience. Roderigo and Don Pedro flew to the rescue, and all were taken out unhurt, though many were speechless with laughter. The excitement had hardly subsided when Hannah appeared, with "Mrs. March's compliments, and would the ladies walk down to supper."

This was a surprise, even to the actors; and, when they saw the table, they looked at one another in rapturous amazement. It was like Marmee to get up a little treat for them; but anything so fine as this was unheard of since the departed days of plenty.

There was ice cream—actually two dishes of it, pink and white—and cake and fruit and French bonbons, and, in the middle of the table, four great bouquets of hot-house flowers!

It quite took their breath away; and they stared first at the table and then at their Mother, who looked as if she enjoyed it immensely.

"Is it fairies?" asked Amy.

"It's Santa Claus," said Beth.

"Mother did it," and Meg smiled her sweetest, in spite of her gray beard and white eyebrows.

"Aunt March had a good fit, and sent the supper," cried Jo, with a sudden inspiration.

"All wrong. Old Mr. Laurence sent it," replied Mrs. March.

"The Laurence boy's grandfather! What in the world put such a thing into his head? We don't know him!" exclaimed Meg.

"Hannah told one of his servants about your breakfast party. He is an odd old gentleman, but that pleased him. He knew my Father, years ago; and he sent me a polite note this afternoon, saying he hoped I would allow him to express his friendly feeling toward my children by sending them a few trifles in honor of the day. I could not refuse; and so you have a little feast at night to make up for the bread-and-milk breakfast."

"That boy put it into his head, I know he did! He's a fine fellow, and I wish we could get acquainted. He looks as if he'd like to know us; but he's bashful, and Meg is so prim she won't let me speak to him when we pass," said Jo, as the plates went round with "Ohs!" and "Ahs!" of satisfaction.

"You mean the people who live in the big house next door, don't you?" asked one of the girls. "My Mother knows old Mr. Laurence but says he's very proud, and doesn't like to mix with his neighbors. He keeps his grandson shut up, when he isn't riding or walking with his tutor, and makes him study very hard. We invited him to our party, but he didn't come. Mother says he's very nice, though he never speaks to us girls."

"Our cat ran away once, and he brought her back, and we talked over the fence, and were getting on beautifully when he saw Meg coming, and walked off. I mean to know him some day; for he needs fun, I'm sure he does," said Jo decidedly.

"I like his manners so I've no objection to your knowing him, if a proper opportunity comes. He brought the flowers himself; and I should have asked him in, if I had been sure what was going on upstairs. He looked so wistful as he went away, hearing the frolic, and evidently having none of his own."

"It's a mercy you didn't, Mother!" laughed Jo, looking at her boots. "But we'll have another play, some time, that he *can* see. Perhaps he'll help act; wouldn't that be jolly?"

"I never had such a fine bouquet before! How pretty it is!" And Meg examined her flowers with great interest.

"They *are* lovely! But Beth's roses are sweeter to me," said Mrs. March, smelling the half-dead posy in her belt.

Beth nestled up to her, and whispered softly, "I wish I could send my bunch to Father. I'm afraid he isn't having such a merry Christmas as we are."

Alice's Adventures in Wonderland

By Lewis Carroll

There are people who decide whether or not someone is worthy of being their friend on the basis of whether or not he or she appreciates ALICE'S ADVENTURES IN WONDER-LAND and ALICE THROUGH THE LOOKING-GLASS.

Trying to explain what we find so deliciously funny about Lewis Carroll's books is a little like trying to explain why our favorite ice-cream flavor is our favorite. If that particular flavor is the kind you like, you will find it delicious. If it isn't, you won't; that's all.

It's just like that with ALICE. People with no taste for fantasy or nonsense simply will not be able to understand why other people find the funny words and ridiculous happenings so delightful.

If you enjoy ALICE in the first place, you will want to read about her incredible adventures many times. And every time you do, you will find more to delight you. Except for the Bible and the plays of Shakespeare, ALICE IN WONDERLAND (including ALICE THROUGH THE LOOKING-GLASS) is probably the most quoted book in the world. People who appreciate its wit and humor want other people to enjoy it too. That is why so many families read it aloud to each other. Incidentally, it's a book that grows on you. The older and wiser you get, the more wisdom and sense you will see in the inspired nonsense.

ALICE was beginning to get very tired of sitting by her sister on the bank and of having nothing to do. Once or twice she had peeped into the book her sister was reading, but it had no pictures or conversations in it, "and what is the use of a book," thought Alice, "without pictures or conversations?"

She was considering, in her own mind (as well as she could, for the hot day made her feel very sleepy and stupid), whether the pleasure of making a daisy-chain would be worth the trouble of getting up and picking the daisies, when suddenly a White Rabbit with pink eyes ran close by her.

There was nothing so *very* remarkable in that; nor did Alice think it so *very* much out of the way to hear the Rabbit say to itself "Oh dear! Oh dear! I shall be too late!" But when the Rabbit actually *took a watch out of its waistcoat pocket,* and looked at it, and then hurried on, Alice started to her feet. Burning with curiosity, she ran across the field after it, and was just in time to see it pop down a large rabbit-hole under the hedge.

In another moment down went Alice after it, never once considering how in the world she was to get out again.

The rabbit-hole went straight on like a tunnel for some way, and then dipped suddenly down, so suddenly that Alice had not a moment to think about stopping herself before she found herself falling down what seemed to be a very deep well.

Either the well was very deep, or she fell very slowly, for she had plenty of time as she went down to look about her, and to wonder what was going to happen next.

First, she tried to look down and make out what she was coming to, but it was too dark to see anything. Then she looked at the sides of the well and noticed that they were filled with cupboards and book-shelves. Here and there she saw maps and pictures hung on pegs. She took down a jar from one of the shelves; it was labeled Orange Marmalade. To her great disappointment it was empty

Down, down, down. Would the fall *never* come to an end? "I wonder how many miles I've fallen by this time?" she said aloud. "I must be getting somewhere near the center of the earth. Let me see: that would be four thousand miles down—but then I wonder what Latitude or Longitude I've got to?" (Alice had not the slightest idea what Latitude was, or Longitude either, but she thought they were nice words to say.) "I wonder if I shall fall right *through* the earth! How funny it'll seem to come out among the people that walk with their heads downwards!"

Down, down, down. There was nothing else to do, so Alice soon began talking

again. "Dinah'll miss me very much tonight, I should think!" (Dinah was the cat.) "I hope they'll remember her saucer of milk at tea-time."

Here Alice began to get rather sleepy. She had just begun to dream that she was walking hand in hand with Dinah when suddenly, thump! thump! down she came upon a heap of sticks and dry leaves, and the fall was over.

Alice was not a bit hurt, and she jumped up on to her feet in a moment. She looked up, but it was all dark overhead. Before her was another long passage, and the White Rabbit was still in sight, hurrying down it.

Alice was just in time to hear the Rabbit say, as it turned a corner, "Oh my ears and whiskers, how late it's getting!" She was close behind it when she turned the corner, but the Rabbit was no longer to be seen. Alice found herself in a long low hall, which was lit up by a row of lamps hanging from the roof.

There were doors all round the hall, but they were all locked; and when Alice had been all the way down one side and up the other, trying every door, she walked sadly down the middle, wondering how she was ever to get out again.

Suddenly she came upon a little three-legged table, all made of solid glass. There

was nothing on it but a tiny golden key, and Alice's first idea was that this might belong to one of the doors of the hall. But, alas! either the locks were too large, or the key was too small, but at any rate it would not open any of them. However, on the second time round, she came upon a low curtain she had not noticed before, and behind it was a little door about fifteen inches high. She tried the little golden key in the lock, and to her great delight it fitted!

Alice opened the door and found that it led into a small passage, not much larger than a rat-hole. She knelt down and looked along the passage into the loveliest garden you ever saw. How she longed to get out of that dark hall, and wander about among those beds of bright flowers and those cool fountains! But she could not even get her head through the doorway. "And even if my head *would* go through," thought poor Alice, "it would be of very little use without my shoulders. Oh, how I wish I could shut up like a telescope! I think I could, if I only knew how to begin."

There seemed to be no use in waiting by the little door, so she went back to the table, half hoping she might find another key on it, or at any rate a book of rules for shutting people up like telescopes. This time she found a little bottle on it ("which certainly was not here before," said Alice), and tied round the neck of the bottle was a paper label, with the words DRINK ME beautifully printed on it in large letters.

It was all very well to say "Drink me," but the wise little Alice was not going to do *that* in a hurry. "No, I'll look first," she said, "and see whether it's marked POISON or not."

However, this bottle was *not* marked POISON; so Alice ventured to taste it, and,

finding it very nice (it had, in fact, a sort of mixed flavor of cherry-tart, custard, pineapple, roast turkey, toffy, and hot buttered toast), she very soon finished ſt off.

"What a curious feeling!" said Alice. "I must be shutting up like a telescope!"

And so it was indeed: she was now only ten inches high, and her face brightened up at the thought that she was now the right size for going through the little door into that lovely garden. She waited for a few minutes to see if she was going to shrink any further.

After a while, finding that nothing more happened, she decided on going into the garden at once. But, alas for poor Alice. When she got to the door, she found she had forgotten the little golden key, and when she went back to the table for it, she found she could not possibly reach it. She could see it quite plainly through the glass, and she tried her best to climb up one of the legs of the table, but it was too slippery; and when she had tired herself out with trying, the poor little thing sat down and cried.

"Come, there's no use in crying like that!"

said Alice to herself rather sharply. "I advise you to leave off this minute!" She generally gave herself very good advice (though she seldom followed it).

Soon her eye fell on a little glass box that was lying under the table. She opened it, and found in it a very small cake, on which the words EAT ME were beautifully marked in currants.

"Well, I'll eat it," said Alice. "If it makes me grow larger, I can reach the key; and if it makes me grow smaller, I can creep under the door. Either way I'll get into the garden."

She ate a little bit and said anxiously to herself "Which way? Which way?", holding her hand on the top of her head to feel which way it was growing; and she was quite surprised to find that she remained the same size.

So she finished off the cake.

THE POOL OF TEARS

"Curiouser and curiouser!" cried Alice (she was so much surprised, that for the moment she quite forgot how to speak good English). "Now I'm opening out like the largest telescope that ever was! Good-bye, feet!" (for when she looked down at her feet, they seemed to be almost out of sight, they were getting so far off).

Just at this moment her head struck against the roof of the hall. She was now rather more than nine feet high. She at once took up the little golden key and hurried off to the garden door.

Poor Alice! It was as much as she could do, lying down on one side, to look through into the garden with one eye; but to get through was more hopeless than ever. She sat down and began to cry again.

"You ought to be ashamed of yourself," said Alice to herself. "A great girl like you to go on crying in this way! Stop this moment, I tell you!" But she went on all the same, shedding gallons of tears, until there was a large pool all round her.

After a time she heard a little pattering of feet in the distance, and she hastily dried her eyes to see what was coming. It was the White Rabbit returning, splendidly dressed, with a pair of white kid-gloves in one hand and a large fan in the other: he came trotting along in a great hurry, muttering to himself, as he came, "Oh! The Duchess, the Duchess! Oh! *Won't* she be savage if I've kept her waiting!"

Alice felt so desperate that she was ready to ask help of any one; so, when the Rabbit came near her, she began, in a low, timid voice, "If you please, Sir——"

The Rabbit started violently, dropped the white kid-gloves and the fan, and scurried away into the darkness.

Alice took up the fan and gloves, and, as the hall was very hot, she kept fanning herself all the time she went on talking. "Dear, dear! How queer everything is to-day! And yesterday things went on just as usual. I wonder if I've changed in the night? I'll try to know all the things I used to know. I'll try and say '*How doth the little—*'." She crossed her hands on her lap, as if she were saying lessons, and began to repeat it, but her voice sounded hoarse and strange, and

the words did not come the same as they used to do.

> *How doth the little crocodile*
> *Improve his shining tail,*
> *And pour the waters of the Nile*
> *On every golden scale!*

> *How cheerfully he seems to grin,*
> *How neatly spreads his claws,*
> *And welcomes little fishes in,*
> *With gently smiling jaws!*

"I'm sure those are not the right words," said poor Alice, and her eyes filled with tears again. "Oh dear! I am so *very* tired of being all alone here!"

As she said this she looked down at her hands, and was surprised to see that she had put on one of the Rabbit's little white kid-gloves while she was talking. "How *can* I have done that?" she thought. "I must be growing small again." She got up and went to the table to measure herself by it, and found that, as nearly as she could guess, she was now about two feet high, and was shrinking rapidly. She soon found out that the cause of this was the fan she was holding, and she dropped it just in time to save herself from shrinking away altogether.

"That *was* a narrow escape!" said Alice, a good deal frightened at the sudden change, but very glad to find herself still in existence. "And now for the garden!" And she ran with all speed back to the little door. But, alas! the little door was shut again, and the little golden key was lying on the glass table as before. "And things are worse than ever," thought the poor child, "for I never was so small as this before, never!"

As she said these words her foot slipped, and in another moment, splash! she was up to her chin in salt-water. Her first idea was that she had somehow fallen into the sea. However, she soon made out that she was

189

in the pool of tears which she had wept when she was nine feet high.

"I wish I hadn't cried so much!" said Alice, as she swam about, trying to find her way out. "I shall be punished for it now, I suppose, by being drowned in my own tears! That *will* be a queer thing, to be sure! However, everything is queer to-day."

Just then she heard something splashing about in the pool a little way off, and she swam nearer to make out what it was. At first she thought it must be a walrus or hippopotamus, but then she remembered how small she was now, and she soon made out that it was only a mouse, that had slipped in like herself.

"Would it be of any use, now," thought Alice, "to speak to this mouse? Everything is so out-of-the-way down here, that I should think very likely it can talk. At any rate, there's no harm in trying." So she began: "O Mouse, do you know the way out of this pool? I am very tired of swimming about here, O Mouse!"

The mouse looked at her rather inquisitively, and seemed to her to wink with one of its little eyes, but it said nothing.

"Perhaps it doesn't understand English," thought Alice. "I daresay it's a French mouse." So she began again: *"Où est ma chatte?"* which was the first sentence in her French lesson-book. The Mouse gave a sudden leap out of the water, and seemed to quiver all over with fright.

"Oh, I beg your pardon!" cried Alice hastily, afraid that she had hurt the poor animal's feelings. "I quite forgot you didn't like cats."

"Our family always *hated* cats: nasty, low, vulgar things!" cried the Mouse, who was trembling down to the end of its tail. "Don't let me hear the name again!"

"I won't indeed!" said Alice, in a great hurry to change the subject of conversation. "Are you — are you fond — of — of dogs?"

The Mouse did not answer, so Alice went on eagerly: "There is such a nice little dog, near our house, I should like to show you! A little bright-eyed terrier, you know, with oh, such long curly brown hair! It belongs to a farmer, you know, and he says it's so useful. He says it kills all the rats and—oh dear!" cried Alice in a sorrowful tone. "I'm afraid I've offended it again!" For the Mouse was swimming away from her as hard as it could go, and making quite a commotion in the pool as it went.

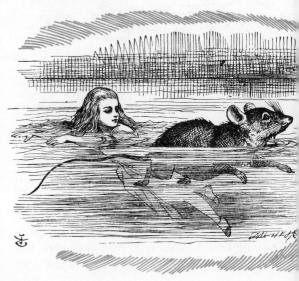

So she called softly after it, "Mouse dear! Do come back again, and we won't talk about cats, or dogs either, if you don't like them!" When the Mouse heard this, it turned round and swam slowly back to her: its face was quite pale and it said, in a low trembling voice, "Let us get to the shore."

It was high time to go, for the pool was getting quite crowded with the birds and animals that had fallen into it: there was a Duck and a Dodo, a Lory and an Eaglet, and several other curious creatures. Alice led the way, and the whole party swam to the shore.

THE WHITE RABBIT

In a little while Alice heard a little pattering of footsteps in the distance, and she looked up eagerly. It was the White Rabbit. It looked anxiously about as if it had lost something; and Alice heard it muttering to itself, "The Duchess! The Duchess! Oh my dear paws! Oh my fur and whiskers! She'll get me executed, as sure as ferrets are ferrets! Where *can* I have dropped them, I wonder?"

Alice guessed in a moment that the Rabbit was looking for the fan and the pair of white kid-gloves, and she very good-naturedly began hunting about for them. But they were nowhere to be seen—everything seemed to have changed since her swim in the pool; and the great hall, with the glass table and the little door, had vanished completely.

Very soon the Rabbit noticed Alice, as she went hunting about, and called out to her, in an angry tone, "Why, Mary Ann, what *are* you doing out here? Run home this moment, and fetch me a pair of gloves and a fan! Quick, now!"

Alice was so much frightened that she ran off at once in the direction the Rabbit pointed to.

"He took me for his housemaid," she said to herself as she ran. "How surprised he'll be when he finds out who I am! But I'd better take him his fan and gloves—that is, if I can find them." As she said this, she came upon a neat little house, on the door of which was a bright brass plate with the name W. RABBIT engraved upon it. She went in without knocking, and hurried upstairs, in great fear lest she should meet the real Mary Ann, and be turned out of the house before she had found the fan and gloves.

"How queer it seems," Alice said to herself, "to be going messages for a rabbit! I suppose Dinah'll be sending me on messages next!"

By this time she had found her way into a tidy little room with a table in the window, and on it (as she had hoped) a fan and two or three pairs of tiny white kid-gloves. She took up the fan and a pair of the gloves, and was just going to leave the room, when her eye fell upon a little bottle that stood near the looking-glass. There was no label this time with the words DRINK ME, but nevertheless she uncorked it and put it to her lips. "I know *something* interesting is sure to happen," she said to herself, "whenever I eat or drink anything: so I'll just see what this bottle does. I do hope it'll make me grow large again, for really I'm quite tired of being such a tiny little thing!"

It did so indeed, and much sooner than she had expected. Before she had drunk half the bottle, she found her head pressing against the ceiling, and had to stoop to save her neck from being broken. She hastily put down the bottle, saying to herself, "I hope I shan't grow any more. As it is, I can't get out at the door. I do wish I hadn't drunk quite so much!"

Alas! It was too late to wish that! She went on growing, and growing, and very soon had to kneel down on the floor. In another minute there was not even room for this, and she tried lying down with one elbow against the door, and the other arm curled round her head. Still she went on growing, and, as a last resource, she put one arm out of the window, and one foot up the chimney, and said to herself "Now I can do no more, whatever happens. What *will* become of me?"

Luckily for Alice, the little magic bottle had now had its full effect, and she grew no larger. Still it was very uncomfortable, and, as there seemed to be no sort of chance of her ever getting out of the room again, no wonder she felt unhappy.

"It was much pleasanter at home," thought poor Alice, "when one wasn't always growing larger and smaller, and being ordered about by mice and rabbits. I almost wish I hadn't gone down that rabbit-hole. And yet—it's rather curious, this sort

of life! I do wonder what *can* have happened to me! When I used to read fairy tales, I fancied that kind of thing never happened, and now here I am in the middle of one!"

After a few minutes she heard a voice outside.

"Mary Ann! Mary Ann!" said the voice. "Fetch me my gloves this moment!" Then came a little pattering of feet on the stairs. Alice knew it was the Rabbit coming to look for her, and she trembled till she shook the house, quite forgetting that she was now about a thousand times as large as the Rabbit, and had no reason to be afraid of it.

Presently the Rabbit came up to the door and tried to open it; but, as the door opened inwards, and Alice's elbow was pressed hard against it, that attempt proved a failure. Alice heard it say to itself "Then I'll go round and get in at the window."

"*That* you won't!" thought Alice, and, after waiting till she fancied she heard the Rabbit just under the window, she suddenly spread out her hand and made a snatch in the air. She did not get hold of anything, but she heard a little shriek and a fall, and a crash of broken glass, from which she concluded that it was just possible it had fallen into a cucumber-frame, or something of the sort.

Next came an angry voice—the Rabbit's—"Pat! Pat! Where are you?" And then a voice she had never heard before, "Sure then I'm here! Digging for apples, yer honor!"

"Digging for apples, indeed!" said the Rabbit angrily. "Here! Come and help me out of *this!*" (Sounds of more broken glass.)

After a minute or two they began moving about again, and Alice heard the Rabbit say "A barrowful will do, to begin with."

"A barrowful of *what?*" thought Alice.

But she had not long to doubt, for the next moment a shower of little pebbles came rattling in at the window, and some of them hit her in the face. "I'll put a stop to this," she said to herself, and shouted out "You'd better not do that again!"

Alice noticed, with some surprise, that the pebbles were all turning into little cakes as they lay on the floor, and a bright idea came into her head. "If I eat one of these cakes," she thought, "it's sure to make *some* change in my size; and, as it can't possibly make me larger, it must make me smaller, I suppose."

So she swallowed one of the cakes, and was delighted to find that she began shrinking directly. As soon as she was small enough to get through the door, she ran out of the house, and found quite a crowd of little animals and birds waiting outside. They all made a rush at Alice; but she ran off as hard as she could, and soon found herself safe in a thick wood.

"The first thing I've got to do," said Alice to herself, as she wandered about in the wood, "is to grow to my right size again; and the second thing is to find my way into that lovely garden. I think that will be the best plan."

It sounded an excellent plan, no doubt, and very neatly and simply arranged. The only difficulty was that she had not the smallest idea how to set about it. "I suppose I ought to eat or drink something or other," she said; "but the great question is 'What?'"

The great question certainly was "What?" Alice looked all round her at the flowers and grass, but she could not see anything that looked like the right thing to eat or drink under the circumstances. There was a large mushroom growing near her, about the same height as herself; and, when she had looked under it, and on both sides of it, and behind it, it occurred to her that she might as well look and see what was on the top of it.

She stretched herself up on tiptoe, and peeped over the edge of the mushroom, and her eyes immediately met those of a large blue caterpillar, that was sitting on the top, with its arms folded, quietly smoking a long hookah, and taking not the smallest notice of her or of anything else.

ADVICE FROM A CATERPILLAR

The Caterpillar and Alice looked at each other for some time in silence. At last the Caterpillar took the hookah out of its mouth, and addressed her in a languid sleepy voice.

"Who are *you?*" said the Caterpillar.

This was not an encouraging opening for a conversation. Alice replied, rather shyly, "I—I hardly know, Sir, just at present. I know who I *was* when I got up this morning, but I think I must have been changed several times since then."

"What do you mean by that?" said the

193

Caterpillar, sternly. "Explain yourself!"

"I can't explain *myself*, I'm afraid, Sir," said Alice, "because I'm not myself, you see."

"I don't see," said the Caterpillar.

"I'm afraid I can't put it more clearly," Alice replied, very politely, "for I can't understand it myself. Being so many different sizes in a day is very confusing."

"It isn't," said the Caterpillar.

Alice felt a little irritated at the Caterpillar's making such *very* short remarks, and she drew herself up and said gravely, "I think you ought to tell me who *you* are, first."

"Why?" said the Caterpillar.

Here was another puzzling question; and, as Alice could not think of any good reason, and the Caterpillar seemed to be in a *very* unpleasant state of mind, she turned away.

"Come back!" the Caterpillar called after her. "I've something important to say!"

Alice turned and came back.

"Keep your temper," said the Caterpillar.

"Is that all?" said Alice, swallowing down her anger as well as she could.

"No," said the Caterpillar. "What size do you want to be?"

"Well, I should like to be a *little* larger, Sir, if you wouldn't mind," said Alice. "Three inches is such a wretched height to be."

"It is a very good height indeed!" said the Caterpillar angrily, rearing itself upright as it spoke (it was exactly three inches high).

"But I'm not used to it!" pleaded poor Alice in a piteous tone. And she thought to herself "I wish the creatures wouldn't be so easily offended!"

"You'll get used to it in time," said the Caterpillar. And it put the hookah into its mouth, and began smoking again.

This time Alice waited patiently until it chose to speak again. In a minute or two the Caterpillar took the hookah out of its mouth, and yawned once or twice, and shook itself. Then it got down off the mushroom, and crawled away into the grass, merely remarking, as it went, "One side will make you grow taller, and the other side will make you grow shorter."

"One side of *what?* The other side of *what?*" thought Alice to herself.

"Of the mushroom," said the Caterpillar, just as if she had asked it aloud; and in another moment it was out of sight.

Alice remained looking thoughtfully at the mushroom for a minute, trying to make out which were the two sides of it; and, as it was perfectly round, she found this a very difficult question. However, at last she stretched her arms round it as far as they would go, and broke off a bit of the edge with each hand.

"And now which is which?" she said to

herself, and nibbled a little of the right-hand bit to try the effect. The next moment she felt a violent blow underneath her chin: it had struck her foot!

She was a good deal frightened by this very sudden change; but she felt that there was no time to be lost, as she was shrinking rapidly: so she set to work at once nibbling first at one piece and then at the other, and growing sometimes taller, and sometimes shorter, until she succeeded in bringing herself to her usual height.

It was so long since she had been anything near the right size, that it felt quite strange at first. But she got used to it in a few minutes, and began talking to herself as usual, "Come, there's half my plan done now! The next thing is, to get into that beautiful garden—how *is* that to be done, I wonder?"

As she said this, she came suddenly upon an open place, with a little house in it about four feet high. "Whoever lives there," thought Alice, "it'll never do to come upon them *this* size. It should frighten them out of their wits!" So she began nibbling at the right-hand bit again, and did not venture to go near the house till she had brought herself down to nine inches high.

For a minute or two Alice stood looking at the house, and wondering what to do next, when suddenly a footman in livery came running out of the wood—(she considered him to be a footman because he was in livery; otherwise, judging by his face only, she would have called him a fish) —and rapped loudly at the door with his knuckles. It was opened by another footman in livery, with a round face, and large eyes like a frog. And both footmen, Alice noticed, had powdered hair that curled all over their heads. She felt very curious to

know what it was all about, and crept a little way out of the wood to listen.

The Fish-Footman began by producing from under his arm a great letter, nearly as large as himself, and this he handed over to the other, saying, in a solemn tone, "For the Duchess. An invitation from the Queen to play croquet." The Frog-Footman repeated, in the same solemn tone, only changing the order of the words a little, "From the Queen. An invitation for the Duchess to play croquet."

Then they both bowed low, and their curls got entangled together.

Alice laughed so much at this that she had to run back into the wood for fear of their hearing her; and, when she next peeped out, the Fish-Footman was gone, and the other was sitting on the ground near the door, staring stupidly up into the sky.

Alice went timidly up to the door, and knocked.

"There's no sort of use in knocking," said the Footman, "and that for two reasons. First, because I'm on the same side of the door as you are; secondly, because they're making such a noise inside, no one could possibly hear you."

And certainly there *was* a most extraordinary noise going on within—a constant howling and sneezing, and every now and then a great crash, as if a dish or kettle had been broken to pieces.

"Please, then," said Alice, "how am I to get in?"

"*Are* you to get in at all?" said the Footman. "That's the first question, you know."

"There's no use in talking to him," said Alice desperately to herself. "He's perfectly idiotic!" And she opened the door and went in.

The door led right into a large kitchen, which was full of smoke from one end to the other. The Duchess was sitting on a three-legged stool in the middle, nursing a baby. The cook was leaning over the fire, stirring a large cauldron which seemed to be full of soup.

"There's certainly too much pepper in that soup!" Alice said to herself, as well as she could for sneezing.

There was certainly too much of it in the *air*. Even the Duchess sneezed occasionally; and the baby was sneezing and howling alternately without a moment's pause. The only two creatures in the kitchen that did *not* sneeze were the cook, and a large cat, which was lying on the hearth and grinning from ear to ear.

"Please would you tell me," said Alice, a little timidly, for she was not quite sure whether it was good manners for her to speak first, "why your cat grins like that?"

"It's a Cheshire-Cat," said the Duchess, "and that's why. Pig!"

She said the last word with such sudden violence that Alice quite jumped; but she saw, in another moment, that it was addressed to the baby, and not to her. So she took courage and went on again.

"I didn't know that Cheshire-Cats always grinned. In fact, I didn't know that cats *could* grin."

"They all can," said the Duchess; "and most of 'em do."

"I don't know of any that do," Alice said very politely, feeling quite pleased to have got into a conversation.

"You don't know much," said the Duchess, "and that's a fact."

Alice did not at all like the tone of this remark, and thought it would be as well to introduce some other subject of conversation. While she was trying to fix on one, the cook took the cauldron of soup off the fire, and at once set to work throwing everything within her reach at the Duchess and the baby—the fire-irons came first; then followed a shower of sauce-pans, plates, and dishes. The Duchess took no notice of them even when they hit her; and the baby was howling so much already that it was quite impossible to say whether the blows hurt it or not.

"Oh, *please* mind what you're doing!" cried Alice, jumping up and down in terror. "Oh, there goes his *precious* nose!" as an unusually large sauce-pan flew close by.

"If everybody minded their own business," the Duchess said in a hoarse growl, "the world would go round a deal faster than it does."

And with that she began nursing her child again, singing a sort of lullaby to it as she did so, and giving it a violent shake at the end of every line:

> *Speak roughly to your little boy,*
> *And beat him when he sneezes:*
> *He only does it to annoy,*
> *Because he knows it teases.*

"Here You may nurse it a bit if you like!" the Duchess said to Alice, flinging the baby at her as she spoke. "I must go and get ready to play croquet with the Queen." And she hurried out of the room. The cook threw a frying-pan after her as she went, but it just missed her.

Alice caught the baby with some difficulty, as it was a queer-shaped little creature and held out its arms and legs in all directions.

She carried it out into the open air. "If I don't take this child away with me," thought Alice, "they're sure to kill it in a day or two."

The baby grunted, and Alice looked very anxiously into its face to see what was the matter with it. There could be no doubt that it had a *very* turn-up nose, much more like a snout than a real nose; also its eyes were getting extremely small for a baby. Altogether Alice did not like the look of the thing at all.

She was just beginning to think, "Now, what am I to do with this creature when I get it home?" when it grunted again, so violently, that she looked down into its face in some alarm. This time there could be *no* mistake about it: it was neither more nor less than a *pig,* and she felt that it would be quite absurd for her to carry it any further.

So she set the little creature down, and felt quite relieved to see it trot away quietly into the wood. "If it had grown up," she said to herself, "it would have made a dreadfully ugly child; but it makes rather a handsome pig, I think." And she began thinking over other children she knew, who might do very well as pigs, when she was a little startled by seeing the Cheshire-Cat sitting on a bough of a tree a few yards off.

The Cat only grinned when it saw Alice.

It looked good-natured, she thought. Still it had *very* long claws and a great many teeth, so she felt that it ought to be treated with respect.

"Cheshire-Puss," she began, rather timidly, "would you tell me, please, which way I ought to go from here?"

"That depends a good deal on where you want to get to," said the Cat.

"I don't much care where——" said Alice.

"Then it doesn't matter which way you go," said the Cat.

"——so long as I get *somewhere*," Alice added as an explanation.

"Oh, you're sure to do that," said the Cat, "if you only walk long enough."

Alice felt that this could not be denied, so she tried another question. "What sort of people live about here?"

"In *that* direction," the Cat said, waving its right paw round, lives a Hatter; and in *that* direction," waving the other paw, "lives a March Hare. Visit either you like, they're both mad."

"But I don't want to go among mad people," Alice remarked.

"Oh, you can't help that," said the Cat: "we're all mad here. I'm mad. You're mad."

"How do you know I'm mad?" said Alice.

"You must be," said the Cat, "or you wouldn't have come here. Do you play croquet with the Queen today?"

"I should like it very much," said Alice, "but I haven't been invited yet."

"You'll see me there," said the Cat, and vanished.

Alice was not much surprised at this, she was getting so used to queer things happening. While she was still looking at the place where it had been, it suddenly appeared again.

"By-the-bye, what became of the baby?" said the Cat. "I'd nearly forgotten to ask."

"It turned into a pig," Alice answered very quietly, just as if the Cat had come back in a natural way.

"I thought it would," said the Cat.

"I wish you wouldn't keep appearing and vanishing so suddenly," said Alice. "You make one quite giddy!"

"All right," said the Cat; and this time it vanished quite slowly, beginning with the tail, and ending with the grin, which remained some time after the rest of it had gone.

"Well! I've often seen a cat without a grin," thought Alice, "but a grin without a cat! It's the most curious thing I ever saw in all my life!"

Alice walked on. She had not gone very far before she came in sight of the house of the March Hare. She thought it must be the right house, because the chimneys were shaped like ears and the roof was thatched with fur. It was so large a house that she did not like to go nearer till she had nibbled some more of the left-hand bit of mushroom, and raised herself to about two feet high. Even then she walked up towards it rather timidly, saying to herself, "Suppose it should be raving mad after all! I almost wish I'd gone to see the Hatter instead!"

A MAD TEA-PARTY

There was a table set out under a tree in front of the house, and the March Hare and the Hatter were having tea at it. A Dormouse was sitting between them, fast asleep, and the other two were using it as a cushion, resting their elbows on it, and talking over its head. "Very uncomfortable for the Dormouse," thought Alice, "but as it's asleep, I suppose it doesn't mind."

The table was a large one, but the three were all crowded together at one corner of it. "No room! No room!" they cried out when they saw Alice coming. "There's *plenty* of room!" said Alice indignantly, and she sat down in a large arm-chair at one end of the table.

"Have some wine," the March Hare said in an encouraging tone.

Alice looked all round the table, but there was nothing on it but tea. "I don't see any wine," she remarked.

"There isn't any," said the March Hare.

"Then it wasn't very civil of you to offer it," said Alice.

"It wasn't very civil of you to sit down without being invited," said the March Hare.

"I didn't know it was *your* table," said Alice; "it's laid for a great many more than three."

"Your hair wants cutting," said the Hatter. He had been looking at Alice for some time with great curiosity, and this was his first speech.

"You should learn not to make personal remarks," Alice said. "It's very rude."

The Hatter opened his eyes very wide on hearing this; but all he *said* was, "Why is a raven like a writing desk?"

"Come, we shall have some fun now!" thought Alice. "I'm glad they've begun asking riddles. I believe I can guess that," she added aloud.

"Do you mean you think you can find out the answer to it?" said the March Hare.

"Exactly so," said Alice.

"Then you should say what you mean," the March Hare went on.

"I do," Alice hastily replied. "At least—at least I mean what I say—that's the same thing, you know."

"You might just as well say," added the March Hare, "that 'I like what I get' is the same thing as 'I get what I like'!"

"You might just as well say," added the Dormouse, which seemed to be talking in its sleep, "that 'I breathe when I sleep' is the same thing as 'I sleep when I breathe'!"

"It *is* the same thing with you," said the Hatter, and here the conversation dropped, and the party sat silent for a minute, while Alice thought over all she could remember about ravens and writing-desks, which wasn't much.

"The Dormouse is asleep again," said the Hatter, and he poured a little hot tea upon its nose.

The Dormouse shook its head impatiently, and said, without opening its eyes, "Of course: just what I was going to remark myself."

"Have you guessed the riddle yet?" the Hatter said, turning to Alice again.

"No, I give it up," Alice replied. "What's the answer?"

"I haven't the slightest idea," said the Hatter.

"Nor I," said the March Hare.

Alice sighed wearily. "I think you might do something better with the time," she said, "than wasting it in asking riddles that have no answers."

"If you knew Time as well as I do," said the Hatter, "you wouldn't talk about wasting *it*. It's *him*."

"I don't know what you mean," said Alice.

"Of course you don't!" the Hatter said, tossing his head contemptuously. "I dare say you never even spoke to Time!"

"Perhaps not," Alice cautiously replied; "but I know I have to beat time when I learn music."

"Ah! That accounts for it," said the Hatter. "He won't stand beating. We quarrelled last March—just before *he* went mad, you know—" (pointing with his teaspoon at the March Hare) "—it was at the great concert given by the Queen of Hearts, and I had to sing:

> *Twinkle, twinkle, little bat!*
> *How I wonder what you're at!*

You know the song, perhaps?"

"I've heard something like it," said Alice.

"It goes on, you know," the Hatter continued, "in this way:

> *Up above the world you fly,*
> *Like a tea-tray in the sky.*
> *Twinkle, twinkle— —*

Here the Dormouse shook itself, and began singing in its sleep *"Twinkle, twinkle, twinkle, twinkle——"* and went on so long that they had to pinch it to make it stop.

"Well, I'd hardly finished the first verse," said the Hatter, "when the Queen bawled out 'He's murdering the time! Off with his head!'"

"How dreadfully savage!" exclaimed Alice.

"And ever since that," the Hatter went on in a mournful tone, "Time won't do a thing I ask! It's always six o'clock now."

"Suppose we change the subject," the March Hare interrupted, yawning. "I'm getting tired of this. I vote the young lady tells us a story."

"I'm afraid I don't know one," said Alice, rather alarmed.

"Then the Dormouse shall!" they both cried. "Wake up, Dormouse!" And they pinched it on both sides at once.

The Dormouse slowly opened its eyes. "I wasn't asleep," it said in a hoarse, feeble voice, "I heard every word you fellows were saying."

"Tell us a story!" said the March Hare.

"Yes, please do!" pleaded Alice.

"And be quick about it," added the Hatter, "or you'll be asleep again before it's done."

"Once upon a time there were three little sisters," the Dormouse began in a great hurry; "and their names were Elsie, Lacie, and Tillie; and they lived at the bottom of a well——"

"What did they live on?" said Alice, who always took a great interest in questions of eating and drinking.

"They lived on treacle," said the Dormouse, after thinking a minute or two.

"They couldn't have done that, you know," Alice gently remarked. "They'd have been ill."

"So they were," said the Dormouse; "*very* ill."

Alice tried a little to fancy to herself what such an extraordinary way of living would be like, but it puzzled her too much; so she went on: "But why did they live at the bottom of a well?"

"Take some more tea," the March Hare said to Alice, very earnestly.

"I've had nothing yet," Alice replied in an offended tone, "so I can't take more."

"You mean you can't take *less*," said the Hatter. "It's very easy to take *more* than nothing."

Alice did not quite know what to say to this, so she helped herself to some tea and bread-and-butter, and then turned to the Dormouse, and repeated her question. "Why did they live at the bottom of a well?"

The Dormouse again took a minute or two to think about it, and then said "It was a treacle-well."

"There's no such thing!" Alice began angrily, but the Hatter and the March Hare went "Sh! Sh!" and the Dormouse sulkily remarked "If you can't be civil, you'd better finish the story for yourself."

"No, please go on!" Alice said very humbly. "I won't interrupt you again. I dare say there may be *one*."

"One, indeed!" said the Dormouse indignantly. However, he consented to go on. "And so these three little sisters—they were learning to draw, you know——"

"What did they draw?" said Alice, quite forgetting her promise.

"Treacle," said the Dormouse.

"I want a clean cup," interrupted the Hatter. "Let's all move one place on."

He moved on as he spoke, and the Dormouse followed him. The March Hare moved into the Dormouse's place, and Alice rather unwillingly took the place of the March Hare. The Hatter was the only one who got any advantage from the change; and Alice was a good deal worse off than before, as the March Hare had just upset the milk-jug into his plate.

Alice did not wish to offend the Dormouse again, so she began very cautiously:

"But I don't understand. Where did they draw the treacle from?"

"You can draw water out of a water-well," said the Hatter, "so I should think you could draw treacle out of a treacle-well,"—eh, stupid?"

"But they were *in* the well," Alice said to the Dormouse, not choosing to notice this last remark.

"Of course they were," said the Dormouse, "well in."

This answer so confused poor Alice, that she let the Dormouse go on for sometime without interrupting.

"They were learning to draw," the Dormouse went on, yawning and rubbing its eyes, for it was getting very sleepy, "and they drew all manner of things—everything that begins with an M—"

"Why with an M?" said Alice.

"Why not?" said the March Hare. Alice was silent.

The Dormouse had closed its eyes by this time, and was going off into a doze; but, on being pinched by the Hatter, it woke up again with a little shriek, and went on: "—that begins with an M, such as mouse-traps, and the moon, and memory, and muchness — you know you say things are 'much of a muchness'—did you ever see a drawing of a muchness!"

"Really, now you ask me," said Alice, very much confused, "I don't think—"

"Then you shouldn't talk," said the Hatter.

This piece of rudeness was more than Alice could bear. She got up in great disgust, and walked off. The Dormouse fell asleep instantly, and neither of the others took the least notice of Alice's going, though she looked back once or twice, half hoping that they would call after her. The last time she saw them, they were trying to put the Dormouse into the teapot.

"At any rate I'll never go *there* again!" said Alice, as she picked her way through the wood. "It's the stupidest tea-party I ever was at in all my life!"

Just as she said this, she noticed that one of the trees had a door leading right into it. "That's very curious!" she thought. "But everything's curious to-day. I think I may as well go in at once." And in she went.

Once more she found herself in the long hall, and close to the little glass table. "Now, I'll manage better this time," she said to herself, and began by taking the little golden key, and unlocking the door that led into the garden. Then she set to work nibbling at the mushroom (she had kept a piece of it in her pocket) till she was about a foot high. Then she walked down the little passage, and *then*—she found herself at last in the beautiful garden, among the bright flower-beds and the cool fountains.

THE QUEEN'S CROQUET GROUND

A large rose-tree stood near the entrance of the garden. The roses growing on it were white, but there were three gardeners at it, busily painting them red. Alice thought this a very curious thing, and she went nearer to watch them, and, just as she came up to them, she heard one of them say "Look out now, Five! Don't go splashing paint over me like that!"

"I couldn't help it," said Five, in a sulky tone. "Seven jogged my elbow."

On which Seven looked up and said "That's right, Five! Always lay the blame on others!"

"*You'd* better not talk!" said Five. "I heard the Queen say only yesterday you deserved to be beheaded."

"Would you tell me, please," said Alice, a little timidly, "why you are painting those roses?"

Five and Seven said nothing, but Two began, in a low voice, "Why, the fact is, you see, Miss, this here ought to have been a *red* rose-tree, and we put a white one in by mistake; and, if the Queen was to find it out, we should all have our heads cut off." At this moment, Five called out "The Queen! The Queen!" and the three gardeners instantly threw themselves flat upon their faces. There was a sound of many footsteps, and Alice looked round, eager to see the Queen.

First came ten soldiers carrying clubs. These were all shaped like the three gardeners, oblong and flat, with their hands and feet at the corners. Next came the ten courtiers ornamented all over with diamonds. They walked two and two, as the soldiers did. After these came the royal children. There were ten of them and the little dears came jumping merrily along, hand in hand, in couples: they were all ornamented with hearts. Next came the guests, mostly Kings and Queens, and among them Alice recognized the White Rabbit talking in a hurried nervous manner, smiling at everything that was said. He went by without noticing her. Then followed the Knave of Hearts, carrying the King's crown on a crimson velvet cushion; and, last of all in this grand procession, came THE KING AND THE QUEEN OF HEARTS.

When the procession came opposite to Alice, they all stopped and looked at her, and the Queen said, severely, "Who is this?" She said it to the Knave of Hearts, who only bowed and smiled in reply.

"Idiot!" said the Queen, tossing her head impatiently; and, turning to Alice, she went on: "What's your name, child?"

"My name is Alice, so please your Majesty," said Alice very politely. But she added, to herself, "Why, they're only a pack of cards, after all. I needn't be afraid of them!"

"And who are *these?*" said the Queen, pointing to the three gardeners who were lying round the rose-tree; for, you see, as they were lying on their faces, and the pattern on their backs was the same as the rest of the pack, she could not tell whether they were gardeners, or soldiers, or courtiers, or three of her own children.

"How should *I* know?" said Alice, surprised at her own courage. "It's no business of *mine*."

The Queen turned crimson with fury, and, after glaring at her for a moment like

"Yes!" shouted Alice.

"Come on, then!" roared the Queen, and Alice joined the procession, wondering what would happen next.

"It's—it's a very fine day!" said a timid voice at her side. She was walking by the White Rabbit, who was peeping anxiously into her face.

a wild beast, began screaming "Off with her head! Off with—"

"Nonsense!" said Alice, very loudly and decidedly, and the Queen was silent.

The King laid his hand upon her arm, and timidly said, "Consider, my dear: she is only a child!"

The Queen turned angrily away from him. "Can you play croquet?" shouted the Queen to Alice.

"Very," said Alice. "Where's the Duchess?"

"Hush! Hush!" said the Rabbit in a low hurried tone. He looked anxiously over his shoulder as he spoke, and then raised himself upon tiptoe, put his mouth close to her ear, and whispered, "She's under sentence of execution."

"Get to your places!" shouted the Queen in a voice of thunder, and people began running about in all directions. However, in a minute or two the game began.

Alice thought she had never seen such a curious croquet-ground in her life. It was all ridges and furrows; the croquet balls were live hedgehogs, and the mallets live flamingoes, and the soldiers had to double themselves up and stand on their hands and feet, to make the arches.

The players all played at once, without waiting for turns, quarreling all the while, and fighting for the hedgehogs; and in a very short time the Queen was stamping about, and shouting "Off with his head!" or "Off with her head!" about once in a minute.

Alice began to feel very uneasy. She was looking about for some way of escape when she noticed a curious appearance in the air. It puzzled her very much at first, but after watching it a minute or two she made it out to be a grin, and she said to herself, "It's the Cheshire-Cat; now I shall have somebody to talk to."

"How are you getting on?" said the Cat,

as soon as there was mouth enough for it to speak with.

"I don't think they play at all fairly," Alice began, in rather a complaining tone, "and they all quarrel so dreadfully one can't hear oneself speak—and they don't seem to have any rules in particular."

"How do you like the Queen?" said the Cat in a low voice.

"Not at all," said Alice.

"Who *are* you talking to?" said the King, coming up to Alice, and looking at the Cat's head with great curiosity.

"It's a friend of mine—a Cheshire-Cat," said Alice: "Allow me to introduce it."

"I don't like the look of it at all," said the King. "However, it may kiss my hand, if it likes."

"I'd rather not," the Cat remarked.

"Don't be impertinent," said the King, "and don't look at me like that!" He got behind Alice as he spoke.

"A cat may look at a King," said Alice. "I've read that in some book, but I don't remember where."

"Well, it must be removed," said the King very decidedly; and he called to the Queen, "My dear! I wish you would have this cat removed!"

The Queen had only one way of settling all difficulties, great or small. "Off with his head!" she said without even looking around. And the rest of the party went back to the game.

The Queen said to Alice, "Have you seen the Mock Turtle yet?"

"No," said Alice. "I don't even know what a Mock Turtle is."

"It's the thing Mock Turtle Soup is made from," said the Queen.

"I never saw one, or heard of one," said Alice.

"Come on, then," said the Queen, "and he shall tell you his history."

They very soon came upon a Gryphon, lying fast asleep in the sun. "Up, lazy thing!" said the Queen, "and take this young lady to see the Mock Turtle. I must go back and see after some executions I have ordered." And she walked off, leaving Alice alone with the Gryphon.

The Gryphon sat up, rubbed its eyes, and watched the Queen till she was out of sight. Then it chuckled, "What fun!"

"What *is* the fun?" said Alice.

"Why, *she,*" said the Gryphon. "It's all her fancy, that. They never executes nobody, you know. Come on!"

"Everybody says 'come on!' here," thought Alice, as she went slowly after the Gryphon. "I never was so ordered about in all my life, never!"

They had not gone far before they saw the Mock Turtle in the distance, sitting sad and lonely on a little ledge of rock, and, as they came nearer, Alice could hear him sighing as if his heart would break. She pitied him deeply. "What is his sorrow?" she asked the Gryphon.

And the Gryphon answered, very nearly in the same words as before, "It's all his fancy, that. He hasn't got no sorrow, you know. Come on!"

They went up to the Mock Turtle. "This here young lady," said the Gryphon, "she wants for to know your history, she do."

"I'll tell it her," said the Mock Turtle in a deep, hollow tone. "Sit down, both of you, and don't speak a word till I've finished."

Alice thought to herself, "I don't see how he can *ever* finish if he doesn't begin." But she waited patiently.

"Once," said the Mock Turtle at last, with a deep sigh, "I was a real Turtle. When we were very little, we went to school in the sea. The master was an old Turtle—we used to call him Tortoise—"

"Why did you call him Tortoise, if he wasn't one?" Alice asked.

"We called him Tortoise because he taught us," said the Mock Turtle angrily.

"Really you are very dull! Yes, we went to school in the sea, though you mayn't believe it. We had the best of educations—in fact, we went to school in the sea, in fact, we went to school every day—"

"*I've* been to a day-school, too," said Alice. "You needn't be so proud as all that."

"With extras?" asked the Mock Turtle, a little anxiously.

"Yes," said Alice. "We learned French and music."

"And washing?" said the Mock Turtle.

"Certainly not!" said Alice indignantly.

"Ah! Then yours wasn't a really good school," said the Mock Turtle in a tone of great relief. "Now, at *ours,* they had, at the end of the bill, 'French, music, *and washing* —extra.' "

"You couldn't have wanted it much," said Alice, "living at the bottom of the sea."

"I couldn't afford to learn it," said the Mock Turtle with a sigh. "I only took the regular course."

"What was that?" inquired Alice.

"Reeling and Writhing, of course, to begin with," the Mock Turtle replied, "and then the different branches of Arithmetic —Ambition, Distraction, Uglification, and Derision."

"I never heard of 'Uglification,' " Alice ventured to say. "What is it?"

The Gryphon lifted both its paws in surprise. "Never heard of uglifying!" it exclaimed. "You know what to beautify is, I suppose?"

"Yes," said Alice doubtfully: " it means —to—make—anything—prettier."

"Well, then," the Gryphon went on, "if you don't know what to uglify is, you *are* a simpleton."

Alice did not feel encouraged to ask any more questions about it: so she turned to the Mock Turtle, and said "What else had you to learn?"

"Well, there was Mystery," the Mock Turtle replied, counting off the subjects on his flappers,—"Mystery, ancient and modern, with Seaography: then Drawling— the Drawling-master was an old conger-eel, that used to come once a week: *he* taught us Drawling, Stretching, and Fainting in Coils."

"And how many hours a day did you do lessons?" said Alice.

"Ten hours the first day," said the Mock Turtle, "nine the next, and so on."

"What a curious plan!" exclaimed Alice.

"That's the reason they're called lessons," the Gryphon remarked, "because they lessen from day to day."

This was quite a new idea to Alice, and she thought it over a little before she made her next remark. "Then the eleventh day must have been a holiday?"

"Of course it was," said the Mock Turtle.

"And how did you manage on the twelfth?" Alice went on eagerly.

"That's enough about lessons," the Gryphon interrupted in a very decided tone.

THE LOBSTER-QUADRILLE

The Mock Turtle sighed deeply, and drew the back of one flapper across his eyes. He looked at Alice and tried to speak, but, for a minute or two, sobs choked his voice. "Same as if he had a bone in his throat," said the Gryphon; and it set to work shaking him and punching him in the back. At last the Mock Turtle recovered his voice, and, with tears running dow~ his cheeks, he went on again:

"You may not have lived much under the sea—" ("I haven't," said Alice)—"and perhaps you were never even introduced to a lobster—" (Alice began to say "I once tasted—" but checked herself hastily, and said "No, never") "—so you can have no idea what a delightful thing a Lobster-Quadrille is!"

"It must be a very pretty dance," said Alice timidly.

"Would you like to see a little of it?" said the Mock Turtle.

"Very much indeed," said Alice.

"Come, let's try the first figure!" said the Mock Turtle to the Gryphon. "We can do it without lobsters, you know. Which shall sing?"

"Oh, *you* sing," said the Gryphon. "I've forgotten the words."

So they began solemnly dancing round and round Alice, every now and then treading on her toes when they passed too close, and waving their fore-paws to mark the time, while the Mock Turtle sang this, very slowly and sadly:

"Will you walk a little faster?" said a
whiting to a snail,
"There's a porpoise close behind us,
and he's treading on my tail.

See how eagerly the lobsters and the
turtles all advance!
They are waiting on the shingle—will
you come and join the dance?

Will you, won't you, will you, won't
you, will you join the dance?
Will you, won't you, will you, won't
you, won't you join the dance?

"Thank you, it's a very interesting dance to watch," said Alice, feeling very glad that it was over at last. "And I do so like that curious song about the whiting!"

"Do you know why it's called a whiting?" asked the Gryphon.

"I never thought about it," said Alice. "Why?"

"It does the boots and shoes," the Gryphon replied very solemnly.

Alice was thoroughly puzzled. "Does the boots and shoes?" she repeated in a wondering tone.

"Why, what are *your* shoes done with?" said the Gryphon. "I mean, what makes them so shiny?"

Alice looked down at them, and considered a little before she gave her answer. "They're done with blacking, I believe."

"Boots and shoes under the sea," the Gryphon went on in a deep voice, "are done with whiting. Now you know."

"And what are they made of?" Alice asked in a tone of great curiosity.

"Soles and eels, of course," the Gryphon replied, rather impatiently. "Any shrimp could have told you that."

"If I'd been the whiting," said Alice, whose thoughts were still running on the song, "I'd have said to the porpoise 'Keep back, please! We don't want *you* with us!'"

"They were obliged to have him with them," the Mock Turtle said. "No wise fish would go anywhere without a porpoise."

"Wouldn't it, really?" said Alice, in a tone of great surprise.

"Of course not," said the Mock Turtle. "Why if a fish came to *me*, and told me he was going a journey, I should say 'With what porpoise?'"

"Don't you mean 'purpose?'" said Alice.

"I mean what I say," the Mock Turtle replied, in an offended tone.

"Shall we try another figure of the Lobster-Quadrille?" the Gryphon asked Alice. "Or would you like the Mock Turtle to sing you another song?"

"Oh, a song, please, if the Mock Turtle would be so kind," Alice replied, so eagerly that the Gryphon said, in a rather offended tone, "Hm! No accounting for tastes! Sing her *Turtle Soup*, will you, old fellow?"

The Mock Turtle sighed deeply, and began, in a voice choked with sobs, to sing:

Beautiful Soup, so rich and green,
Waiting in a hot tureen!
Who for such dainties would not stoop?
Soup of the evening, beautiful Soup!
Beau-ootiful Soo-oop!
Beau-ootiful Soo-oop!
Soo-oop of the e - e - evening,
Beautiful, beautiful Soup!

"Chorus again!" cried the Gryphon, and the Mock Turtle had just begun to repeat it, when a cry of "The trial's beginning!"

was heard in the distance.

"Come on!" cried the Gryphon, and, taking Alice by the hand, it hurried off, without waiting for the end of the song.

"What trial is it?" Alice panted as she ran; but the Gryphon only answered "Come on!" and ran the faster, while more and more faintly came, carried on the breeze that followed them, the melancholy words:

Soo-oop of the e - e - evening,
Beautiful, beautiful Soup!

ALICE'S EVIDENCE

The King and Queen of Hearts were seated on their throne when they arrived, with a great crowd assembled about them —all sorts of little birds and beasts, as well as the whole pack of cards. The Knave was standing before them, in chains, with a soldier on each side to guard him; and near the King was the White Rabbit, with a trumpet in one hand and a scroll of parchment in the other. In the very middle of the court was a table, with a large dish of tarts upon it. It made Alice quite hungry to look

at them—"I wish they'd get the trial done," she thought, "and hand round the refreshments!" But there seemed to be no chance of this; so she began looking at everything about her to pass away the time.

Alice had never been in a court of justice before, but she had read about them in books, and she was quite pleased to find that she knew the name of nearly everything there. "That's the judge," she said to herself, "because of his great wig."

The judge, by the way, was the King; and, as he wore his crown over the wig, he did not look at all comfortable, and it was certainly not becoming.

"And that's the jury-box," thought Alice, "and those twelve creatures" (she was obliged to say "creatures," you see, because some of them were animals and some were birds) "I suppose they are the jurors."

The twelve jurors were all writing very busily on slates. "What are they doing?" Alice whispered to the Gryphon. "They can't have anything to put down yet, before the trial's begun."

"They're putting down their names," the Gryphon whispered in reply, "for fear they should forget them before the end of the trial."

"Stupid things!" Alice began in a loud indignant voice. But she stopped herself hastily, for the White Rabbit cried out "Silence in the court!"

"Call the first witness," said the King.

The first witness was the Hatter. He came in with a teacup in one hand and a piece of bread-and-butter in the other. "I beg pardon, your Majesty," he began, "for bringing these in; but I hadn't quite finished my tea when I was sent for."

"Take off your hat," the King said to the Hatter.

"It isn't mine," said the Hatter.

"*Stolen!*" the King exclaimed, turning to the jury, who instantly made a memorandum of the fact.

"I keep them to sell," the Hatter added as an explanation. "I've none of my own. I'm a hatter."

"Give your evidence," said the King, "and don't be nervous, or I'll have you executed on the spot."

This did not seem to encourage the witness at all. He kept shifting from one foot to the other, and in his confusion he bit a large piece out of his teacup instead of the bread-and-butter.

Just at this moment Alice felt a very curious sensation, which puzzled her a good deal until she made out what it was. She was beginning to grow larger again, and she thought at first she would have to get up and leave the court; but on second thought she decided to remain as long as there was room for her.

"I'm a poor man, your Majesty," the Hatter began again in a trembling voice, "and I hadn't but just begun my tea—not above a week or so—and what with the bread-and-butter getting so thin—"

"You're a *very* poor *speaker*," said the King. "You may stand down."

"I can't go no lower," said the Hatter. "I'm on the floor, as it is."

"Then you may *sit* down," the King replied. "Call the next witness!"

Alice watched the White Rabbit as he fumbled over the list, feeling very curious to see what the next witness would be like, "—for they haven't got much evidence *yet*," she said to herself. Imagine her surprise, when the White Rabbit read out, at the top of his shrill little voice, the name "Alice!"

"Here!" cried Alice, quite forgetting in the flurry of the moment how large she had grown in the last few minutes.

The King called out "Silence!" and read out from his book, "Rule Forty-two. *All persons more than a mile high to leave the court.*"

Everybody looked at Alice.

"*I'm* not a mile high," said Alice.

"You are," said the King.

"Nearly two miles high," added the Queen.

"Well, I shan't go, at any rate," said Alice.

The King shut his note-book hastily. "Consider your verdict," he said to the jury, in a low trembling voice.

"There's more evidence to come yet, please your Majesty," said the White Rabbit, jumping up in a great hurry. "This paper has just been picked up."

"What's in it?" said the Queen.

"I haven't opened it yet," said the White Rabbit. "But it seems to be a letter, written by the prisoner to—to somebody."

"It must have been that," said the King, "unless it was written to nobody, which isn't usual, you know."

"Who is it directed to?" said one of the jurymen.

"It isn't directed at all," said the White Rabbit. "In fact, there's nothing written on the *outside*." He unfolded the paper as he spoke, and added, "It isn't a letter, after all; it's a set of verses."

"Are they in the prisoner's handwriting?" asked another of the jurymen.

"No, they're not," said the White Rabbit.

"Please, your Majesty," said the Knave, "I didn't write it, and they can't prove that I did; there's no name signed at the end."

"If you didn't sign it," said the King, "that only makes the matter worse. You *must* have meant some mischief, or else you'd have signed your name like an honest man."

"That *proves* his guilt, of course," said the

Queen: "so, off with—"

"It doesn't prove anything of the sort!" said Alice. "Why, you don't even know what they're about!"

"Read them," said the King.

The White Rabbit put on his spectacles. "Where shall I begin, please your Majesty?" he asked.

"Begin at the beginning," the King said gravely, "and go on till you come to the end; then stop."

There was dead silence in the court, whilst the White Rabbit read out these verses:

> They told me you had been to her,
> And mentioned me to him:
> She gave me a good character,
> But said I could not swim.
>
> He sent them word I had not gone
> (We know it to be true):
> If she should push the matter on,
> What would become of you?
>
> I gave her one, they gave him two,
> You gave us three or more;
> They all returned from him to you,
> Though they were mine before.
>
> My notion was that you had been
> (Before she had this fit)
> An obstacle that came between
> Him, and ourselves, and it.

"That's the most important piece of evidence we've heard yet," said the King, rubbing his hands; "so now let the jury—"

"If any one of them can explain it," said Alice (she had grown so large in the last rupting him) "I'll give him sixpence. *I* don't believe there's an atom of meaning in it."

"If there's no meaning in it," said the King, "that saves a world of trouble, you know, as we needn't try to find any. And yet I don't know," he went on, spreading out the verses on his knee, and looking at them with one eye; "I seem to see some meaning in them, after all. '—*said I could not swim*—'you can't swim, can you?" he added, turning to the Knave.

The Knave shook his head sadly. "Do I look like it?" he said. (Which he certainly did *not*, being made entirely of cardboard.)

"All right, so far," said the King; and he went on muttering over the verses to himself: " '*We know it to be true*'—that's the jury, of course—'*If she should push the matter on*'— that must be the Queen—'*What would become of you?*'—What, indeed!—'*I gave her one, they gave him two*'—why, that must be what he did with the tarts, you know—"

"But it goes on '*They all returned from him to you*,' " said Alice.

"Why, there they are!" said the King triumphantly, pointing to the tarts on the table. "Nothing can be clearer than *that*. Then again —'*before she had this fit*'— you never had *fits*, my dear, I think?" he said to the Queen.

"Never!" said the Queen, furiously, throwing an inkstand at the Lizard as she spoke.

"Then the words don't *fit* you," said the King, looking round the court with a smile. There was a dead silence.

"It's a pun!" the King added in an angry tone, and everybody laughed. "Let the jury consider their verdict," the King said, for about the twentieth time that day.

"No, no!" said the Queen. "Sentence first —verdict afterwards."

"Stuff and nonsense!?" said Alice. "The idea of having the sentence first!"

"Hold your tongue!" said the Queen, turning purple.

"I won't!" said Alice.

"Off with her head!" the Queen shouted at the top of her voice. Nobody moved.

"Who cares for *you?*" said Alice (she had

grown to her full size by this time). "You're nothing but a pack of cards!"

At this the whole pack rose up into the air, and came flying down upon her. She gave a little scream, half of fright and half of anger, and tried to beat them off, and found herself lying on the bank, with her head in the lap of her sister, who was gently brushing away some dead leaves that had fluttered down from the trees upon her face.

"Wake up, Alice dear!" said her sister. "Why, what a long sleep you've had!"

"Oh, I've had such a curious dream!" said Alice. And she told her sister, as well as she could remember them, all these strange adventures of hers that you have just been reading about. When she had finished, her sister kissed her, and said "It *was* a curious dream, dear, certainly; but now run in to your tea. It's getting late." So Alice got up and ran off, thinking, as well she might, what a wonderful dream it had been.

Through the Looking-Glass

By Lewis Carroll

LOOKING-GLASS HOUSE

ONE thing was certain, that the *white* kitten had had nothing to do with it—it was the black kitten's fault entirely. For the white kitten had been having its face washed by the old cat for the last quarter of an hour (and bearing it pretty well, considering); so you see it *couldn't* have had any hand in the mischief.

The way Dinah washed her children's faces was this: First she held the poor thing down by its ear with one paw, and then with the other paw she rubbed its face all over, the wrong way, beginning at the nose. Just now she was hard at work on the white kitten, which was lying quite still and trying to purr.

But the black kitten had been finished with earlier in the afternoon, and so, while Alice was sitting curled up in a corner of the great armchair, half talking to herself and half asleep, the kitten had been having a grand game of romps with the ball of worsted Alice had been trying to wind up, and had been rolling it up and down till it had all come undone again; and there it was, spread over the hearth-rug, all knots and tangles, with the kitten running after its own tail in the middle.

"Do you know what to-morrow is, Kitty?" Alice began. "You'd have guessed if you'd been up in the window with me—only Dinah was making you tidy, so you couldn't. I was watching the boys getting in sticks for the bonfire—and it needs plenty of sticks, Kitty! Only it got so cold, and it

snowed so, they had to leave off. Never mind, Kitty, we'll go and see the bonfire tomorrow." Here Alice wound two or three turns of the worsted round the kitten's neck, just to see how it would look.

"Do you hear the snow against the window-panes, Kitty? How nice and soft it sounds! Just as if some one was kissing the window all over outside. I wonder if the snow *loves* the trees and fields, that it kisses them so gently? And then it covers them up snug, you know, with a white quilt; and perhaps it says 'Go to sleep, darlings, till the summer comes again.' And when they wake up in the summer, Kitty, they dress themselves

all in green, and dance about—whenever the wind blows—oh, that's very pretty!" cried Alice, dropping the ball of worsted to clap her hands. "And I do so *wish* it was true! I'm sure the woods look sleepy in the autumn when the leaves are getting brown.

"Kitty, can you play chess? Now, don't smile, my dear, I'm asking it seriously. Because, when we were playing just now, you watched just as if you understood it: and when I said 'Check!' you purred! Well, it *was* a nice check, Kitty, and really I might have won, if it hadn't been for that nasty Knight, that came wriggling down among my pieces. Let's pretend that you're the Red Queen, Kitty! Do you know, I think if you sat up and folded your arms, you'd look exactly like her. Now do try, there's a dear!" And Alice took the Red Queen from among the chess pieces on the table, and set it up before the kitten as a model for it to imitate. However, the thing didn't succeed, principally, Alice said, because the kitten wouldn't fold its arms properly. So, to punish it, she held it up to the Looking-glass, that it might see how sulky it was, "—and if you're not good directly," she added, "I'll put you through into Looking-glass House. How would you like *that?*

"Now, if you'll only attend, Kitty," Alice went on, "I'll tell you all my ideas about Looking-glass House. First, there's the room you can see through the glass—that's just the same as our drawing-room, only the things go the other way. I can see all of it when I get upon a chair—all but the bit just behind the fireplace. Oh! I do so wish I could see *that* bit! I want so much to know whether they've a fire in the winter: you never *can* tell, you know, unless our fire smokes, and then smoke comes up in that room too—but that may be only pretense,

just to make it look as if they had a fire. Well then, the books are something like our books, only the words go the wrong way: I know *that,* because I've held up one of our books to the glass, and then they hold up one in the other room.

"How would you like to live in Looking-glass House, Kitty? I wonder if they'd give you milk in there? Perhaps Looking-glass milk isn't good to drink—but oh, Kitty! now we come to the passage. You can just see a little *peep* of the passage in Looking-glass House, if you leave the door of our drawing-room wide open. It's very like our passage as far as you can see, only you know it may be quite different on beyond.

"Oh, Kitty, how nice it would be if we could only get through into Looking-glass House! Let's pretend there's a way of get-

215

ting through into it. Let's pretend the glass
has got all soft like gauze, so that we can
get through. Why, it's turning into a sort
of mist now, I declare! It'll be easy enough
to get through—" She was up on the chimney-piece while she said this, though she
hardly knew how she had got there. And
certainly the glass *was* beginning to melt
away, just like a bright silvery mist.

In another moment Alice was through
the glass, and had jumped lightly down
into the Looking-glass room. The very first
thing she did was to look whether there was
a fire in the fireplace, and she was quite
pleased to find that there was a real one,
blazing away as brightly as the one she had
left behind. "So I shall be as warm here as
I was in the old room," thought Alice.
"Warmer, in fact, because there'll be no
one here to scold me away from the fire.
Oh, what fun it'll be, when they see me
through the glass in here, and can't get at
me!"

Then she began looking about, and
noticed that what could be seen from the
old room was quite common and uninteresting, but that all the rest was as different
as possible. For instance, the pictures on the
wall next the fire seemed to be all alive,
and the very clock on the chimney-piece
(you know you can see only the back of it
in the Looking-glass) had got the face of a
little old man, and grinned at her.

"They don't keep this room so tidy as the
other," Alice thought to herself, as she
noticed several of the chessmen down in the
hearth among the cinders. But in another
moment, with a little "Oh!" of surprise,
she was down on her hands and knees
watching them. The chessmen were walking about, two and two!

"Here are the Red King and the Red

Queen," Alice said (in a whisper, for fear
of frightening them), "and there are the
White King and the White Queen sitting
on the edge of the shovel—and here are two
Castles walking arm in arm. I don't think
they can hear me," she went on, as she put
her head closer down, "and I'm nearly sure
they can't see me. I feel somehow as if I
were getting invisible—"

Here something began squeaking on the
table behind Alice, and made her turn her
head just in time to see one of the White
Pawns roll over and begin kicking.

"It is the voice of my child!" the White
Queen cried out, as she rushed past the
King, so violently that she knocked him
over among the cinders. "My precious Lily!
"My imperial kitten!" and she began
scrambling wildly up the side of the fender.

"Imperial fiddlestick!" said the King,
rubbing his nose, which had been hurt by
the fall. He had a right to be a *little* an-
noyed with the Queen, for he was covered
with ashes from head to foot.

Alice was very anxious to be of use, and
as the poor little Lily was nearly screaming herself into a fit, she hastily picked up
the Queen and set her on the table by the

side of her noisy little daughter.

The Queen gasped, and sat down. The rapid journey through the air had quite taken away her breath, and for a minute or two she could do nothing but hug the little Lily in silence. As soon as she had recovered her breath a little, she called out to the White King, who was sitting sulkily among the ashes, "Mind the volcano!"

"What volcano?" said the King, looking up anxiously into the fire, as if he thought that was the most likely place to find one.

"Blew—me—up," panted the Queen, who was still a little out of breath. "Mind you come up—the regular way—don't get blown up!"

Alice watched the White King as he slowly struggled up from bar to bar, till at last she said "Why, you'll be hours and hours getting to the table, at that rate. I'd far better help you, hadn't I?"

But the King took no notice of the question. It was clear that he could neither hear her nor see her.

So Alice picked him up very gently, and lifted him across more slowly than she had

lifted the Queen, that she mightn't take his breath away. But before she put him on the table, she thought she might as well dust him a little, he was so covered with ashes.

She said afterwards that she had never seen in all her life such a face as the King made, when he found himself held in the air by an invisible hand, and being dusted.

"Oh! *please* don't make such faces, my dear!" she cried out, quite forgetting that the King couldn't hear her. "You make me laugh so that I can hardly hold you! And don't keep your mouth so wide open! All the ashes will get into it. There, now I think you're tidy enough!" she added, as she smoothed his hair, and set him upon the table near the Queen.

The King immediately fell flat on his back, and lay perfectly still. Alice was a little alarmed at what she had done, and went round the room to see if she could find any water to throw over him. However, she could find nothing but a bottle of ink, and when she got back with it she found he had recovered, and he and the Queen were talking together in a frightened whisper.

The King was saying "I assure you, my dear, I turned cold to the very ends of my whiskers!"

To which the Queen replied "You haven't got any whiskers."

"The horror of that moment," the King went on, "I shall never, *never* forget!"

"You will, though," the Queen said, "if you don't make a memorandum of it."

Alice looked on with great interest as the King took an enormous memorandum-book out of his pocket, and began writing. A sudden thought struck her, and she took hold of the end of the pencil, which came some way over his shoulder, and began writing for him.

The poor King looked puzzled and un-happy, and struggled with the pencil for some time without saying anything. But Alice was too strong for him, and at last he panted out "My dear! I really *must* get a thinner pencil. I can't manage this one a bit; it writes all manner of things that I don't intend—"

There was a book lying near Alice on the table, and while she sat watching the White King (for she was still a little anxious about him, and had the ink all ready to throw over him, in case he fainted again), she turned over the leaves, to find some part that she could read, "—for it's all in some language I don't know," she said to herself.

It was like this.

ꞲᴚƆOᴡᴚƎᙠᙠAꞀ

ᴢɘvoɟ ɣʜɟiɭƨ ɘʜɟ bnɒ ,ᵷillิᴎd ƨɒwᴛ'
;ɘdɒw ɘʜɟ ni ɘldmiᵷ bnɒ ɘᴎɣᵷ biᗡ
,ᴢɘvoᵷoᴚod ɘʜɟ ɘᴚɘw ɣᴢmim llA
.ɘdɒᴚᵷɟuo ᴢʜɟɒᴚ ɘmom ɘʜɟ bnA

She puzzled over this for some time, but at last a bright thought struck her. "Why, it's a Looking-glass book, of course! And, if I hold it up to a glass, the words will all go the right way again."

This was the poem that Alice read.

JABBERWOCKY

'Twas brillig, and the slithy toves
Did gyre and gimble in the wabe;
All mimsy were the borogoves,
And the mome raths outgrabe.

"Beware the Jabberwock, my son!
The jaws that bite, the claws that catch!
Beware the Jubjub bird, and shun
The frumious Bandersnatch!"

He took his vorpal sword in hand;
Long time the manxome foe he sought—
So rested he by the Tumtum tree,
And stood awhile in thought.

And, as in uffish thought he stood,
The Jabberwock, with eyes of flame,
Came whiffling through the tulgey wood,
And burbled as it came!

One, two! One, two! And through and through
The vorpal blade went snicker-snack!
He left it dead, and with its head
He went galumphing back.

"And hast thou slain the Jabberwock?
Come to my arms, my beamish boy!
O frabjous day! Callooh! Callay!"
He chortled in his joy.

'Twas brillig, and the slithy toves
Did gyre and gimble in the wabe;
All mimsy were the borogoves,
And the mome raths outgrabe.

"It seems very pretty," she said when she had finished it, "but it's *rather* hard to under-stand!" (You see she didn't like to confess, even to herself, that she couldn't make it out at all.) "Somehow it seems to fill my head with ideas—only I don't exactly know what they are! However, *somebody* killed *something;* that's clear, at any rate—"

"But oh!" thought Alice, suddenly jump-ing up, "if I don't make haste, I shall have to go back through the Looking-glass, be-fore I've seen what the rest of the house is like! Let's have a look at the garden first!"

She was out of the room in a moment, and ran down stairs—or, at least, it wasn't exactly running, but a new invention for getting down stairs quickly and easily, as Alice said to herself. She just kept the tips of her fingers on the hand-rail, and floated gently down without even touching the stairs with her feet. Then she floated on through the hall, and would have gone straight out at the door in the same way, if she hadn't caught hold of the door-post. She was getting a little giddy with so much floating in the air, and was rather glad to find herself walking again in the natural way.

THE GARDEN OF LIVE FLOWERS

"I should see the garden far better," said Alice to herself, "if I could get to the top of that hill: and here's a path that leads straight to it—at least, no, it doesn't do *that*—" (after going a few yards along the path, and turning several sharp corners), "but I suppose it will at last. But how curiously it twists! It's more like a corkscrew than a path! Well, *this* turn goes to the hill, I suppose—no, it doesn't! This goes straight back to the house! Well then, I'll try it the other way."

And so she did: wandering up and down, and trying turn after turn, but always coming back to the house, do what she would. Indeed, once, when she turned a corner rather more quickly than usual, she ran against it before she could stop herself.

"It's no use talking about it," Alice said, looking up at the house and pretending it was arguing with her. "I'm *not* going in again yet. I know I should have to get through the Looking-glass again—back into the old room—and there'd be an end of all my adventures!"

Turning her back upon the house, Alice set out once more down the path, determined to keep straight on till she got to the hill.

She had not been walking a minute before she found herself face to face with the Red Queen, and full in sight of the hill she had been so long aiming at.

"Where do you come from?" said the Red Queen. "And where are you going? Look up, speak nicely, and don't twiddle your fingers all the time."

Alice attended to all these directions, and explained, as well as she could, that she had lost her way.

"I don't know what you mean by *your* way," said the Queen. "All the ways about here belong to *me*—but why did you come out here at all?" she added in a kinder tone. "Curtsey while you're thinking what to say. It saves time."

"I'll try it when I go home," thought Alice to herself, "the next time I'm a little late for dinner."

"It's time for you to answer now," the Queen said, looking at her watch. "Open

219

your mouth a *little* wider when you speak, and always say 'your Majesty.'"

"I only wanted to see what the garden was like, your Majesty—"

"That's right," said the Queen, patting her on the head, which Alice didn't like at all, "though, when you say 'garden'—*I've* seen gardens, compared with which this would be a wilderness."

Alice didn't dare to argue the point, but went on "—and I thought I'd try and find my way to the top of that hill—"

"When you say 'hill,'" the Queen interrupted, "*I* could show you hills, in comparison with which you'd call that a valley."

"No, I shouldn't," said Alice, surprised into contradicting her at last. "A hill *can't* be a valley, you know. That would be nonsense—"

The Red Queen shook her head. "You may call it 'nonsense' if you like," she said, "but *I've* heard nonsense, compared with which that would be as sensible as a dictionary!"

Alice curtseyed again, as she was afraid from the Queen's tone that she was a *little* offended, and they walked on in silence till they got to the top of the little hill.

For some minutes Alice stood without speaking, looking out in all directions over the country—and a most curious country it was. There were a number of tiny little brooks running straight across it from side to side, and the ground between was divided up into squares by a number of little green hedges that reached from brook to brook.

"I declare it's marked out just like a large chess-board!" Alice said at last. "There ought to be some men moving about somewhere—and so there are!" she added in a tone of delight, and her heart began to beat quick with excitement as she went on. "It's

a great huge game of chess that's being played—all over the world—if this *is* the world at all, you know. Oh, what fun it is! How I *wish* I was one of them! I wouldn't mind being a Pawn, if only I might join—though of course I should *like* to be a Queen, best."

She glanced rather shyly at the real Queen as she said this, but her companion only smiled pleasantly, and said "That's easily managed. You can be the White Queen's Pawn, if you like, as Lily's too young to play; and you're in the Second Square to begin with. When you get to the Eighth Square you'll be a Queen—" Just at this moment, somehow or other, they began to run.

Alice never could quite make out, in thinking it over afterwards, how it was that they began. All she remembers is that they were running hand in hand, and the Queen went so fast that it was all she could do to keep up with her. Still the Queen kept crying "Faster! Faster!" But Alice felt she *could not* go faster, though she had no breath left to say so.

The most curious part of the thing was that the trees and the other things around them never changed their places at all; however fast they went, they never seemed to pass anything. "I wonder if all the things move along with us?" thought poor puzzled Alice.

And the Queen seemed to guess her thoughts, for she cried "Faster! Don't try to talk!"

Not that Alice had any idea of doing *that*. She felt as if she would never be able to talk again, she was getting so much out of breath. But still the Queen cried "Faster! Faster!", and dragged her along.

"Are we nearly there?" Alice managed .to pant out at last.

"Nearly there!" the Queen repeated. "Why, we passed it ten minutes ago! Faster!" And they ran on for a time in silence, with the wind whistling in Alice's ears, and almost blowing her hair off.

"Now! Now!" cried the Queen. "Faster! Faster!" And they went so fast that at last they seemed to skim through the air, hardly touching the ground with their feet, till suddenly, just as Alice was getting quite exhausted, they stopped, and she found herself sitting on the ground, breathless and giddy.

The Queen propped her up against a tree, and said kindly, "You may rest a little, now."

Alice looked around her in surprise. "Why, I do believe we've been under this tree the whole time! Everything's just as it was!"

"Of course it is," said the Queen. "What would you have it?"

"Well, in *our* country," said Alice, still panting a little, "you'd generally get to somewhere else—if you ran very fast for a long time as we've been doing."

"A slow sort of country!" said the Queen. "Now, *here*, you see, it takes all the running *you* can do to keep in the same place. If you want to get somewhere else, you must run at least twice as fast as that!"

"I'd rather not try, please!" said Alice. "I'm quite content to stay here—only I *am* so hot and thirsty!"

"I know what *you'd* like!" the Queen said good-naturedly, taking a little box out of her pocket. "Have a biscuit?"

Alice thought it would not be civil to say "No," though it wasn't at all what she wanted. So she took it, and ate it as well as she could. It was *very* dry; she thought she had never been so nearly choked in all her life.

"Have another biscuit?" the Queen said.

"No, thank you," said Alice. "One's *quite* enough!"

"Thirst quenched, I hope?" said the Queen.

Alice did not know what to say to this, but luckily the Queen did not wait for an answer.

How it happened, Alice never knew, but suddenly the Queen was gone. Where she had vanished to there was no way of guessing but Alice began to remember that it would soon be time for her to move on.

She went on a long way, but, wherever the road divided, there were two fingerposts pointing the same way, one marked

221

TO TWEEDLEDUM'S HOUSE, and the other TO THE HOUSE OF TWEEDLE-DEE.

"I do believe," said Alice at last, "that they live in the *same* house! I wonder I never thought of that before—But I can't stay there long. I'll just call and say 'How d'ye do?'" So she wandered on, talking to herself as she went, till, on turning a sharp corner, she suddenly came upon two fat little men.

TWEEDLEDUM AND TWEEDLEDEE

They were standing under a tree, each with an arm around the other's neck, and Alice knew which was which in a moment, because one of them had DUM embroidered on his collar, and the other DEE. "I suppose they've each got TWEEDLE round at the back of the collar," she said to herself.

They stood so still that she quite forgot they were alive, and she was just going round to see if the word TWEEDLE was written at the back of each collar, when she was startled by a voice coming from the one marked DUM.

"If you think we're wax-works," he said, "you ought to pay, you know. Wax-works weren't made to be looked at for nothing. Nohow!"

"Contrariwise," added the one marked DEE, "if you think we're alive, you ought to speak."

"I'm sure I'm very sorry," was all Alice could say, for the words of the old song kept ringing through her head like the ticking of a clock, and she could hardly help saying them out loud:

> *"Tweedledum and Tweedledee*
>   *Agreed to have a battle,*
> *For Tweedledum said Tweedledee*
>   *Had spoiled his nice new rattle.*
>
> *Just then flew down a monstrous crow,*
>   *As black as a tar-barrel,*
> *Which frightened both the heroes so,*
>   *They quite forgot their quarrel."*

"I know what you're thinking about," said Tweedledum. "But it isn't so, nohow."

"Contrariwise," continued Tweedledee. "If it was so, it might be; and if it were so, it would be; but as it isn't, it ain't. That's logic."

"I was thinking," Alice said very politely, "which is the best way out of this place. It's getting so dark. Would you tell me, please?"

But the fat little men only looked at each other and grinned.

"You've begun wrong!" cried Tweedledum. "The first thing in a visit is to say 'How d'ye do?' and shake hands!" And here the two brothers gave each other a hug, and then they held out the two hands that were free, to shake hands with her.

Alice did not like shaking hands with either of them first, for fear of hurting the other one's feelings; so, as the best way out of the difficulty, she took hold of both hands at once. The next moment they were dancing round in a ring.

The dancers were fat, and very soon out of breath. "Four times round is enough for one dance," Tweedledum panted out, and they left off dancing as suddenly as they had begun.

Then they let go of Alice's hands, and stood looking at her for a minute. There was a rather awkward pause, as Alice didn't know how to begin a conversation with people she had just been dancing with. "It would never do to say 'How d'ye do?' *now,*" she said to herself. "We seem to have got beyond that!"

"I hope you're not much tired?" she said at last.

"Nohow. And thank you *very* much for asking," said Tweedledum.

"So *much* obliged!" added Tweedledee. "You like poetry?"

"Ye-es, pretty well—*some* poetry," Alice said doubtfully. "Would you tell me which road leads out of this place?"

"What shall I repeat to her?" said Tweedledee, looking round at Tweedledum with great solemn eyes, and not noticing Alice's question.

" 'The Walrus and the Carpenter' is the longest," Tweedledum replied, giving his brother an affectionate hug.

Tweedledee began instantly:

"The sun was shining—"

Here Alice ventured to interrupt him. "If it's *very* long," she said, as politely as she could, "would you please tell me first which road—"

Tweedledee smiled gently, and began again:

"The sun was shining on the sea,
Shining with all his might:
He did his very best to make
The billows smooth and bright—
And this was odd, because it was
The middle of the night.

The moon was shining sulkily,
Because she thought the sun
Had got no business to be there
After the day was done—
'It's very rude of him,' she said,
'To come and spoil the fun!'

The sea was wet as wet could be,
The sands were dry as dry.
You could not see a cloud, because
No cloud was in the sky:
No birds were flying overhead—
There were no birds to fly.

The Walrus and the Carpenter
Were walking close at hand;
They wept like anything to see
Such quantities of sand:
'If this were only cleared away,'
They said, 'it would be grand!'

If seven maids with seven mops
Swept it for half a year,
Do you suppose,' the Walrus said,
'That they could get it clear?'
'I doubt it,' said the Carpenter,
And shed a bitter tear.

'O Oysters, come and walk with us!'
    The Walrus did beseech.
'A pleasant walk, a pleasant talk,
    Along the briny beach:
We cannot do with more than four,
    To give a hand to each.'

The eldest Oyster looked at him,
    But never a word he said:
The eldest Oyster winked his eye,
    And shook his heavy head—
Meaning to say he did not choose
    To leave the oyster-bed.

But four young Oysters hurried up,
    All eager for the treat:
Their coats were brushed, their faces washed,
    Their shoes were clean and neat—
And this was odd, because, you know,
    They hadn't any feet.

Four other Oysters followed them,
    And yet another four;
And thick and fast they came at last,
    And more, and more, and more—
All hopping through the frothy waves,
    And scrambling to the shore.

The Walrus and the Carpenter
    Walked on a mile or so,
And then they rested on a rock
    Conveniently low:
And all the little Oysters stood
    And waited in a row.

'The time has come,' the Walrus said,
    'To talk of many things:
Of shoes—and ships—and sealing-wax—
    Of cabbages—and kings—
And why the sea is boiling hot—
    And whether pigs have wings.'

'But wait a bit,' the Oysters cried,
    'Before we have our chat;
For some of us are out of breath,
    And all of us are fat!'
'No hurry!' said the Carpenter.
    They thanked him much for that.

'A loaf of bread,' the Walrus said,
    'Is what we chiefly need:
Pepper and vinegar besides
    Are very good indeed—
Now, if you're ready, Oysters dear,
    We can begin to feed.'

'But not on us!' the Oysters cried,
    Turning a little blue.
'After such kindness, that would be
    A dismal thing to do!'
'The night is fine,' the Walrus said.
    'Do you admire the view?

'It was so kind of you to come!
    And you are very nice!'
The Carpenter said nothing but
    'Cut us another slice.
I wish you were not quite so deaf—
    I've had to ask you twice!'

'It seems a shame,' the Walrus said.
 'To play them such a trick.
After we've brought them out so far,
 And made them trot so quick!'
The Carpenter said nothing but
 'The butter's spread too thick!'

'I weep for you,' the Walrus said:
 'I deeply sympathize.'
With sobs and tears he sorted out
 Those of the largest size,
Holding his pocket-handkerchief
 Before his streaming eyes.

'O Oysters,' said the Carpenter,
 'You've had a pleasant run!
Shall we be trotting home again?'
 But answer came there none—
And this was scarcely odd, because
 They'd eaten every one."

"I like the Walrus best," said Alice, "because he was a *little* sorry for the poor oysters."

"He ate more than the Carpenter, though," said Tweedledee. "You see he held his handkerchief in front, so that the Carpenter couldn't count how many he took. Contrariwise."

"That was mean!" Alice said indignantly. "Then I like the Carpenter best—if he didn't eat so many as the Walrus."

"But he ate as many as he could get," said Tweedledum.

This was a puzzler. After a pause, Alice began, "Well! They were *both* very unpleasant characters—" Here she checked herself in some alarm, at hearing something that sounded to her like the puffing of a steam-engine in the wood near them, though she feared it was more likely to be a wild beast. "Are there any lions or tigers about here?" she asked timidly.

"It's only the Red King snoring," said Tweedledee.

"Come and look at him!" the brothers cried, and they each took one of Alice's hands, and led her up to where the King was sleeping.

"Isn't he a *lovely* sight?" said Tweedledum.

Alice couldn't say honestly that he was. He had a tall red night-cap on, with a tassel, and he was lying crumpled up into a sort of untidy heap, and snoring loud—"fit to snore his head off!" as Tweedledum remarked

"I'm afraid he'll catch cold lying on the damp grass," said Alice, who was a very thoughtful little girl.

"He's dreaming now," said Tweedledee. "And what do you think he's dreaming about?"

Alice said, "Nobody can guess that."

"Why, about *you!*" Tweedledee exclaimed, clapping his hands. "And if he left off dreaming about you, where do you suppose you'd be?"

"Where I am now, of course," said Alice.

"Not you!" Tweedledee retorted contemptuously. "You'd be nowhere. Why, you're only a sort of thing in his dream!"

"If that there King was to wake," added Tweedledum, "you'd go out—bang!—just like a candle!"

"I shouldn't!" Alice exclaimed indignantly. "Besides, if *I'm* only a sort of thing in his dream, what are *you*, I should like to know?"

"Ditto," said Tweedledum.

"Ditto, ditto!" cried Tweedledee.

He shouted this so loud that Alice couldn't help saying "Hush! You'll be waking him, I'm afraid, if you make so much noise."

"Well, it's no use *your* talking about waking him," said Tweedledum, "when you're only one of the things in his dream. You know very well you're not real."

"I *am* real!" said Alice, and began to cry.

"You won't make yourself a bit realer by crying," Tweedledee remarked. "There's nothing to cry about."

"If I wasn't real," Alice said, half-laughing through her tears, because it all seemed so ridiculous, "I shouldn't be able to cry."

"I hope you don't suppose those are *real* tears?" Tweedledum interrupted in a tone of great contempt.

"I know they're talking nonsense," Alice thought to herself, "and it's foolish to cry about it." So she brushed away her tears, and went on, as cheerfully as she could, "At any rate I'd better be getting on, for really

it's becoming very dark. Do you think it's going to rain?"

Tweedledum spread a large umbrella over himself and his brother, and looked up into it. "No, I don't think it is," he said: "at least—not under *here*. Nohow."

"But it may rain *outside?*"

"It may—if it chooses," said Tweedledee. "We've no objection. Contrariwise."

"Selfish things!" thought Alice, and she was just going to say "Good-night" and leave them, when Tweedledum sprang out from under the umbrella, and seized her by the wrist.

"Do you see *that?*" he said, in a voice choking with passion. His eyes grew large and yellow all in a moment, as he pointed with a trembling finger at a small white thing lying under the tree.

"It's only an old rattle," Alice said, after a careful examination of the little white thing. "Not a rattle-*snake,* you know," she added hastily, thinking that he was frightened.

"I knew it was!" cried Tweedledum, beginning to stamp about wildly and tear his hair. "It's spoilt, of course!" Here he looked at Tweedledee, who immediately sat down on the ground, and tried to hide himself under the umbrella.

Alice laid her hand upon his arm, and said, in a soothing tone, "You needn't be so angry about an old rattle."

"But it *isn't* old!" Tweedledum cried, in a greater fury than ever. "It's *new*, I tell you—I bought it yesterday—my nice NEW RATTLE!" and his voice rose to a perfect scream.

All this time Tweedledee, was trying his best to fold up the umbrella, with himself in it, and that was such an extraordinary thing to do that it quite took off Alice's attention from the angry brother. But he couldn't quite succeed, and it ended in his rolling over, bundled up in the umbrella, with only his head out; and there he lay, opening and shutting his mouth and his large eyes—"looking more like a fish than anything else," Alice thought.

"Of course you agree to have a battle?" Tweedledum said in a calmer tone.

"I suppose so," the other sulkily replied, as he crawled out of the umbrella. "Only *she* must help us to dress up, you know."

So the two brothers went off hand-in-hand into the wood, and returned in a minute with their arms full of things—such as bolsters, blankets, hearth-rugs, table-cloths, dish-covers, and coal-scuttles. "I hope you're good at pinning and tying strings?" Tweedledum remarked. "Every one of these things has got to go on, some-how or other."

Alice said afterwards she had never seen such a fuss made about anything in all her life— the way those two bustled about— and the quantity of things they put on—and the trouble they gave her in tying strings and fastening buttons—"Really they'll be more like bundles of old clothes than any-thing else, by the time they're ready!" she said to herself as she arranged a bolster

round the neck of Tweedledee, "to keep his head from being cut off," as he said.

"You know," he added gravely, "it's one of the most serious things that can possibly happen to one in a battle—to get one's head cut off."

Alice laughed loud; but she managed to turn it into a cough, for fear of hurting his feelings.

"Do I look very pale?" said Tweedledum, coming up to have his helmet tied on. (He *called* it a helmet, though it certainly looked much more like a saucepan.)

"Well—yes—a *little*," Alice replied gently.

"I'm very brave, generally," he went on in a low voice. "Only today I happen to have a headache."

"And *I've* got a toothache!" said Tweedle-dee, who had overheard the remark. "I'm far worse than you!"

"Then you'd better not fight to-day," said Alice, thinking it a good opportunity to make peace.

"We *must* have a bit of a fight, but I don't care about going on long," said Tweedle-dum. "What's the time now?"

Tweedledee looked at his watch, and said "Half-past four."

"Let's fight till six, and then have dinner," said Tweedledum.

"Very well," the other said, rather sadly. "And *she* can watch us—only you'd better not come *very* close," he added. "I generally hit everything I can see—when I get really excited."

"And *I* hit everything within reach," cried Tweedledum, "whether I can see it or not!"

Alice laughed. "You must hit the *trees* pretty often, I should think," she said.

Tweedledum looked round him with a satisfied smile. "I don't suppose," he said, "there'll be a tree left standing for ever so far around, by the time we've finished!"

"And all about a rattle!" said Alice, still hoping to make them a *little* ashamed of fighting for such a trifle.

"I shouldn't have minded it so much," said Tweedledum, "if it hadn't been a new one."

"There's only one sword, you know," Tweedledum said to his brother; "but *you* can have the umbrella—it's quite as sharp. Only we must begin quick. It's getting as dark as it can."

"And darker," said Tweedledee.

It was getting dark so suddenly that Alice thought there must be a thunderstorm coming on. "What a thick black cloud that is!" she said. "And how fast it comes! Why, I do believe it's got wings!"

"It's the crow!" Tweedledum cried out in a shrill voice of alarm; and the two brothers took to their heels and were out of sight in a moment.

Alice ran a little way into the wood, and stopped under a large tree. "It can never get at me *here*," she thought. "It's far too large to squeeze itself in among the trees. But I wish it wouldn't flap its wings so—it makes quite a hurricane in the wood—here's somebody's shawl being blown away!"

WOOL AND WATER

She caught the shawl as she spoke, and looked about for the owner. In another moment the White Queen came running wildly through the wood, with both arms stretched out wide, as if she were flying, and Alice very civilly went to meet her with the shawl.

"I'm very glad I happened to be in the way," Alice said, as she helped her to put on her shawl again.

The White Queen only looked at her in a helpless frightened sort of way, and kept repeating something in a whisper to herself that sounded like "Bread-and-butter, bread-and-butter," and Alice felt that if there was to be any conversation at all, she must manage it herself. So she began rather timidly, "Am I addressing the White Queen?"

"Well, yes, if you call that a-dressing," the Queen said. "It isn't *my* notion of the thing, at all."

Alice thought it would never do to have an argument at the very beginning of their conversation, so she smiled and said "If your Majesty will only tell me the right way to begin, I'll do it as well as I can."

"But I don't want it done at all!" groaned the poor Queen. "I've been a-dressing myself for the last two hours."

It would have been all the better, as it seemed to Alice, if she had got someone else to dress her, she was so dreadfully untidy. "Every single thing's crooked," Alice thought to herself, "and she's all over pins!" "May I put your shawl straight for you?" she added aloud.

"I don't know what's the matter with it!" said the Queen in a melancholy voice. "It's

the Queen said. "The rule is, jam tomorrow and jam yesterday—but never jam *today.*"

"It *must* come sometimes to 'jam today,'" Alice objected.

"No, it can't," said the Queen. "It's jam every *other* day. Today isn't any *other* day you know."

"I don't understand you," said Alice. "It's dreadfully confusing!"

"That's the effect of living backwards," the Queen said kindly. "It always makes one a little giddy at first—"

"Living backwards!" Alice repeated in great astonishment. "I never heard of such a thing!"

"There's one great advantage in it: one's memory works both ways."

"I'm sure *mine* works only one way," Alice remarked. "I can't remember things before they happen."

"It's a poor sort of memory that only works backwards," the Queen remarked.

"What sort of things do *you* remember best?" Alice ventured to ask.

"Oh, things that happened the week after next," the Queen replied in a careless tone.

"For instance, now," she went on, sticking a large piece of plaster on her finger as she spoke, "there's the King's Messenger. He's in prison now, being punished; and

out of temper, I think. I've pinned it here, and I've pinned it there, but there's no pleasing it!"

"It *can't* go straight, you know, if you pin it all on one side," Alice said, as she gently put it right for her. "And, dear me, what a state your hair is in!"

"The brush has got entangled in it!" the Queen said with a sigh. "And I lost the comb yesterday."

Alice carefully released the brush, and did her best to get the hair into order. "Come, you look rather better now!" she said, after altering most of the pins. "But really you should have a lady's-maid!"

"I'm sure I'll take *you* with pleasure!" the Queen said. "Twopence a week, and jam every other day."

Alice couldn't help laughing, as she said, "I don't want you to hire *me*—and I don't care for jam."

"It's very good jam," said the Queen.

"Well, I don't want any *today,* at any rate."

"You couldn't have it if you *did* want it,"

229

the trial doesn't even begin till next Wednesday; and of course the crime comes last of all."

"Suppose he never commits the crime?" said Alice.

"That would be all the better, wouldn't it?" the Queen said, as she bound the plaster round her finger with a bit of ribbon.

Alice felt there was no denying *that.* "Of course it would be all the better," she said. "But his being punished wouldn't be all the better."

"You're wrong *there,* at any rate," said the Queen. "Were *you* ever punished?"

"Only for faults," said Alice.

"And you were all the better for it, I know!" the Queen said triumphantly.

"Yes, but then I *had* done the things I was punished for," said Alice. "That makes all the difference."

"But if you *hadn't* done them," the Queen said, "that would have been better still: better and better and better!" Her voice went higher with each "better," till it got quite to a squeak at last.

Alice was just beginning to say "There's a mistake somewhere," when the Queen began screaming so loud that she had to leave the sentence unfinished. "Oh, oh, oh!" shouted the Queen, shaking her hand about as if she wanted to shake it off. "My finger's bleeding! Oh, oh, oh, oh!"

Her screams were so exactly like the whistle of a steam-engine, that Alice had to hold both her hands over her ears.

"What *is* the matter?" she said, as soon as there was a chance of making herself heard. "Have you pricked your finger?"

"I haven't pricked it *yet,*" the Queen said, "but I soon shall—oh, oh, oh!"

"When do you expect to do it?" Alice asked, feeling very much inclined to laugh.

"When I fasten my shawl again," the poor Queen groaned out, "the brooch will come undone directly. Oh, oh!" As she said the words the brooch flew open, and the Queen clutched wildly at it and tried to clasp it again.

"Take care!" cried Alice. "You're holding it all crooked!" She caught at the brooch; but it was too late: the pin had slipped, and the Queen had pricked her finger.

"That accounts for the bleeding, you see," she said to Alice with a smile. "Now you understand the way things happen here."

"But why don't you scream *now?*" Alice asked, holding her hands ready to put over her ears again.

"Why, I've done all the screaming already," said the Queen. "What would be the good of having it all over again?"

By this time it was getting light. "The crow must have flown away, I think," said Alice. "I'm so glad it's gone. I thought it was the night coming on."

"I wish *I* could manage to be glad!" the Queen said. "Only I never can remember the rule. You must be very happy, living in this wood, and being glad whenever you like!"

"Only it is so *very* lonely here!" Alice said in a melancholy voice; and, at the thought of her loneliness, two large tears came rolling down her cheeks.

"Oh, don't go on like that!" cried the poor Queen, wringing her hands in despair. "Consider what a great girl you are. Consider what a long way you've come today. Consider what o'clock it is. Consider anything, only don't cry!"

Alice could not help laughing at this, even in the midst of her tears. "Can *you* keep from crying by considering things?" she asked.

"That's the way it's done," the Queen said with great decision. "Nobody can do two things at once, you know. Let's consider your age to begin with—how old are you?"

"I'm seven and a half, exactly."

"You needn't say 'exactually,'" the Queen remarked. "I can believe it without that. Now I'll give *you* something to believe. I'm just one hundred and one, five months and a day."

"I can't believe *that!*" said Alice.

"Can't you?" the Queen said in a pitying tone. "Try again."

Alice laughed. "There's no use trying," she said. "One *can't* believe impossible things."

"I daresay you haven't had much practice," said the Queen. "When I was your age, I always did it for half-an-hour a day. Why, sometimes I've believed as many as six impossible things before breakfast. There goes the shawl again!"

The brooch had come undone as she spoke, and a sudden guest of wind blew the Queen's shawl across a little brook. The Queen spread out her arms again, and went flying after it, and this time she succeeded in catching it for herself. "I've got it!" she cried in a triumphant tone. "Now you shall see me pin it on again, all by myself!"

"Then I hope your finger is better now?" Alice said very politely, as she crossed the little brook after the Queen.

"Oh, much better!" cried the Queen, her voice rising into a squeak as she went on. "Much be-etter! Be-etter! Be-e-e-etter! Be-e-ehh!" The last word ended in a long bleat, so like a sheep that Alice quite started.

She looked at the Queen, who seemed to have suddenly wrapped herself up in wool. Alice rubbed her eyes, and looked again. She couldn't make out what had happened at all. Was she in a shop? And was that really a *sheep* that was sitting on the other side of the counter? Rub as she would, she could make nothing more of it. She was in a little dark shop, leaning with her elbows on the counter, and opposite to her was an old Sheep, sitting in an arm-chair, knitting, and every now and then leaving off to look at her through a great pair of spectacles.

"What is it you want to buy?" the Sheep said at last, looking up for a moment from her knitting.

"I don't *quite* know yet," Alice said very gently. "I should like to look all round me first, if I might."

"You may look in front of you, and on both sides, if you like," said the Sheep; "but you can't look *all* round you—unless you've got eyes at the back of your head."

But these, as it happened, Alice had *not* got; so she contented herself with turning around, looking at the shelves as she came to them.

The shop seemed full of all manner of curious things—but the odd part of it all was that whenever she looked hard at any shelf to make out exactly what it had on it, that particular shelf was always quite empty, though the others were crowded as full as they could hold.

"Things flow about so here!" she said at last in a plaintive tone, after she had spent a minute or so in vainly pursuing a large bright thing that was always in the shelf next above the one she was looking at. "I'll follow it up to the very top shelf of all," she said to herself.

But the 'thing' went right through the ceiling, as if it were quite used to it.

"Are you a child or a teetotum?" the Sheep said, as she took up another pair of needles. "You'll make me giddy soon, if you go on turning round like that." She was now working with fourteen pairs at once, and Alice couldn't help looking at her in great astonishment.

"How *can* she knit with so many?" the puzzled child thought to herself. "She gets more and more like a porcupine every minute!"

"Can you row?" the Sheep asked, handing her a pair of knitting-needles as she spoke.

"Yes, a little—but not on land—and not with needles—" Alice was beginning to say, when suddenly the needles turned into oars in her hands, and she found they were in a little boat, gliding along between banks.

"Feather!" cried the Sheep, as she took up another pair of needles.

This didn't sound like a remark that needed any answer; so Alice said nothing, but pulled away.

"Feather! Feather!" the Sheep cried again, taking more needles. "You'll be catching a crab directly."

"A dear little crab!" thought Alice. "I should like that."

"Didn't you hear me say 'Feather'?" the Sheep cried angrily, taking up quite a bunch of needles.

"Indeed I did," said Alice. "Please, where *are* the crabs?"

"In the water, of course!" said the Sheep, sticking some of the needles into her hair, as her hands were full. "Feather, I say!"

"*Why* do you say 'Feather' so often?" Alice asked at last, rather vexed. "I'm not a bird!"

"You are," said the Sheep: "you're a little goose."

This offended Alice a little, so there was no more conversation for a minute or two, while the boat glided gently on, sometimes among beds of weeds (which made the oars stick fast in the water) and sometimes under trees, but always with the same tall river-banks frowning over their heads.

"Oh, please! There are some scented rushes!" Alice cried in a sudden transport of delight. "There really are—and *such* beauties!"

"You needn't say 'please' to *me* about 'em," the Sheep said, without looking up from her knitting. "I didn't put 'em there, and I'm not going to take 'em away."

"No, but I meant—please, may we wait and pick some?" Alice pleaded. "If you don't mind stopping the boat for a minute."

"How am *I* to stop it?" said the Sheep. "If you leave off rowing, it'll stop of itself."

So the boat was left to drift down the stream as it would, till it glided gently in among the waving rushes.

"Oh, *what* a lovely one!" cried Alice.

"Only I couldn't quite reach it." And it certainly *did* seem a little provoking that, though she managed to pick plenty of beautiful rushes as the boat glided by, there was always a more lovely one that she couldn't reach.

They hadn't gone much farther before the blade of one of the oars got fast in the water and *wouldn't* come out again, and the handle of it caught her under the chin, and, in spite of a series of little shrieks of 'Oh, oh, oh!' from poor Alice, it swept her straight off the seat, and down among the heap of rushes.

But she was soon up again. The Sheep went on with her knitting all the while, just as if nothing had happened. "That was a nice crab you caught!" she remarked, as Alice got back into her place, very much relieved to find herself still in the boat.

"Was it? I didn't see it," said Alice, peeping cautiously over the side of the boat into the dark water. "I wish it hadn't let go—I should so like a little crab to take home with me!"

But the Sheep only laughed scornfully, and went on with her knitting.

"Are there many crabs here?" said Alice.

"Crabs, and all sorts of things," said the Sheep. "Plenty of choice, only make up your mind. Now, what *do* you want to buy?"

"To buy!" Alice echoed in a tone that was half astonished and half frightened—for the oars, and the boat, and the river, had vanished all in a moment, and she was back again in the little dark shop.

"I should like to buy an egg, please," she said timidly. "How do you sell them?"

"Fivepence farthing for one—twopence for two," the Sheep replied.

"Then two are cheaper than one?" Alice said in a surprised tone, taking out her purse.

"Only you *must* eat them both, if you buy two," said the Sheep.

"Then I'll have *one*, please," said Alice, as she put the money down on the counter. For she thought to herself, "They mightn't be at all nice, you know."

The Sheep took the money, and put it away in a box. Then she said "I never put things into people's hands—that would never do." And so saying, she went off to the other end of the shop, and set the egg upright on a shelf.

"I wonder *why* it wouldn't do?" thought Alice, as she groped her way among the tables and chairs, for the shop was very dark towards the end. "The egg seems to get farther away the more I walk towards it. Let me see, is this a chair? Why, it's got branches, I declare! How very odd to find trees growing here! And actually here's a little brook! Well, this is the very queerest shop I ever saw!"

So she went on, wondering more and more at every step, as everything turned into a tree the moment she came up to it, and she quite expected the egg to do the same.

HUMPTY DUMPTY

However, the egg only got larger and larger, and more and more human. When Alice had come within a few yards of it, she saw that it had eyes and a nose and mouth; and, when she had come close to it, she saw clearly that it was HUMPTY DUMPTY himself.

Humpty Dumpty was sitting, with his legs crossed like a Turk, on the top of a high wall—such a narrow one that Alice quite wondered how he could keep his balance—and, as his eyes were steadily fixed in the opposite direction, and he didn't take the least notice of her, she thought he must be a stuffed figure, after all.

"And how exactly like an egg he is!" she said aloud, standing with her hands ready to catch him, for she was every moment expecting him to fall.

"It's *very* provoking," Humpty Dumpty said after a long silence, looking away from Alice as he spoke, "to be called an egg."

"I said you *looked* like an egg, Sir," Alice gently explained. "And some eggs are very pretty, you know," she added, hoping to turn her remark into a sort of compliment.

"Some people," said Humpty Dumpty, looking away from her as usual, "have no more sense than a baby!"

Alice didn't know what to say to this. It wasn't at all like conversation, she thought, as he never said anything to *her*. In fact, his last remark was evidently addressed to a tree—so she stood and softly repeated to herself:

"Humpty Dumpty sat on a wall:
Humpty Dumpty had a great fall.
All the King's horses and all the King's men
Couldn't put Humpty Dumpty in his place again."

"That last line is much too long for the poetry," she added, almost out loud, forgetting that Humpty Dumpty would hear her.

"Don't stand chattering to yourself like that," Humpty Dumpty said, looking at her for the first time, "but tell me your name and your business."

"My *name* is Alice, but——"

"It's a stupid name enough!" Humpty Dumpty interrupted impatiently. "What does it mean?"

"*Must* a name mean something?" Alice asked doubtfully.

"Of course it must," Humpty Dumpty said with a short laugh. "My name means the shape I am—and a good handsome shape it is, too. With a name like yours, you might be any shape, almost."

"Why do you sit out here all alone?" said Alice, not wishing to begin an argument.

"Why, because there's nobody with me!" cried Humpty Dumpty. "Did you think I didn't know the answer to *that?* Ask another."

"Don't you think you'd be safer down on the ground?" Alice went on, not with any idea of making another riddle, but simply in her good-natured anxiety for the queer creature. "That wall is so *very* narrow!"

"What tremendously easy riddles you ask!" Humpty Dumpty growled. "Of course I don't think so! Why, if ever I *did* fall off—which there's no chance of—but *if* I did—" Here he pursed up his lips, and looked so solemn and grand that Alice could hardly help laughing. "*If* I *did* fall," he went on, "*the King has promised me*—ah, you may turn pale, if you like! You didn't think I was going to say that, did you? *The King has promised me—with his very own mouth*—to—to—"

"To send all his horses and all his men," Alice interrupted, rather unwisely.

"Now I declare that's too bad!" Humpty Dumpty cried, breaking into a sudden passion. "You've been listening at doors—and behind trees—and down chimneys—or you couldn't have known it!"

"I haven't, indeed!" Alice said very gently. "It's in a book."

"Ah, well! They may write such things in a *book*," Humpty Dumpty said in a calmer tone. "But to show you I'm not proud,

234

just as if it was a game!" thought Alice.) "So here's a question for you. How old did you say you were?"

Alice made a short calculation, and said "Seven years and six months."

"Wrong!" Humpty Dumpty exclaimed triumphantly. "You never said a word like it!"

"I thought you meant 'How old *are* you?'" Alice explained.

"If I'd meant that, I'd have said it," said Humpty Dumpty.

Alice didn't want to begin another argument, so she said nothing.

"Seven years and six months!" Humpty Dumpty repeated thoughtfully. "An uncomfortable sort of age. Now if you'd asked *my* advice, I'd have said 'Leave off at seven'— but it's too late now."

"I never ask advice about growing," Alice said indignantly. "One can't help growing older."

"*One* can't, perhaps," said Humpty Dumpty; "but *two* can. With proper assistance, you might have left off at seven."

"What a beautiful belt you've got on!" Alice suddenly remarked. (They had had quite enough of the subject of age, she thought, and, if they really were to take turns in choosing subjects, it was *her* turn now.) "At least," she corrected herself, "a beautiful cravat, I should have said—no, a belt, I mean—I beg your pardon!" she added in dismay, for Humpty Dumpty looked thoroughly offended, and she began to wish she hadn't chosen that subject. "If only I knew," she thought to herself, "which was neck and which was waist!"

"It is a—*most—provoking*—thing," said Humpty Dumpty, "when a person doesn't know a cravat from a belt!"

"I know it's very ignorant of me," Alice

you may shake hands with me!" And he grinned almost from ear to ear, as he leant forwards (nearly falling off the wall as he did so) and offered Alice his hand. She watched him a little anxiously as she took it. "If he smiled much more the ends of his mouth might meet behind," she thought, "and then I don't know *what* would happen to his head! I'm afraid it would come off!"

"Yes, all his horses and all his men," Humpty Dumpty went on. "They'd pick me up again in a minute, *they* would! However, this conversation is going on a little too fast. Let's go back to the last remark but one."

"I'm afraid I can't quite remember it," Alice said, very politely.

"In that case we start afresh," said Humpty Dumpty, "and it's my turn to choose a subject—" ("He talks about it

235

said, in so humble a tone that Humpty Dumpty relented.

"It's a cravat, child, and a beautiful one, as you say. It's a present from the White King and Queen. There now!"

"Is it really?" said Alice, quite pleased to find that she *had* chosen a good subject, after all.

"They gave it to me," Humpty Dumpty continued thoughtfully, as he crossed one knee over the other and clasped his hands round it, "for an un-birthday present."

"I beg your pardon?" Alice said with a puzzled air.

"I'm not offended," said Humpty Dumpty.

"I mean, what *is* an un-birthday present?"

"A present given when it isn't your birthday, of course."

Alice considered a little. "I like birthday presents best," she said at last.

"You don't know what you're talking about!" cried Humpty Dumpty. "How many days are there in a year?"

"Three hundred and sixty-five," said Alice.

"And how many birthdays have you?"

"One."

"And if you take one from three hundred and sixty-five, what remains?"

"Three hundred and sixty-four, of course."

"So there are three hundred and sixty-four days when you might get un-birthday presents—"

"Certainly," said Alice.

"And only *one* for birthday presents. There's glory for you!"

"I don't know what you mean by 'glory,'" Alice said.

Humpty Dumpty smiled contemptuously. "Of course you don't—till I tell you. I meant 'there's a nice knock-down argument for you!'"

"But 'glory' doesn't mean 'a nice knock-down argument,'" Alice objected.

"When *I* use a word," Humpty Dumpty said, in rather a scornful tone, "it means just what I choose it to mean—neither more nor less."

"The question is," said Alice, "whether you *can* make words mean so many different things."

"The question is," said Humpty Dumpty, "which is to be master—that's all."

Alice was too much puzzled to say anything. So after a minute Humpty Dumpty began again. "They've a temper, some of them—particularly verbs; they're the proudest. Adjectives you can do anything with, but not verbs. However, *I* can manage the whole lot of them! Impenetrability! That's what *I* say!"

"Would you tell me, please," said Alice, "what *that* means?"

"Now you talk like a reasonable child," said Humpty Dumpty, looking very much pleased. "I meant by 'impenetrability' that we've had enough of that subject, and it would be just as well if you'd mention what you mean to do next, as I suppose you don't mean to stop here all the rest of your life."

"That's a great deal to make one word mean," Alice said in a thoughtful tone.

"When I make a word do a lot of work like that," said Humpty Dumpty, "I always pay it extra."

"Oh!" said Alice. She was too much puzzled to make any other remark.

"Ah, you should see 'em come round me of a Saturday night," Humpty Dumpty went on, wagging his head gravely from side to side, "for to get their wages, you know."

"You seem very clever at explaining words, Sir," said Alice. "Would you kindly tell me the meaning of the poem called 'Jabberwocky'?"

"Let's hear it," said Humpty Dumpty. "I can explain all the poems that ever were invented—and a good many that haven't been invented yet."

This sounded very hopeful, so Alice repeated the first verse:

> "'Twas brillig, and the slithy toves
>   Did gyre and gimble in the wabe:
> All mimsy were the borogoves,
>   And the mome raths outgrabe."

"That's enough to begin with," Humpty Dumpty interrupted: "there are plenty of hard words there. 'Brillig' means four o'clock in the afternoon—the time when you begin broiling things for dinner."

"That'll do very well," said Alice: "and 'slithy'?"

'Well, 'slithy' means 'lithe and slimy.' 'Lithe' is the same as 'active.' You see it's like a portmanteau—there are two meanings packed up into one word."

"I see it now," Alice remarked thoughtfully. "And what are 'toves'?"

"Well, 'toves' are something like badgers —they're something like lizards—and they're something like corkscrews."

"They must be very curious-looking creatures."

"They are that," said Humpty Dumpty. "Also they make their nests under sundials—also they live on cheese."

"And what's to 'gyre' and to 'gimble'?"

"To 'gyre' is to go round and round like a gyroscope. To 'gimble' is to make holes like a gimblet."

"And 'the wabe' is the grass-plot round a sun-dial, I suppose?" said Alice, surprised at her own ingenuity.

"Of course it is. It's called 'wabe,' you know, because it goes a long way before it, and a long way behind it____"

"And a long way beyond it on each side," Alice added.

"Exactly so. Well then, 'mimsy' is 'flimsy and miserable' (there's another portmanteau for you). And a 'borogove' is a thin shabby-looking bird with its feathers sticking out all round—something like a live mop."

"And then 'mome raths'?" said Alice. "I'm afraid I'm giving you a great deal of trouble."

"Well, a 'rath' is a sort of green pig; but 'mome' I'm not certain about. I think it's short for 'from home'—meaning that they'd lost their way, you know."

"And what does *'outgrabe'* mean?"

"Well, *'outgribing'* is something between bellowing and whistling, with a kind of sneeze in the middle. However, you'll hear it done, maybe—down in the wood yonder —and, when you've once heard it, you'll be *quite* content."

Alice thought that she ought to be going. So she got up and held out her hand. "Goodbye, till we meet again!" she said as cheerfully as she could.

"I shouldn't know you again if we *did* meet," Humpty Dumpty replied in a discontented tone, giving her one of his fingers to shake. "You're so exactly like other people."

"The face is what one goes by, generally," Alice remarked in a thoughtful tone.

"That's just what I complain of," said Humpty Dumpty. "Your face is the same as everybody's: two eyes, nose in the middle, mouth under. It's always the same. Now if you had the two eyes on the same side of the nose, for instance—or the mouth at the top —that would be *some* help."

"It wouldn't look nice," Alice objected.

But Humpty Dumpty only shut his eyes and said, "Wait till you've tried."

Alice waited a minute to see if he would speak again, but, as he never opened his eyes or took any further notice of her, she said "Good-bye!" once more, and, getting no answer to this, she quietly walked away. But she couldn't help saying to herself, as she went, "Of all the unsatisfactory—" (she repeated this aloud, as it was a great comfort to have such a long word to say) "of all the unsatisfactory people I *ever* met —" She never finished the sentence, for at this moment a heavy crash shook the forest from end to end.

THE LION AND THE UNICORN

The next moment soldiers came running through the wood, at first in twos and threes, then ten or twenty together, and at last in such crowds that they seemed to fill the whole forest. Alice got behind a tree, for fear of being run over.

She thought that in all her life she had never seen soldiers so uncertain on their feet. They were always tripping over something or other, and whenever one went down, several more always fell over him, so that the ground was soon covered with little heaps of men.

Then came the horses. Having four feet, these managed rather better than the foot-soldiers; but even *they* stumbled now and then; and it seemed to be a regular rule that, whenever a horse stumbled, the rider fell off instantly. The confusion got worse every moment, and Alice was very glad to get out of the wood into an open place, where she found the White King seated on the ground, busily writing in his memorandum-book.

"I've sent them all!" the King cried in a tone of delight, on seeing Alice. "Did you happen to meet any soldiers, my dear, as you came through the wood?"

"Yes, I did," said Alice: "several thousand, I should think."

"Four thousand two hundred and seven is the exact number," the King said, referring to his book. "I couldn't send all the horses, you know, because two of them are wanted in the game. And I haven't sent the two Messengers, either. They've both gone to the town. Just look along the road, and tell me if you can see either of them."

"I see nobody on the road," said Alice.

"I only wish *I* had such eyes," the King remarked in a fretful tone. "To be able to see Nobody! And at that distance too! Why, it's as much as *I* can do to see real people, by this light!"

"I see somebody now!" Alice exclaimed. "But he's coming very slowly—and what curious attitudes he goes into!" (For the Messenger kept skipping up and down, and wriggling like an eel, as he came along, with his great hands spread out like fans on each side.)

"Not at all," said the King. "He's an Anglo-Saxon Messenger — and those are Anglo-Saxon attitudes. He only does them when he's happy. His name is Haigha." (He pronounced it so as to rhyme with 'mayor.')

"I love my love with an H," Alice couldn't help beginning, "because he is Happy. I hate him with an H, because he is Hideous. I fed him with—with—with Ham-sand-wiches and Hay. His name is Haigha, and he lives____"

"He lives on the Hill," the King remarked simply, without the least idea that he was joining in the game, while Alice was still hesitating for the name of a town beginning with H. "The other Messenger's called Hatta. I must have *two*, you know—to come and go. One to come, and one to go."

"I beg your pardon?" said Alice.

"It isn't respectable to beg," said the King.

"I only meant that I didn't understand," said Alice. "Why one to come and one to go?"

"Don't I tell you?" the King repeated impatiently. "I must have *two*—to fetch and carry. One to fetch, and one to carry."

At this moment the Messenger arrived.

He was far too much out of breath to say a word. He could only wave his hands about and make the most fearful faces at the poor King.

"This young lady loves you with an H," the King said, introducing Alice in the hope of turning off the Messenger's attention from himself—but it was of no use—the Anglo-Saxon attitudes only got more extraordinary every moment, while the great eyes rolled wildly from side to side.

"You alarm me!" said the King. "I feel faint—Give me a ham sandwich!"

On which the Messenger, to Alice's great amusement, opened a bag that hung round his neck, and handed a sandwich to the King, who devoured it greedily.

"Another sandwich!" said the King.

"There's nothing but hay left now," the Messenger said, peeping into the bag.

"Hay, then," the King murmured in a faint whisper.

Alice was glad to see that it revived him a good deal. "There's nothing like eating hay when you're faint," he remarked to her, as he munched away.

"I should think throwing cold water over

you would be better," Alice suggested.

"I didn't say there was nothing *better*," the King replied. "I said there was nothing *like* it." Which Alice did not venture to deny.

"Who did you pass on the road?" the King went on, holding out his hand to the Messenger for some more hay.

"Nobody," said the Messenger.

"Quite right," said the King. "This young lady saw him too. So of course Nobody walks slower than you."

"I do my best," the Messenger said. "I'm sure nobody walks much faster than I do!"

"He can't do that," said the King, "or else he'd have been here first. However, now you've got your breath, you may tell us what's happened in the town."

"I'll whisper it," said the Messenger, putting his hands to his mouth in the shape of a trumpet and stooping so as to get close to the King's ear. Alice was sorry for this, as she wanted to hear the news too. However, instead of whispering, he simply shouted, at the top of his voice, "They're at it again!"

"Do you call *that* a whisper?" cried the poor King, jumping up and shaking himself. "If you do such a thing again, I'll have you buttered! It went through and through my head like an earthquake!"

"It would have to be a very tiny earthquake!" thought Alice. "Who are at it again?" she ventured to ask.

"Why, the Lion and the Unicorn, of course," said the King.

"Fighting for the crown?"

"Yes, to be sure," said the King: "and the best of the joke is, that it's *my* crown all the while! Let's run and see them."

"Would you—be good enough—" Alice panted, "to stop a minute—just to get— one's breath again?"

"I'm *good* enough," the King said, "only I'm not *strong* enough. You see, a minute goes by so fearfully quick."

Alice had no more breath for talking; so they trotted on in silence till they came into sight of a great crowd, in the middle of which the Lion and the Unicorn were fighting. They were in such a cloud of dust that at first Alice could not make out which was which; but she soon managed to distinguish the Unicorn by his horn.

They placed themselves close to where Hatta, the other Messenger, was standing watching the fight, with a cup of tea in one hand and a piece of bread-and-butter in the other.

"He's only just out of prison, and he hadn't finished his tea when he was sent in," Haigha whispered to Alice. "And they only give them oyster-shells in there—so you see he's very hungry and thirsty. How are you, dear child?" he went on, putting his arm affectionately round Hatta's neck.

Hatta looked round and nodded, and went on with his bread-and-butter.

"Were you happy in prison, dear child?" said Haigha.

Hatta looked round once more, and this time a tear or two trickled down his cheek; but not a word would he say.

"Speak, can't you?" Haigha cried impatiently. But Hatta only munched away, and drank some more tea.

"Speak, won't you!" cried the King. "How are they getting on with the fight?"

Hatta made a desperate effort, and swallowed a large piece of bread-and-butter. "They're getting on very well," he said in a choking voice. "Each of them has been down about eighty-seven times."

There was a pause in the fight just then, and the Lion and the Unicorn sat down, panting, while the King called out "Ten minutes allowed for refreshments!" Haigha and Hatta set to work at once, carrying round trays of white and brown bread.

"I don't think they'll fight any more to-day," the King said to Hatta. "Go and order the drums to begin." And Hatta went bounding away like a grasshopper.

For a minute or two Alice stood silent, watching him. Suddenly she brightened up. "Look, look!" she cried, pointing eagerly. "There's the White Queen running across the country! She came flying out of .the wood over yonder—How fast those Queens *can* run!"

"There's some enemy after her, no doubt," the King said, without even looking round. "That wood's full of them."

"But aren't you going to run and help her?" Alice asked, very much surprised at his taking it so quietly.

"No use, no use!" said the King. "She runs so fearfully quick. But I'll make a memorandum about her, if you like— She's a dear good creature," he repeated softly to himself, as he opened his memorandum-book. "Do you spell 'creature' with a double 'e'?"

At this moment the Unicorn sauntered by them, with his hands in his pockets. "I had the best of it this time!" he said to the King, glancing at him as he passed.

"A little—a little," the King replied, rather nervously. "You shouldn't have run him through with your horn, you know."

"It didn't hurt him," the Unicorn said carelessly, and he was going on, when his eye happened to fall upon Alice. He turned around and looked at her with the deepest disgust.

"What—is—this?" he said at last.

"This is a child!" Haigha replied eagerly,

coming in front of Alice to introduce her, and spreading out both his hands towards her in an Anglo-Saxon attitude. "We only found it today. It's as large as life, and twice as natural!"

"I always thought they were fabulous monsters!" said the Unicorn. "Is it alive?"

"It can talk," said Haigha solemnly.

The Unicorn looked dreamily at Alice, and said "Talk, child."

Alice could not help smiling. "Do you know," she said, "I always thought *Unicorns* were fabulous monsters. I never saw one alive before!"

"Well, now that we *have* seen each other," said the Unicorn, "if you'll believe in me, I'll believe in you. Is that a bargain?"

"Yes, if you like," said Alice.

"Come, fetch out the plum-cake, old man!" the Unicorn went on, turning from her to the King. "None of your brown bread for me!"

"Certainly—certainly!" the King muttered, and beckoned to Haigha. "Open the bag!" he whispered. "Quick! Not that one —that's full of hay!"

Haigha took a large cake out of the bag, and gave it to Alice to hold, while he got out a dish and carving-knife. How they all

241

came out of it Alice couldn't guess. It was just like a conjuring-trick, she thought.

The Lion had joined them while this was going on: he looked very tired and sleepy, and his eyes were half shut. "What's this!" he said, blinking lazily at Alice, and speaking in a deep hollow tone that sounded like the tolling of a great bell.

"Ah, what *is* it, now?" the Unicorn cried eagerly. "You'll never guess! *I* couldn't."

The Lion looked at Alice wearily. "Are you animal—or vegetable—or mineral?" he said, yawning at every other word.

"It's a fabulous monster!" the Unicorn cried out, before Alice could reply.

"Then hand round the plum-cake, Monster," the Lion said, lying down and putting his chin on his paws. "And sit down, both of you" (to the King and the Unicorn): "fair play with the cake, you know!"

The King was evidently very uncomfortable at having to sit down between the two great creatures; but there was no other place for him.

"What a fight we might have for the crown, *now!*" the Unicorn said, looking slyly up at the crown, which the poor King was nearly shaking off his head, he trembled so much.

"I should win easy," said the Lion.

"I'm not so sure of that," said the Unicorn.

"Why, I beat you all round the town!" the Lion replied angrily, half getting up as he spoke.

Here the King interrupted, to prevent the quarrel going on. He was very nervous, and his voice quite quivered. "All round the town?" he said. "That's a good long way. Did you go by the old bridge, or the market-place? You get the best view by the old bridge."

"I'm sure I don't know," the Lion growled out as he lay down again. "There was too much dust to see anything. What a time the Monster is, cutting up that cake!"

Alice had seated herself on the bank of a little brook, with the great dish on her knees, and was sawing away diligently with the knife. "It's very provoking!" she said, in reply to the Lion (she was getting quite used to being called 'the Monster'). "I've cut several slices already, but they always join on again!"

"You don't know how to manage Looking-glass cakes," the Unicorn remarked. "Hand it round first, and cut it afterwards."

This sounded like nonsense, but Alice very obediently got up, and carried the dish round, and the cake divided itself into three pieces as she did so. "*Now* cut it up," said the Lion, as she returned to her place with the empty dish.

"I say, this isn't fair!" cried the Unicorn, as Alice sat with the knife in her hand, very much puzzled how to begin. "The Monster has given the Lion twice as much as me!"

"She's kept none for herself, anyhow," said the Lion. "Do you like plum-cake, Monster?"

Before Alice could answer, the drums began.

Where the noise came from, she couldn't make out. The air seemed full of it, and it rang through her head till she felt quite deafened. She started to her feet and sprang across the little brook in terror, and had just time to see the Lion and the Unicorn rise to their feet, with angry looks at being interrupted in their feast, before she dropped to her knees, and put her hands over her ears, vainly trying to shut out the dreadful uproar.

"If *that* doesn't 'drum them out of town,' "

she thought to herself, "nothing ever will!"

"IT'S MY OWN INVENTION"

After a while the noise seemed gradually to die away, till all was dead silence, and Alice lifted up her head in some alarm. There was no one to be seen, and her first thought was that she must have been dreaming about the Lion and the Unicorn and those queer Anglo-Saxon Messengers.

But her thoughts were interrupted by a loud shouting of "Ahoy! Check!" and a Knight, dressed in crimson armour, came galloping down upon her, brandishing a great club. Just as he reached her, the horse stopped suddenly. "You're my prisoner!" the Knight cried, as he tumbled off his horse.

Startled as she was, Alice was more frightened for him than for herself, and she watched him with some anxiety as he mounted again. As soon as he was comfortably in the saddle, he began once more "You're my——"but here another voice broke in "Ahoy! Check!" and Alice looked round in some surprise for the new enemy.

This time it was a White Knight. He drew up at Alice's side, and tumbled off his horse just as the Red Knight had done. Then he got on again, and the two Knights sat and looked at each other for some time without speaking. Alice looked from one to the other in some bewilderment.

"She's *my* prisoner, you know!" the Red Knight said at last.

"Yes, but then *I* came and rescued her!" the White Knight replied.

"Well, we must fight for her, then," said the Red Knight.

"I don't want to be anybody's prisoner." Alice said, "I want to be a Queen."

"So you will, when you've crossed the next brook," said the White Knight. "I'll see you safe to the end of the wood—and then I must go back."

Alice thought she had never seen such a strange-looking soldier in all her life.

He was dressed in tin armour, which seemed to fit him very badly, and he had a queer-shaped little box fastened across his shoulders, upside-down, and with the lid hanging open. Alice looked at it with great curiosity.

"I see you're admiring my little box," the Knight said in a friendly tone. "It's my own invention—to keep clothes and sandwiches in. You see I carry it upside-down, so that the rain can't get in."

"But the things can get *out*," Alice gently remarked. "Do you know the lid's open?"

"I didn't know it," the Knight said, a shade of vexation passing over his face. "Then all the things must have fallen out! And the box is no use without them." He unfastened it as he spoke, and was just going to throw it into the bushes when a sud-

243

den thought seemed to strike him, and he hung it carefully on a tree. "Can you guess why I did that?" he said to Alice.

Alice shook her head.

"In hopes some bees may make a nest in it—then I should get the honey."

"But you've got a bee-hive—or something like one—fastened to your saddle," said Alice.

"Yes, it's a very good bee-hive," the Knight said in a discontented tone, "one of the best kind. But not a single bee has come near it yet. And the other thing is a mouse-trap. I suppose the mice keep the bees out—or the bees keep the mice out, I don't know which."

"I was wondering what the mouse-trap was for," said Alice. "It isn't very likely there would be any mice on the horse's back."

"Not very likely, perhaps," said the Knight. "But if they *do* come, I don't choose to have them running all about."

"You see," he went on after a pause, "it's as well to be provided for *everything*. That's the reason the horse has all those anklets round his feet."

"But what are they for?" Alice asked in a tone of great curiosity.

"To guard against the bites of sharks," the Knight replied. "It's an invention of my own. And now help me on. I'll go with you to the end of the wood——What's that dish for?"

"It's meant for plum-cake," said Alice.

"We'd better take it with us," the Knight said. "It'll come in handy if we find any plum-cake. Help me to get it into this bag."

This took a long time to manage, though Alice held the bag open very carefully, because the Knight was so *very* awkward in putting in the dish. The first two or three times he tried, he fell in himself instead. "It's rather a tight fit, you see," he said, as they got it in at last; "there are so many candlesticks in the bag." And he hung it to the saddle, which was already loaded with bunches of carrots and fire-irons and many other things.

"I hope you've got your hair well fastened on?" he continued, as they set off.

"Only in the usual way," Alice said, smiling.

"That's hardly enough," he said, anxiously. "You see the wind is so *very* strong here. It's as strong as soup."

"Have you invented a plan for keeping the hair from being blown off?" Alice inquired.

"Not yet," said the Knight. "But I've got a plan for keeping it from *falling* off."

"I should like to hear it, very much."

"First you take an upright stick," said the Knight. "Then you make your hair creep up it, like a fruit-tree. Now the reason hair falls off is because it hangs *down*—things never fall *upwards,* you know. It's a plan of my own invention. You may try it if you like."

It didn't sound like a comfortable plan to Alice, and for a few minutes she walked on in silence, puzzling over the idea, and every now and then stopping to help the poor Knight, who certainly was *not* a good rider.

Whenever the horse stopped (which it did very often), he fell off in front; and, whenever it went on again (which it generally did rather suddenly), he fell off behind. Otherwise he kept on pretty well, except that he had a habit of now and then falling off sideways; and, as he generally did this on the side on which Alice was walking, she soon found that it was the best plan not to walk *quite* close to the horse.

"I'm afraid you've not had much practice in riding," she ventured to say, as she was helping him up from his fifth tumble.

The Knight looked very much surprised, and a little offended at the remark. "What makes you say that?" he asked, as he scrambled back into the saddle, keeping hold of Alice's hair with one hand, to save himself from falling over on the other side.

"Because people don't fall off quite so often when they've had much practice."

"I've had plenty of practice," the Knight said very gravely, "plenty of practice!"

Alice could think of nothing better to say than "Indeed?" but she said it as heartily as she could. They went on a little way in silence after this, the Knight with his eyes shut, muttering to himself, and Alice watching anxiously for the next tumble.

"The great art of riding," the Knight suddenly began in a loud voice, waving his right arm as he spoke, "is to keep——" Here the sentence ended as suddenly as it had begun, as the Knight fell heavily on the top of his head exactly in the path where Alice was walking. She was quite frightened this time, and said in an anxious tone, as she picked him up, "I hope no bones are broken?"

"None to speak of," the Knight said, as if he didn't mind breaking two or three of them. "The great art of riding, as I was saying, is—to keep your balance properly. Like this, you know——"

He let go the bridle, and stretched out both his arms to show Alice what he meant, and this time he fell flat on his back, right under the horse's feet.

"Plenty of practice!" he went on repeating, all the time that Alice was getting him on his feet again. "Plenty of practice!"

"It's too ridiculous!" cried Alice, losing all her patience. "What you ought to have is a wooden horse on wheels!"

"Does that kind go smoothly?" the Knight asked in a tone of great interest, clasping his arms round the horse's neck as he spoke, just in time to save himself from tumbling off again.

"Much more smoothly than a live horse," Alice said, with a little scream of laughter, in spite of all she could do to prevent it.

"I'll get one," the Knight said thoughtfully.

There was a short silence and then the Knight went on, "I'm a great hand at inventing things."

"What a curious helmet you've got!" said Alice cheerfully. "Is that your invention too?"

The Knight looked down proudly at his helmet, which hung from the saddle. "Yes," he said; "but I've invented a better one than that—like a sugar-loaf. When I used to wear it, if I fell off the horse, it always touched the ground directly. So I had a *very* little way to fall, you see—But there *was* the danger of falling *into* it, to be sure."

245

He raised his hands in some excitement as he said this, and instantly rolled out of the saddle, and fell headlong into a deep ditch.

Alice ran to the side of the ditch to look for him. She was afraid he might be hurt this time. However, though she could see nothing but the soles of his feet, she was much relieved to hear him talking on in his usual tone.

"How *can* you go on talking so quietly, head downwards?" Alice asked, as she dragged him out by the feet, and laid him in a heap on the bank.

The Knight looked surprised at the question. "What does it matter where my body happens to be?" he said. "My mind goes on working all the same. In fact, the more head-downwards I am, the more I keep inventing new things."

"Now the cleverest thing of the sort that I ever did," he went on after a pause, "was inventing a new pudding during the meat course."

"In time to have it cooked for the next course?" said Alice.

"Well, not the *next* course," the Knight said.

"Then it would have to be the next day."

"Well, not the *next* day," the Knight admitted. "In fact," he went on, holding his head down, his voice getting lower and lower, "I don't believe that pudding ever *was* cooked! In fact, I don't believe that pudding ever *will* be cooked! And yet it was a very clever pudding to invent."

"What did you mean it to be made of?" Alice asked, hoping to cheer him up.

"It began with blotting-paper," the Knight answered with a groan.

"That wouldn't be very nice, I'm afraid——"

"Not very nice *alone*," he interrupted,

"but you've no idea what a difference it makes when you mix it with other things—such as gunpowder and sealing-wax. And here I must leave you." They had just come to the end of the wood.

The Knight gathered up the reins, and turned his horse's head along the road by which they had come. "You've only a few yards to go," he said, "down the hill and over that little brook, and then you'll be a Queen. But you'll stay and see me off first?" he added as Alice turned with an eager look in the direction to which he pointed. "I shan't be long. You'll wait and wave your handkerchief when I get to that turn in the road! I think it'll encourage me."

"Of course I'll wait," said Alice.

They shook hands, and then the Knight rode slowly away into the forest. "It won't

take long to see him *off,* I expect," Alice said as she watched the horse walking leisurely along the road, and the Knight tumbling off, first on one side and then on the other. After the fourth or fifth tumble he reached the turn, and then she waved her handkerchief to him, and waited till he was out of sight.

"I hope it encouraged him," she said, as she turned to run down the hill. "And now for the last brook, and to be a Queen! How grand it sounds!" A very few steps brought her to the edge of the brook. She bounded across, and threw herself down to rest on a lawn as soft as moss, with little flower-beds dotted about it here and there. "Oh, how glad I am to get here! And what *is* this on my head?" she exclaimed in a tone of dismay, as she put her hands up to something very heavy, that fitted tight all round her head.

"But how *can* it have got there without my knowing it?" she said to herself, as she lifted it off, and set it on her lap to make out what it could possibly be.

It was a golden crown.

QUEEN ALICE

"Well, this *is* grand!" said Alice. "I never expected I should be a Queen so soon. And I'll tell you, your Majesty," she went on in a severe tone (she was always rather fond of scolding herself): "It'll never do for you to be lolling about on the grass like that. Queens have to be dignified, you know!"

So she got up and walked about—rather stiffly at first, as she was afraid that the crown might come off. "But if I really am a Queen," she said as she sat down again, "I shall be able to manage it quite well in time."

Everything was happening so oddly that she didn't feel a bit surprised at finding the Red Queen and the White Queen sitting close to her, one on each side. "Please, would you tell me——" she began, looking timidly at the Red Queen.

"Speak when you're spoken to!" the Queen sharply interrupted her.

"But if everybody obeyed that rule," said Alice, "and if you only spoke when you were spoken to, and the other person always waited for *you* to begin, nobody would ever say anything."

"Ridiculous!" cried the Queen. "Besides, what do you mean by 'If I really am a Queen'? What right have you to call yourself so? You can't be a Queen till you've passed the proper examination. And the sooner we begin it, the better."

"I only said 'if'!" poor Alice pleaded in a piteous tone.

The two Queens looked at each other, and the Red Queen remarked, "She *says* she only said 'if'——"

"But she said a great deal more than that!" the White Queen moaned, wringing her hands. "Oh, ever so much more than that!"

"So you did, you know," the Red Queen said to Alice. "Always speak the truth—think before you speak—and write it down afterwards."

"I'm sure I didn't mean——" Alice was beginning, but the Red Queen interrupted her impatiently.

"That's just what I complain of! You *should* have meant! What do you suppose is the use of a child without any meaning? Even a joke should have some meaning—and a child's more important than a joke, I hope."

There was an uncomfortable silence for

a minute or two. Then the Red Queen said to the White Queen, "I invite you to Alice's dinner-party this afternoon."

The White Queen smiled feebly, and said "And I invite *you.*"

"I didn't know I was to have a party," said Alice. "But, if there *is* to be one, I think *I* ought to invite the guests."

"We gave you the opportunity of doing it," the Red Queen remarked; but I daresay you've not had many lessons in manners yet."

"Manners are not taught in lessons," said Alice. "Lessons teach you to do sums and things like that."

"Can you do Addition?" the White Queen asked. "What's one and one and one and one and one and one and one and one and one and one?"

"I don't know," said Alice. "I lost count."

"She can't do Addition," the Red Queen interrupted. "Can you do Subtraction? Take nine from eight."

"Nine from eight I can't, you know," Alice replied.

"She can't do Substraction," said the White Queen. "Can you do Division? Divide a loaf by a knife—what's the answer to *that?*"

"I suppose——" Alice was beginning, but the Red Queen answered for her. "Bread-and-butter, of course. Try another Subtraction sum. Take a bone from a dog; what remains?"

Alice considered. "The bone wouldn't remain, of course, if I took it—and the dog wouldn't remain; it would come to bite me —and I'm sure *I* shouldn't remain!"

"Then you think nothing would remain?" said the Red Queen.

"I think that's the answer."

"Wrong, as usual," said the Red Queen;

"the dog's temper would remain."

"But I don't see how——"

"Why, look here!" the Red Queen cried. "The dog would lose its temper, wouldn't it?"

"Perhaps it would," Alice replied cautiously.

"Then if the dog went away, its temper would remain!" the Queen exclaimed triumphantly.

Alice said, as gravely as she could, "They might go different ways." But she couldn't help thinking to herself "What dreadful nonsense we *are* talking!"

"She can't do sums a *bit!*" the Queens said together, with great emphasis.

"Can *you* do sums?" Alice said, turning suddenly on the White Queen, for she didn't like being found fault with so much.

The Queen gasped and shut her eyes. "I can do Addition," she said, "if you give me time—but I can't do Substraction under *any* circumstances!"

"Of course you know your A B C?" said the Red Queen.

"To be sure I do," said Alice.

"So do I," the White Queen whispered: "we'll often say it over together, dear. And I'll tell you a secret—I can read words of one letter! Isn't *that* grand? However, don't be discouraged. You'll come to it in time."

Here the Red Queen began again. "Can you answer useful questions?" she said. "How is bread made?"

" I know *that!*" Alice cried eagerly. "You take some flour——"

"Where do you pick the flower?" the White Queen asked. "In a garden or in the hedges?"

"Well, it isn't *picked* at all," Alice explained: "it's *ground*——"

"How many acres of ground?" said the White Queen. "You mustn't leave out so many things."

"Fan her head!" the Red Queen anxiously interrupted. "She'll be feverish after so much thinking." So they set to work and fanned her with bunches of leaves, till she had to beg them to leave off, it blew her hair about so.

"She's all right again now," said the Red Queen. "Do you know Languages? What's the French for fiddle-de-dee?"

"Fiddle-de-dee's not English," Alice replied gravely.

"Who ever said it was?" said the Red Queen.

Alice thought she saw a way out of the difficulty, this time. "If you'll tell me what language 'fiddle-de-dee' is, I'll tell you the French for it!" she exclaimed triumphantly.

But the Red Queen drew herself up rather stiffly, and said "Queens never make bargains."

" I wish Queens never asked questions," Alice thought to herself.

"Don't let us quarrel," the White Queen said in an anxious tone. "What is the cause of lightning?"

"The cause of lightning," Alice said very decidedly, for she felt quite certain about this, "is the thunder. No, no!" she hastily corrected herself. "I meant the other way."

"It's too late to correct it," said the Red Queen. "When you've once said a thing, that fixes it, and you must take the consequences."

"Which reminds me——" the White Queen said, nervously clasping and unclasping her hands, "we had *such* a thunderstorm last Tuesday—I mean one of the last set of Tuesdays, you know."

Alice was puzzled. "In *our* country," she remarked, "there's only one day at a time."

The Red Queen said "That's a poor thin way of doing things. Now *here*, we mostly have days and nights two or three at a time, and sometimes in the winter we take as many as five nights together—for warmth, you know."

"Are five nights warmer than one night?" Alice ventured to ask.

"Five times as warm, of course."

"But they should be five times as *cold*, by the same rule——"

"Just so!" cried the Red Queen. "Five times as warm, *and* five times as cold—just as I'm five times as rich as you are, *and* five times as clever!"

Alice sighed and gave it up. "It's exactly like a riddle with no answer!" she thought.

"Humpty Dumpty saw it too," the White Queen went on in a low voice, more as if she were talking to herself. "He came to the door with a corkscrew in his hand——"

"What did he want?" said the Red Queen.

"He said he *would* come in," the White Queen went on, "because he was looking for a hippopotamus. Now, as it happened, there wasn't such a thing in the house, that morning."

"Is there generally?" Alice asked in an astonished tone.

"Well, only on Thursdays," said the Queen.

"I know what he came for," said Alice: "he wanted to punish the fish, because——"

Here the White Queen began again. "It was *such* a thunderstorm, you can't think!" ("She *never* could, you know," said the Red Queen.) "And part of the roof came off, and ever so much thunder got in—and it went rolling round the room in great lumps —and knocking over the tables and things— till I was so frightened, I couldn't remember my own name!"

Alice thought to herself "I never should *try* to remember my name in the middle of an accident! Where would be the use of it?" but she did not say this aloud, for fear of hurting the poor Queen's feelings.

"Your Majesty must excuse her," the Red Queen said to Alice, taking one of the White Queen's hands in her own, and gently stroking it. "She means well, but she can't help saying foolish things."

The White Queen looked timidly at Alice, who felt she *ought* to say something kind, but really couldn't think of anything at the moment.

"She never was really well brought up," the Red Queen went on, "but it's amazing how good-tempered she is! Pat her on the head, and see how pleased she'll be!" But this was more than Alice had courage to do.

"A little kindness—and putting her hair in papers—would do wonders for her——"

The White Queen gave a deep sigh, and laid her head on Alice's shoulder. "I *am* so sleepy!" she moaned.

"She's tired, poor thing!" said the Red Queen. "Smooth her hair—lend her your nightcap—and sing her a soothing lullaby."

"I haven't got a nightcap with me," said Alice, "and I don't know any soothing lullabies."

"I must do it myself, then," said the Red Queen, and she began:

"Hush-a-by lady, in Alice's lap!
Till the feast's ready, we've time for a nap.
When the feast's over, we'll go to the ball—
Red Queen, and White Queen, and Alice, and all!

"And now you know the words," she added, as she put her head down on Alice's other shoulder, "just sing it through to *me*. I'm getting sleepy, too." In another moment both Queens were fast asleep, and snoring loud.

"What *am* I to do?" exclaimed Alice, looking about as first one round head, and then the other, rolled down from her shoulder, and lay like a heavy lump in her lap. "I don't think it *ever* happened before, that any one had to take care of two Queens asleep at once! Do wake up, you heavy things!" she went on in an impatient tone. But there was no answer but a gentle snoring.

The snoring got more distinct every minute, and sounded more like a tune. At last Alice could even make out words, and she listened so eagerly that, when the two great heads suddenly vanished from her lap,

250

she hardly missed them.

She was standing before an arched doorway, over which were the words "QUEEN ALICE" in large letters, and on each side of the arch there was a bell-handle. One was marked "Visitors' Bell," and the other "Servants' Bell."

"I'll wait till the song's over," thought Alice, "and then I'll ring the—the—*which* bell must I ring?" she went on, very much puzzled by the names. "I'm not a visitor, and I'm not a servant. There *ought* to be one marked 'Queen,' you know——"

Just then the door opened a little way, and a creature with a long beak put its head out for a moment and said "No admittance till the week after next!" and shut the door again with a bang.

Alice knocked and rang for a long time. At last a very old Frog, who was sitting under a tree, got up and hobbled slowly towards her.

"Where's the servant whose business it is to answer the door?" Alice began angrily.

"Which door?" said the Frog.

"*This* door, of course!"

"To answer the door?" said the Frog. "What's it been asking of?" He was so hoarse that Alice could scarcely hear him.

"I don't know what you mean," said Alice.

"I speaks English, doesn't I?" the Frog went on. "Or are you deaf? What did it ask you?"

"Nothing!" Alice said impatiently. "I've been knocking at it!"

"Shouldn't do that—shouldn't do that—" the Frog muttered. "Vexes it, you know." At this moment the door was flung open, and a shrill voice was heard singing:—

"To the Looking-Glass world it was Alice that said
    'I've a sceptre in hand I've a crown on my head.
Let the Looking-Glass creatures, whatever they be
Come and dine with the Red Queen, the White Queen, and me!'"

And hundreds of voices joined in the chorus:

"Then fill up the glasses as quick as you can,
    And sprinkle the table with buttons and bran;
Put cats in the coffee, and mice in the tea—
And welcome Queen Alice with thirty-times-three!"

Then followed a confused noise of cheering, and Alice thought to herself "Thirty times three makes ninety. I wonder if any one's counting?" In a minute there was silence again, and the same shrill voice sang another verse:

" 'O Looking-Glass creatures,' quoth Alice, 'draw near!
    'Tis an honour to see me, a favour to hear:
'Tis a privilege high to have dinner and tea
Along with the Red Queen, the White Queen, and me!'"

Then came the chorus again:

"Then fill up the glasses with treacle and ink,
Or anything else that is pleasant to drink;
Mix sand with the cider, and wool with the
wine—
And welcome Queen Alice with ninety-times-
nine!"

"Ninety times nine!" Alice repeated in despair. "I'd better go in at once——" and in she went, and there was a dead silence the moment she appeared.

Alice glanced nervously along the table, as she walked up the large hall, and noticed that there were about fifty guests, of all kinds: some were animals, some birds, and there were even a few flowers among them.

"I'm glad they've come without waiting to be asked," she thought. "I should never have known who were the right people to invite!"

There were three chairs at the head of the table. The Red and White Queens had already taken two of them, but the middle one was empty. Alice sat down in it, rather uncomfortable at the silence.

At last the Red Queen spoke. "You've missed the soup and fish," she said. "Put on the joint!" And the waiters set a leg of mutton before Alice, who looked at it rather anxiously, as she had never had to carve a joint before.

"You look a little shy: let me introduce you to that leg of mutton," said the Red Queen. "Alice——Mutton; Mutton—— Alice." The leg of mutton got up in the dish and made a little bow to Alice; and Alice returned the bow, not knowing whether to be frightened or amused.

"May I give you a slice?" she said, taking up the knife and fork, and looking from one Queen to the other.

"Certainly not," the Red Queen said, very decidedly. "It isn't etiquette to cut any one you've been introduced to. Remove the joint!" And the waiters carried it off, and brought a large plum-pudding in its place.

"I won't be introduced to the pudding, please," Alice said rather hastily, "or we shall get no dinner at all. May I give you some?"

But the Red Queen looked sulky, and growled "Pudding——Alice; Alice——Pudding. Remove the pudding!", and the waiters took it away so quickly that Alice couldn't return its bow.

However, she didn't see why the Red Queen should be the only one to give orders; so, as an experiment, she called out "Waiter! Bring back the pudding!", and there it was again in a moment, like a conjuring-trick. It was so large that she couldn't help feeling a *little* shy with it, as she had been with the mutton. However, she cut a slice and handed it to the Red Queen.

"What impertinence!" said the Pudding. "I wonder how you'd like it, if I were to cut a slice out of *you,* you creature!"

It spoke in a thick suety sort of voice, and Alice hadn't a word to say in reply.

"Make a remark," said the Red Queen. "It's ridiculous to leave all the conversation to the pudding!"

Alice was a little frightened at finding that, the moment she opened her lips, there was dead silence, and all eyes were fixed upon her.

Then the Red Queen screamed at the top of her voice. "We'll drink your health— Queen Alice's health!" And all the guests began drinking it directly, and very queerly too: some of them put their glasses upon their heads like extinguishers, and drank all that trickled down their faces; others upset the decanters, and drank the wine as it ran off the edges of the table; and three of them (who looked like kangaroos) scrambled into the dish of roast mutton, and began eagerly lapping up the gravy, "just like pigs in a trough!" thought Alice.

"You ought to return thanks in a neat speech," the Red Queen said, frowning at Alice.

"We must support you, you know," the White Queen whispered, as Alice got up to do it.

It was rather difficult for her to keep in her place while she made her speech; the two Queens kept pushing her so. "I rise to return thanks——" Alice began. And she really *did* rise as she spoke, several inches; but she got hold of the edge of the table, and managed to pull herself down again.

"Take care of yourself!" screamed the

White Queen, seizing Alice's hair with both her hands. "Something's going to happen!"

At this moment Alice heard a hoarse laugh at her side, and turned to see what was the matter with the White Queen. But instead of the Queen, there was the leg of mutton sitting in the chair. "Here I am!" cried a voice from the soup-tureen, and Alice turned again, just in time to see the Queen's broad good-natured face grinning at her for a moment over the edge of the tureen, before she disappeared into the soup.

There was not a moment to be lost. Already several of the guests were lying down in the dishes, and the soup-ladle was walking up the table towards Alice's chair, and beckoning to her impatiently to get out of its way.

"I can't stand this any longer!" she cried, as she jumped up and seized the tablecloth with both hands. One good pull, and plates, dishes, guests, and candles came crashing down together in a heap on the floor.

"And as for *you*," she went on, turning fiercely upon the Red Queen, whom she considered as the cause of all the mischief— but the Queen was no longer at her side— she had suddenly dwindled down to the size of a little doll, and was now on the table, merrily running round and round after her own shawl, which was trailing behind her.

At any other time, Alice would have felt surprised at this, but she was far too much excited to be surprised at anything *now*. "As for *you*," she repeated, catching hold of the little creature in the very act of jumping over a bottle which had just lighted upon the table, "I'll shake you into a kitten, that I will!"

She took her off the table as she spoke, and shook her backwards and forwards with all her might.

when she was explaining the thing afterwards to her sister. "It turned away its head and pretended not to see it; but it looked a *little* ashamed of itself, so I think it *must* have been the Red Queen.")

"Sit up a little more stiffly, dear!" Alice cried with a merry laugh. "And curtsy while you're thinking what to—what to purr." And she caught it up and gave it one little kiss, just in honour of its having been a Red Queen.

The Red Queen made no resistance whatever. Only her face grew very small, and her eyes got large and green; and still, as Alice went on shaking her, she kept on growing shorter—and fatter—and softer—and rounder—and——and it really *was* a kitten, after all.

WHICH DREAMED IT?

"Your Red Majesty shouldn't purr so loud," Alice said, rubbing her eyes, and addressing the kitten. "You woke me out of such a nice dream! And you've been along with me, Kitty—all through the Looking-Glass world. Did you know it, dear?"

The kitten only purred, and it was impossible to guess whether it meant "yes" or "no."

So Alice hunted among the chessmen on the table till she had found the Red Queen. The she went down on her knees on the hearth-rug and put the kitten and the Queen to look at each other. "Now, Kitty!" she cried, clapping her hands triumphantly. "Confess that was what you turned into!"

("But it wouldn't look at it," she said,

"Snowdrop, my pet!" she went on, looking over her shoulder at the White Kitten, "when *will* Dinah have finished with your White Majesty, I wonder? That must be the reason you were so untidy in my dream. ——Dinah! Do you know that you're scrubbing a White Queen? Really, it's most disrespectful of you!

"And what did *Dinah* turn to, I wonder?" she prattled on, as she settled comfortably down, with one elbow on the rug, and her chin in her hand, to watch the kittens. "Tell me, Dinah, did you turn to Humpty

254

Dumpty? I *think* you did, but you'd better not mention it to your friends just yet, for I'm not sure.

"By the way, Kitty, if only you'd been really with me in my dream, there was one thing you *would* have enjoyed——I had such a quantity of poetry said to me, all about fishes! Tomorow morning you shall have a real treat. All the time you're eating your breakfast, I'll repeat 'The Walrus and the Carpenter' to you.

"Now, Kitty, let's consider who it was that dreamed it all. This is a serious question, my dear, and you should *not* go on licking your paw like that—as if Dinah hadn't washed you this morning! You see, Kitty, it *must* have been either me or the Red King. He was part of my dream, of course—but then I was part of his dream, too! *Was* it the Red King, Kitty? You were his wife, my dear, so you ought to know—— Oh, Kitty, *do* help to settle it! I'm sure your paw can wait!"

But the provoking kitten only began on the other paw, and pretended it hadn't heard the question.

Which do *you* think it was?

255

The Green Grass Growing All Around

THERE was a tree stood in the ground
The prettiest tree you ever did see;
The tree in the wood, and the wood in the ground,
And the green grass growing all around.

And on this tree there was a limb,
The prettiest limb you ever did see;
The limb on the tree, and the tree in the wood,
The tree in the wood, and the wood in the ground,
And the green grass growing all around.

And on this limb there was a bough,
The prettiest bough you ever did see;
The bough on the limb, and the limb on the tree,
The limb on the tree, and the tree in the wood,
The tree in the wood, and the wood in the ground,
And the green grass growing all around.

Now on this bough there was a nest,
The prettiest nest you ever did see;
The nest on the bough, and the bough on the limb,
The bough on the limb, and the limb on the tree,
The limb on the tree, and the tree in the wood,
The tree in the wood, and the wood in the ground,
And the green grass growing all around.

And in the nest there were some eggs,
The prettiest eggs you ever did see;
Eggs in the nest, and the nest on the bough,
The nest on the bough, and the bough on the limb,
The bough on the limb, and the limb on the tree,
The limb on the tree, and the tree in the wood,
The tree in the wood, and the wood in the ground,
And the green grass growing all around.

Tom Whitewashes the Fence

From TOM SAWYER

By Mark Twain

If you like stories about a very real boy who thinks up the most marvelously mischievous things to do, you'll want to read Mark Twain's famous book TOM SAWYER.

You will find two stories from TOM SAWYER here: "The Glorious Whitewasher" and "The Cat and the Pain Killer." You may find it hard, at first, to read the things Tom says because he talks the way small-town boys talked in midwest America two generations ago. But you will find it worth while to try to get the hang of it because it is wonderfully funny.

You'll admire Tom too, in spite of his ragged clothes and his unruly ways, for he has courage and honor. He protects the weak and he keeps his word to his friend.

Three generations of boys and girls have all but "died laughing" over the adventures of the irrepressible Tom Sawyer. And probably he will go on delighting us for ever.

" Tom!"

"Tom!"

No answer.

"What's gone with that boy, I wonder! You TOM!"

No answer.

The old lady pulled her spectacles down and looked over them about the room; then she put them up and looked out under them. She seldom or never looked *through* them for so small a thing as a boy. They were her state pair, the pride of her heart, and were built for "style," not service—she could have seen through a pair of stove-lids just as well. She looked perplexed for a moment, and then said, not fiercely but still loud enough for the furniture to hear, "Well, if I get hold of you I'll—"

She did not finish, for by this time she was bending down and punching under the bed with the broom, and so she needed breath to punctuate the punches with. She resurrected nothing but the cat.

"I never did see the beat of that boy!"

She went to the open door and stood in it and looked out among the tomato vines and "jimpson" weeds that constituted the garden. No Tom. So she lifted up her voice at an angle calculated for distance, and shouted, "Y-o-u-u *Tom!*"

There was a slight noise behind her and she turned just in time to seize a small boy by the slack of his roundabout and arrest his flight.

"There! I might 'a' thought of that closet. What you been doing in there?"

"Nothing."

"Nothing! Look at your hands. And look at your mouth. What *is* that truck?"

"*I* don't know, aunt."

"Well, *I* know. It's jam—that's what it is. Forty times I've said if you didn't let that jam alone I'd skin you. Hand me that switch."

The switch hovered in the air—the peril was desperate.

"My! Look behind you, aunt!"

The old lady whirled around, and snatched her skirts out of danger. The lad

fled, on the instant, scrambled up the high board fence, and disappeared over it.

His Aunt Polly stood surprised a moment, and then broke into a gentle laugh.

"Hang the boy, can't I never learn anything? Ain't he played me tricks enough like that for me to be looking out for him by this time? But old fools is the biggest fools there is. Can't learn an old dog new tricks, as the saying is. But my goodness, he never plays them alike two days, and how is a body to know what's coming? He 'pears to know just how long he can torment me before I get my dander up, and he knows if he can make out to put me off for a minute or make me laugh, it's all down again and I can't hit him a lick. I ain't doing my duty by that boy, and that's the Lord's truth, goodness knows. Spare the rod and spoil the child, as the Good Book says. I'm a-laying up sin and suffering for us both, *I* know. He's full of the Old Scratch, but laws-a-me! he's my own dead sister's boy, poor thing, and I ain't got the heart to lash him, somehow. Every time I let him off, my conscience does hurt me so, and every time I hit him my old heart most breaks. Well-a-well, man that is born of woman is of few days and full of trouble, as the Scripture says, and I reckon it's so. He'll play hookey this evening, and I'll be obleeged to make him work, tomorrow, to punish him. It's mighty hard to make him work Saturdays, when all the boys is having holiday, but he hates work more than he hates anything else, and I've *got* to do some of my duty by him, or I'll be the ruination of the child."

Tom did play hookey, and he had a very good time. He got back home barely in season to help Jim, the small colored boy, saw next-day's wood and split the kindlings before supper. At least he was there in time to tell his adventures to Jim while Jim did three-fourths of the work. Tom's younger brother (or rather, half-brother), Sid, was already through with his part of the work (picking up chips), for he was a quiet boy, and had no adventurous troublesome ways.

While Tom was eating his supper, and stealing sugar as opportunity offered, Aunt Polly asked him questions that were full of guile, and very deep — for she wanted to trap him into damaging revealments. Like many other simple-hearted souls, it was her pet vanity to believe she was endowed with a talent for dark and mysterious diplomacy, and she loved to contemplate her most transparent devices as marvels of low cunning. Said she:

"Tom, it was middling warm in school, warn't it?"

"Yes'm."

"Powerful warm, warn't it?"

"Yes'm."

"Didn't you want to go in a-swimming, Tom?"

A bit of a scare shot through Tom—a touch of uncomfortable suspicion. He searched Aunt Polly's face, but it told him nothing. So he said:

"No'm—well, not very much."

The old lady reached out her hand and felt Tom's shirt, and said: "But you ain't too warm now, though." And it flattered her to reflect that she had discovered that the shirt was dry without anybody knowing that that was what she had in her mind. But in spite of her, Tom knew where the wind lay now. So he forestalled what might be the next move:

"Some of us pumped on our heads—mine's damp yet. See?"

Aunt Polly was vexed to think she had overlooked that bit of circumstantial evidence and missed a trick. Then she had a new inspiration: "Tom, you didn't have to undo your shirt-collar where I sewed it, to pump on your head, did you? Unbutton your jacket!"

The trouble vanished out of Tom's face. He opened his jacket. His shirt-collar was securely sewed.

"Bother! Well, go 'long with you. I'd made sure you'd played hookey and been a-swimming. But I forgive ye, Tom. I reckon you're kind of a singed cat, as the saying is —better'n you look. *This* time."

She was half sorry her sagacity had miscarried, and half glad that Tom had stumbled into obedient conduct for once.

But Sidney said: "Well, now, if I didn't think you sewed his collar with white thread, but it's black."

"Why, I did sew it with white! Tom!"

But Tom did not wait for the rest. As he went out at the door he said: "Siddy, I'll lick you for that."

In a safe place Tom examined two large needles which were thrust into the lapels of his jacket, and had thread bound about them—one needle carried white thread and the other black. He said:

"She'd never noticed if it hadn't been for Sid. Confound it! sometimes she sews it with white, and sometimes she sews it with black. I wish to gee-miny she'd stick to one or t'other—*I* can't keep the run of 'em. But I bet you I'll lam Sid for that. I'll learn him!"

Tom was not the Model Boy of the village. He knew the model boy very well though—and loathed him.

Within two minutes, or even less, he had forgotten all his troubles. Not because his troubles were one whit less heavy and bitter to him than a man's are to a man, but because a new and powerful interest bore them down and drove them out of his mind for the time—just as men's misfortunes are forgotten in the excitement of new enterprises. This new interest was a valued novelty in whistling, which he had just acquired from a Negro, and he was suffering to practise it undisturbed. It consisted in a peculiar birdlike turn, a sort of liquid warble, produced by touching the tongue to the roof of the mouth at short intervals in the midst of the music. The reader probably remembers how to do it, if he has ever been a boy. Diligence and attention soon gave him the knack of it, and he strode down the street with his mouth full of harmony and his soul full of gratitude. He felt much as an astronomer feels who has discovered a new planet. No doubt, as far as strong deep pleasure is concerned, the advantage was with the boy, not the astronomer.

The summer evenings were long. It was not dark yet. Presently Tom checked his whistle. A stranger was before him—a boy a shade larger than himself. A newcomer of any age or either sex was an impressive curiosity in the poor little shabby village of St. Petersburg. This boy was well dressed, too—well dressed on a week-day. This was simply astounding. His cap was a dainty thing, his close-buttoned blue cloth roundabout was new and natty, and so were his pantaloons. He had shoes on—and it was only Friday. He even wore a necktie, a bright bit of ribbon. He had a citified air about him that ate into Tom's vitals. The more Tom stared at the splendid marvel, the higher he turned up his nose at his finery and the shabbier and shabbier his own outfit seemed to him to grow. Neither boy spoke. If one moved, the other moved—but only sideways, in a circle. They kept face to face and eye to eye all the time.

Finally Tom said, "I can lick you!"

"I'd like to see you try it."

"Well, I can do it."

"No you can't either."

"Yes I can."

"No you can't."

"I can."

"You can't."

"Can!"

"Can't!"

An uncomfortable pause. Then Tom said, "What's your name?"

" 'Tisn't any of your business, maybe."

"Well, I'll *make* it my business."

"Well, why don't you?"

"If you say much, I will."

"Much—much—*much*. There now."

"Oh, you think you're mighty smart, *don't* you? I could lick you with one hand tied behind me, if I wanted to."

"Well, why don't you *do* it? You *say* you can do it."

"Well, I *will*, if you fool with me."

"Oh, yes—I've seen whole families in the same fix."

"Smarty! You think you're *some* now, *don't* you? Oh, what a hat!"

"You can lump that hat if you don't like it. I dare you to knock it off—and anybody that'll take a dare will suck eggs."

"You're a liar!"

"You're another."

"You're a fighting liar and dasn't take it up."

"Aw—take a walk!"

"Say—if you give me much more of your sass, I'll take and bounce a rock off'n your head."

"Oh, of *course* you will."

"Well, I *will*."

"Well, why don't you *do* it then? What do you keep *saying* you will for? Why don't you *do* it? It's because you're afraid."

"I *ain't* afraid."

"You are."

"I ain't."

"You are."

Another pause, and more eyeing and sidling around each other. Presently they were shoulder to shoulder. Tom said, "Get away from here!"

"Go away yourself!"

"I won't."

"*I* won't either."

So they stood, each with a foot placed at an angle as a brace, and both shoving with might and main, and glowering at each other with hate. But neither could get an advantage. After struggling till both were hot and flushed, each relaxed his strain with watchful caution, and Tom said, "You're a coward and a pup. I'll tell my big brother on you. He can thrash you with his little finger, and I'll make him do it, too."

"What do I care for your big brother? I've got a brother that's bigger than he is —and what's more, he can throw him over that fence, too." (Both brothers were imaginary.)

"That's a lie."

"*Your* saying so don't make it so."

Tom drew a line in the dust with his big toe, and said, "I dare you to step over that, and I'll lick you till you can't stand up. Anybody that'll take a dare will steal sheep."

The new boy stepped over promptly, and said, "Now you said you'd do it, let's see you do it."

"Don't you crowd me now; you better look out."

"Well, you *said* you'd do it—why don't you do it?"

"By jingo! For two cents I *will* do it."

The new boy took two broad coppers out of his pocket and held them out with derision. Tom struck them to the ground. In an instant both boys were rolling and tumbling in the dirt, gripped together like cats; and for the space of a minute they tugged and tore at each other's hair and clothes, punched and scratched each other's noses, and covered themselves with dust and glory. Presently the confusion took form and through the fog of battle Tom appeared, seated astride the new boy, and pounding him with his fists.

"Holler 'nuff!" said he.

The boy only struggled to free himself. He was crying—mainly from rage.

"Holler 'nuff!"—and the pounding went on.

At last the stranger got out a smothered " 'Nuff!" and Tom let him up and said, "Now that'll learn you. Better look out who you're fooling with next time."

The new boy went off brushing the dust from his clothes, sobbing, snuffling, and

occasionally looking back and shaking his head and threatening what he would do to Tom the "next time he caught him out."

Tom responded with jeers, started off in high feather, and as soon as his back was turned the new boy snatched up a stone, threw it and hit him between the shoulders and then turned tail and ran like an antelope. Tom chased the traitor home and thus found out where he lived. He then held a position at the gate for some time, daring the enemy to come outside, but the enemy only made faces at him through the window and declined. At last the enemy's mother appeared, and called Tom a bad vicious vulgar child, and ordered him away. So he went away, but he said he " 'lowed to lay for" that boy.

He got home pretty late that night, and when he climbed cautiously in at the window, he uncovered an ambuscade, in the person of his aunt. When she saw the state his clothes were in, her resolution to turn his Saturday holiday into captivity at hard labor became adamantine in its firmness.

Saturday morning was come, and all the summer world was bright and fresh and brimming with life. There was a song in every heart; and if the heart was young the music issued at the lips. There was cheer in every face and a spring in every step. The locust trees were in bloom and the fragrance of the blossoms filled the air. Cardiff Hill, beyond the village and above it, was green with vegetation, and it lay just far enough away to seem a Delectable Land, dreamy, reposeful, and inviting.

Tom appeared on the sidewalk with a bucket of whitewash and a long-handled brush. He surveyed the fence. All gladness left him and a deep melancholy settled down upon his spirit. Thirty yards of board fence nine feet high! Life to him seemed hollow, and existence but a burden. Sighing he dipped his brush and passed it along the topmost plank. He repeated the operation; did it again; compared the insignificant whitewashed streak with the far-reaching continent of unwhitewashed fence, and sat down on a tree-box discouraged.

Jim came skipping out at the gate with a tin pail. He was singing "Buffalo Gals."

Bringing water from the town pump had always been hateful work in Tom's eyes, before, but now it did not strike him so. He remembered that there was company at the pump. White and Negro boys and girls were always there waiting their turns, resting, trading playthings, quarreling, fighting, skylarking. And he remembered that although the pump was only a hundred and fifty yards off, Jim never got back with a bucket of water under an hour — and even then somebody generally had to go after him.

Tom said, "Say, Jim, I'll fetch the water if you'll do some whitewashing."

Jim shook his head and said, "Can't, Mars' Tom. Ole Missis, she tole me I got to go an' git dis water an' not stop foolin' roun' wid anybody. She says she spec' Mars' Tom gwine to ax me to whitewash, an' so she tole me go 'long an' 'tend to my own business—she 'lowed *she'd* tend to de whitewashin'."

"Oh, never you mind what she said, Jim. That's the way she always talks. Gimme the bucket—I won't be gone only a minute. *She* won't ever know."

"Oh, I dasn't, Mars' Tom. Ole Missis she'd take an' tar de head off'n me. 'Deed she would."

"*She!* She never licks anybody. She

262

whacks 'em over the head with her thimble —but who cares for that, I'd like to know? She talks awful, but talk don't hurt—anyways it don't if she don't cry. Jim, I'll give you a marvel. I'll give you a white alley!"

Jim began to waver.

"White alley, Jim! And it's a bully taw."

"My! Dat's a might gay marvel, *I* tell you! But, Mars' Tom, I's powerful 'fraid ole Missis—"

"And besides, if you will, I'll show you my sore toe."

Jim was only human—this attraction was too much for him. He put down his pail, took the white alley, and bent over the toe with absorbing interest while the bandage was being unwound. In another moment he was flying down the street with his pail and a tingling rear. Tom was whitewashing

with vigor, and Aunt Polly was retiring from the field with a slipper in her hand and triumph in her eye.

But Tom's energy did not last. He began to think of the fun he had planned for this day, and his sorrows multiplied. Soon the free boys would come tripping along on all sorts of delicious expeditions, and they would make fun of him for having to work. The very thought of it burnt him like fire. He got out his worldly wealth and examined it—bits of toys, marbles, and trash; enough to buy an exchange of *work*, maybe, but not half enough to buy so much as half an hour of pure freedom. So he returned his straitened means to his pocket, and gave up the idea of trying to buy the boys.

At this dark and hopeless moment an inspiration burst upon him! It was nothing

less than a great, magnificent inspiration.

He took up his brush and went tranquilly to work. Ben Rogers hove in sight presently—the very boy, of all boys, whose ridicule he had been dreading. Ben's gait was the hop-skip-and-jump—proof enough that his heart was light and his anticipations high. He was eating an apple, and giving a long melodious whoop, at intervals, followed by a deep-toned ding-dong-dong, ding-dong-dong, for he was personating a steamboat. As he drew near, he slackened speed, took the middle of the street, leaned far over to starboard and rounded to ponderously and with laborious pomp and circumstance — for he was personating the *Big Missouri* and he considered himself to be drawing nine feet of water. He was boat and captain and engine-bells combined, so he had to imagine himself standing on his own hurricane-deck giving the orders and executing them: "Stop her, sir! Ting-a-ling-ling!"

The headway ran almost out and he drew up slowly toward the sidewalk. "Ship up to back! Ting-a-ling-ling!" His arms straightened and stiffened down his sides. "Set her back on the stabboard! Ting-a-ling-ling! Chow! Ch-chow-wow! Chow!" His right hand, meantime, described stately circles—for it was representing a forty-foot wheel. "Let her go back on the labboard! Ting-a-ling-ling! Chow-ch-chow-chow!" The left hand began to describe circles. "Stop the stabboard! Ting-a-ling-ling! Stop the labboard! Come ahead on the stabboard! Stop her! Let your outside turn over slow! Ting-a-ling-ling! Chow-ow-ow! Get out that headline! *Lively* now! Come—out with your springline—what're you about there! Take a turn round that stump with the

bight of it! Stand by that stage, now—let her go! Done with the engines, sir! Ting-a-ling-ling!"

Tom went on whitewashing — paid no attention to the steamboat.

Ben stared a moment and then said, *"Hi-yi! You're* up a stump, ain't you!"

No answer. Tom surveyed his last touch with the eye of an artist, then he gave his brush another gentle sweep and surveyed the result, as before.

Ben ranged up alongside of him.

Tom's mouth watered for the apple, but he stuck to his work.

Ben said, "Hello, old chap, you got to work, hey?"

Tom wheeled suddenly and said, "Why, it's you, Ben! I warn't noticing."

"Say—*I'm* going in a-swimming, I am. Don't you wish you could? But of course you'd druther *work*—wouldn't you? Course you would!"

Tom contemplated the boy a bit, and said, "What do you call work?"

"Why, ain't *that* work?"

Tom resumed his whitewashing and answered carelessly, "Well, maybe it is, and maybe it ain't. All I know, is, it suits Tom Sawyer."

"Oh come, now, you don't mean to let on that you *like* it?"

The brush continued to move.

"Like it? Well, I don't see why I oughtn't to like it. Does a boy get a chance to whitewash a fence every day?"

That put the thing in a new light. Ben stopped nibbling his apple.

Tom swept his brush daintily back and forth — stepped back to note the effect — added a touch here and there — criticized the effect again.

Ben was watching every move and getting more and more interested, more and more absorbed. Presently he said, "Say, Tom, let *me* whitewash a little."

Tom considered, was about to consent; but he altered his mind. "No—no—I reckon it wouldn't hardly do, Ben. You see, Aunt Polly's awful particular about this fence—right here on the street, you know. If it was the back fence I wouldn't mind and *she* wouldn't. Yes, she's awful particular about this fence. It's got to be done very careful. I reckon there ain't one boy in a thousand, maybe two thousand, that can do it the way it's got to be done."

"No—is that so? Oh come, now—lemme just try. Only just a little—I'd let *you* if you was me, Tom."

"Ben, I'd like to, honest Injun; but Aunt Polly—well, Jim wanted to do it, but she wouldn't let him. Sid wanted to do it, and she wouldn't let Sid. Now don't you see how I'm fixed? If you was to tackle this fence and anything was to happen to it—"

"Oh, shucks, I'll be just as careful. Now lemme try. Say—I'll give you the core of my apple."

"Well, here — no, Ben, now don't. I'm afeard—"

"I'll give you *all* of it!"

Tom gave up the brush with reluctance in his face but alacrity in his heart. And while the late steamer *Big Missouri* worked and sweated in the sun, the retired artist sat on a barrel in the shade close by, dangled his legs, munched his apple, and planned the slaughter of more innocents. There was no lack of material; boys happened along every little while. They came to jeer, but remained to whitewash. By the time Ben was fagged out, Tom had traded the next chance to Billy Fisher for a kite, in good repair; and when *he* played out, Johnny Miller bought in for a dead rat and a string to swing it with—and so on, and so on, hour after hour. And when the middle of the afternoon came, from being a poor poverty-stricken boy in the morning, Tom was literally rolling in wealth. He had, besides the things before mentioned, twelve marbles, part of a jew's harp, a piece of blue bottle-glass to look through, a spool cannon, a key that wouldn't unlock anything, a fragment of chalk, a glass stopper of a decanter, a tin soldier, a couple of tadpoles, six fire-crackers, a kitten with only one eye, a brass door-knob, a dog-collar—but no dog—the handle of a knife, four pieces of orange-peel, and a dilapidated old window-sash.

He had had a nice good idle time all the while—plenty of company—and the fence had three coats of whitewash on it! If he hadn't run out of whitewash, he would have bankrupted every boy in the village.

Tom said to himself that it was not such a hollow world after all. He had discovered a great law of human action, without knowing it — namely, that in order to make a man or boy covet a thing, it is only necessary to make the thing difficult to attain. If he had been a great wise philosopher, like the writer of this story, he would now have comprehended that Work consists of whatever a body is *obliged* to do, and that Play consists of whatever a body is not obliged to do. And this would help him to understand why constructing artificial flowers or performing on a treadmill is work, while rolling ten-pins or climbing Mont Blanc is only amusement.

The boy mused awhile over the substantial change which had taken place in his worldly circumstances, and then wended toward headquarters to report.

266

The Cat and the Painkiller

From TOM SAWYER

By Mark Twain

ONE of the reasons why Tom's mind had drifted away from its secret troubles was that it had found a new and weighty matter to interest itself about. Becky Thatcher had stopped coming to school. Tom had struggled with his pride a few days, and tried to "whistle her down the wind," but failed.

He began to find himself hanging around her father's house, nights, and feeling very miserable. She was ill. What if she should die! There was distraction in the thought. He no longer took an interest in war, nor even in piracy. The charm of life was gone; there was nothing but dreariness left. He put his hoop away, and his bat; there was no joy in them any more.

His aunt was concerned. She began to try all manner of remedies on him. She was one of those people who are infatuated with patent medicines and all newfangled methods of producing health or mending it. When something fresh in this line came out she was in a fever, right away, to try it; not on herself, for she was never ailing, but on anybody else that came handy. She was a subscriber for all the "Health" periodicals and phrenological frauds; and the solemn ignorance they were inflated with was breath to her nostrils. All the "rot" they contained about ventilation, and how to go to bed, and how to get up, and what to eat, and what to drink, and how much exercise to take, and what frame of mind to keep one's self in, and what sort of clothing to wear, was all gospel to her, and she never observed that her health journals of the current month customarily upset everything they had recommended the month before. She was as simple-hearted and honest as the day was long, and so she was an easy victim. She gathered together her quack periodicals and her quack medicines, and thus armed with death, went about on her pale horse, metaphorically speaking, with "hell following after." But she never suspected that she was not an angel of healing and the balm of Gilead in disguise to the suffering neighbors.

The water treament was new, now, and Tom's low condition was a windfall to her. She had him out at daylight every morning, stood him up in the woodshed and drowned him with a deluge of cold water; then she scrubbed him down with a towel like a file, and so brought him to. Then she rolled him up in a wet sheet and put him away under blankets till she sweated his soul clean and "the yellow stains of it came through his pores"—as Tom said.

Yet notwithstanding all this, the boy grew more and more melancholy and pale. She added hot baths, sitz baths, shower baths, and plunges. The boy remained as dismal as a hearse. She began to assist the water with a slim oatmeal diet and blister plasters. She calculated his capacity as she would a jug's, and filled him up every day with quack cure-alls.

Tom had become indifferent to persecution by this time. This phase filled the old lady's heart with consternation. This indifference must be broken up at any cost. Now she heard of Painkiller for the first time. She ordered a lot of it at once. She tasted it and was filled with gratitude. It was simply fire in liquid form. She dropped the water treatment and everything else, and pinned her faith to Painkiller. She gave Tom a teaspoonful and watched with the deepest anxiety for the result. Her troubles were instantly at rest, her soul at peace again, for the "indifference" was broken up. The boy could not have shown a wilder or heartier interest if she had built a fire under him.

Tom felt that it was time to wake up. This sort of life might be romantic enough, in his blighted condition, but it was getting to have too little sentiment and too much distracting variety about it. So he thought over various plans for relief, and finally hit upon professing to be fond of Painkiller. He asked for it so often that he became a nuisance, and his aunt ended by telling him to help himself and quit bothering her. But she watched the bottle. She found that the medicine did really diminish, but it did not occur to her that the boy was mending the health of a crack in the sitting-room floor with it.

One day Tom was in the act of dosing the crack when his aunt's yellow cat came along, purring, eying the teaspoon avariciously, and begging for a taste.

Tom said, "Don't ask for it unless you want it, Peter."

But Peter signified that he did want it.

"You better make sure."

Peter was sure.

"Now you've asked for it, and I'll give it to you, because there ain't anything mean about *me*. But if you find you don't like it, you mustn't blame anybody but your own self."

Peter was agreeable. So Tom pried his mouth open and poured down the Pain-

268

killer. Peter sprang a couple of yards in the air, and then delivered a war whoop and set off round and round the room, banging against furniture, upsetting flowerpots, and making general havoc. Next he rose on his hind feet and pranced around, in a frenzy of enjoyment, with his head over his shoulder and his voice proclaiming his unappeasable happiness. Then he went tearing around the house again spreading chaos and destruction in his path. Aunt Polly entered in time to see him throw a few double somersaults, deliver a final mighty hurrah, and sail through the open window, carrying the rest of the flowerpots with him. The old lady stood petrified with astonishment, peering over her glasses. Tom lay on the floor expiring with laughter.

"Tom, what on earth ails that cat?"

"I don't know, aunt," gasped the boy.

"Why, I never see anything like it. What *did* make him act so?"

" 'Deed I don't know, Aunt Polly. Cats always act so when they're having a good time."

"They do, do they?" There was something in the tone that made Tom apprehensive.

"Yes'm. That is, I believe they do."

"You *do?*"

"Yes'm."

The old lady was bending down, Tom watching with interest emphasized by anxiety. Too late he divined her "drift." The handle of the telltale teaspoon was visible under the bed valance. Aunt Polly took it, held it up. Tom winced, and dropped his eyes. Aunt Polly raised him by the usual handle—his ear—and cracked his head soundly with her thimble.

"Now, sir, what did you want to treat that poor dumb beast so for?"

"I done it out of pity for him—because he hadn't any aunt."

"Hadn't any aunt? You numbskull! What has that got to do with it?"

"Heaps. Because if he'd 'a' had one, she'd 'a' burnt him out herself! She'd 'a' roasted his bowels out of him 'thout any more feeling than if he was a human!"

Aunt Polly felt a sudden pang of remorse. This was putting the thing in a new light. What was cruelty to a cat *might* be cruelty to a boy too. She began to soften; she felt sorry. Her eyes watered a little, and she put her hand on Tom's head and said gently, "I was meaning for the best, Tom. And, Tom, it *did* do you good."

Tom looked up in her face with just a perceptible twinkle peeping through his gravity; and said, "I know you was meaning for the best, Auntie, and so was I with Peter. I done *him* good, too. I never see him get around so since—"

"Oh, go 'long with you, Tom, before you aggravate me again. And you try and see if you can't be a good boy, for once, and you needn't take any more medicine."

Tom reached school ahead of time. It was noticed that this strange thing had been occurring every day lately. And now, as usual of late, he hung about the gate of the schoolyard instead of playing with his comrades. He was sick, he said, and he looked it. He tried to seem to be looking everywhere but where he really was looking — down the road. Presently Jeff Thatcher hove in sight, and Tom's face lighted. He gazed a moment, then turned sorrowfully away.

When Jeff arrived, Tom "led up" warily to opportunities for remarks about Becky.

But the giddy lad never could see the bait. Tom watched and watched, hoping whenever a frisking frock came in sight, and hating the owner of it as soon as he saw she was not the right one. At last frocks ceased to appear, and he dropped hopelessly into the dumps. He entered the empty schoolhouse and sat down to suffer. Then one more frock passed in at the gate, and Tom's heart gave a great bound. The next instant he was out and "going on" like an Indian, yelling, laughing, chasing boys, jumping over the fence at risk of life and limb, throwing handsprings, standing on his head—doing all the heroic things he could conceive of, and keeping a furtive eye out all the while to see if Becky Thatcher was noticing.

But she seemed to be unconscious of it all; she never looked.

Could it be possible that she was not aware that he was there? He carried his exploits to her immediate vicinity; came war-whooping around, snatched a boy's cap, hurled it to the roof of the schoolhouse, broke through a group of boys, tumbling them in every direction, and fell sprawling, himself, under Becky's nose, almost upsetting her. She turned, with her nose in the air, and he heard her say: "Mf! some people think they're mighty smart—always showing off!"

Tom's cheeks burned. He gathered himself and sneaked off, crushed and crestfallen.

September

By Helen Hunt Jackson

The goldenrod is yellow,
  The corn is turning brown,
The trees in apple orchards
  With fruit are bending down;

The gentian's bluest fringes
  Are curling in the sun;
In dusty pods the milkweed
  Its hidden silk has spun;

The sedges flaunt their harvest
  In every meadow nook,
And asters by the brookside
  Make asters in the brook.

From dewy lanes at morning
  The grapes' sweet odors rise;
At noon the roads all flutter
  With yellow butterflies.

By all these lovely tokens
September's days are here,
With summer's best of weather
And autumn's best of cheer.

Apple-Seed John

By Lydia Maria Child

Poor Johnny was bended well nigh double
With years of toil and care and trouble;
But his large old heart still felt the need
Of doing for others some kindly deed.

"But what can I do," old Johnny said,
"I who work so hard for daily bread?
It takes heaps of money to do much good;
I am far too poor to do as I would."

The old man sat thinking deeply a while,
Then over his features gleamed a smile,
And he clapped his hands with a boyish glee,
And said to himself: "There's a way for me!"

He worked and he worked with might and
    main,
But no one knew the plan in his brain.
He took ripe apples in pay for chores,
And carefully cut from them all the cores.

He filled a bag full, then wandered away,
And no man saw him for many a day.
With knapsack over his shoulder slung,
He marched along, and whistled or sung.

He seemed to roam with no object in view,
Like one who had nothing on earth to do;
But journeying thus o'er the prairies wide,
He paused now and then and his bag untied.

With pointed cane deep holes he bore,
And in every hole he placed a core;
Then covered them well, and left them
    there
In keeping of sunshine, rain, and air.

Sometimes for days he waded through grass,
And saw not a living creature pass,
But often, when sinking to sleep in the dark,

He heard the owls hoot and the prairie-
dogs bark.

Sometimes an Indian of sturdy limb
Came striding along and walked with him;
And he who had food shared with the other,
As if he had met a hungry brother.

When the Indian saw how the bag was
    filled,
And looked at the holes that the white man
    drilled,
He thought to himself 'twas a silly plan
To be planting seed for some future man.

Sometimes a log cabin came in view,
Where Johnny was sure to find jobs to do,
By which he gained stores of bread and
    meat,
And welcome rest for his weary feet.

He had full many a story to tell,
And goodly hymns that he sung right well;
He tossed up the babes and joined the boys
In many a game full of fun and noise.

And he seemed so hearty in work or play,
Men, women, and boys all urged him to stay;
But he always said, "I have something to do,
And I must go on to carry it through."

The boys who were sure to follow him round,
Soon found what it was he put in the ground;
And so, as time passed and he travelled on,
Everyone called him "Old Apple-Seed
    John."

Whenever he'd used the whole of his store,
He went into cities and worked for more;
Then he marched back to the wilds again,
And planted seed on hillside and plain.

In cities, some said the old man was crazy
While others said he was only lazy;
But he took no notice of jibes and jeers,
He knew he was working for future years.

He knew that trees would soon abound
Where once a tree could not have been
    found,
That a flickering play of light and shade
Would dance and glimmer along the glade,

That blossoming sprays would form fair
    bowers
And sprinkle the grass with rosy showers,
And the little seeds his hands had spread,
Would become ripe apples when he was
    dead.

So he kept on travelling far and wide,
Till his old limbs failed him, and he died.
He said at the last, "'Tis a comfort to feel
I've done good in the world, though not a
    great deal."

Weary travellers, journeying west,
In the shade of his trees find pleasant rest;
And they often start, with glad surprise,
At the rosy fruit that around them lies.

And if they inquire whence came such trees,
Where not a bough once swayed in the
    breeze,
The answer still comes, as they travel on:
"These trees were planted by Apple-Seed
    John."

Robinson Crusoe's Adventure on a Desert Island

Retold from ROBINSON CRUSOE

By Daniel Defoe

When a book remains a favorite with boys and girls for over two centuries, we may be pretty sure it tells an exciting and satisfying story.

Such a book is ROBINSON CRUSOE. Generation after generation of children and grown-ups too have been thrilled by this tale of a man marooned on a desert island, having to conquer nature to stay alive.

How Robinson Crusoe fought off wild animals, how he provided himself with food and clothes and shelter, how he cultivated a garden, kept himself going physically and mentally, and finally how he found his faithful and loyal "man Friday"—all this is a story as exciting today as it has always been.

Robinson Crusoe's heroic and successful efforts to win a place for himself by his courage and resourcefulness and friendliness has always been an inspiration to all who read this story of his exploits.

ROBINSON CRUSOE wanted to go to sea. His parents did not want him to go because in his time, long ago, the life of a sailor was hard and dangerous. So he ran away.

He set sail as a passenger on a sailing ship from England. He wanted adventure, but he had more of it than he bargained for. He ran into more trouble and danger than a traveler could expect even in those rough days. He rode out storms that threw the little ship about like a bean bag in the high waves. He fell into the hands of pirates who made him a slave. He escaped, but he began to think he'd had enough of the sea.

He settled down on a tobacco plantation in Brazil. There he did so well that he thought the sea would hold no more dangers for him. So with a light heart he embarked on a sailing ship to go home to York in England. He had no idea that the real adventure of his life was just begin-

ning. He expected that the voyage home would take about three months. He did not dream that twenty-eight long years would go by before he saw England again. He was a tall, strong, healthy young man when he went aboard. He was still tall and strong when he arrived, but his hair was gray.

His ship had not gone far from Brazil when she ran into a hurricane that, like an angry giant, tore off the ship's masts and smashed her hull. The crew leaped into the ship's boats. They could see an island to the west, but their boats turned over in the mountainous waves. All the crew and Captain were drowned. Only one man escaped — Robinson Crusoe. He was young and strong and a fine swimmer, so he managed to swim to the island. Utterly worn out he lay on the sandy beach, soaking wet and bruised by the waves. He had no idea where he was. He hoped he would find friendly natives who would give him dry clothes and something to eat. "But," he thought, "the natives may be cannibals and perhaps fierce animals will be on the prowl in the darkness of the night."

Wearily he trudged, seeking a safe place where he could look about. He came to a tall strong tree, clambered up, and lay on its broad branches and slept.

In the morning he climbed a hill nearby and looked about for signs of people and houses. But everywhere he saw only rocks and trees.

He said to himself, "I am all alone on this island." He wandered about and found a fresh spring and drank cool water, but he was hungry and there was nothing to eat.

In despair he turned and looked out to sea, and his joy was great that the broken ship was still afloat. Perhaps there was someone left aboard. And perhaps there was something to eat that had not been spoiled by the salt water.

The sun was shining and the sea, so cruel the night before, was calm and smooth. Without a moment's wait, he threw off his salt-soaked clothes and swam out to the ship. Her masts were gone, and she was lying deep in the water. Even so her deck rose high above him. He swam about until he came across a rope hanging over the side. He managed to clamber aboard, calling out as he went. But there was no answer, only silence. Sad at heart, he started to search about him. And he was relieved to find many things still undamaged that would be a help to him.

He found bread and meat. Some of that he gulped down in great swallows. When he was no longer hungry, he began to think and plan. He must find a way to get supplies from the ship to shore. He could not keep swimming in and out, taking a little at a time. He must make a raft. There was plenty of timber from the broken masts and the stove-in sides of the ship. It was a hard job to drag these together and to tie them with stout stiff rope. But at last he had a good solid raft. On the raft he piled the hard bread which people ate at sea. Then great slabs of salted meat. These would keep a long time without spoiling. He took rice and barley and flour. Carefully he wrapped the ship's Bible. And over all on the raft he laid an old sail. On shore that night he made a tent of the sail and slept in it.

Next day he swam to the ship again, pushing the raft before him. This time he brought back guns and powder, for he might find animals that he could kill for food. He made many trips to the wrecked boat. On one trip he found two cats and a dog that had been hiding below still afraid of the storm. He was delighted and took them along for company. And he took the ship's tool box, with hammers and axes and nails. There was money in the Captain's cabin, but it could buy nothing on his island. One of the best things he found and brought ashore was the Captain's fine spy-glass, which had not been damaged at all. Many a time afterward this spy-glass was to save his life. He was glad he had done all this as fast as he could, for one day he woke up and saw that the wreck was gone, washed out to sea.

His next job was to build himself a place to keep off rain and to sleep safely. He used a hillside for a wall, then made sides of heavy sail-cloth he had brought from the wreck. He had brought blankets too, and these made a good bed. All round his tent he pounded a fence of sharp pointed sticks, so that no animal could get through. He made no gate; to get in and out he used a ladder that he pulled in after him each night. In back of the tent he dug a deep cave. There he kept his guns and powder dry.

As day after day went by, and no ship came in sight, he began to wonder: "Shall I ever get back home again? Shall I ever have anybody to talk to?" At first he was worried when he thought, "How can I tell what day it is? How will I know how long I have been here? I have no calendar. And no church bells ring to tell me when Sunday comes. How shall I know?" But he thought of a way. At the side of his house he put up a large cross. Each week day he cut a small line on it. On Sundays he cut a long line.

But he had little time to worry because he had a great deal to do. He went for long walks around the island searching for anything that might help him. He found some fine fruits, especially grapes. These he dried and so he had raisins. He found some tobacco plants too and was glad to be able to smoke his pipe again. He planted some of the seeds of barley and rice that he had saved from the ship, but the first ones did not come up. A Boy Scout of our own time would know many things that Robinson Crusoe had to learn the hard way by himself. If he had been a country boy he would have had an easier time. But he had grown up in the city of York in England and he did not know the simplest farming ways. He planted his seeds at the wrong time of year. Some baked in the sun and some were drowned out in the rainy season. But he

tried again and again and he learned from his failures. After awhile he had grain from the barley. He ground it between blocks of hard wood and he was able to bake a sort of bread.

In his search of the island he caught turtles and fish, and one day he found a goat and her kids. From the goat he got plenty of good milk. He caught and tamed a parrot and taught it to speak.

He hammered together a rough chair. That was simple. And it was easy for him to weave baskets to hold solid objects. But baskets would not do for meat and flour and bread. For those he needed jars of earthenware with no openings for rain or crawling insects or prying animals. He found some clay and formed it into jars. These he set out in the sun to dry. But when he went to pick them up they crumbled in his hands. He found a different kind of clay and he made a different mixture with water and he baked the pots longer. It took many experiments and much patience but at last he had a fine row of good jars.

He began to feel that he was learning how to manage on his island. But then came the hardest work of all. He must have a boat. He must be able to sail around the island to explore. And perhaps some day a ship would appear and he could row or sail out to her. First he thought the longboat he had brought from the ship would do. It was lying on its side and half-rotted. He worked on it for weeks but he had to give it up. He couldn't save it and it was too heavy to handle. Then he set out to make a canoe. For six months he worked on the canoe. It was good and solid. Indeed it was too solid, for he could not move it into the water.

A year went by and another year and more years. By this time Robinson Crusoe looked like a wild man. He had made himself clothes of goatskins. A pointed cap of goatskin sat on his head, and on his feet he wore rough goatskin boots. He had no way of getting the hair off the skins so goat's hair stuck out all around him from head to foot. But these rough clothes kept off the rain and cold and he was pleased with them. He even made an umbrella of the goatskins. In those days hardly anybody had an umbrella. The umbrella was a new invention. But in Brazil in South America he had seen the natives make umbrellas. He wanted one now to keep off the sun when it was too hot and the rain when it came down in tropic torrents. The umbrella he made of the hairy goatskins was a strange-looking object indeed but he found that the hair side shed the rain and the skin side kept off the sun. He even found a way to open and close it.

And so he made himself comfortable and resigned himself to patient waiting. He even found ways to have a little fun. The parrot learned to say Robin Crusoe. The dog from the wreck was a friend until he died of old age. The old cats died too, but they had kittens and the kittens had kittens; so he always had some as pets, though some of the cats did run off into the woods and become wild. The young kids were frisky.

You can imagine Robinson Crusoe then, dressed in his rough fur clothes, sitting on the chair he had made. He is reading the Bible he had brought from the ship. The parrot is sitting on his shoulder, talking loud as parrots do. The dog is at his feet and the kittens are chasing each other and pretending to fight. The kids are dancing about. And Crusoe would look up over the sea and hope for a ship.

For five years he worked and learned and longed for a friendly voice. Yet when he saw the first sign of a human visitor he was not glad at all. Instead he was frightened. He was walking along the beach a long way from his house, when he stopped as though struck. For in the sand he had seen the print of a human foot! Just the print of one foot, but that meant that someone had been here, someone might be here now. Someone might be waiting to catch him and perhaps eat him! He ran in a panic all the way back to his house. After that, he kept his guns loaded beside him day and night. But days and weeks and months went by and nothing more happened, until he had counted two whole years by the marks on his cross. Once again he began to feel safe.

So one day he set out for a part of the island he had never explored before. There he was horrified to see the bones of human beings scattered on the shore. He saw hands and feet and even skulls. Nearby he found the ashes of a fire. He was sure then of something he had guessed at before, that the natives who had come here were cannibals.

He was so sick at the thought of such cruelty that he forgot to be afraid, but he did rush away as fast as he could to his own sheltered spot. Luckily, he had chosen to live on this side of the island, where the savages never had come. He was filled with new fear as he thought how these savages had come and gone, and that with all his watching he had seen and heard nothing. There was always the danger that they might come upon his rough home.

He began to take new care for his own safety. He built a new shelter on a hilltop with a double wall of sharp stakes around it. From this he watched the shore through his spyglass day after day. He loaded each of his guns and kept them all ready pointed toward the place where he had found the bones. He stayed as close to his refuge as he could, but whenever he had to go out he carried his loaded pistols.

He was beginning to grow less fearful when through his glass he saw a band of naked savages. These were waving spears and dancing wildly on the distant beach. Suppose he had wandered near them without his guns! But these came no nearer and after awhile they got into their canoes and went off.

Suppose, he thought, even one cannibal saw the smoke of his cooking fires. He must do something about that. He sought out a small cave in the rocks near his shelter and from that time he always built his fires inside the cave. That helped him to feel a little safer. But he knew that all this care was not enough. He must find some way to frighten off the savages. He could not think of a way. Of course, if they came closer he would fire his guns. They were used to bows and arrows and would be put into panic by guns. But he was only one man and they were many. And there was another danger. His powder might run out and he had no way to make more. In order to save powder, he had long ago given up shooting game for food.

Then, one day something happened that made him forget all about hiding the fire. As he was bending over his cooking he heard a shot from a gun. Not in many long years had he heard any gun but his own.

He rushed to the hilltop and looked out. And there off in the water he saw a large ship. He thought this must mean that the ship carried civilized men who would be his friends. But the ship was pounding to pieces on the rocks. If he hurried, he might rescue the crew. Swiftly he built up a huge fire on the hill. He ran to the shore to pull in any man who could swim ashore. He waited and waited but not one came. He felt sad and lonely indeed as, one by one, the bodies of the sailors were washed up on the beach, dead. So once more he lived alone, finding what comfort and pleasure he could in his Bible and the company of his animals.

And then came a great change. It happened like this: He was looking from his shelter when he was alarmed to see that five canoes were lying on the beach. They were not ten minutes' walk from his shelter. This could be worse than anything he had seen before. He could not tell whether the men from the canoes were white men or savage cannibals, because he could see only the canoes and not the men they had brought. He climbed to the hilltop and looked through the spyglass. Then he saw the men who belonged to the canoes. And a sad and terrifying sight it was. These were no friends. These were naked savages, South American Indians. There must have been as many as thirty of them. They had built a fire and were screaming and dancing around it. But there was worse, for they were dragging two poor wretches toward the fire. One they knocked on the head ready to throw him in. But while they were busy with this, the savages turned their backs on the other captive, for they thought he could not escape. As far as they knew, there was no one on the island. The man

thought he saw a chance to escape and at once he turned and ran away. And to Crusoe's horror, he saw that the man was running straight toward him and his shelter.

Crusoe was indeed frightened. All the plans he had made to fight off invaders were of no use now. How could one man fight off thirty? All he could do was to stay in his shelter and keep his guns trained on the savages. But in a moment he was glad to see that only three of the savages were giving chase. Against three men he might be able to do something since he had guns and they had only bows and arrows.

Between his shelter and the savages there was a deep narrow creek. The fugitive jumped into the creek and swam across. The men jumped after him. But one of them who could not swim crawled out and ran back. The others swam across. Crusoe caught up a pistol and a gun and raced toward the creek. He moved fast, but he was careful to keep under the trees. Now only two men were in pursuit and the men around the fire could no longer see any of the runners.

Crusoe came close enough to shoot the pursuers with his gun; but if he did that, he knew the men around the fire would hear the shot. Besides, Crusoe did not want to kill even a cannibal unless he had to. So he crept up close enough to hit the nearest savage over the head with the stock of his gun. The man fell and the other cannibal lifted his bow, ready to fire an arrow. Crusoe had to shoot and kill him. When the cannibals around the fire heard the crash of the shots, they did not come closer, as Crusoe feared they would, but fled to their boats and hurried off.

The poor escaping savage had never seen a gun and he was so frightened by Crusoe's

shot that he stood as though made of stone. Crusoe made all the friendly signs he could and step by step the man came forward. At last he said a few words. The language was strange, but it sounded as though he wanted to be friendly. He threw himself down on the ground and placed one of Robinson's feet on his head to show that he meant to be his slave forever.

Crusoe motioned him to rise and pointed to the savage who had been stunned. He could mean danger to them. The rescued man pointed to the sword which Crusoe wore. Crusoe gave it to him and then, without a word, he dashed back and killed the stunned savage. Then they buried both the slain men.

Crusoe led the way to his shelter. He was happy indeed. For the first time in twenty-five years he was hearing a human voice even though he could not understand a word.

The man was tall and well made, and his face was both handsome and kindly. Crusoe took him to his cave to hide him from the savages, if any should come back. He gave the man raisins and bread. He made a rough bed and the man lay down and slept.

While he slept Crusoe wondered what he should call him. He thought that this day was Friday and it would be fitting to call the man by the name of his rescue day. So Friday was his name. For a while they were both very busy, for Crusoe had to teach his man Friday his way of living. Crusoe took Friday on all his trips, taught him how to shoot a gun and how to care for crops. He also had to teach him English. This was hard, but it was also fun, since they both laughed heartily over Crusoe's strange gestures and Friday's queer pronunciations. After he got over his fear, Friday was a merry soul. This was the most pleasant year of Crusoe's stay on the island.

One day, when the sky was clear, Crusoe

looked through his spyglass and saw land in the distance. He knew it was the continent of South America. He handed the spyglass to Friday, and after the Indian had looked through it he jumped for joy and said this was his homeland, the place where he had lived before he had been captured by the enemy Indians.

While he was still alone Crusoe had built two boats, but both were too heavy to be useful. Now Crusoe taught Friday how to use his tools, and the two men set out to build a new boat. When it was finished, Crusoe wanted to try out Friday's loyalty. He offered to give him the new boat if he wanted to go home to his people. Friday looked very sad and said he would not go unless his master went with him.

Friday pointed to his home place and said, "More white men over there." He tried to count them on his fingers but could not. Crusoe guessed there might be twelve. He thought that if he could reach the mainland he would get the help of these white men to find a way to go home. But the rainy season came, with storms that made such a journey dangerous. Before he could do anything further, Friday came rushing up to the little fort one day crying and wringing his hands.

"Master," he wailed, "bad . . . bad," and he pointed to the shore. There Crusoe made out twenty-one savages and three prisoners. They were getting ready to build their fires and to throw the prisoners in.

Crusoe decided at once to go to the rescue. He told Friday not to be afraid. He gave Friday a pistol to put in his belt and three guns for his shoulders. He and Friday were two and the others were twenty-one, but he knew from Friday's rescue how afraid of guns the savages were. He and Friday would make a surprise attack and perhaps the savages would flee. The two men ran at the savages, waving guns and knives and screaming in the manner the savages used themselves. They fired off their guns, so that the savages thought there were many of them.

Some of the Indians ran at once to their boats. Some stayed and fought, but the fight was short. Only two of the prisoners were left alive. Quickly Crusoe cut their ropes and freed them. Both had been captured on the mainland. One was Spanish; the other was an Indian. Friday went to the Indian and began to jump for joy. "This is my father," he shouted, "my own father."

Crusoe tended the Spaniard, while Friday took care of his father. For a while then there were four men on the island and Crusoe began to feel like a King. When both the prisoners were well and strong again, Crusoe said they could now help to get word to the white men on the mainland. Then all together they would plan a way to get home. Crusoe sent the Spaniard and Friday's father off to the mainland in the canoe they had built. And Crusoe and Friday waited for them to come back. Eight days went by. Then on the ninth day, they could see a boat off shore.

But when Crusoe looked at it through his spyglass, it was not the small canoe at all, but a big English merchant ship. She was anchored in the offing, her sails furled. Rowing in to the shore was her long boat, filled with English sailors. Robinson was so happy he almost danced. Here, at last, was his chance to go home. He was just ready to run down to welcome them when he saw that three of the men were being shoved and beaten by eight others. One of the prisoners was kneeling, pleading. Then all three were bound and thrown on the beach.

"See," said Friday, "see, the white men will throw their prisoners on the fire and eat them, just as my people do."

"No, no," said Crusoe, "white men are not cannibals. They may kill the captives, or they may leave them on the island and sail away."

As the two watched, they saw the sailors leave the prisoners while they went off to explore the island. They stayed away so long that the tide went out and their boat was grounded. When they saw this they went off again under the trees. As soon as they were out of sight Crusoe hurried down to speak to the captives. When the tied-up men saw him looking so wild in his queer

goatskin clothes, they were afraid of him and would have run away if they could.

"I will not hurt you," said Robinson, "I am an Englishman too. I have been shipwrecked on this island for twenty-eight years. But what is wrong here? Why are you prisoners?"

One of the three spoke up, though he was almost choked with tears, "I am the Captain of this ship. This is my mate and the other is a passenger. My crew has mutinied. They have brought us here to maroon us, in the hope that we will starve."

He said a few of the crew were loyal but were afraid of the mutineers.

"We will help you," said Crusoe. "We have guns and we will give you arms. But you must promise two things. One is that you will obey me in all things. The other is that you will take me and my friends home to England." He told the Captain about Friday and the white men on the mainland.

The Captain was only too glad to make

281

the promises. He said, "You must have been sent from heaven, for we had given up all hope of help from fellowmen."

"First," said Crusoe, "we must find the men who brought you to the island."

He sent Friday to find out where they were. Friday reported that they were fast asleep in the woods. Crusoe then told the Captain that they should fire on the men to frighten them, and perhaps kill the ringleaders. But the Captain did not want to kill any of them even though two of the ringleaders were dangerous. But he took a musket. The mate and passenger went along. When they reached the men, it was they who shot and killed the ringleaders of the mutiny. They captured the rest and tied them up and left them in the cave.

Crusoe then sent Friday with the Captain's mate to take the sails and oars out of the longboat and to make a hole in her bottom. While all this was going on, the mother ship that was anchored off shore kept sending signals, ordering the first boatload of men to come back to the ship. At last, when they got no answer, they sent another boatful to find out what had happened to the first one. The men in the second boat were armed.

The Captain said that three of the men in this boat were honest fellows who had not wanted to mutiny. The rest were evil men. When they landed and saw the hole in the first longboat, they were stunned with surprise. They fired off their guns as a signal to the missing longboat crew. When they got no answer, they got into their own boat and hurried back to the ship.

The Captain did not like this. He thought the terrified longboat men would go aboard the ship again, set sail, and leave all of them behind. But soon they came ashore once again, and this time they went off to search the woods for their fellows. They came farther into the island and kept shouting to their friends. Since the friends were prisoners they got no answer; so once more they turned toward their boat.

"We must stop them," said Crusoe.

The Captain then thought of a trick to keep them from going off. The Captain, his mate, the passenger, and Friday would go off a distance and halloo as loud as they could, but would stay out of sight. The men from the second boat would think them friends and would halloo back. Thus the Captain and the three would lead the mutineers toward Crusoe who was hiding ready to catch them one by one.

All but five of the mutineers were caught when it began to grow dark. Crusoe knew the island so well that this did not bother him but it confused the mutineers. Crusoe said that this was a good time to show themselves to the five remaining mutineers and offer to parley with them. "We will not fire on them unless they fire on us first."

The Captain said that was good, but to be careful of the boatswain, Will Atkins, who had started the mutiny.

So they crept up on the five men with hardly a sound. Then as they got close, they leaped up and ran at them yelling, taking them utterly by surprise.

Will Atkins, who was a coward, cried and wrung his hands and begged for mercy. But all of them were tied up and taken back to camp to join the other prisoners. The Captain talked to them and said that about twelve of the prisoners wanted no part of the mutiny and that he could trust them.

All went well, but the most important

part of all had still to be done. They must capture the ship from the men still aboard her. But Crusoe had made a plan for this. Crusoe and Friday stayed on the island to guard the prisoners. The Captain and the friendly sailors got into the second long-boat and approached the ship. It was now late at night and while there was a moon, the men aboard could not see the boat clearly and thought they were the mutineers coming back. The Captain and the loyal men, after a short hard fight, took back the ship. They then fired the ship's guns as a signal to Crusoe that all was well. When Crusoe heard them, he knew that at last he would be able to go home to England.

Happy and tired, Crusoe slept. When he woke, he saw that the Captain had brought the ship close to shore. Neither he nor the Captain wished to kill the rest of the mutineers. They supplied them with food, guns, and clothes, and left them on the island, saying that since Crusoe had been able to live, so should they too.

And so at last Crusoe went on board, taking Friday with him. He took also his parrot and his goatskin hat and his umbrella. They then sailed for the mainland, the home of Friday's father. There they rescued the white sailors who had been left.

And so they reached England and home. Crusoe had been on the island for twenty-eight years. Many of his friends were dead. But the money he had made in his tobacco plantation in Brazil had been saved for him. So he was able to live a life of ease for the rest of his days.

Ozymandias
By Percy Bysshe Shelley

I met a traveler from an antique land
Who said: Two vast and trunkless legs of stone
Stand in the desert. Near them on the sand
Half sunk, a shattered visage lies, whose frown
And wrinkled lip and sneer of cold command
Tell that its sculptor well those passions read
Which yet survive, stamped on these lifeless things,
The hand that mocked them and the heart that fed.

And on the pedestal these words appear:
"My name is Ozymandias, king of kings:
Look on my works, ye Mighty and despair!"

Nothing beside remains. Round the decay
Of that colossal wreck, boundless and bare,
The lone and level sands stretch far away.

How Arthur Became King

From KING ARTHUR AND HIS NOBLE KNIGHTS

By Mary MacLeod

There were tales about King Arthur and his noble knights told many centuries ago, long before printing had been invented. The tales were carried by messengers from village to village, and later from country to country. Soldiers returning from wars, minstrels and other travelers added to them. Early in the ninth century a Welsh priest wrote down in Latin the essential facts of the King Arthur story.

Other versions of the story appeared from time to time in England and in France, but it was not until the late fifteenth century that a first-rate English writer, Sir Thomas Malory, collected all the stories and legends that he could find about King Arthur and wrote what has ever since been considered the best and most fruitful source of the stories. Caxton, the famous early printer, set Malory's book in type and gave it the title of "Le Morte d'Arthur," meaning "The Death of Arthur." Why Caxton called it that, and why in French, no one seems to know exactly since Malory had apparently meant to call it THE BOOK OF KING ARTHUR AND HIS NOBLE KNIGHTS OF THE ROUND TABLE.

At any rate, Malory's book has served as the source of stories about King Arthur by many great writers, including the English poets, Chaucer, Spenser, Milton and Tennyson.

The stories have been described as "great and joyous," and they are so indeed, although no one is quite sure just who King Arthur actually was. But all the stories show his great longing to do good and to right wrongs. For this the stories have lived and will live among the great tales of literature. Here is part of the story.

THE MARVEL OF THE SWORD

WHEN Uther Pendragon, King of England, died, the country for a long while stood in danger, for every lord that was mighty gathered his forces, and many wished to be King. King Uther's own son, Prince Arthur, who *should* have succeeded him, was but a child, and Merlin, the mighty magician, had hidden him away.

Now a strange thing had happened at Arthur's birth, and this was how it was.

Some time before, Merlin had done Uther a great service, on condition that the King should grant him whatsoever he wished for. This the King swore a solemn oath to do.

Then Merlin made him promise that when his child was born it should be delivered to Merlin to bring up as he chose, for this would be to the child's own great advantage. The King had given his promise so he was obliged to agree. Then Merlin said he knew a very true and faithful man, one of King Uther's lords, by name of Sir Ector, who had large possessions in many parts of England and Wales, and that the child should be given to him to bring up.

On the night the baby was born, while it was still unchristened, King Uther commanded two knights and two ladies to take it, wrap it in a cloth of gold, and deliver it to a poor man whom they would find waiting at the postern gate of the Castle.

This poor man was Merlin in disguise, although they did not know it. So the child was delivered unto Merlin and he carried him to Sir Ector, and made a holy man christen him Arthur. Sir Ector's wife cherished him as her own child.

Within two years King Uther fell sick, and for three days and nights he was speechless. All the barons were in much sorrow and asked Merlin what was to be done.

"There is no remedy," said Merlin. "God will have His will. But look ye all, barons, come before King Uther tomorrow, and God will make him speak."

So the next day Merlin and all the barons came before the King, and Merlin said aloud to King Uther, "Sir, after your days are over, shall your son Arthur be King of this realm and all that belongs to it?"

Then Uther Pendragon said, "I give my son, Arthur, God's blessing and mine, and bid him pray for my soul, and righteously and honorably claim the Crown, on forfeiture of my blessing."

And with those words on his lips, King Uther died.

But Arthur was still only a baby, not two years old, and Merlin knew it would be no use to proclaim him King. There were many powerful nobles in England who were all trying to get the kingdom for themselves, and perhaps they would kill the little Prince. So there was much strife and debate in the land for a long time.

When several years had passed, Merlin went to the Archbishop of Canterbury and counselled him to send for all the lords of the realm, and all the gentlemen of arms,

that they should come to London at Christmas, and for this cause—that a miracle would show who should be rightly the King of the realm. So all the lords and gentlemen made themselves ready and came to London, and long before dawn on Christmas day they were all gathered in the giant Church of St. Paul's to pray.

When the first service was over, there was seen in the churchyard a large stone, four-square, like marble, and in the midst of it was an anvil of steel a foot high. Into this stone was stuck by the point a beautiful sword, with naked blade and there were letters written in gold about the sword which said thus:

"WHOSO PULLETH THIS SWORD OUT OF THIS STONE AND ANVIL IS RIGHTLY KING OF ALL ENGLAND."

Then the people marvelled, and told it to the Archbishop.

"I command," said the Archbishop, "that you stay within the church and pray, and that no man touch the sword till the service is over."

So when the prayers in church were over all the lords went to behold the stone and the sword, and when they read the writing some of them—such as wished to be King—tried to pull the sword out of the anvil. But not one could make it stir.

"The man is not here who shall achieve the sword," said the Archbishop, "but doubt not God will make him known. Let us provide ten knights of good fame to keep guard over the sword."

So it was ordained, and proclamation was made that every one who wished might try to win the sword.

On New Year's day the barons arranged

to have a great tournament in which all knights who would joust or tourney might take part so that it could be made known who would win the sword.

HOW ARTHUR WAS CROWNED KING

On New Year's day after church, the barons rode to the field to joust, and some to tourney, and it happened that Sir Ector came also to the tournament. With him rode Sir Kay, his son, with young Arthur, his foster brother.

As they rode Sir Kay found he had lost his sword, for he had left it at his father's lodging, so he begged young Arthur to go and fetch it for him.

"That I will gladly," said Arthur, and he rode fast away.

But when he came to the house he found no one at home to give him the sword, for everyone had gone to the jousting.

Then Arthur was angry and said to himself, "I will ride to the churchyard and take the sword with me that sticketh in the stone, for my brother, Sir Kay, shall not be without a sword this day."

When he came to the churchyard he alighted and tied his horse to the stile and went to the tent. But he found there no knights who should have been guarding the sword, for they were all away at the joust. Seizing the sword by the handle he lightly and fiercely pulled it out of the stone, then took his horse and rode his way, till he came to Sir Kay, to whom he delivered the sword.

As soon as Sir Kay saw it, he knew well it was the sword of the stone, so he rode to his father, Sir Ector, and said, "Sir, lo here is the sword of the stone, wherefore I must be King of this land."

When Sir Ector saw the sword he turned back and came to the church, and there they all three alighted and went into the church, and he made his son swear truly how he got the sword.

"From my brother, Arthur," said Sir Kay, "for he brought it to me."

"How did you get this sword!" said Sir Ector to Arthur.

And the boy told him.

"Now," said Sir Ector, "I understand you must be King of England."

"Wherefore," said Arthur, "and for what cause?"

"Sir," said Ector, "because God will have it so, for never man could draw out this sword but he that should rightly be King. Now let me see whether you can put the sword there as it was and pull it out again."

"There is no difficulty," said Arthur, and he put it back into the stone.

Then Sir Ector tried to pull out the sword and failed. Sir Kay also tried with all his might but could not move it.

"Now you try," said Sir Ector to Arthur.

"I will," said Arthur and pulled the sword out easily.

At this Sir Ector and Sir Kay knelt on the ground before him.

"Alas," said Arthur, "mine own dear father and brother, why do you kneel to me?"

"Nay, nay, my lord Arthur, it is not so. I was never your father, nor of your blood, but I know well you are of higher blood than I thought you were."

Then Sir Ector told him how he had taken him to bring him up, and by whose command, and how he had received him from Merlin. And when he understood that

Ector was not his father Arthur was deeply grieved.

"Will you be my good gracious lord when you are King?" asked the knight.

"If not, I should be to blame," said Arthur, "for you are the man in the world to whom I am most beholden, and my good lady and mother, your wife, who has fostered and kept me as well as her own children. And if ever it be God's will that I be King, as you say, you shall desire of me what I shall do, and God forbid that I should fail you."

"Sir," said Sir Ector, "I will ask no more of you but that you will make my son, your foster brother, seneschal of all your lands."

"That shall be done," said Arthur, "and by my faith, no other man shall have that office while he and I live."

Then they went to the Archbishop and told him how the sword was achieved.

On Twelfth Day all the barons came to the stone in the churchyard, so that anyone who wished might try to win the sword. But not one of them could take it.

Many of them, therefore, were very angry, and said it was a great shame to be governed by a boy not of high blood, for as yet none of them knew that he was the son of King Uther Pendragon. So they agreed to delay the decision until Candlemas which is the second day of February.

But when Candlemas came and Arthur once more was the only one who could pull out the sword, they put it off until the Feast of Pentecost.

Then by Merlin's advice the Archbishop summoned some of the best knights to be found—such knights as in his own day King Uther Pendragon had best loved and trusted most—and there were appointed to attend young Arthur, and never to leave him night or day until the Feast of Pentecost.

When the great day came, all manner of men once more made the attempt and once more none could prevail but Arthur. Before all the Lords and Commons there assembled he pulled out the sword, whereupon all cried out at once, "We will have Arthur for our King! We will no more delay, for we see it is God's will that he shall be our King."

Therewith they knelt down at once, both rich and poor, and besought pardon of Arthur because they had delayed him so long.

And Arthur forgave them, and took the sword in both his hands and offered it on the altar where the Archbishop was. After that, he was crowned at once, and he swore to be a true King, and to govern with true justice from thenceforth all of his life.

England

By William Shakespeare

This royal throne of Kings, this sceptred isle,
This earth of majesty, this seat of Mars,
This other Eden, demi-paradise;
This fortress, built by nature for herself,
Against infection and the hand of war;
This happy breed of men, this little world;
This precious stone set in the silver sea,
Which serves it in the office of a wall,
Or as a moat defensive to a house,
Against the envy of less happier lands,
This blessed plot, this earth, this realm,
   this England.

288

I Wandered Lonely as a Cloud

By William Wordsworth

I wandered lonely as a cloud
   That floats on high o'er vales and hills,
When all at once I saw a crowd,
   A host of golden daffodils:
Beside the lake, beneath the trees,
Fluttering and dancing in the breeze.

Continuous as the stars that shine
   And twinkle on the milky way,
They stretched in never-ending line
   Along the margin of a bay:
Ten thousand saw I at a glance,
Tossing their heads in sprightly dance.

The waves beside them danced, but they
   Outdid the sparkling waves in glee;
A poet could not but be gay,
   In such a jocund company.
I gazed—and gazed—but little thought
What wealth the show to me had brought.

For oft, when on my couch I lie
   In vacant or in pensive mood,
They flash upon that inward eye
   Which is the bliss of solitude;
And then my heart with pleasure fills,
And dances with the daffodils.

Chartless

By Emily Dickinson

I never saw a moor,
I never saw the sea;
Yet know I how the heather looks,
And what a wave must be.

I never spoke with God,
Nor visited in heaven;
Yet certain am I of the spot
As if the chart were given.

The Year's Round

By Coventry Patmore

The crocus, while the days are dark,
   Unfolds its saffron sheen;
At April's touch the crudest bark
   Discovers gems of green.

Then sleep the seasons, full of night,
   While slowly swells the pod
And round the peach, and in the night
   The mushroom bursts the sod.

The winter falls, the frozen rut
   Is bound with silver bars;
The snowdrift heaps against the hut,
   And night is pierced with stars.

Adventures of Don Quixote

Retold from DON QUIXOTE

By Miguel De Cervantes

The author of the great book from which we present these few exciting episodes, was a Spaniard named Miguel de Cervantes. His own life was full of misery. He was seriously wounded in a naval battle, then captured by pirates and held prisoner for years in Algiers. Finally, back in Spain, he tried to keep himself out of debtors' prison by writing.

Though ill and all but penniless, he wrote his immortal DON QUIXOTE in a spirit of gayety and romance. It is the story of an erratic hunting-gentleman who called himself Don Quixote and it tells of his adventures as he rode through the world on his bony horse Rosinante, righting wrongs and tilting at windmills; of his lady-love Dulcinea del Toboso; and of his long-suffering squire, Sancho Panza.

Their escapades are hilarious indeed, but there is a serious purpose underlying this story that has made DON QUIXOTE an immortal classic for well over four hundred years.

ABOUT three hundred years ago a strange old gentleman named Quixada lived in Spain. His niece and his housekeeper lived with him. He had a horse and a small farm.

Quixada never spent his time thinking about breakfast or dinner or supper. Instead, he thought about fairies and giants and magicians and the wonderful adventures men sometimes have. He found the plain ordinary everyday things, like eating and sleeping, very dull, and longed for the excitement of the days when Knights, all clad in armor, sallied forth on prancing steeds to fight for ladies to whom they had sworn loyalty. Often the Knights did not know the ladies at all, but that made the adventure the more exciting. Besides, Quixada didn't have a thing in the world to do, because he hired a man to work the farm.

Quixada read so many stories about giants and Knights and thrilling adventures that at last he could no longer endure the stupid life he was living. He determined to set forth on his "fine white steed"—which was really a decrepit old farm-horse—in quest of adventure.

"I have a charger," said he, "but where shall I find armor?" And he proceeded to rummage in the old house where he lived until he found the armor which had belonged to his great-grandfather. He spent days polishing and mending it.

Quixada looked at himself with pride and satisfaction when he had donned his complete suit of armor. He had made his helmet himself, out of pasteboard, lined with thin metal; but he was sure it looked like the real thing!

"Now," said Quixada, drawing himself up proudly, "it remains to name myself and my noble steed." For days he pondered, and then he cried, "My charger shall answer to the name of Rozinante, and I shall be known as Don Quixote de la Mancha.

"But who shall be the lady I shall defend, and whose glove I shall wear on my helmet as token of my devotion?"

This was indeed a hard question, for Don Quixote knew no ladies.

"There's Aldonza Lorenzo," he mused. "She's just a healthy country girl, but I guess she'll do. She must change her name, though. Henceforth, Aldonza Lorenzo shall be known as Dulcinea del Toboso! And I, her faithful Knight, Don Quixote de la Mancha, will proclaim her everywhere the fairest lady in the land. Who dares deny it does so at his peril!"

The very next morning Don Quixote fared forth on Rozinante. He was terribly upset when he suddenly thought, "I've not yet been knighted!" He knew, however, that adventurers were sometimes knighted by persons they happened to meet.

"My first duty," he swore, "shall be to earn my knighthood. Come, Rozinante, go any way you please, but let it be in the way of adventure!"

All day Don Quixote jogged along on Rozinante but, sad to relate, without any kind of an adventure. Fortunately, Rozinante's instinct directed him to an inn where he thought he could spend a comfortable night. Horse and rider were both very tired when they approached the inn at nightfall.

"Ah! A castle!" cried Don Quixote, when he saw the inn before him. "What! I hear no trumpet sounding to announce our approach!"

If Don Quixote had had his way he would have waited for a trumpet to sound, but Rozinante made straight for the stable and supper.

"Toot! toot!" Just as the horse started off, a horn sounded. Don Quixote did not know it was merely a swineherd summoning his pigs. He was satisfied that a watchful dwarf had spied him out and very properly announced his coming to the castle.

At the door of the inn were two village girls. To Don Quixote they were charming ladies of the castle, enjoying the evening glories of nature.

"Good evening to you, fair ladies," said Don Quixote in his best knight-errant manner, and he entered upon a long speech about everything imaginable. Don Quixote was exceedingly gallant and entirely in earnest, but the girls did not understand him at all, and they laughed rudely in his face. Such treatment did not at all suit Don Quixote's idea of his own dignity, and something quite terrible might have happened had not the inn-keeper come out in the nick of time.

The inn-keeper was a jolly good-natured fellow, a friend to every man. So, although he thought Don Quixote the strangest guest he had ever had, he did not laugh at him, but did his best to make him feel at home.

Don Quixote dismounted with difficulty. He was stiff from his long ride.

"If it please you, most honorable governor of the castle," he said to the inn-keeper, handing Rozinante over to him, "see that my good steed wants for nothing. There has not been his like in the whole world since Alexander the Great rode horseback. As for me, my only comfort is in arms, and by choice my bed is a battlefield."

One look at Rozinante, whose bones stuck out, and the inn-keeper lost his last doubt that Don Quixote was stark staring mad.

Then Don Quixote learned some of the inconveniences of wearing armor. He could not get his helmet off without cutting the ribbons with which it was tied. Nothing could persuade him to cut the ribbons, so the inn-keeper had to get a long funnel, through which he poured Don Quixote's supper.

When supper was over Don Quixote turned suddenly to the landlord and said, "Most gracious Sir, will you honor me by meeting me in the stable?"

The inn-keeper obediently followed Don Quixote to the stable, wondering what he would do next.

"Noble and valorous Knight," cried Don Quixote, shutting the stable door, and flinging himself at the inn-keeper's feet, "I shall kneel before you like this until you grant me a boon."

"'Tis granted before you ask it," said the inn-keeper, determined to play his part in the strange game of his guest.

"Sir Castle-Keeper, the boon is this: Pray let me watch my armor all night long in the chapel of your castle, and in the morning give me my knighthood."

Used to fobbing off all sorts of unreasonable guests, the inn-keeper looked about for some excuse to get Don Quixote out of his inn, and so be rid of him. "Our chapel," he said, keeping a straight face, "is out of repair. But better for your purpose, we have a great paved courtyard, directly under heaven itself."

The night was fine, the moon was shining. Don Quixote was well content with his appointed watch. He laid his armor in the horse trough, because he could find no better place, and began to stalk solemnly up and down the courtyard in the moonlight. He kept looking at his armor with the utmost gravity and affection, his thoughts running undisturbed on knightly matters.

The inn-keeper had told the other guests what was going on, and they enjoyed the performance greatly—but from a safe distance!

It was well after midnight when a mule-driver, grumpy with fatigue and sleepiness, clattered across the cobbled courtyard to water his mules at the trough.

"Hold, rash Knight," warned Don Quixote spinning on his heel. "Touch with your defiling hand that armor and you risk your life!"

The mule-driver batted his eyes, stuck out his jaw, and swung the armor up by its straps, flinging it from him as far as it would go.

At this insult, Don Quixote called upon his fair lady.

"My Lady Dulcinea del Toboso, be gracious to me as I risk my life to defend your honor and mine!" he cried. And he brought down his spear upon the poor mule-driver's head.

The man fell down senseless. Don Quixote put his armor back in the trough, and continued his march up and down the court.

In a few moments another driver came up to water his mules. Without any warning, Don Quixote struck at him with his spear. But it had no quieting effect. Unfortunately, the fellow bawled so loudly that all his friends at the inn heard him. They came out of every door and window to stone poor Don Quixote—though from a respectful distance.

The Knight, undaunted, did not budge an inch. Protecting himself with his shield, he drew his sword and shouted, "Lay on, base knaves, if ye dare!"

At this point the inn-keeper appeared as peacemaker. He stopped the stone-throwing and soothed Don Quixote's ruffled dignity. He resumed his watch.

The inn-keeper, who wanted to get back to sleep and feared that another alarm in

the courtyard might unpave every stone in it, assured Don Quixote that his long vigil was over. He was ready for knighthood.

"You have proved yourself so valiant," said the inn-keeper, "that you need watch your armor no longer. I will knight you at once. Kneel!"

Quixote knelt, while the landlord of the inn fetched an account book in which he reckoned the price of hay and barley. The village girls stood by to rearm Don Quixote and the stable-boy held a candle, for the moon was now low in the skies.

"Mumble, mumble, mumble, mumble," said the inn-keeper and he struck the lank kneeling figure of Quixote a smart blow on the shoulder with the flat of his sword. "Mutter, mutter. Rise Sir Knight."

Quixote's own sword was belted around him, his spurs buckled on. Rozinante was brought forward and Quixote was ready to ride forth—a Knight!

"Have you got any money, Sir Knight?" asked the landlord.

"Not a penny." Quixote raised himself to his full height. "Should a Knight-errant carry base money about him?"

"He should, indeed," replied the inn-keeper. "Also clean shirts, for which you need a squire to attend you."

Quixote determined to go home in search of these. He embraced and thanked the landlord for his advice and service. As Don

Quixote took to the field again in quest of adventures, the landlord was more than relieved to see the last of that guest.

So delighted was Quixote to find himself a Knight, and with so little trouble, that he had spirits enough for two. He spurred Rozinante under him and the poor horse paced and pranced along. Still Quixote kept his eyes and ears open for adventure on the way.

An adventure was at hand. In a wood near the road Quixote heard a pitiful outcry.

"Halt! I hear the moans of one in distress!" Don Quixote exclaimed. He turned Rozinante into the wood, thankful that he had so soon found an opportunity to prove himself worthy of his knighthood. Sure enough, he found a boy tied to a tree, and a man beating him angrily, and calling out, "I'll teach you! I'll teach you!"

Don Quixote lost no time in making his presence known. "Sir Knight," he said decidedly, "the laws of knighthood forbid a Knight to strike one who cannot defend himself. I challenge you to combat! I will show you that you are a coward."

The countryman, who had never seen the like of Don Quixote before, was so terrified that his legs shook beneath him. "The lad is my servant, Sir," he quavered, "and he is indeed a poor one." (At this the lad howled again.) "I tell him to watch my sheep, but he goes off and plays and lets the sheep stray and get lost."

"But, Sir," the lad protested to Don Quixote, "not a cent has he paid me in wages."

"Scoundrel!" cried Don Quixote. "So you beat the lad and cheat him as well! But now the defenseless has a defender. I command you to pay the boy and let him go."

"Nine months have I worked for him, Sir, and not a cent has he paid me!"

"The boy does not tell the truth to you," whined the countryman, "for I owe him much less than he says. Nevertheless, to show you that I am a kind master, I will take the boy home and pay him the full nine months' wages. I cannot pay him here, for I have no money."

"No, no! Don't let him do that!" Andreo begged. "I am afraid to go home with him!"

"Be not afraid, Andreo," said Don Quixote. "He will not dare harm you, for I command him to treat you well. Sir," said he to the man, "swear by your knighthood that you will deal fairly with the boy."

"I swear," said the fellow. "Come on, Andreo."

"Remember your oath, for I am Don Quixote de la Mancha, the righter of wrongs." And the Knight spurred his horse and set off at a gallop.

"Sir! Sir!" Andreo called after him. "My master's no knight; he is John the farmer, and his oaths are as bad as his blows."

Little did Don Quixote guess that as soon as his back was turned the countryman seized the lad again and punished him more severely than before. Then he set him free, but he did not pay him.

Delighted to have made such a good beginning Don Quixote continued on his way carolling to himself, "Beauty of beauties, Dulcinea del Toboso. How happy you are to have captivated a Knight-errant who has so perfectly righted the greatest wrong ever known."

He did not have to wait long for his next adventure. Six silk merchants appeared on the road, each riding a fine horse, and each shading himself with a big umbrella. They had four servants on horseback and three on foot.

"What a chance," thought the Knight, "to prove that my lady is most lovely of all!"

"Halt!" he shouted to the men. "I hold this road against all who do not declare that in the whole universe there is no more beautiful damsel than the peerless Dulcinea del Toboso."

"Who is this lady? Without seeing her, we cannot pass judgment on her beauty." So spoke the silk merchants, who were quite puzzled by the strange encounter.

"I will fight anyone who dares say he does not know the famous beauty of Lady Dulcinea del Toboso," roared the Knight, who was furious that the men had not given in to his demand without question. "Prepare to defend yourselves."

With this, Don Quixote rode at full speed toward the men, who had nothing but their umbrellas with which to defend themselves.

He would have sent them flying before him except that, in full swoop, Rozinante stumbled and fell, rolling poor Don Quixote off into a ditch in a manner most unseemly for a Knight. His armor was so heavy that he could not get up.

"Cowards! Rascals! Do not fly!" said Quixote still unable to rise. "It's not my fault that I lie here, but the fault of my horse. Rozinante stumbled, you poltroons!"

An ill-natured mule-driver came up to him where he lay fallen and entangled. He broke the Knight's good lance and beat him with the pieces. Quixote bellowed threats at every blow as loudly as he could.

Then the merchants set off on their business and Quixote was left bruised and battered. Yet Don Quixote was happy for *he* had not been overthrown. It was his

horse that had stumbled.

A plowman from his own village, passing with a sack of wheat some hours later, stopped to investigate the man in armor sprawled in the road and making such an uproar. He opened the broken helmet visor and stared at a neighbor he well knew.

When it became dark, the plowman led Quixote, slung over the plowman's donkey, back to the Knight's own house. Here his good friends, the barber, who was somewhat of a doctor of bodies, and the curate, who was somewhat of a doctor of heads, put the returned Knight-errant to bed where he lay down, bruised from head to foot. The curate and barber discussed Quixote's behavior with the Knight's housekeeper and his niece.

"My uncle reads sometimes for forty-eight hours at a stretch," complained his niece, "which is too much reading for any man's head. It sets him to fencing with his shadow on the wall, acting out all manner of misadventures, and saying he has killed four giants as tall as steeples. He gets it all out of books—and they all deserve to be burned!"

That night, the curate and the barber decided that the only way to keep Don Quixote from starting off again in search of new adventures was to destroy the books where he had read all the tales of Knights, Ladies and Enchanters.

This they did while the poor Knight lay helpless on his bed of pain. They not only made a bonfire of the books, but they bricked up the library door, making it appear as if there had never been a library there.

No sooner was Don Quixote back on his feet again, however, than he set out to visit his beloved books. He searched in vain for his library and, much disturbed, asked his niece about it.

"No, dear Uncle," she said "there is no library here now. While you were away an Enchanter flew here on a dragon. He entered your library and what he did in there we do not know. We were too frightened to stop him," she continued making it all up, "but in a little while he fled out of the roof of the house, leaving it filled with smoke. And when we went to see what he had done, we found neither room nor books."

"Freston! It must have been Freston, the notorious Enchanter, for he hates me bitterly," exclaimed Don Quixote. "But I tell him it is useless to oppose me. I shall get the better of him yet!"

"But Uncle," said his niece, "what makes you run after these quarrels? Hadn't you better stay at home and live in peace? Remember the proverb that those who go seeking wool often come home shorn."

"Shorn?" said Quixote. "Before I am shorn I will pluck the beards of all who think to tweak but a hair tip of my mustachios."

While he was recovering, Don Quixote spent his time patching his helmet, mending his lance and otherwise preparing for further adventure. He set about to provide himself with money, pawning one thing, selling another, and mortgaging his good acres.

Convinced that a Knight's iron breeches were no place for jingling coins, Quixote recruited a squire to ride behind him and carry his wallet.

This squire was a haunchy, paunchy farm laborer named Sancho Panza. Before his simple eyes Don Quixote dangled such allurements of fame and riches as dazzled his simple soul.

He promised him nothing less than the governorship of an island—the first that came to hand.

"Or," said the generous Don Quixote, "I may even crown you King."

"King? said Sancho. "We'll stick to the island. An island governor's wife is as much as my Teresa could handle."

"Don't think small thoughts," replied Quixote.

So, one dark and windy night when everyone was asleep, they sallied forth without telling anyone of their plans. Don Quixote clattered along on Rozinante, while close behind them sat Sancho Panza, like a patriarch, on his faithful little gray donkey Dapple, who was the delight of his lazy master.

A large wallet that held not only money for their journey, but also bandages, ointment, bread, cheese, and clean shirts was fastened to Dapple's saddle. Sancho would have preferred more food and less laundry, but he consoled himself with the thought of his island that would be overflowing with good things to eat.

As they rode along squire and master talked of the great conquests that lay before them.

Suddenly at the first glimmer of daylight, Sancho jogged Don Quixote's armored elbow till it clanked. "Do you see any islands in the mist?"

Aroused from his meditations so suddenly, what Don Quixote saw all about him was not islands, but enemies.

"Sancho," he cried, "our fortunes could not be better! We'll get enormous booty when I overthrow those huge giants on the plain below." And he pointed to some thirty or forty windmills flapping their wings in the breeze.

"What giants?" Sancho stopped short, amazed.

Don Quixote pointed straight ahead. "See their long arms stretched to bar our path? I've read that such giants can reach out and catch people two leagues away."

"Then we're much too close," and Sancho made himself small on Dapple's back, and peeped between the donkey's ears.

"It seems to me," he said cautiously, "that those things you're pointing at are windmills. They can't hurt us at all!"

"You know very little about giants to be mistaking them for windmills, ignoramus! I tell you they are giants and if you are afraid, I'll ride them down and conquer them alone!"

Without waiting another instant, he rode furiously at the windmills, lance in hand, to attack them while Sancho bawled, "Windmills! What's he up to now?"

Just then a breeze sprang up, moving the great windmill arms, and Don Quixote thought his enemies were threatening him with their long arms.

"Though you should wield more arms than the Giant Briareus, I shall make you pay for your insolence!" he cried. And thundering his watchword, "Dulcinea," he charged full tilt with his lance leveled at the first of them.

As Quixote thrust his lance through the whirling sail, the wind turned it with such violence that the weapon broke into splinters. Rozinante toppled after a glancing blow on the shoulder, while Don Quixote executed a spectacular series of cartwheels across the field as the whirling sails caught him.

Sancho Panza hurried to the rescue as quickly as Dapple could go. "Bless me," he said, "didn't I tell you they were windmills? How was I to know you'd go frolicking with them?"

Don Quixote opened his helmet. "Peace, friend Sancho," he said sadly. "Fortune of war. They really are giants to whom Freston, that wicked enchanter who robbed me of my library and books, has given the shape of windmills to rob me of victory. But next time I shall win!"

"It may be so," said Sancho who didn't know enough about magic to argue the point. And he helped his master rise and pulled up Rozinante, who, poor horse, was himself much bruised by the fall.

Don Quixote was quiet as they rode, worrying over the loss of his lance. "Sancho," he said, "I shall get me a new spear in a manner befittting a Knight. The next oak tree we meet shall be my spear."

"What, Sir, will you pick up a whole big tree for your spear?"

"Perhaps a branch will do," said Don Quixote. "Whatever it is, it will bring me fame, as did the sword which the Bruiser, famous Knight that he was, made for himself of a tree limb."

That night he fixed his spear end on a branch he tore from a tree, and he was well pleased with his make-shift lance.

Adventures now came thick and fast for Don Quixote. In the very next encounter his helmet was ruined, although he conquered his opponent. Don Quixote swore he would not rest until he took a helmet just as good from another Knight. He did not have long to wait.

"Sancho," he called eagerly, as they rode along one morning, "do you see the Knight on a fine gray charger, wearing a helmet of gold? That helmet is the helmet of Mambrino and it shall be mine!"

Sancho was skeptical, as usual. "The man's riding on an old donkey, Sir, and that's no helmet on his head."

Don Quixote would not listen to such nonsense, and rushed at his opponent with Rozinante at full gallop. The man jumped from his donkey in an effort to save himself. His helmet, which was too big for him, rolled off. The man fled, too frightened to protest, and left the coveted gold helmet and donkey behind.

Sancho ran quickly to pick up the booty.

"This is a strange helmet," said Don Quixote, trying it on.

"Why, master, it's not a helmet at all," said Sancho. "The fellow must have been a barber, for that's the sort of a basin they use in their trade. He must have put it on to keep the rain off, for it's raining hard."

"It may look like such a basin," said Don Quixote, decidedly, "but it is not. It's an enchanted helmet of pure gold."

Don Quixote was proud and happy as he rode along with his new helmet on his head.

Not many days later the Knight was greatly excited by a cloud of dust on the road ahead.

"It must be a mighty army, and they are marching this way," said he.

"There must be two armies then," said Sancho, "for I see another cloud of dust just like it over there." Don Quixote was mightily pleased, thinking a great battle was about to take place before their eyes.

"What shall we do, master, if they fight?"

"Help the weaker side, of course," said Don Quixote. "What else could brave men do? Do you see that valiant Knight, Laurcalio, and the giant Braudabarbaray, and do you hear the horses neigh? It will be a glorious battle."

"But, master, not a horse do I see or hear. I believe it is two flocks of sheep. Yes, I hear them bleating. Come, do not attack them!"

Sancho's words had no effect on Don Quixote, who rushed off to the attack, leaving Sancho behind, protesting.

Sheep or not, he charged whole squadrons of them with such vigor that he thrust down seven and scattered the rest.

The shepherds, astounded to have an armed man bearing down on their flocks, shouted to him to stop and when he did not, they unloosed their slings and let fly in the direction of the Knight with a hailstorm of stones as big as their fists.

When Sancho Panza, who had stayed behind, saw Don Quixote plunge to earth, he came scampering down the hill toward his master.

"This comes of not taking my advice," he bawled, half in annoyance and half in solicitude. "See what you've done to the sheep!"

"See what your sheep have done to me," said Don Quixote, battered and bruised and lifting himself a little so that Sancho could take a good look. "Is this the work of peaceful flocks?" Don Quixote inquired severely. "Show me a sheep!"

This Sancho was unable to do for the shepherds had lugged off the dead sheep along with the live ones. Sancho was doubly regretful, for he was both mortified and hungry. Substantial mutton would have consoled him and satisfied his hunger as well.

"But, master," he said, "why did you attack them when I told you they were sheep?"

"They were not really sheep, Sancho, but Knights whom Freston disguised as sheep to shame me. Over that hill you may see them, I wager, returned to their real knightly shapes."

The encounter with the shepherds, and many other adventures, left Don Quixote weak and sick, so they rode away to rest awhile. One night they even fell sound asleep before they got off their mounts.

Sancho's loud snores attracted a passing adventurer, who wanted a donkey. He placed four long sticks under Sancho's saddle, loosened the straps, raised the saddle and Sancho above Dapple's back, and led the animal off, leaving Sancho and the saddle behind, high in the trees!

These were but the beginning of the adventures of this strange pair. Sancho got back his beloved donkey, and Don Quixote had many other encounters.

At last the curate and the barber found the Knight and took him home, in a very ordinary cart, but Don Quixote insisted that it was an enchanted chariot.

The curate and the barber could take Don Quixote home, but they could not keep him there. It was not long before he started off for a third journey, with the faithful Sancho in attendance. This time the purpose was a visit to the Lady Dulcinea del Toboso.

They reached the town at midnight. "Lead me to her palace, Sancho," the Knight directed.

"Palace!" exclaimed the matter-of-fact squire. "When last I saw her she lived in a very small cottage in a very poor part of the village. Besides, this is no time of day to go calling."

"Leave that to me, Sancho," said Don Quixote in his sternest manner. "This very building before us must be my lady's palace."

With this the Knight smote mightily on the door of a huge building, which happened to be the church of Toboso. Not a trace of Dulcinea's palace did they find, although they hunted all night. Toward morning they rested in a grove of trees well out of the village. There could be no rest for Don Quixote, however, until he should find the peerless Dulcinea. At daybreak Sancho was sent to the village to look for her again.

The idea of hunting through Toboso again for Dulcinea did not appeal to Sancho at all. He was sure he could not recognize her, if, as Don Quixote said, she was a beautiful lady and lived in a palace. The girl that Sancho had known was a simple country maid.

"My master is surely mad," he thought. "He never sees things as they are. Sheep to him are Knights, and windmills are giants. I believe any country maid might seem to him to be his Dulcinea. What's the use in hunting? I'll wait here until a country girl comes along, and then I'll take her to the master."

It was still very early in the morning when they came near the tumbled-down quarter of the village where the Lorenzos lived.

Exclaimed Sancho, "Speak of the dev—I mean Dulcinea—here she comes now!" Sancho saw three peasant lasses riding along on donkeys.

"Such favor I never deserved," said Don Quixote humbly as he swung out of his saddle. "Down on your knees with me, Sancho. Dulcinea graciously rides to meet me, with her two fairest damsels on palfreys no less fine than hers."

A blinding sun was rising behind the three damsels, but Sancho was pretty sure they were mounted on donkeys and he was also sure that Aldonza Lorenzo was on her way to the woods to look after her father's pigs.

Everyone but Don Quixote knew Aldonza's father kept swine and that she had the best hand for salting pork in all La Mancha.

When she called out, "Who's that block-
ing the road?" Sancho knew it was indeed
Aldonza Lorenzo. The last time he had
heard her was when she climbed to the
church steeple to summon some ploughmen
two miles away.

Don Quixote had never heard her voice
raised above a church whisper, and now
its thunderous tone came as a shock to him.
Also upon closer inspection he was equally
amazed to see that the face he had known
in its youth was more weather-beaten than
his own. Strangest of all was her figure. She
had never been exactly a willow-wand, but
neither had he imagined his love was as
thick in the waist as the trunk of an old
tree!

Don Quixote swallowed his amazement.
"Peerless beauty, accept your poor Knight's
homage," he said, and he loyally rose and
bowed in his clattering armor, still wondering how this red-faced fat country lass could
be his fair Dulcinea.

Dulcinea's donkey took fright at the
strange figure of the Knight. Up went its
heels and down in the road, flat on her
face, came Don Quixote's fair lady love.
The Knight ran to help her, but she was
even more frightened by his armor than her
donkey had been.

Up she jumped and off she ran. Overtak-
ing her donkey, she put both hands on its
rump and vaulted into the pack-saddle,
astride like a man. A cloud of dust rose

301

over the plain where she and her two companions whipped it up.

"She rides like a woman bewitched!" Sancho Panzo muttered to himself admiringly.

"The deceit of those unscrupulous Enchanters! My heart almost failed me, Sancho," mourned Don Quixote. "To make my lovely Dulcinea, fairest and daintiest lady in all the world, look and act like that! There are changes in the world that a man can scarcely face, unless he is a firm believer in black magic. What I have seen can be only a passing enchantment, and I shall die believing that Dulcinea is still most fair."

"Would that we could make way with all the evil crew of Enchanters, and force them to do penance for their foul deeds!" Sancho echoed heartily.

One day as Don Quixote journeyed along with Sancho they were overtaken by a gentleman in a green suit, who rode a fine horse. The gentleman was interested in the Knight, and rode along with him. They had not gone far when they saw a large high-boarded wagon approaching, drawn by mules, and gay with little red-and-yellow flags.

"An adventure!" cried Don Quixote. "Bring me my helmet, Sancho!" Sancho heard the shout and came up, not knowing what was wanted. He had just filled Don Quixote's helmet with milk, which he had bought of some shepherd. He dared not hesitate to hand it to the Knight when he asked for it, and Don Quixote clapped it on his head, full of milk as it was.

"The Enchanter has sent this adventure against me, and, coward that he is, would give my opponent the odds by blinding me before the combat! Or, Sancho, perhaps you put this milk in my helmet?"

"I, Sir?" asked Sancho, mournfully. "I'd much rather put it in my mouth!" Sancho was depressed by seeing the milk he had paid for go to waste. "The devil himself must have done that deed," he said.

The wagon was coming nearer. Don Quixote rode up and spoke to the driver.

"What have you in this wagon, and where are you taking it? What do the flags mean?"

"In the wagon I have a lion, which we are taking to the King, and the flags mean it is royal Spanish property," the driver answered, politely enough.

"Is it a large lion?" asked Don Quixote, rather taken aback.

"Large! It's by far the biggest lion I've ever seen, and I've seen a lot of them, too." This was from the keeper, who sat on top of the wagon. "Pray clear the road so we can pass. The lion's dinner-time is past, and he is getting hungrier and more savage every minute."

"I am not to be frightened by such talk, young man," said Don Quixote, proudly. "I'll show that wicked enemy of mine the stuff of which I am made! Mr. Keeper, kindly let the lion out of his cage so I can engage him in combat."

Sancho appealed to the gentleman who had joined their party. "Pray, Sir, keep my master from this dangerous and foolish act! We shall all be torn to pieces!"

"Is your master mad, then?"

"No, Sir, only rash, very very rash."

"I'll fix it," said the gentleman, and remonstrated with Don Quixote. The Knight told him quite bluntly not to interfere.

"Mr. Keeper," cried Don Quixote, "open that cage at once, or I'll give you reason to regret it."

"My mules!" cried the driver. "If the

lion is to be let out, they will be eaten. This wagon and team are all I have. Pray let me take them to a safe distance."

"Very well," said the Knight, "but be quick about it."

"Everybody get out of the way!" shouted the keeper. "This gentleman, against my will, makes me let the lion loose. Everybody for himself now. Remember, if the lion gets you, it's this gentleman's fault, not mine."

"Pray let the men take their lion off in peace," the gentleman in green begged.

"Sir, let not my acts concern you. I know what I do. If you are afraid, ride quickly to a place of safety," said Don Quixote, haughtily.

"Dear master," pleaded Sancho, who was quite upset, "what shall I do if the lion kills you?"

"Go to Dulcinea and tell her—I have often told you what to tell her!"

So everyone but the keeper and Don Quixote scurried off to safety. Don Quixote dismounted, determined to meet the lion on foot, because he felt sure Rozinante would be more timid than he. He placed himself, sword in hand, before the door of the cage.

Still protesting, the keeper threw the door as far open as it would go, after Don Quixote had pricked him gently with the point of his lance.

"Now he won't harm me," the keeper warned Don Quixote, "because I feed him, but he'll gnaw you right out of your armor."

The lion thrust up its bristling head. Its eyes flamed in the sunlight. Its great claws bit into the planking and its fangs shone like tarnished steel.

Before the beast could roar, Don Quixote shouted his battle cry straight into the lion's teeth. "Dulcinea," the cry rang out, louder and clearer than it had ever sounded before.

The lion saw the open door, and, looking straight at Don Quixote, stretched himself, and thrust out his great paws. He stuck out his huge tongue and licked his chops. He rose to his feet, walked to the door, and put his great shaggy head out. He gazed with his blazing eyes at Don Quixote. He turned and walked toward the rear of the cage. Then he opened his huge jaws and yawned a great lazy yawn, and proceeded to lie down.

"Force him to come out and do battle," cried Don Quixote to the keeper.

"I will not. I dare not. And, indeed, Sir, you have conquered. What more can a man do than persuade his enemy by the fierceness of his manner that it were best he did not fight?"

"You are right, my man," said Don Quixote. "Shut the door, then, and see that you give a true account of this happening, that all men may know how even a lion fears to fight Don Quixote de la Mancha." And the Knight waved a white cloth on the end of his spear to let the others know that the danger was over.

Sancho and the rest came hurrying up, and the keeper told them what had happened. He lost no opportunity to show how brave Don Quixote had been.

"The big lion turned tail as soon as he heard your master shout that terrible word," the admiring keeper told Sancho. "Now he's curled up in his cage with his paws clapped over his ears. When I get to court," he declared, "I shall tell the King himself of this gentleman's bravery."

"If," said Don Quixote, drawing himself up, "the King should ask who did this thing, you may say that the Knight of the Lions did it, for that shall be my name from this day on."

The gentleman in green now begged Don Quixote to spend some time at his mansion, and they all went there together.

When Don Quixote and Sancho set out again, they decided to go to the fair at Saragossa. Chariots rolled by, decked for the carnival. Strolling players, clowns, farmers and country people, added to the gayety along the way.

They stopped one night at an inn. They had hardly arrived when another guest appeared. This man was clad in leather and wore a green patch over one eye so it was hard to see what his face looked like. Master Peter, as he called himself, was a sort of fortune-teller and magician. He did a thriving business with a show of cardboard puppets, but when Don Quixote first saw him, Peter was telling fortunes outside the inn. To help him, he used a live ape, which would leap to his shoulder and whisper the answer to questions. (Of course Peter had interviewed the landlord first about his guests).

The landlord explained to Don Quixote that Master Peter had the cleverest ape in the world. "Just try him, Sir," he urged. "Ask it any question, and it will jump on its master's shoulder and tell him the answer."

Sancho was all agog to know his fortune, and the ape was soon chattering away in Peter's ear. As soon as the ape finished, Master Peter fell on his knees, not to Sancho, but to Sancho's master.

"Oh, wonderful Knight of the Lions! Restorer of Knight-errantry," cried Peter in admiration. "Who can sufficiently praise the great Don Quixote de la Mancha?"

"Now that's very wonderful. Even the ape has heard of my master's glory," marvelled Sancho. "But what did the ape say about me?"

Master Peter thought a moment. He said, "You are honest, Sancho Panza, the best squire in the world."

"So I am," Sancho said smugly, "but I knew that already. Did he say anything about Teresa? It is no great matter, even for an ape, to know such famous people as me and my master. But can he tell us the name of my wife?"

"Teresa Panza?" asked Peter.

"The very same." Sancho was all admiration for the knowledge whispered by this clever ape.

Later in the evening he begged Don Quixote to visit Master Peter's puppet show, set up in one of the rooms of the inn.

Soon the puppet show, called "Melisendra's Deliverance," began. Master Peter moved the puppets, and a boy in front explained to the audience what was happening on the stage. The story was exciting. The hero, who had just rescued his wife from captivity, was being set upon by the enemy. There seemed no escape from death for hero and heroine.

Don Quixote could not endure this triumph of might over right. He rose in his seat and cried, "Halt! No harm shall befall that fair lady and her brave husband! I myself will defend them against the enemy host!" He drew his sword and attacked the puppets violently. Master Peter himself had hardly time to get out of his way.

Nothing could stop the Knight, who in his rage, broke the entire show into bits. When no puppet was left whole, he cried: "I rejoice that this trial did not find me wanting. I could never have called myself Knight again had I let those wicked Moors destroy the lovely Melisendra and her husband."

Master Peter wailed loudly over his loss. "Cheer up, Master Peter," Sancho said, "my master will repay you when he realizes that the Moors he thinks he killed are only your puppets."

"His puppets?" said the Knight.

"See, Master, there before you, and all about you are the broken wooden pieces that were this man's puppet show."

"Those Enchanters have been trying to outwit me again! All that was acted I believed to be real. Now the Enchanters have turned my enemies to wooden puppets. I will give you money to buy you new puppets, Master Peter."

Don Quixote did not know that Master Peter happened to be the very thief who had taken Sancho's donkey from under him. Do you suppose the story would have ended so well for Master Peter if he had known?

Soon after this, Don Quixote and Sancho were invited to join a group of picnickers whom they met in the woods. The men and women were dressed as shepherds and shepherdesses. The Knight was very grateful for their kindness, and, as a sign of his appreciation, announced that for two days he would remain in the middle of the high road leading to Saragossa and make everyone who came admit that the ladies in the party, disguised as shepherdesses as they were, had no rival in beauty save the unequaled Lady Dulcinea.

The very first thing to pass along the road was a great herd of wild bulls, driven by several men on horseback. Even for them Don Quixote would not step aside. He stayed in the middle of the road and ordered them to halt. The bulls paid no attention, but ran right ahead, knocking horse and rider, squire and donkey, into the ditch, and trampling on them.

Don Quixote got up and ran after the herd, begging them to stop and fight him. They did not even stop to listen.

Knight and squire were in very low spirits when they reached the inn where they intended to spend the night. Sancho's spirits sank even lower when he found that the fare at the inn was very poor, but the Knight ate with other guests who had wisely brought their supper with them.

From this place the Knight went to Barcelona, which lies on the Mediterranean Sea.

One morning Don Quixote rode, fully armed, on the road along the shore. A Knight similarly armed came toward him. A bright moon was painted on his shield, and he announced in a loud voice:

"I am the Knight of the White Moon, most famous Don Quixote de la Mancha. You have doubtless heard of my exploits. Be it known to you now that the lady of my heart — whoever she is — is far more lovely than your Lady Dulcinea del Toboso. Confess it, and you may go free. Deny it, and I shall overcome you. If I win, my prize must be that for a year you stay at home. Conquer me, and all that I have, even my fame, is yours."

"Your challenge, unknown Knight, is accepted. Your terms, also, I accept. But I will never add the fame of your deeds to my own, because my own are enough, and yours I know not. Had you ever, even once, seen my Lady Dulcinea, however, you would never have challenged me thus. Choose your ground, and let us speedily to the fray!"

Just then the Governor of Barcelona, who knew Don Quixote, came on the scene. He would have stopped the battle, but when he heard why they were fighting he decided it must be a joke, and stopped to watch what would happen.

In a moment the Knight of the White Moon had Don Quixote on the ground and stood over him.

"Kill me!" Don Quixote exclaimed, "for I will never yield."

"Not so," said the Knight of the White Moon. "But you must do as you agreed and return home for a year."

The Knight did not tell Don Quixote, but the only reason he wanted to fight him was in order to make him go home and be cured of his mad desire for adventure.

After this battle Don Quixote was very sick. As soon as they could safely move him they took him to his home. There a fever set in, and he had to stay in bed. The doctor said he was in great danger. When Don Quixote heard this he asked everyone to leave the room so that he could sleep. He awoke a different man.

"Those fairy tales are all gone. I am as I used to be before I knew of Knights and giants and great adventures. Bring me a lawyer, that I may make my will as a wise man."

In his will, Don Quixote left almost everything to his niece. But even though he had decided that all his adventures were madness, he did not forget to leave the devoted Sancho Panza a small sum of money. We can hardly imagine, though, that any amount of money would have comforted Sancho for the loss of the master with whom he had passed through so many strange adventures.

Gulliver's Adventures in Lilliput

Retold from GULLIVER'S TRAVELS

By Jonathan Swift

Jonathan Swift, Dean of the Established Church of England, took a great part in politics as well as the church. But he is remembered best as a writer. His most famous book is GULLIVER'S TRAVELS.

Swift wrote GULLIVER'S TRAVELS in 1726, but even today grown people as well as children everywhere love to read about the strange adventures of its hero, Lemuel Gulliver.

One of the most wonderful of Gulliver's adventures was his journey to Lilliput, the land of the Lilliputians. You can read this story here.

But Lemuel Gulliver was hungry for more adventure. On another exciting voyage he found himself in a land of giants, the Brobdingnags, where, waking up in a grain field, he was seized between the thumb and finger of a farmer who carried him home in his pocket to show to his family.

Later Gulliver went to an island in the sky, and then to a land of horses who talked and acted like men. His adventures were fearful and wonderful. Many of you will want to read about them all in Jonathan Swift's big book, GULLIVER'S TRAVELS.

ABOARD the good ship *Antelope* we set sail from Bristol, England, on May 4, 1699, bound for the South Seas. At first our voyage was very prosperous. But one day we were driven by a violent storm onto a rock, and our ship split. Six of us were able to get into a small boat and we rowed for days. Then the boat upset and I lost the other men.

I swam, pushed forward by wind and tide till no strength was left in my arms or legs. My eyes were blinded by the great wave that broke over my head. I was almost gone when I found myself finally able to stand. The shore sloped so gradually I waded nearly a mile till I reached dry land. I continued forward for half a mile but could not discover any sign of houses or inhabitants.

By this time darkness was coming on and, weakened and tired as I was, I lay down and fell asleep on the grass. When I awakened it was daylight. I was lying on my back and when I tried to rise I could not. I found my arms and legs were tightly fastened to the ground. Across my body were thin but strong cords, and even my hair, which was long and thick, was tied down in the same manner.

All around me was a confused sound of voices, but in the position in which I lay I could see nothing but the sky. In a little while I felt something alive crawling up my left leg, gently advancing almost to my chin. Bending my eyes downward as far as I could, I saw a human creature not six inches high, with a bow and arrow in his hands and a quiver on his back. Then I felt at least forty more of the same kind following the first. I roared so loud they all ran back in fright, and some of them, I heard afterwards, were hurt by the falls they got by leaping from my sides to the ground. But very quickly the little people came back again.

Struggling to get loose, I managed at

last to wrench out the pegs that fastened my left arm to the ground. At the same time, by a violent pull that gave me great pain, I loosened the strings that tied my hair on the left side so that I was able to turn my head about two inches. But the tiny creatures ran off a second time before I could seize them.

Then I heard a great shouting. In an instant I felt more than a hundred arrows on my left hand. They pricked me like needles. The little people shot a volley of arrows into the air and some fell on my face. When this shower of arrows was over, I fell a-groaning with pain. When I stirred again to get loose, they discharged another volley larger than the first. Some of them attempted to stick me in the sides with spears. But by good luck I had on a buff jerkin which they could not pierce. I found that the more I struggled the more I was hurt; so I thought it best to lie still, and they discharged no more arrows. My plan was to continue to lie still till night when, my left hand being already loose, I could easily free myself. But by the noise I heard, I knew that more and more of the little soldiers were coming around me.

Soon, about four yards from me, over against my right ear, I heard a continued sound of hammering. Turning my head that way, as well as the pegs and strings would let me, I saw a stage erected about a foot and a half from the ground. When it was finished, four men climbed up to it by ladders. One of them (who seemed to be a very important person, for he had a little page boy to hold up his train) made a long speech. I did not understand one word; but he seemed to be giving an order, for at once about fifty of the little people came and cut the strings that fastened the left side of my head. I was thankful that I could now easily look to the right and observe the person who was speaking. He appeared to be middle-aged and taller than the others, and from his manner of speaking it seemed to me that the little man sometimes threatened and sometimes made promises of pity and kindness.

I answered in a few words, but in the most submissive manner. Then, being almost famished with hunger, I kept putting my fingers to my mouth to show I wanted food.

The speaker understood me very well. He commanded that several ladders be put against my sides, and soon about a hundred little people, laden with baskets of meat and bread, climbed up and walked toward my mouth. I observed there was the flesh of several animals, but I could not distinguish them by the taste. There were shoulders, legs, and loins, shaped like those of mutton, but so small—smaller than the wings of a lark—that I ate them two or three at a mouthful. And each loaf of bread being about the size of a small bullet, I easily swallowed three of them at a time. The little creatures supplied me as fast as they could, showing wonder at my bulk and my appetite.

I then made another sign showing I wanted drink. They slung up two of their largest hogsheads, and rolled them towards my hand. I drank them off at a draught, for together they did not hold half a pint. The little people shouted for joy and danced on my chest. They made a sign that I should throw down the two hogsheads, warning the people below me to stand out of the way. I confess I was often tempted, while they were pressing back-

wards and forwards on my body, to seize forty or fifty of them and dash them against the ground. But the pain I had already suffered from their arrows made me think better of it. Besides I now considered myself bound by the laws of hospitality to a people who had treated me with so much expense and magnificence.

I wondered at the courage of these diminutive mortals who ventured to mount and walk upon my body, while one of my hands was free, without trembling at the sight of such a huge creature as I must have seemed to them.

After some time there appeared another small man who, from his brilliant uniform, seemed to be an officer of very high rank. He mounted on my right leg, advanced forwards up to my face, with about a dozen of his retinue, and held up to my eyes a paper which I understood to be a royal order. He spoke, and I learned later, as he often pointed toward something a long way off, that I was to be taken to the capital city, half a mile distant.

I asked, by signs, that my hands be loosed. The officer shook his head and refused, showing that I must be carried as a prisoner. However, he made other signs to let me understand that I would have enough to eat and very good treatment. I once more thought of breaking my bonds, but, my face and hands being all in blisters from the arrows, with many of the darts still sticking to them, I let them know they might do with me what they pleased.

Soon afterwards I felt great numbers of people on my left side relaxing the cords until I was able to turn on my right side. After this the little people drew out the arrows that still stuck in my hands and face

and daubed them with a pleasant-smelling ointment which removed all the pain. Soon I fell asleep and slept for eight hours. This was no great wonder for, I afterwards understood, the Emperor's physician had mixed a very strong sleeping potion in my drink.

I awoke with a violent fit of sneezing, and with the feeling of small feet running off my chest. I was still bound but no longer lying on the ground. I was greatly puzzled to find myself on a sort of platform. Soon I began to realize what had happened, and later, when I had learned the language, I found out what had been done while I slept.

Before I dropped off to sleep, I had heard a rumbling as of wheels, and the shouts of many drivers. This, it seemed, was caused by the arrival of a kind of vehicle driven up alongside of me. It was a frame of wood raised three inches from the ground, seven feet long and four feet wide and moving on twenty-two tiny wheels. Fifteen hundred of the Emperor's horses, each just four and a half inches high, were harnessed to this trolley. It had taken five hundred carpenters and engineers to make it!

On this vehicle I was supposed to be taken to the city. The principal difficulty the little people had was in raising me and placing me in it. They did it in about three hours while I slept. By the use of eighty strong poles fixed in the ground, to which were attached many pulleys and the strongest cords to be found in the country, nine hundred men managed to hoist me aboard the trolley. There I was tied fast.

We were far on our way to the city when I awoke. The vehicle had stopped for a little to rest the horses. An officer of the Emperor's Guard had climbed up my body and, looking at my face, had not been able to resist the temptation to put his sword up my nose. This tickled me so that I woke, sneezing violently.

We did not reach the city till the following day, and I had to spend the night lying where I was, guarded by five hundred men on each side of me, half with torches, half with bows and arrows, all ready to shoot me if I should attempt to move.

In the morning, the Emperor and all his court and thousands of his people came out to gaze at the wonderful sight. The trolley stopped outside the walls, alongside a very large building, which had once been used as a temple, though that use of it had been given up since a murder had been committed in it.

The door of this temple was about four feet high and two feet wide, so I could creep through it. On each side was a small window about six inches from the ground. Inside the building blacksmiths fashioned many chains which they then brought through one of these little windows and fastened with thirty-six padlocks around my left ankle.

Opposite the temple, on the other side of a great highway, there was a turret at least five feet high. Here the Emperor ascended, with many lords of his court, to get a view of me, as I was later told, for I could not see them. In fact, over a hundred thousand inhabitants came out of the town on the same errand.

In spite of my guards, not fewer than ten thousand of them mounted my body several times with the help of ladders. But a proclamation was soon issued forbidding it, upon pain of death. When the workmen found it was impossible for me to break loose, they cut the strings that bound me. When I rose

up, the noise and astonishment of the people at seeing me rise and walk cannot be expressed. A chain about two feet long still held my left leg, but I could walk backwards and forwards in a semicircle. Since I was fastened by the ankle to within four inches of the temple gate, I could creep in and lie at my full length in the temple.

Once on my feet I looked about me and I must confess I never saw a prettier view. The country looked like a continuous garden, and the enclosed fields, which were generally forty feet square, resembled so many beds of flowers. These fields were mingled with woods of half an acre, and the tallest trees appeared to be about seven feet high. The town on my left looked like the painted scene of a city in a theater.

The Emperor had already come down from the tower and was advancing on horseback toward me. This nearly cost him dear, for the beast, though very well trained, was wholly unused to such a sight. It must have appeared as if a mountain moved before him, and he reared up on his hind feet. But the Emperor, who was an excellent horseman, kept his seat till his attendants ran in and held the bridle, giving His Majesty time to dismount. When he alighted, he looked me up and down with great admiration, but he kept beyond the length of my chain.

The Emperor was taller, by almost the breadth of my nail, than any of his court. His features were strong and masculine, his complexion was olive. At that time he was twenty-eight years old and he had reigned happily for seven of these years. His clothes were plain, but on his head he had a light helmet of gold, adorned with jewels and a plume. He held his sword in his hand to defend himself in case I should break loose. The sword was not three inches long. The ladies and courtiers were magnificently clad, so that the spot where they stood resembled a gay coverlet spread on the ground, embroidered with figures of gold and silver.

His Imperial Majesty spoke often to me, and I returned answers. But neither of us could understand a word of the other's. Several of his priests and lawyers were present and the Emperor commanded them to address themselves to me. I spoke to them in as many languages as I had the least knowledge of, but all to no purpose.

The Emperor ordered his cooks and butlers, who were already prepared, to give me food and drink, which they pushed forward in carts on wheels until I could reach them. I took up these carts and soon emptied them all. Twenty of them were filled with meat, and ten with things to drink.

After about two hours the court retired, and I was left with a strong guard, to prevent the crowd from harming me. They were very impatient to crowd about me as near as they dared, and some of them had the impudence to shoot their arrows at me as I sat on the ground by the door of my house. One arrow narrowly missed my left eye. But the Colonel in command ordered six of the ringleaders to be seized and, as punishment, delivered them bound into my hands. I took them all in my right hand, put five of them into my coat pocket, and as to the sixth, I pretended I would eat him alive. The poor man squalled terribly, and the Colonel and his officers were in great pain, especially when they saw me take out my penknife. But I soon put them out of fear, for I immediately cut the strings he was bound with, and set him gently on the ground. Away he ran. I treated the rest in the same manner, taking them one by one out of my pocket, and I saw that both the soldiers and the other people were pleased at this sign of my mercy, which they reported to the Emperor.

Towards night I got with some difficulty into my house, where I lay on the ground. I continued to sleep thus for about a fortnight, during which time the Emperor gave orders to have a bed prepared for me. Six hundred beds of common size were brought in a carriage for my house. A hundred and fifty of their beds, sewn together, made up the length and breadth; and they protected me none too well from the hardness of the floor that was of smooth stone.

As the news of my arrival spread through the land, it brought huge numbers of rich, idle, and curious people to see me. In the meantime, as I later learned, the Emperor had frequent councils to debate what course should be taken with me. The courtiers were afraid I might break loose and that my food would be very expensive and cause a famine in their land. Sometimes they determined to starve me, or at least shoot me in the face and hands with poisoned arrows.

Others, however, argued that if this were done it would be a very difficult thing to get rid of so large a dead body. But in the midst of the consultations, several officers of the army gave an account of my behavior which made so favorable an impression on His Majesty and the whole Council that an Imperial Command was issued on my behalf.

It ordered all villages nine hundred yards around the city to deliver each morning six oxen, forty sheep, and a sufficient quantity of bread and wine. It was also commanded that six hundred persons should act as my servants, and tents were built for them very conveniently on each side of my door. It was likewise ordered that three hundred tailors should make me a suit of clothes and that six of His Majesty's greatest scholars should teach me the language of the country.

All these orders were duly carried out and in about three weeks I had made good progress in learning the language. I now began to find out a good deal about this land in which I found myself. It was called Lilliput and the people in it were called Lilliputians.

These Lilliputians believed that their kingdom and the neighboring country of Blefuscu were the whole world. Blefuscu, to these little people, lay far over the sea, dim and blue on the horizon, though to me the distance appeared not more than a mile. The Lilliputians thought I must have fallen from the moon, or perhaps from one of the stars. It was impossible, they said, that so big a race of men could live on the earth. They were quite certain there could not be enough food for them.

While I was learning the language, the Emperor frequently honored me with his visits and was pleased to assist my masters in teaching me. We began to converse and the first thing I learned was how to ask for my liberty, which I every day repeated on my knees. His answer, as I understood it, was that this would take time and the advice of his Council, and that first I must "swear a peace" with the kingdom of Lilliput, and afterward, if by continued good behavior I gained their confidence, I might be freed. He hoped that I would not mind if he gave orders to certain officers to search

me. I took up the two officers in my hands, put them first into my coat pockets, and then into every other pocket except my two fobs.

These gentlemen made an inventory of everything they found there and wrote an account of it for the Emperor. They referred to my pocket-comb as "a sort of huge bar from the back of which twenty long poles stuck out like fence posts." My pistols they called "hollow pillars of iron fastened to strong pieces of timber." The use of my bullets and my powder (which I had been lucky enough to bring ashore dry, owing to the fact that my powder pouch was watertight), they could not understand at all. Of my watch they could make nothing. They called it a "wonderful kind of engine, which makes an incessant noise like a water-wheel. We think it is some unknown god he worships, for he made us understand that he seldom did anything without consulting it. He said it pointed out the time for every action of his life."

When the whole inventory was read over to the Emperor, he ordered three thousand men to surround me and then asked me to draw my scimitar which, although it had got some rust on it from the sea-water, was still exceedingly bright. I did so and immediately all the troops gave a great shout, between terror and surprise; for the sun was shining and the reflection dazzled their eyes. His Majesty ordered me to return the scimitar into the scabbard and cast it on the ground as gently as I could.

Next he demanded one of the "hollow iron pillars," by which he meant my pistols. As his request I explained their purpose as well as I could. I charged one of them with powder and told the Emperor not to be afraid. Then I fired it into the air.

At once hundreds of little people fell down as if they had been struck dead. Even the Emperor, although he stood his ground, could not recover himself for some time.

I gave him my pistols as I had my scimitar, and then my pouch of powder and bullets. These were put, for safety, under strict guard. The rest of my goods were returned to me.

In one private pocket, which had escaped their search, I still retained a pair of spectacles, a pocket telescope, and some other little conveniences which, being of no consequence to the Emperor, I did not feel honor bound to reveal. I fancied they might be lost or spoiled if they left my possession.

My good behavior had made such an impression on the Emperor and the people that I began to have hopes of getting my liberty in a short time.

Little by little the Lilliputians came to be less afraid of me. I would sometimes lie down and let five or six of them dance on my hand; and at last the boys and girls would venture to come and play hide-and-seek in my hair. The horses of the army were no longer shy and their riders would leap them over my hand. One jumped over my foot, shoe and all, and that was indeed a prodigious leap.

One day the Emperor took into his head a curious fancy. He ordered a review of troops to be held. First he directed that I should stand with my legs as far apart as I could. He then commanded his general to draw up his troops of three thousand foot soldiers and a thousand horsemen and march them under me, the foot soldiers by twenty-four abreast, and the horsemen by

sixteen, with drums beating and colors flying.

Shortly after this I was set free, and this is how it came about. There had been a meeting of the Emperor's Council, and the Lord High Admiral was the only member in favor of still keeping me in chains. This important officer was my bitter enemy, and though on this occasion he was out-voted, yet he was allowed to draw up the conditions which I had to swear to uphold before my chains were struck off.

These were his conditions:

First: The Man-Mountain shall not leave our domain without our permission.

Second: He shall not come into the city without express order; at which time the inhabitants shall have two hours' warning to keep within their doors.

Third: He shall take the utmost care not to trample on anybody, or on any horses or carriages, or take any of our subjects into his hands without our consent.

Fourth: He shall be our ally against our enemies in the Island of Blefuscu, and do his utmost to destroy their fleet, which is now preparing to invade us.

Fifth: The Man-Mountain shall assist our workmen in moving certain great stones needed to repair some of the public buildings.

Sixth: He shall make an exact survey of the circumference of our dominions by counting how many of his own paces it took him to go all around the coast.

Lastly: On his swearing to the above conditions, the said Man-Mountain shall have the daily ration of meat and drink ordinarily allowed for seventeen hundred and twenty-eight of our subjects.

Though some of these rules did not quite

please me, I nevertheless agreed. I signed the document and my chains were immediately unlocked.

The first request I made, after I had obtained my liberty, was that I might be allowed to see Milendo, the metropolis of Lilliput. This permission the Emperor granted me, but with a special charge to do no harm to the inhabitants or their houses. The people had notice by proclamation of my plan to visit the town.

The great wall which surrounded it was two and a half feet high and at least eleven inches broad so that a coach and horses could be driven very safely round it, and it was flanked with strong towers ten feet apart.

I stepped over the great Western Gate and passed through the two principal streets very gently and sideways for fear of damaging the roofs or chimneys of the houses. Wherever I went the tops of the houses and the attic windows were crowded with wondering spectators. The houses were from three to five stories high, and the shops and markets were well stocked.

In the center of the city, where the two chief streets met, stood the Emperor's palace, a very fine building surrounded by a wall. But I was not able to see the whole palace that day, because the royal apartments were shut off by another wall nearly five feet in height, which I could not get over without a risk of doing damage.

Some days later I did climb over it with the help of two stools which I made from some trees which I was allowed to cut down for the purpose. By putting one of the stools at each side of the wall, I was able to step across. Then, by lying down on my side, and putting my face close to the open win-

dows of the middle stories, I looked in and saw the most splendid apartments than can be imagined. The Empress and the young Princes had their chief attendants about them. Her Imperial Majesty smiled very graciously upon me, and gave me her hand out of the window to kiss.

One morning, about a fortnight after I had obtained my liberty, the Emperor's Chief Secretary, Reldresal, a very great man, came to my house for a conference, attended by only one servant. I offered to lie down so that Reldresal could reach my ear. But he chose to let me hold him in my hand, during our conversation about the state of the country.

He said that though to the outward eye things in Lilliput seemed very settled and prosperous, yet in reality there were troubles, both internal and external, that threatened the safety of the nation.

"There are two struggling parties in this Empire," he said, "under the names of *Trameck'san* and *Slamecksan*. The names come from the high and low heels of their shoes, by which they distinguish themselves. His Majesty has determined to make use of only those with low heels in his government and all offices. You must have observed that His Majesty's Imperial heels are lower by at least a *drurr* than any of his court. (A *drurr* is a measure of about a fourteenth of an inch). The enmity between the two parties has for long been so bitter that they will neither eat nor drink nor talk with each other. In addition, the heir to the crown has some tendency toward those who wear high heels. At least we can plainly see that one of his heels is higher than the other, giving him a hobble in his walk."

Continued the Secretary, "That is evil

316

enough. But we are threatened now with an invasion from the island of Blefuscu, which is the other great Empire of the universe, almost as large and powerful as this. You affirm that there are other kingdoms inhabited by human creatures as large as yourself, but we do not believe this. We think you must have dropped from the moon or one of the stars. *Our* histories make no mention of any regions other than the two great Empires of Lilliput and Blefuscu."

He went on, "The war with Blefuscu began this way. As far back as history goes, our people used to break an egg before eating it, at the larger end. But it came about that the present Emperor's grandfather, while he was a boy, happened to cut his finger as he was breaking an egg in the usual way at the large end. Thereupon the Emperor, his father, at once gave strict commands that in future all his subjects should break their eggs at the small end.

"This greatly angered the people, who thought the Emperor had no right to give such an order. There have been six rebellions on account of this law. Many have been killed and thousands have fled as exiles to take refuge in Blefuscu rather than obey the hated order.

"Now, the Big End exiles have found so much assistance from the Emperor of Blefuscu's court that a bloody war has been carried on between the two Empires for three years. We have lost many ships and thirty thousand of our best seamen and soldiers. The enemy has lost even more. Now the Blefuscudians have equipped a great fleet and are preparing to attack us. His Imperial Majesty has confidence in your valor and depends on the help you swore to give us against our enemies. He com-

manded me to lay this account of his affairs before you."

I asked the Secretary to let the Emperor know that I was ready, at the risk of my life, to defend him and the country against all invaders.

The Empire of Blefuscu is an island, to the northeast side of Lilliput, from which it is separated by a channel eight hundred yards wide. I had not yet seen it, and, since all communication between the two countries had been forbidden during the war, the Blefuscudians had not heard of me.

I told His Majesty of a plan I had for seizing the enemy's whole fleet. It lay at anchor in the harbor, our scouts assured us, ready to sail with the first fair wind. The channel between us, I was told, was about six feet deep at high water. I walked toward the coast opposite Blefuscu, and lay down behind a hillock so that I might not be seen by any of the enemy's ships should they happen to be cruising nearby. I could see the cliffs of Blefuscu, and with my pocket telescope I could see the whole fleet of about fifty men-of-war and a great many transports.

Coming back to the city, I ordered a great length of the strongest cable and a quantity of bars of iron. The cable was hardly thicker than packing string, and the bars of iron much about the length and size of knitting needles. Twisting three of the iron bars together, I bent them into a hook at one end. I wound three lengths of cable together making fifty shorter cables and to these I fastened the hooks.

Taking off my coat, shoes and stockings, I walked in my leather jerkin into the sea about an hour before high tide. In the middle I swam for about thirty yards till I felt ground. I reached the fleet in less than half an hour.

The enemy was so frightened when they saw me that they leaped out of their ships and swam to shore in terror. Never had any of them seen or dreamed of so monstrous a giant. I then took my tackling and, fastening a hook to the hole at the prow of each ship, I tied all the cords together at the end.

While I was thus occupied, the Blefuscudian soldiers on the shore plucked up courage and began to discharge thousands of arrows, many of which stuck in my hands and face. I should have lost my eyes had I not suddenly thought of a way out. I had kept my spectacles in a private pocket which had escaped the Emperor's searchers. These I fastened as strongly as I could upon my nose. Thus armed, I went on boldly with my work in spite of the enemy's arrows.

I now fastened the cable together and pulled, but the ships held fast by their anchors. But I cut the cables that fastened the anchors with my knife, and easily drew fifty of the enemy's men-of-war after me.

The Blefuscudians, who had not the least idea of what I intended, were at first simply astonished. But when they saw their great fleet being steadily drawn out to sea, their grief was terrible, as I could hear from their cries of despair. By the time I got well away from their land the tide had fallen a little, and I was able to wade across the channel with my cargo. I arrived safe at the royal port of Lilliput.

The Emperor and his whole court stood on the shore. They saw the ships move forward in a large half-moon and as the channel grew shallower, I soon came within hearing and, holding up the end of the cable by which the fleet was fastened, I cried in a loud voice, "Long live the Emperor of Lilliput!"

The Emperor was so pleased that when I landed he created me a *Nordac,* the highest honor in his power to bestow. But my success over the Blefuscudians turned out to be the beginning of trouble for me. The Emperor was so puffed up by the victory that he formed plans for me to bring all the rest of his enemy's ships into his ports. And it was now his wish to crush Blefuscu completely—to destroy the Big End exiles and thus compel all people to break the smaller end of their eggs. In this way, he thought, he would be monarch of the whole world.

In this scheme I refused to take part. "I will never be an instrument to bringing a free and brave people into slavery," I protested.

This open declaration of mine angered the Emperor so much that he never forgave me.

But about this time there came to Lilliput ambassadors from Blefuscu, asking for peace. When a treaty had been made and signed (greatly to Lilliput's advantage) the Blefuscudian ambassadors asked to see the great Man-Mountain of whom they had heard so much. They asked me to give them further proof of my strength, which I did. The ambassadors, who had privately been told how friendly I had been to them, invited me to visit their country in the name of *their* Emperor. This I promised to do.

Accordingly the next time I saw the Emperor of Lilliput, I asked his permission to leave the country for a time to go to Blefuscu. The Emperor did not refuse, but his manner was very cold. Later I learned from friendly sources that my enemies in the Council had told the Emperor lying tales of

318

my meetings with the ambassadors from Blefuscu. This aroused his anger still further.

It happened, too, most unfortunately at this time, that by a well-meant but badly managed effort to do the Empress a service I had offended her and thus lost her friendship too. But though I was now out of favor with the court, I was still a subject of great interest.

Three hundred cooks prepared my food, and these men, with their families, lived in small huts built near my house. I had made a chair and table for myself. Onto this table I lifted twenty waiters who then, by means of ropes and pulleys, drew up all my food and drink which a hundred other servants had in readiness on the ground. I often ate my meals with hundreds of the little people looking on.

One day, the Emperor, who had not seen me since this table had been built, sent a message that he and the Empress and their sons desired to dine with me. They arrived just before dinner and I placed them in chairs of state upon my table just facing me, with their guards about them.

Their Majesties sat in their chairs all the time, fascinated as whole roasts of beef and mutton, and whole flocks of geese and turkeys and fowl disappeared into my mouth.

But Flimnap, the Lord High Treasurer, who had always been one of my enemies, pointed out to the Emperor that my meals had cost His Majesty about a million-and-a-half *sprugs*, the largest Lilliputian gold coin, and that it would be advisable for him to dismiss me.

While I was preparing for my visit to the Emperor of Blefuscu, an important personage of the court of Lilliput, to whom I had been of great service, came to my house secretly one night.

To a servant I could trust I gave orders that no one else was to be admitted, and having set this Courtier upon my table, so that we might better converse, he unfolded the following information:

"You are to know that the Emperor and his Council have charged you as a traitor in that you did aid and comfort their enemies, the Empire of Blefuscu; that having brought the fleet of Blefuscu into port, and being afterwards commanded by His Majesty to seize all the other Blefuscudian ships, you refused. It was also said that you would not join in crushing the Empire of Blefuscu, nor give aid when it was proposed to put to death not only all the Big Endians who had fled there for refuge but all the Blefuscudians themselves who were friends of the Big Endians.

"You are also accused," continued the Courtier, "of being over-friendly with the ambassadors of Blefuscu; that, though His Majesty has not given you written permission to visit Blefuscu, yet you are preparing to go there to give help to the Emperor against Lilliput."

The Courtier went on to say that the Lord High Admiral and Flimnap, the treasurer, had made violent speeches, strongly advising that I should be put to death by having my house set on fire at night. One general offered to attend, with twenty thousand men armed with poisoned arrows.

"It must be confessed," the Courtier admitted, "that His Majesty urged leniency considering the services you had performed for the country. One of your friends on the Council, Reldresal, then spoke. He allowed that your crimes were great, but there was still room for mercy. His Majesty might spare your life and instead merely put out both your eyes. He thought this would not prevent you from still being useful. Certain of the Council then said that your care and food had put Lilliput to great expense. They thought they might gradually lessen your food so that in the course of two or three months you would die of starvation. And now," continued my friend the Courtier, "I must depart as secretly as I came."

With this he left me to decide what I should do. It would have been possible for me to destroy all of Lilliput, once I had been warned, while I still had my liberty. But this I rejected with horror, remembering the oath I had made to the Emperor and the favors I had received from him.

However, the Emperor of Blefuscu had asked me to pay him a visit because of my saving his people. To this the Emperor of Lilliput had consented, as it was to be for only a brief stay, and as he supposed me ignorant of the plans against me. I therefore took this opportunity, before three days had elapsed, to send a letter to my friend, the Courtier, signifying my intention of setting out for Blefuscu.

Without waiting for an answer I went to the coast where our fleet lay. I seized a large man-of-war which was at anchor there, tied a cable to the prow, and then putting my clothes and my coverlet on board, I drew the ship after me as I waded and swam toward Blefuscu.

There I was well received. The Emperor and his train alighted from their horses to greet me. I lay on the ground to kiss His Majesty's and the Empress's hands.

Three days after my arrival, when walking along the seashore, I observed, about half a league off in the sea, something that looked like a boat overturned. Wading out, I saw that it was a real boat, blown there by some tempest. I asked the Emperor to lend me twenty of the tallest vessels he had left and three thousand seamen. With their help I brought the boat in toward shore and turned it right side up. I found that but little damage had been done. The populace wondered at the sight of so prodigious a vessel. I told the Emperor that "my good fortune has thrown this boat my way to carry me toward my native country." I begged him to order it to be fitted up, and this he was pleased to do.

I did very much wonder, in all this time, why I had not heard from the Emperor of Lilliput. But I learned that since he thought his designs against me had been kept secret, he expected me to return. As my stay in Blefuscu lengthened, however, the Emperor sent word demanding that I be sent back to Lilliput, bound hand and foot, there to be punished as a traitor.

To this message the Emperor of Blefuscu replied that it was not possible to bind me, that moreover, though I had deprived him of his fleet, he owed me great obligations for many good offices I had done him in making the peace. "Besides," he said, "the great Man-Mountain has found a vessel of size great enough to carry him over the sea and it is his purpose to leave Blefuscu in a few weeks."

In about a month I was prepared to sail. I loaded the boat with the carcasses of one hundred oxen and three hundred sheep, a quantity of bread and wine, and as much other food as four hundred cooks could provide. I also took with me six cows, two bulls, and a flock of sheep, intending to carry them to my own country, and propagate the breed. To feed them on board I had a good bundle of hay and a bag of corn. I would gladly have taken a dozen of the natives, but this the Emperor would not permit.

Everything being ready, I set sail on the 24th day of September, 1701, and two days later I sighted a sail. I came up to her between five and six in the evening and my heart leaped to see her English colors. It is not easy to express my joy at the unexpected hope of once more seeing my own beloved country.

On reaching the vessel I put my live cattle and sheep into my coat pockets and went aboard with all my cargo of provisions. The captain received me very kindly, but when I told him my story he obviously thought the dangers I had undergone had disturbed my head. But the cattle and sheep I took from my pockets convinced him I was speaking the truth. I also showed him gold coins given me by the Emperor of Blefuscu, together with His Majesty's picture, and I promised to make him a present of a cow and a sheep when we got to England.

The vessel did not arrive at the port of London till April, 1702. For the short time I remained in England I made a considerable profit by exhibiting my cattle, and I sold them for six hundred pounds.

Then I set out on another voyage.

Invictus

By William Ernest Henley

Out of the night that covers me,
  Black as the pit from pole to pole,
I thank whatever gods there be
  For my unconquerable soul.

In the fell clutch of circumstance
  I have not winced nor cried aloud.
Under the bludgeonings of chance
  My head is bloody, but unbowed.

Beyond this space of wrath and tears
  Looms but the horror of the shade,
And yet the menace of the years
  Finds and shall find me unafraid.

It matters not how strait the gate,
  How charged with punishments the scroll,
I am the master of my fate:
  I am the captain of my soul.

A Song of Sherwood

By Alfred Noyes

Sherwood in the twilight, is Robin Hood awake?
Gray and ghostly shadows are gliding through the brake,
Shadows of the dappled deer, dreaming of the morn,
Dreaming of a shadowy man that winds a shadowy horn.

Robin Hood is here again; all his merry thieves
Hear a ghostly bugle-note shivering through the leaves,
Calling as he used to call, faint and far away,
In Sherwood, in Sherwood, about the break of day.

Merry merry England has kissed the lips of June;
All the wings of fairyland were here beneath the moon,
Like a flight of rose-leaves fluttering in a mist
Of opal and ruby and pearl and amethyst.

Merry merry England is waking as of old,
With eyes of blither hazel and hair of brighter gold,
For Robin Hood is here again beneath the bursting spray
In Sherwood, in Sherwood, about the break of day.

Love is in the greenwood building him a house
Of wild rose and hawthorn and honeysuckle boughs;
Love is in the greenwood, dawn is in the skies,
And Marian is waiting with a glory in her eyes.

Hark! The dazzled laverock climbs the golden steep!
Marian is waiting; is Robin Hood asleep?
Round the fairy grass-rings frolic elf and fay
In Sherwood, in Sherwood, about the break of day.

Oberon, Oberon, rake away the gold,
Rake away the red leaves, roll away the mold,
Rake away the gold leaves, roll away the red,
And wake Will Scarlett from his leafy forest bed.

Friar Tuck and Little John are riding down together
With quarter-staff and drinking can and gray goose-feather.
The dead are coming back again, the years are rolled away
In Sherwood, in Sherwood, about the break of day.

Softly over Sherwood the south wind blows.
All the heart of England hid in every rose
Hears across the greenwood the sunny whisper leap,
Sherwood in the red dawn, is Robin Hood asleep?

Hark, the voice of England wakes him as of old
And, shattering the silence with a cry of brighter gold,
Bugles in the greenwood echo from the steep,
Sherwood in the red dawn, is Robin Hood asleep?

Where the deer are gliding down the shadowy glen
All across the glades of fern he calls his merry men—
Doublets of the Lincoln green glancing through the May
In Sherwood, in Sherwood, about the break of day—

Calls them and they answer; from aisles of oak and ash
Rings the Follow! Follow! and the boughs begin to crash,
The ferns begin to flutter, and the flowers begin to fly,
And through the crimson dawning the robber band goes by.

Robin! Robin! Robin! All his merry thieves
Answer as the bugle-note shivers through the leaves,
Calling as he used to call, faint and far away,
In Sherwood, in Sherwood, about the break of day.

Lochinvar

By Walter Scott

O, young Lochinvar is come out of the west,
Through all the wide Border his steed was
    the best,
And save his good broadsword he weapons
    had none;
He rode all unarmed, and he rode all alone.
So faithful in love, and so dauntless in war,
There never was knight like the young
    Lochinvar.

He stayed not for brake, and he stopped
    not for stone,
He swam the Eske river where ford there
    was none;
But, ere he alighted at Netherby gate,
The bride had consented, the gallant came
    late;
For a laggard in love, and a dastard in war,
Was to wed the fair Ellen of brave
    Lochinvar.

So boldly he entered the Netherby hall,
'Mong bride's-men and kinsmen, and
    brothers and all;
Then spoke the bride's father, his hand on
    his sword
(For the poor craven bridegroom said never
    a word),
"O come ye in peace here, or come ye in
    war,
Or to dance at our bridal, young Lord
    Lochinvar?"

"I long wooed your daughter, my suit you
    denied;

Love swells like the Solway, but ebbs like
    its tide;
And now I am come, with this lost love of
    mine,
To lead but one measure, drink one cup of
    wine.
There are maidens in Scotland more lovely
    by far,
That would gladly be bride to the young
    Lochinvar."

The bride kissed the goblet; the knight
    took it up;
He quaffed off the wine, and he threw down
    the cup.
She looked down to blush, and she looked
    up to sigh,
With a smile on her lips and a tear in her
    eye.
He took her soft hand, ere her mother
    could bar—
"Now tread we a measure!" said young
    Lochinvar.

So stately his form, and so lovely her face,
That never a hall such a galliard did grace;
While her mother did fret, and her father
    did fume,
And the bridegroom stood dangling his
    bonnet and plume;
And the bride-maidens whispered, " 'Twere
    better by far
To have matched our fair cousin with
    young Lochinvar."

One touch to her hand, and one word in
    her ear,
When they reached the hall door, and the
    charger stood near;
So light to the croup the fair lady he
    swung,
So light to the saddle before her he sprung!

"She is won! We are gone, over bank, bush,
    and scaur!
They'll have fleet steeds that follow," quoth
    young Lochinvar.

There was mounting 'mong Graemes of the
    Netherby clan;
Forsters, Fenwicks, and Musgraves, they
    rode and they ran;
There was racing and chasing on Cannobie
    Lee,
But the lost bride of Netherby ne'er did
    they see.
So daring in love, and so dauntless in war,
Have ye e'er heard of gallant like young
    Lochinvar?

Rip Van Winkle

By *Washington Irving*

Here is the complete story of that lovable, lazy, good-natured scalawag, Rip Van Winkle, and of his fabulous adventures in the Kaatskill (now spelled Catskill) mountains.

The story was written well over a century ago by America's best-known writer of Hudson Valley legends, Washington Irving, and it has been amusing and delighting children as well as grown-ups ever since.

Of course Irving wrote the story entirely out of his imagination. But to make it sound real, he pretended he had found it among the papers of an old gentleman whom he called Diedrich Knickerbocker. This gentleman, according to Irving, was a collector of legends about old New York, the Hudson River Valley, and the old Dutch settlers there.

The ever delightful RIP VAN WINKLE was the result of Washington Irving's little joke. Here it is, in its entirety, for your entertainment.

WHOEVER has made a voyage up the Hudson must remember the Kaatskill mountains. They are a dismembered branch of the great Appalachian family, and are seen away to the west of the river, swelling up to a noble height, and lording it over the surrounding country. Every change of season, every change of weather, indeed every hour of the day, produces some change in the magical hues and shapes of these mountains, and they are regarded by all the good wives, far and near, as perfect barometers. When the weather is fair and settled, they are clothed in blue and purple, and print their bold outlines on the clear evening sky; but sometimes, when the rest of the landscape is cloudless, they will gather a hood of gray vapors about their summits, which, in the last rays of the setting sun, will glow and light up like a crown of glory.

At the foot of these fairy mountains, the voyager may have descried the light smoke curling up from a village, whose shingle roofs gleam among the trees, just where the blue tints of the upland melt away into the fresh green of the nearer landscape. It is a little village of great antiquity, having been founded by some of the Dutch colonists, in the early times of the province, just about the beginning of the government of the good Peter Stuyvesant (may he rest in peace!), and there were some of the houses of the original settlers standing within a few years, built of small yellow bricks brought from Holland, having latticed windows and gable fronts, surmounting with weather-cocks.

In that same village, and in one of these very houses (which, to tell the precise truth, was sadly time-worn and weather-beaten), there lived many years since, while the country was yet a province of Great Britain, a simple, good-natured fellow, of the name of Rip Van Winkle. He was a descendant of the Van Winkles who figured so gallantly in the chivalrous days of Peter Stuyvesant, and accompanied him to the siege of Fort Christina. He inherited, however, but little of the martial character of his ancestors. I have observed that he was a simple, good-natured man; he was, moreover, a kind neighbor, and an obedient, henpecked husband. Indeed, to the latter circumstance might be owing that meekness of spirit which gained him such universal popularity; for those men are most apt to be obsequious and conciliating abroad who are under the discipline of shrews at home. Their tempers, doubtless, are rendered pliant and malleable in the fiery furnace of domestic tribulation, and a curtain lecture is worth all the sermons in the world for teaching the virtues of patience and long-suffering. A termagant wife may, therefore, in some respects, be considered a toler-

able blessing; and if so, Rip Van Winkle was thrice blessed.

Certain it is that he was a great favorite among all the good wives of the village, who, as usual with the amiable sex, took his part in all family squabbles; and never failed, whenever they talked those matters over in their evening gossipings, to lay all the blame on Dame Van Winkle. The children of the village, too, would shout with joy whenever he approached. He assisted at their sports, made their playthings, taught them to fly kites and shoot marbles, and told them long stories of ghosts, witches, and Indians. Whenever he went dodging about the village, he was surrounded by a troop of them, hanging on his skirts, clambering on his back, and playing a thousand tricks on him with impunity; and not a dog would bark at him throughout the neighborhood.

The great error in Rip's composition was an insuperable aversion of all kinds of profitable labor. It could not be from the want of assiduity or perseverance; for he would sit on a wet rock, with a rod as long and heavy as a Tartar's lance, and fish all day without a murmur, even though he should not be encouraged by a single nibble. He would carry a fowling-piece on his shoulder for hours together, trudging through woods and swamps, and up hill and down dale, to shoot a few squirrels or wild pigeons. He would never refuse to assist a neighbor even in the roughest toil, and was a foremost man at all country frolics for husking Indian corn or building stone fences. The women of the village, too, used to employ him to run their errands, and to do such little odd jobs as their less obliging husbands would

not do for them. In a word, Rip was ready to attend to anybody's business but his own; but as to doing family duty, and keeping his farm in order, he found it impossible.

In fact, he declared it was of no use to work on his farm; it was the most pestilent little piece of ground in the whole country; everything about it went wrong, and would go wrong, in spite of him. His fences were continually falling to pieces; his cow would either go astry or get among the cabbages; weeds were sure to grow quicker in his fields than anywhere else; the rain always made a point of setting in just as he had some outdoor work to do; so that, though his patrimonial estate had dwindled away under his management, acre by acre, until there was little more left than a mere patch of Indian corn and potatoes, yet it was the worst conditioned farm in the neighborhood.

His children, too, were as ragged and wild as if they belonged to nobody. His son Rip, an urchin begotten in his own likeness, promised to inherit the habits, with the old clothes of his father. He was generally seen trooping like a colt, at his mother's heels, equipped in a pair of his father's castoff galligaskins, which he had much ado to hold up with one hand, as a fine lady does her train in bad weather.

Rip Van Winkle, however, was one of those happy mortals, of foolish, well-oiled dispositions, who take the world easy, eat white bread or brown, whichever can be got with least thought or trouble, and would rather starve on a penny than work for a pound. If left to himself, he would have whistled life away, in perfect contentment; but his wife kept continually dinning in his ears about his idleness, his carelessness, and

the ruin he was bringing on his family. Morning, noon, and night, her tongue was incessantly going, and everything he said or did was sure to produce a torrent of household eloquence.

Rip had but one way of replying to all lectures of the kind, and that, by frequent use, had grown into a habit. He shrugged his shoulders, shook his head, cast up his eyes, but said nothing. This, however, always provoked a fresh volley from his wife; so that he was fain to draw off his forces, and take to the outside of the house—the only side which, in truth, belongs to a henpecked husband.

Rip's sole domestic adherent was his dog

Wolf, who was as much henpecked as his master; for Dame Van Winkle regarded them as companions in idleness, and even looked upon Wolf with an evil eye, as the cause of his master's going so often astray. True it is, in all points of spirit befitting an honorable dog, he was as courageous an animal as ever scoured the woods—but what courage can withstand the ever-during and all-besetting terrors of a woman's tongue? The moment Wolf entered the house his crest fell, his tail drooped to the ground or curled between his legs, he sneaked about with a gallows air, casting many a sidelong glance at Dame Van Winkle, and at the least flourish of a broomstick or ladle, he would fly to the door with yelping precipitation.

Times grew worse and worse with Rip Van Winkle as years of matrimony rolled on. A tart temper never mellows with age, and a sharp tongue is the only edge tool that grows keener with constant use. For a long while he used to console himself, when driven from home, by frequenting a kind of perpetual club of the sages, philosophers, and other idle personages of the village, which held its sessions on a bench before a small inn, designated by a rubicund portrait of his Majesty George the Third. Here they used to sit in the shade, of a long lazy summer's day, talk listlessly over village gossip, or tell endless sleepy stories about nothing. But it would have been worth any stateman's money to have heard the profound discussions that sometimes took place when by chance an old newspaper fell into their hands from some passing traveller. How solemnly they would listen to the contents, as drawled out by Derrick Van Bummel, the schoolmaster, a dapper learned little man, who was not to be daunted by the most gigantic word in the dictionary; and how sagely they would deliberate upon public events some months after they had taken place.

The opinions of this junto were completely controlled by Nicholas Vedder, a patriarch of the village, and landlord of the inn, at the door of which he took his seat from morning till night, just moving sufficiently to avoid the sun, and keep in the shade of a large tree; so that the neighbors could tell the hour by his movements as accurately as by a sun-dial. It is true, he was rarely heard to speak, but smoked his pipe incessantly. His adherents, however (for every great man has his adherents), perfectly understood him, and knew how to gather his opinions. When anything that was read or related displeased him, he was observed to smoke his pipe vehemently, and send forth short, frequent, and angry puffs; but when pleased, he would inhale the smoke slowly and tranquilly, and emit it in light and placid clouds, and sometimes taking the pipe from his mouth, and letting the fragrant vapor curl about his nose, would gravely nod his head in token of perfect approbation.

From even this stronghold the unlucky Rip was at length routed by his termagant wife, who would suddenly break in upon the tranquillity of the assemblage and call the members all to naught; nor was that august personage, Nicholas Vedder himself, sacred from the daring tongue of this terrible virago, who charged him outright with encouraging her husband in habits of idleness.

Poor Rip was at last reduced almost to despair; and his only alternative to escape from the labor of the farm and the clamor of his wife, was to take gun in hand, and stroll away into the woods. Here he would sometimes seat himself at the foot of a tree, and share the contents of his wallet with Wolf, with whom he sympathized as a fellow-sufferer in persecution. "Poor Wolf," he would say, "thy mistress leads thee a dog's life of it; but never mind, my lad, whilst I live thou shalt never want a friend to stand by thee!"

Wolf would wag his tail, look wistfully in his master's face, and if dogs can feel pity, I verily believe he reciprocated the sentiment with all his heart.

In a long ramble of the kind on a fine autumnal day, Rip had unconsciously scrambled to one of the highest parts of the Kaatskill mountains. He was after his favorite sport of squirrel-shooting, and the still solitudes had echoed and reëchoed with the reports of his gun. Panting and fatigued, he threw himself, late in the afternoon, on a green knoll, covered with mountain herbage, that crowned the brow of a precipice. From an opening between the trees he could overlook all the lower country for many a mile of rich woodland. He saw at a distance the lordly Hudson, far far below him, moving on its silent but majestic course, with the reflection of a purple cloud, or the sail of a lagging bark, here and there sleeping on its glassy bosom, and at last losing itself in the blue highlands.

On the other side he looked down into a deep mountain glen, wild, lonely, and shagged, the bottom filled with fragments from the impending cliffs, and scarcely lighted by the reflected rays of the setting sun. For some time Rip lay musing on this scene. Evening was gradually advancing; the mountains began to throw their long blue shadows over the valleys. He saw that it would be dark long before he could reach the village, and he heaved a heavy sigh when he thought of encountering the terrors of Dame Van Winkle.

As he was about to descend, he heard a voice from a distance hallooing, "Rip Van Winkle! Rip Van Winkle!"

He looked around, but could see nothing but a crow winging its solitary flight across the mountain. He thought his fancy must have deceived him and turned again to descend, when he heard the same cry ring through the still evening air: "Rip Van Winkle! Rip Van Winkle!" At the same time Wolf bristling up his back, and giving a low growl, skulked to his master's side, looking fearfully down into the glen. Rip now felt a vague apprehension stealing over him. He looked anxiously in the same direction, and perceived a strange figure slowly toiling up the rocks and bending under the weight of something he carried on his back. He was surprised to see any human being in this lonely and unfrequented place, but supposing it to be someone of the neighborhood in need of his assistance he hastened down to yield it.

On nearer approach, he was still more surprised at the singularity of the stranger's appearance. He was a short, square-built old fellow, with thick, bushy hair, and a grizzled beard. His dress was of the antique Dutch fashion—a cloth jerkin strapped round the waist—several pairs of breeches, the outer one of ample volume, decorated with rows of buttons down the sides; and bunches at the knees. He bore on his shoulder a stout keg, that seemed full of liquor, and made signs for Rip to approach and assist him with the load. Though rather shy and distrustful of this new acquaintance, Rip complied with his usual alacrity, and mutually relieving each other, they clambered up a narrow gully, apparently the dry bed of a mountain torrent. As they ascended, Rip every now and then heard long rolling peals, like distant thunder, that seemed to issue out of a deep ravine, or rather cleft between lofty rocks, toward which their rugged path conducted. He paused for an instant, but supposing it to be the muttering of one of those transient thunder showers which often take place in mountain heights, he proceeded. Passing through the ravine, they came to a hollow, like a small amphitheatre, surrounded by perpendicular precipices over the brinks of which impending trees shot their branches, so that you only caught glimpses of the azure sky, and the bright evening cloud. During the whole time Rip and his companion had labored on in silence; for though the former marvelled greatly what could be the object of carrying a keg of liquor up this wild mountain, yet there was something strange and incomprehensible about the unknown, that inspired awe and checked familiarity.

On entering the amphitheatre, new objects of wonder presented themselves. On a level spot in the center was a company of odd-looking personages playing at ninepins. They were dressed in a quaint, outlandish fashion: some wore short doublets, others jerkins, with long knives in their belts, and most of them had enormous breeches, of similar style with that of the guide's. Their visages, too, were peculiar; one had a large head, broad face, and small piggish eyes; the face of another seemed to consist entirely of nose, and was surmounted by a white sugarloaf hat, set off with a little red cock's tail. They all had beards, of various shapes and colors. There was one who seemed to be the commander. He was a stout old gentleman, with a weather-beaten countenance. He wore a laced doublet, broad belt and hanger, high-crowned hat and feather, red stockings, and high-heeled shoes, with roses in them. The whole group reminded Rip of the figures in an old Flemish painting, in the parlor of Dominie Van Shaick, the village parson, and which had been brought over from Holland at the time of the settlement.

What seemed particularly odd to Rip was that though these folk were evidently amusing themselves, yet they maintained the gravest faces, the most mysterious silence, and were, withal, the most melancholy party of pleasure he had ever witnessed. Nothing interrupted the stillness of the scene but the noise of the balls, which, whenever they were rolled, echoed along the mountains like rumbling peals of thunder.

As Rip and his companion approached them, they suddenly desisted from their play, and stared at him with such fixed, statue-like gaze, and such strange, uncouth, lack-luster countenances, that his heart turned within him, and his knees smote together. His companion now emptied the contents of the keg into large flagons, and made signs to him to wait upon the company. He obeyed with fear and trembling; they quaffed the liquor in profound silence, and then returned to their game.

By degrees Rip's awe and apprehension subsided. He even ventured, when no eye was fixed upon him, to taste the beverage, which he found had much of the flavor of excellent Hollands. He was naturally a thirsty soul, and was soon tempted to repeat the draught. One taste provoked another, and he reiterated his visits to the flagon so often that at length his senses

were overpowered, his eyes swam in his head, his head gradually declined, and he fell into a deep sleep.

On waking, he found himself on the green knoll from whence he had first seen the old man of the glen. He rubbed his eyes—it was a bright sunny morning. The birds were hopping and twittering among the bushes, and the eagle was wheeling aloft and breasting the pure mountain breeze.

"Surely," thought Rip, "I have not slept here all night." He recalled the occurrences before he fell asleep. The strange man with a keg of liquor—the mountain ravine—the wild retreat among the rocks—the woe-begone party at nine-pins—the flagon—"Oh! that flagon! that wicked flagon!" thought Rip. "What excuse shall I make to Dame Van Winkle?"

He looked around for his gun, but in place of the clean, well-oiled fowling-piece, he found an old firelock lying by him, the barrel encrusted with rust, the lock falling off, and the stock worm-eaten. He now suspected that the grave roysterers of the mountain had put a trick upon him, and, having dosed him with liquor, had robbed him of his gun. Wolf, too, had disappeared, but he might have strayed away after a squirrel or partridge. He whistled after him and shouted his name, but all in vain; the echoes repeated his whistle and shout, but no dog was to be seen.

He determined to revisit the scene of the last evening's gambol, and if he met with any of the party, to demand his dog and gun. As he rose to walk he found himself stiff in the joints, and wanting in his usual activity. "These mountain beds do not agree with me," thought Rip, "and if this frolic should lay me up with a fit of rheumatism, I shall have a blessed time with Dame Van Winkle."

With some difficulty he got down into the glen. He found the gully up which he and his companion had ascended the preceding evening; but to his astonishment a mountain stream was now foaming down it, leaping from rock to rock, and filling the glen with babbling murmurs. He, however, made shift to scramble up its sides, working his toilsome way through thickets of birch, sassafras, and witch-hazel, and sometimes tripped up or entangled by the wild grape-vines that twisted their coils and tendrils from tree to tree, and spread a kind of network in his path.

At length he reached to where the ravine had opened through the cliffs, to the amphitheatre; but no traces of such opening remained. The rocks presented a high impenetrable wall, over which the torrent came tumbling in a sheet of feathery foam, and fell into a broad deep basin, black from the shadows of the surrounding forest.

Here poor Rip was brought to a stand. He again called and whistled after his dog. He was answered only by the cawing of a flock of idle crows, sporting high in air about a dry tree that overhung a sunny precipice; and who, secure in their elevation, seemed to look down and scoff at the poor man's perplexities.

What was to be done? The morning was passing away, and Rip felt famished for want of his breakfast. He grieved to give up his dog and gun; he dreaded to meet his wife; but it would not do to starve among the mountains. He shook his head, shouldered the rusty firelock, and, with a heart full of trouble and anxiety, turned his steps homeward.

As he approached the village he met a number of people, but none whom he knew, which somewhat surprised him, for he had thought himself acquainted with everyone in the country around. Their dress, too, was of a different fashion from that to which he was accustomed. They all stared at him with equal marks of surprise, and whenever they cast eyes upon him, instant recurrence of this gesture induced Rip, involuntarily, to do the same, when, to his astonishment, he found his beard had grown a foot long!

He had now entered the skirts of the vil-

lage. A troop of strange children ran at his heels, hooting after him, and pointing at his gray beard. The dogs, too, not one of which he recognized for an old acquaintance, barked at him as he passed. The very village was altered: it was larger and more populous. There were rows of houses which he had never seen before, and those which had been his familiar haunts had disappeared. Strange names were over the doors —strange faces at the windows—everything was strange.

His mind now misgave him; he began to doubt whether both he and the world around him were not bewitched. Surely this was his native village, which he had left but the day before. There stood the Kaatskill mountains—there ran the silver Hudson at a distance—there was every hill and dale precisely as it had always been— Rip was sorely perplexed. "That flagon last night," thought he, "has addled my poor head sadly!"

It was with some difficulty that he found the way to his own house, which he approached with silent awe, expecting every moment to hear the shrill voice of Dame Van Winkle. He found the house gone to decay—the roof fallen in, the windows shattered, and the doors off the hinges. A half-starved dog, that looked like Wolf, was skulking about. Rip called him by name, but the cur snarled, showed his teeth, and passed on. This was an unkind cut indeed —"My very dog," sighed poor Rip, "has forgotten me!"

He entered the house, which, to tell the truth, Dame Van Winkle had always kept in neat order. It was empty, forlorn, and apparently abandoned. This desolateness overcame all his connubial fears. He called loudly for his wife and children—the lonely chambers rang for a moment with his voice, and then all again was silence.

He now hurried forth, and hastened to his old resort, the village inn—but it too was gone. A large rickety wooden building stood in its place, with great gaping windows, some of them broken, and mended with old hats and petticoats, and over the door was painted, "The Union Hotel, by Jonathan Doolittle." Instead of the great tree that used to shelter the quiet little Dutch inn of yore, there now was reared a tall naked pole, with something on the top that looked like a red nightcap, and from it was fluttering a flag, on which was a singular assemblage of stars and stripes—all this was strange and incomprehensible. He recognized on the sign, however, the ruby face of King George, under which he had smoked so many a peaceful pipe, but even this was singularly metamorphosed. The red coat was changed for one of blue and buff, a sword was held in the hand instead of a scepter, the head was decorated with a cocked hat, and underneath was painted in large characters, GENERAL WASHINGTON.

There was, as usual, a crowd of folk about the door, but none that Rip recollected. The very character of the people seemed changed. There was a busy, bustling, disputatious tone about it, instead of the accustomed phlegm and drowsy tranquillity. He looked in vain for the sage Nicholas Vedder, with his broad face, double chin, and fair long pipe, uttering clouds of tobacco smoke instead of idle speeches; or Van Bummel, the schoolmaster, doling forth the contents of an ancient newspaper. In place of these, a lean, bilious-looking fellow, with his pockets full of handbills, was haranguing vehemently about rights of citizens—election—members of Congress—liberty—Bunker Hill—heroes of seventy-six—and other words that were a perfect Babylonish jargon to the bewildered Van Winkle.

The appearance of Rip, with his long grizzled beard, his rusty fowling-piece, his uncouth dress, and the army of women and children that had gathered at his heels, soon attracted the attention of the tavern politicians. They crowded round him, eyeing him from head to foot, with great curiosity. The orator bustled up to him, and drawing him partly aside, inquired "on which side he voted."

Rip stared in vacant stupidity.

Another short but busy little fellow pulled him by the arm, and rising on tip-toe, inquired in his ear, "whether he was Federal or Democrat."

Rip was equally at a loss to comprehend the question when a knowing, self-important gentleman, in a sharp cocked hat, made his way through the crowd, putting them to the right and left with his elbows as he passed, and planting himself before Van Winkle, with one arm akimbo, the other resting on his cane, his keen eyes and sharp hat penetrating, as it were, into his very soul, demanded, in an austere tone, "what brought him to the election with a gun on his shoulder, and a mob at his heels, and whether he meant to breed a riot in the village?"

"Alas! gentlemen," cried Rip, somewhat dismayed, "I am a poor quiet man, a native of the place, and a loyal subject of the King, God bless him!"

Here a general shout burst from the bystanders—"A tory! A tory! A spy! A refugee! Hustle him! Away with him! It was with great difficulty that the self-important man in the cocked hat restored order; and having assumed a tenfold austerity of brow, demanded again of the unknown culprit what he came there for, and whom he was seeking. The poor man humbly assured him that he meant no harm, but merely came there in search of some of his neighbors, who used to keep about the tavern.

"Well—who are they? Name them."

Rip bethought himself a moment, and inquired, "Where's Nicholas Vedder?"

There was silence for a little while, when an old man replied, in a thin piping voice, "Nicholas Vedder? Why he is dead and gone these eighteen years! There was a wooden tombstone in the church-yard that used to tell all about him, but that's rotted and gone too."

"Where's Brom Dutcher?"

"Oh, he went off to the army in the beginning of the war; some say he was killed at the storming of Stony-Point—others say he was drowned in a squall at the foot of Antony's Nose. I don't know—he never came back again."

"Where's Van Bummel, the schoolmaster?"

"He went off to the wars too, was a great militia general, and is now in Congress."

Rip's heart died away at hearing of these sad changes in his home and friends, and finding himself thus alone in the world. Every answer puzzled him, too, by treating of such enormous lapses of time, and of matters which he could not understand: war—Congress—Stony-Point. He had no courage to ask after any more friends, but cried out in despair, "Does nobody here know Rip Van Winkle?"

"Oh, Rip Van Winkle!" exclaimed two or three, "Oh, to be sure! that's Rip Van Winkle yonder, leaning against the tree.

Rip looked, and beheld a precise counterpart of himself, as he went up the mountain: apparently as lazy, and certainly as ragged. The poor fellow was now completely confounded. He doubted his own identity, and whether he was himself or another man. In the midst of his bewilderment, the man in the cocked hat demanded who he was, and what was his name?

"God knows," exclaimed he, at his wit's end. "I'm not myself—I'm somebody else—that's me yonder—no—that's somebody else, got into my shoes—I was myself last night, but I fell asleep on the mountain, and they've changed my gun, and everything's changed, and I'm changed, and I can't tell what's my name, or who I am!"

The bystanders began now to look at each other, nod, wink significantly, and tap their fingers against their foreheads. There was a whisper, also, about securing the gun, and keeping the old fellow from doing mischief, at the very suggestion of which the self-important man in the cocked hat retired with some precipitation. At this critical moment a fresh likely-looking woman pressed through the throng to get a peep at the gray-bearded man. She had a chubby

child in her arm who, frightened at his looks, began to cry. "Hush Rip," cried she, "the old man won't hurt you." The name of the child, the air of the mother, the tone of her voice, all awakened a train of recollection in his mind. "What is your name, my good woman?" asked he.

"Judith Gardenier."

"And your father's name?"

"Ah, poor man, his name was Rip Van Winkle. It's twenty years since he went away from home with his gun, and never has been heard of since—his dog came home without him; but whether he shot himself, or was carried away by the Indians, nobody can tell. I was then but a little girl."

Rip had but one question more to ask; but he put it with a faltering voice:

"Where's your mother?"

Oh, she too had died but a short time since; she broke a blood vessel in a fit of passion at a New England peddler.

There was a drop of comfort, at least in this intelligence. The honest man could contain himself no longer. He caught his daughter and her child in his arms. "I am your father!" cried he—"Young Rip Van Winkle once—old Rip Van Winkle now!—Does nobody know poor Rip Van Winkle?"

All stood amazed, until an old woman, tottering out from among the crowd, put her hand to her brow, and peering under it in his face for a moment, exclaimed, "Sure enough it is Rip Van Winkle—it is himself! Welcome home again, old neighbor. Why, where have you been these twenty long years?"

Rip's story was soon told, for the whole twenty years had been to him as one night. The neighbors stared when they heard it. Some were seen to wink at each other, and put their tongues in their cheeks; and the self-important man in the cocked hat who, when the alarm was over, had returned to the field, screwed down the corners of his mouth, and shook his head—upon which there was a general shaking of the head throughout the assemblage.

It was determined, however, to take the opinion of old Peter Vanderdonk, who was seen slowly advancing up the road. He was a descendant of the historian of that name, who wrote one of the earliest accounts of the province. Peter was the most ancient inhabitant of the village, and well versed in all the wonderful events and traditions of the neighborhood. He recollected Rip at once, and corroborated his story in the most satisfactory manner. He assured the company that it was a fact, handed down from his ancestor the historian, that the Kaatskill mountains had always been haunted by strange beings. That it was affirmed that the great Hendrick Hudson, the first discoverer of the river and country, kept a kind of vigil there every twenty years, with his crew of the *Half Moon*, being permitted in this way to revisit the scenes of his enterprise, and keep a guardian eye upon the river, and the great city called by his name. That his father had once seen them in their old Dutch dresses playing at nine-pins in a hollow of the mountain; and that he himself had heard, one summer afternoon, the sound of their balls like distant peals of thunder.

To make a long story short, the company broke up, and returned to the more important concerns of the election. Rip's daughter took him home to live with her: she had a snug, well-furnished house, and a stout cheery farmer for a husband, whom

Rip recollected for one of the urchins that used to climb upon his back. As to Rip's son and heir, who was the ditto of himself, seen leaning against the tree, he was employed to work on the farm; but evinced an hereditary disposition to attend to anything else but his business.

Rip now resumed his old walks and habits. He soon found many of his former cronies, though all rather the worse for the wear and tear of time; and preferred making friends among the rising generation, with whom he soon grew into great favor.

Having nothing to do at home, and being arrived at that happy age when a man can do nothing with impunity, he took his place once more on the bench, at the inn door, and was reverenced as one of the patriarchs of the village, and a chronicler of the old times "before the war." It was some time before he could get into the regular track of gossip, or could be made to comprehend the strange events that had taken place during his torpor. How that there had been a revolutionary war—that the country had thrown off the yoke of old England—and that, instead of being a subject of His Majesty George the Third, he was now a free citizen of the United States.

Rip, in fact, was no politician; the changes of states and empires made but little impression on him; but there was one species of despotism under which he had long groaned, and that was—petticoat government. Happily, that was at an end; he had got his neck out of the yoke of matrimony, and could go in and out whenever he pleased, without dreading the tyranny of Dame Van Winkle. Whenever her name was mentioned, however, he shook his head, shrugged his shoulders, and cast up his eyes; which might pass either for an expression of resignation to his fate, or joy at his deliverance.

He used to tell his story to every stranger that arrived at Mr. Doolittle's hotel. He was observed, at first, to vary on some points every time he told it, which was, doubtless, owing to his having so recently awakened. It at last settled down precisely to the tale I have related, and not a man, woman, or child in the neighborhood, but knew it by heart. Some always pretended to doubt the reality of it, and insisted that Rip had been out of his head, and that this was one point on which he always remained flighty. The old Dutch inhabitants, however, almost universally gave it full credit. Even to this day they never hear a thunder storm of a summer afternoon, about the Kaatskill, but they say Hendrick Hudson and his crew are at their game of nine-pins; and it is a common wish of all henpecked husbands in the neighborhood, when life hangs heavy on their hands, that they might have a quieting draught out of Rip Van Winkle's flagon.

A Christmas Carol

By Charles Dickens

There is a good reason why we hear this delightful little classic read, Christmas after Christmas, on radio and television, in homes and schools and churches, throughout the English-speaking world. Ever since it was written more than a century ago, it has shamed scoffers into becoming kinder human beings.

It is a spooky and exciting ghost story. But, more important, it tells of the transformation of a man called Scrooge—a man so stingy and flinty-hearted that his very name has come to stand for meanness and cold-heartedness.

But Scrooge was frightened one chilly Christmas Eve when the spirits of Christmas Past, Christmas Present, and Christmas Yet to Come showed him, to his horror, what he was really like.

When he woke up on Christmas Day, Scrooge was a repentant man indeed. After seeing Christmas being celebrated by the family of poor Bob Cratchit, the little clerk to whom he had always been mean to the point of cruelty, the reformed Scrooge made handsome amends.

So moving a story is this CHRISTMAS CAROL that anyone reading or hearing it to the end, and echoing Tiny Tim's "God bless us, every one!" will have a hard time keeping a lump out of his throat.

MARLEY'S GHOST

MARLEY was dead, to begin with. There is no doubt whatever about that. Old Marley was as dead as a door-nail.

Did Scrooge know Marley was dead? Of course he did. Ebenezer Scrooge and he had been partners for I don't know how many years. Scrooge was his sole executor, his sole legatee, his sole mourner. And even Scrooge was not dreadfully cut up by the sad event but on the very day of the funeral he solemnized it with an undoubted bargain.

There is no doubt that Marley was dead. This must be distinctly understood, or nothing wonderful can come of the story I am going to relate.

Scrooge never painted out Old Marley's name. There it stood, years afterwards, above the warehouse door: SCROOGE AND MARLEY, as the firm was known. Sometimes people new to the business called Scrooge Scrooge, and sometimes Marley. He answered to both names; it was all the same to him.

Oh but he was a tight-fisted hand at the grindstone, Scrooge! A squeezing, wrenching, grasping, clutching old sinner! Hard and sharp as flint, from which no steel had ever struck out generous fire; secret and solitary as an oyster. The cold within him froze his old features, nipped his pointed nose, shrivelled his cheek, stiffened his gait.

External heat and cold had little influence on him. No warmth could warm, no cold could chill him. No wind that blew was bitterer than he.

Nobody ever stopped him in the street to say, "My dear Scrooge, how are you? When will you come to see me?" No beggars implored him to bestow a trifle, no children asked him what it was o'clock. No man or woman ever once in all his life inquired the

way to such and such a place of Scrooge. Even the blind men's dogs, when they saw him coming, would tug their owners into doorways and then wag their tails as though they said, "No eye at all is better than an evil eye, dark master!"

But what did Scrooge care! It was the very thing he liked: to edge his way along the crowded paths of life, warning all human sympathy to keep its distance.

Once upon a time—of all the good days in the year upon a Christmas Eve—old Scrooge sat busy in his counting-house. It was cold, bleak, biting, foggy weather. The city clocks had only just gone to three, but it was already dark.

The door of Scrooge's counting-house was open so that he might keep his eye on his clerk, who in a dismal little cell beyond, was copying letters. Scrooge had a very small fire, but the clerk's fire was so much smaller that it looked like one coal. But when the clerk came in with a shovel to replenish the fire, Scrooge said it would be necessary for them to part. Wherefore the clerk put on his white comforter and tried to warm himself at a candle; in which effort he failed.

"A merry Christmas, uncle! God save you!" cried a cheerful voice. It was the voice of Scrooge's nephew, who had come upon him so quickly that Scrooge had not seen him approach.

"Bah!" said Scrooge. "Humbug!"

He had so heated himself with rapid walking in the fog and frost, this nephew of Scrooge's, that he was all in a glow. His face was ruddy and handsome and his eyes sparkled.

"Christmas a humbug, uncle!" he said. "You don't mean that, I am sure."

"I do," said Scrooge. "Merry Christmas indeed.! What reason have *you* to be merry? You're poor enough."

"Come, then," returned the nephew gaily. "What reason have you to be dismal? You're rich enough."

"Scrooge, having no better answer ready, said "Bah!" and "Humbug!" again.

"Don't be cross, uncle," said the nephew.

"What else can I be" returned the uncle, "when I live in such a world of fools as this? Merry Christmas! Out upon merry Christmas! What's Christmas time to you but a time for paying bills without money; a time for finding yourself a year older, and not an hour richer? If I had my will, every idiot who goes about with 'Merry Christmas' on his lips should be boiled with his own pudding, and buried with a stake of holly through his heart."

"Uncle!"

"Nephew, keep Christmas in your own way, and let me keep it in mine."

"Keep it! But you don't keep it."

"Let me leave it alone, then. Much good may it do you! Much good it has ever done you!"

"There are many things from which I have not profited, I dare say, Christmas among the rest," replied the nephew. "But I have always thought of Christmas time as a pleasant time, the only time I know of when men and women open their hearts freely. Though it has never put a scrap of gold or silver in my pocket, I believe it *has* done me good, and *will* do me good; and I say God bless it!"

The clerk in the cell involuntarily applauded. Becoming immediately sensible of the impropriety, he poked the fire, and extinguished the last frail spark forever.

"Let me hear another sound from you," said Scrooge, "and you'll keep your Christmas by losing your situation!" Then, turning to his nephew, he added, "You're quite a powerful speaker. I wonder you don't go into Parliament."

"Don't be angry, uncle. Come dine with us tomorrow."

Scrooge said that he would be seen dead first.

"But why?" cried Scrooge's nephew. "Why?"

"Why did you get married?" asked Scrooge.

"Because I fell in love."

"Because you fell in love!" growled Scrooge. "That's the only thing in the world more ridiculous than a merry Christmas. Good afternoon!"

"I want nothing from you; I ask nothing of you", replied the nephew. "Why cannot we be friends?"

"Good afternoon," said Scrooge.

"I am sorry, with all my heart, to find you so resolute. We have never had any quarrel. But I'll keep my Christmas humor to the last. So a merry Christmas, uncle, and a happy New Year!"

"Good afternoon!" said Scrooge.

His nephew left the room without an angry word, notwithstanding. He stopped at the outer door to bestow the greeting of the season on the clerk who, cold as he was, was warmer than Scrooge. He returned the greetings cordially.

"There's another fellow," muttered Scrooge, "my clerk, with fifteen shillings a week, and wife and family, talking about a merry Christmas. I'll retire to Bedlam."

The clerk, in letting Scrooge's nephew out, hailed two other people in. They were portly gentlemen, pleasant to behold and now stood, with their hats off, in Scrooge's office. They had books and papers in their hands, and bowed to him.

"Scrooge and Marley's, I believe," said one of the gentlemen, referring to his list. "Have I the pleasure of addressing Mr. Scrooge or Mr. Marley?"

"Marley has been dead these seven years," Scrooge replied. "He died seven years ago this very night."

"We have no doubt his liberality is well represented by his surviving partner," said the gentleman.

At the ominous word "liberality," Scrooge frowned, and shook his head.

"At this festive season, Mr. Scrooge," said the gentleman, "it is more than usually desirable that we should make some provision for the poor and destitute. Many thousands are in want of common necessaries; hundreds of thousands are in want of common comforts, sir."

"Are there no prisons?" asked Scrooge.

"Plenty of prisons. But they scarcely furnish Christian cheer of mind or body to the unoffending multitude. A few of us are endeavoring to raise a fund to buy the poor some meat and drink and means of warmth. We choose this time because it is a time, of all others, when want is keenly felt, and abundance rejoices. What shall I put you down for?"

"Nothing!"

"You wish to be anonymous?"

"I wish to be left alone. I don't make merry myself at Christmas, and I can't af-

ford to make idle people merry. I help to support the prisons and the workhouses— they cost enough—and those who are badly off must go there."

"Many can't go there; and many would rather die."

"If they would die, they had better do it, and decrease the surplus population. Good afternoon, gentlemen!"

The gentlemen withdrew and Scrooge resumed his labors with an improved opinion of himself.

At length the hour of shutting up the counting-house arrived. With ill-will Scrooge, dismounting from his stool, tacitly admitted the fact to the clerk who snuffed out his candle and put on his hat.

"You want all day tomorrow, I suppose?"

"If quite convenient, sir."

"It's not convenient, and it's not fair. If I was to stop half a crown for it, you'd think yourself mightily ill-used, I'll be bound?"

The clerk smiled faintly.

"And yet," said Scrooge, "you don't think *me* ill-used when I pay a day's wages for no work."

The clerk observed that it was only once a year.

"A poor excuse for picking a man's pocket every twenty-fifth of December!" said Scrooge, buttoning his great-coat to the chin. "But I suppose you must have the whole day. Be here all the earlier next morning!"

The clerk promised that he would; and Scrooge walked out with a growl. The office was closed in a twinkling, and the clerk, with the long ends of his white comforter dangling below his waist (for he had no great-coat), ran to his home in Camden Town as hard as he could pelt, to play at

345

blindman's-buff with his children.

Scrooge took his melancholy dinner at his usual melancholy tavern and went home to bed. He lived in chambers which had once belonged to his deceased partner. They were gloomy rooms, in a lowering pile of buildings up a yard. Nobody lived in it but Scrooge, the other rooms being all let out as offices.

Now there was nothing at all particular about the knocker on the door of this house, except that it was very large; also, that Scrooge had seen it, night and morning, during his whole residence in that place; also that Scrooge had as little of what is called fancy about him as any man in the City of London.

Let it also be borne in mind that Scrooge had not bestowed one thought on Marley since his last mention of his dead partner that afternoon. And then let any man explain, if he can, how it happened that Scrooge having his key in the lock of the door, saw in the knocker, without its undergoing any intermediate process of change, not a knocker, but Marley's face—Marley's face, with a dismal light about it!

As Scrooge looked fixedly at this phenomenon, it became a knocker again.

To say that he was not startled, would be untrue. But he put his hand upon the key, turned it sturdily, walked in, and lighted his candle.

He *did* pause before he shut the door; and he *did* look cautiously behind first, as if he half-expected to be terrified with the sight of Marley's pigtail sticking out into the hall. But there was nothing on the back of the door except the screws and nuts that held the knocker on; so Scrooge said "Pooh," and closed the door with a bang.

The bang resounded through the house like thunder. Every room above, and every cask in the wine-merchant's cellars below, appeared to have a separate peal of echoes of its own. But Scrooge was not a man to be frightened by echoes. He fastened the door, walked across the hall and up the stairs, trimming his candle as he went.

But before he shut his heavy door, he walked through his room to see that all was right. He had just enough recollection of the face he had seen on the knocker to desire to do that.

Sitting-room, bedroom, lumber-room, all as they should be. Nobody under the table, nobody under the sofa; a small fire in the grate; spoon and basin ready; and the little saucepan of gruel (Scrooge had a cold in his head) upon the hob. Nobody under the bed; nobody in the closet; nobody in his dressing-gown, which was hanging up in a suspicious attitude against the wall.

Quite satisfied, he closed his door, double-locked himself in, which was not his custom. Thus secured against surprise, he put on his dressing-gown and slippers and his nightcap, and sat down before the very low fire to take his gruel.

It was a very low fire indeed; especially for such a bitter cold night. He was obliged to sit close to it before he could extract the least sensation of warmth from such a handful of fuel. The fire-place was an old one, built by some Dutch merchant long ago, and paved all around with quaint Dutch tiles, designed to illustrate the Scriptures. Yet that face of Marley, seven years dead, came like the ancient Prophet's rod, and swallowed up the whole.

"Humbug!" said Scrooge, and walked across the room.

After several turns, he sat down again. As he threw his head back in the chair, his glance happened to rest upon a disused bell that hung in the room, and communicated, for some purpose now forgotten, with a chamber in the highest story of the building. It was with a strange, inexplicable dread that, as he looked, Scrooge saw this bell begin to swing. Soon it rang out loudly, and so did every bell in the house.

This was succeeded by a clanking noise deep down below as if some person were dragging a heavy chain over the casks in the wine-merchant's cellar.

Then he heard the noise much louder, on the floors below; then coming up the stairs; then coming straight towards his door.

It came on through the heavy door, and a ghostly figure passed into the room before his eyes. Upon its coming in, the dying flame leaped up as though it cried, "I know

him! Marley's ghost!"

The same face, the very same. Marley in his pigtail, usual waistcoat, tights, and boots; the tassels on the latter bristling, like his pigtail, and his coat-skirts, and the hair upon his head. The chain he drew was clasped about his middle. It was long and wound about him like a tail; and it was made of cashboxes, keys, padlocks, ledgers, deeds, and heavy purses wrought in steel. The body was transparent, so that Scrooge looking through his waistcoat, could see the two buttons on his coat behind.

Though he looked the phantom through and through, and saw it standing before

him—though he felt the chilling influence of his death-cold eyes, and noticed the very texture of the folded kerchief bound about its head and chin—he was still incredulous.

"How now." said Scrooge, caustic and cold as ever. "What do you want with me?"

"Much!" Marley's voice, no doubt about it.

"Who are you?"

"Ask me who I *was*."

"Who *were* you then?"

"In life I was your partner, Jacob Marley."

"Can you—can you sit down?"

"I can."

"Do it, then."

The ghost sat down on the opposite side of the fireplace as if he were quite used to it.

"You don't believe in me."

"I don't."

"Why do you doubt your senses?"

"Because a little thing affects them. A slight disorder of the stomach makes them cheat. You may be an undigested bit of beef, a crumb of cheese, a fragment of an underdone potato. There's more of gravy than of grave about you, whatever you are!"

Scrooge was not much in the habit of cracking jokes, nor did he feel, in his heart, by any means waggish then. The truth is that he tried to be smart as a means of keeping down his terror, for the ghost's voice disturbed the very marrow in his bones. But how much greater was his horror when the phantom, taking off the bandage round its head as if it were too warm to wear indoors, its lower jaw dropped down upon its breast!

Scrooge fell upon his knees, and clasping his hands before his face, said, "Dreadful apparition, why do you trouble me!"

"Man of the worldly mind," replied the ghost, "do you believe in me or not?"

"I do," said Scrooge. "I must. But why do spirits walk the earth, and why do they come to me?"

"It is required of every man," the ghost returned, "that his spirit should walk abroad among his fellow-men, and if that spirit goes not forth in life, it is condemned to do so after death. It is doomed to wander through the world—oh, woe is me!—and witness what it cannot share, but might have shared on earth and turned to happiness!"

Again the ghost raised a cry, and shook its shadowy hands. "I cannot tell you all I would. A very little more is permitted to me. I cannot rest, I cannot linger anywhere. In life my spirit never roved beyond the narrow limits of our counting-house but weary journeys lie before me!"

"Seven years dead. And traveling all the time? You travel fast?" asked Scrooge.

"On the wings of the wind."

"You must have got over a great quantity of ground in seven years."

"O blind man, blind man! not to know that any Christian spirit will find its mortal life too short for its vast means of usefulness, that no regret can make amends for one life's opportunities misused!"

"But you were always a good man of business, Jacob," faltered Scrooge.

"Business!" cried Marley's ghost, wringing its hands again. "Mankind was my business, the common welfare: charity, mercy, forbearance, benevolence. The dealings of my trade were but a drop of water in the ocean of my business!"

Scrooge, much dismayed, began to quake.

"Hear me! My time is nearly gone."

"I will. But don't be hard upon me, Jacob!"

"I am here to warn you that you have yet a hope of escaping my fate. A chance of *my* procuring, Ebenezer."

"You were always a good friend to me," said Scrooge. "Thanks."

"You will be haunted by three spirits," resumed the ghost.

"Is that the chance you mentioned, Jacob?" demanded Scrooge in a faltering voice.

"It is."

"I—I think I'd rather not," said Scrooge.

"Without their visits," said the ghost, "you cannot hope to shun the path I tread. Expect the first one tomorrow, when the bell strikes one."

"Couldn't I take 'em all at once, and have it over, Jacob?" hinted Scrooge.

"Expect the second on the next night at the same hour. The third upon the next night when the last strike of twelve has ceased to vibrate. Look to see me no more."

The apparition walked backward from him; and at every step it took, the window raised itself a little, so that, when the ghost reached it, it was wide open. It beckoned Scrooge to approach, which he did. When they were within two paces of each other, Marley's ghost held up its hand, warning him to come no nearer.

Scrooge stopped. He became sensible of confused noises in the air, sounds of lamentation and regret. The ghost joined in the mournful dirge and floated out upon the bleak dark night.

Scrooge closed the window and examined the door by which the ghost had entered. It was still double-locked, as he had locked it with his own hands. Scrooge tried to say, "Humbug!" but stopped at the first syllable. And being much in need of repose, he went straight to bed without undressing, and instantly fell asleep.

THE FIRST OF THE THREE SPIRITS

When Scrooge awoke it was so dark that he could scarcely distinguish the window from the walls until suddenly the chuch clock tolled a deep, dull, hollow, melancholy one.

Light flashed up in the room, and a strange figure, like a child, yet not so like a child as like an old man diminished to a child's proportions. Its hair, which hung about its neck and down its back, was white as if with age; and yet the face had not a wrinkle. It held a branch of fresh green holly in its hand and, in singular contradiction of that wintry emblem, had its dress trimmed with summer flowers. But the strangest thing about it was that from the crown of its head there sprung a bright clear jet of light, which was doubtless the occasion for its using, in its duller moments, a great extinguisher for a cap, which it now held under its arm.

"Are you the spirit, sir, whose coming was foretold to me?"

"I am!" The voice was soft and gentle.

"Who and what are you?"

"I am the ghost of Christmas Past."

"Long past?"

"No. Your past."

Scrooge then made bold to inquire what business brought him there.

"Your welfare. Rise and walk with me!"

The spirit's grasp, though gentle as a woman's hand, was not to be resisted. Scrooge rose; but finding that the spirit made towards the window, clasped its robe in supplication.

"I am a mortal, and liable to fall."

"Bear but a touch of my hand *there,*" said the spirit, laying it upon his heart, and you shall be upheld in more than this!"

As the words were spoken, Scrooge and the spirit passed through the wall, and stood upon an open country road, with snowy fields on either hand. The city had entirely vanished.

"Good Heavens!" said Scrooge, clasping his hands together, as he looked about him. "I was bred in this place. I was a boy here!"

They walked along the road, Scroge recognizing every gate and post and tree, until a little market-town appeared in the distance, with its bridge, its church, and winding river. Some shaggy ponies now were seen trotting towards them with boys upon their backs. The boys were in great spirits, and shouted to each other until the broad fields were full of merry music.

"These boys are but shadows of the things that have been" said the ghost. "They have no consciousness of us."

The jocund travellers came on; and as they came, Scrooge knew and named them every one. Why was he rejoiced beyond all bounds to see them? Why did his cold eyes glisten, and his heart leap up as they went past? Why was he filled with gladness when he heard them give each other merry Christmas, as they parted at crossroads and byways for their several homes? What was merry Christmas to Scrooge?

"The school is not quite deserted," said the ghost. "A solitary child, neglected by his friends is left there still."

Scrooge said he knew it. And he sobbed.

They left the highroad by a well-remembered lane and soon approached a mansion of dull red brick, with a little weather-cock surmounted cupola on the roof, and a bell hanging in it. They went to a door at the back of the house. It opened before them, and disclosed a long bare melancholy room, made barer still by lines of plain deal forms and desks. At one of these a lonely boy was reading near a feeble fire; and Scrooge sat down and wept to see his poor forgotten self as he used to be.

The spirit touched him on the arm and pointed to his younger self intent upon his reading.

"I wish," Scrooge muttered, putting his hand in his pocket and looking about him, after drying his eyes with his cuff, "but it's too late now."

"What is the matter?" asked the spirit.

"Nothing," said Scrooge. "Nothing. There was a boy singing a Christmas carol at my door last night. I should like to have given him something, that's all."

The ghost smiled and waved its hand, saying as it did so, "Let us see another Christmas!"

Scrooge's former self grew larger at the words, and the room became a little darker and more dirty. The panels shrunk, the windows cracked; fragments of plaster fell out of the ceiling, and the naked laths were shown instead. How all this was brought about Scrooge knew no more than you do. He only knew that everything had happened just so; that there he was, alone again, when all the other boys had gone home for the jolly holidays.

The boy was not reading now, but walking up and down despairingly. Scrooge looked at the ghost and, with a mournful shaking of his head, glanced anxiously to-

ward the door.

It opened, and a little girl much younger than the boy came darting in, put her arms about his neck, and kissed him.

"I have come to bring you home, dear brother!" said the child, clapping her tiny hands, and bending down to laugh. "To bring you home, home, home!"

"Home, little Fan?" returned the boy.

"Yes!" said the child, brimful of glee. "Home for ever and ever. Father is so much kinder than he used to be. He spoke so gently to me one night when I was going to bed, that I was not afraid to ask him once more if you might come home; and he said yes, you should; and sent me in a coach to bring you. We're to be together all the Christmas long, and have the merriest time in all the world."

Just then a terrible voice in the hall cried, "Bring down Master Scrooge's box!" And in the hall appeared the schoolmaster himself who glared at Master Scrooge and threw him into a dreadful state of mind by shaking hands with him. He then conveyed him and his sister into the best parlor.

Master Scrooge's trunk being by this time tied on to the top of the chaise, the children bade the schoolmaster goodbye right willingly; and they drove gaily down the garden sweep; the quick wheels dashing the frost from the dark leaves of the evergreens like spray.

"Always a delicate creature," said the ghost. "But she had a large heart!"

"So she had," cried Scrooge.

"She died a woman," said the ghost, "and I think had children."

"One child," Scrooge returned.

"True," said the ghost. "Your nephew!"

Scrooge, uneasy in his mind, answered briefly, "Yes."

Although they had but that moment left the school behind them, they were now in

351

the busy thoroughfares of a city. It was made plain enough, by the dressing of the shops, that here, too, it was Christmas time again; but it was evening, and the streets were lighted up.

The ghost stopped at a certain warehouse door, and asked Scrooge if he knew it.

"Know it!" said Scrooge. "Was I not apprenticed here?"

They went in. At the sight of an old gentleman sitting behind a high desk, Scrooge cried in great excitement, "Why, it's old Fezziwig! Bless his heart, it's Fezziwig alive again!"

Old Fezziwig laid down his pen, and looked up at the clock, which pointed to seven. He rubbed his hands, adjusted his waistcoat, laughed all over himself, and called out, in a rich, fat, jovial voice: "Yo ho, there! Ebenezer Scrooge! Dick Wilkins!"

Scrooge's former self, now grown a young man, came briskly in, accompanied by his fellow-'prentice, Dick Wilkins.

"Yo ho, my boys!" said Fezziwig. "No more work tonight. It's Christmas Eve! Let's have the shutters up."

You wouldn't believe how those two fellows went at it!

"Hilli-ho!" cried old Fezziwig. "Clear away, my lads, and let's have lots of room here!"

Clear away! It was done in a minute. Every movable was packed off, the floor was swept, fuel was heaped upon the fire, and the warehouse was as snug and warm and dry and bright a ball-room as you would desire to see upon a winter's night.

In came a fiddler with a music book, and went up to the lofty desk, and made an orchestra of it. In came Mrs. Fezziwig,

one vast substantial smile. In came the three Miss Fezziwigs, beaming. In came the six young followers whose hearts they broke. In came all the young men and women employed in the business, one after another; some shyly, some boldly, some gracefully, some awkwardly, some pushing, some pulling; in they all came, any how and every how. Away they all went, twenty couples at once half around and back again the other way; down the middle and up again; 'round and 'round.

Old Fezziwig, clapping his hands to stop the dance, cried out, "Well done!"

There was food and drink in great quantities for everyone.

When the clock struck eleven, this domestic ball broke up. Mr. and Mrs. Fezziwig shook hands with everyone and wished him or her a merry Christmas.

During the whole of this time Scrooge had acted like a man out of his wits. His heart and soul were in the scene, and with his former self. He remembered everything and enjoyed everything. It was not until the bright faces of his former self and Dick were turned from them, that he remembered the ghost.

"A small matter," said the ghost, "Fezziwig has spent but a few pounds of money to make these silly folks so full of gratitude."

"Small!" echoed Scrooge. "He has the power to render us happy or unhappy; to make our service a pleasure or a toil. The happiness he gives is quite as great as if it cost a fortune."

He felt the spirit's glance, and stopped.

"What is the matter?" asked the ghost.

"Nothing particular," said Scrooge.

"Something, I think?" insisted the ghost.

"No, no. I should like to be able to say a word or two to my clerk just now. That's all."

"My time grows short," observed the spirit. "Quick!"

"Spirit!" said Scrooge in a broken voice. "Remove me from this place."

"I told you there were shadows of the things that have been," said the ghost. "Do not blame me that they are what they are!"

"Remove me!" Scrooge exclaimed. "I cannot bear it! Leave me! Haunt me no longer!"

As he struggled with the spirit he was conscious of being exhausted, and overcome by an irresistible drowsiness; and further, of being in his own bedroom. He had barely time to reel to bed before he sank into a heavy sleep.

THE SECOND OF THE THREE SPIRITS

Scrooge awoke in his own bedroom. There was no doubt about that. But it and his own adjoining sitting-room, into which he shuffled in his slippers, attracted by a great light there, had undergone a surprising transformation. The walls and ceiling were so hung with living green, that it looked a perfect grove. The leaves of holly, mistletoe, and ivy reflected back the light, as if so many little mirrors had been scattered there; and such a mighty blaze went roaring up the chimney as had never been known in Scrooge's time or Marley's or for many and many a winter gone. Heaped upon the floor to form a kind of throne, were turkeys,

geese, suckling pigs, long wreaths of sausages, mince-pie, plum-puddings, barrels of oysters, red-hot chestnuts, cherry-cheeked apples, juicy oranges, luscious pears, immense cakes, and great bowls of punch. Upon a couch there sat a jolly giant glorious to see who raised high a glowing torch to shed its light on Scrooge, as he came peeping round the door.

"Come in!" exclaimed the ghost. "Come in and know me better, man!"

Scrooge entered timidly, and hung his head before this spirit.

"I am the ghost of Christmas Present," said the spirit. "Look upon me!"

Scrooge reverently did so. It was clothed in one simple robe bordered with white fur. On its head it wore a holly wreath set with shining icicles. Its dark brown curls were long and free as its genial face, its sparkling eye, its open hand, its cheery voice and joyful air.

"You have never seen the likes of me before!" exclaimed the spirit.

"Never," Scrooge made answer to it.

The ghost of Christmas Present rose.

"Spirit," said Scrooge submissively, "conduct me where you will. Last night I learnt a lesson which is working now. Tonight, if you have aught to teach me, let me profit by it."

"Touch my robe!"

Scrooge did as he was told, and held it fast.

Holly, mistletoe, red berries, ivy, turkeys, geese, game, poultry, meat, pigs, sausages, oysters, pies, puddings, fruit, and punch, all vanished instantly, and Scrooge and the spirit stood in the city streets upon a snowy Christmas morning.

They passed on, invisible, straight to Scrooge's clerk's; and on the threshold of the door the spirit smiled, and stopped to bless Bob Cratchit's dwelling with the sprinklings of his torch.

"Think of that! Bob had but fifteen bob a week himself; and yet the ghost of Christmas Present blessed his four-room house!

Mrs. Cratchit's wife, dressed out but poorly in a twice-turned gown, but brave in ribbons, laid the cloth, assisted by Belinda Cratchit, second of her daughters, also brave in ribbons; while Master Peter Cratchit plunged a fork into the saucepan of potatoes. And now two smaller Cratchits, boy and girl, came tearing in, and, basking in luxurious thoughts of sage and onion, danced about the table, and exalted Master Peter Cratchit to the skies, while he blew the fire, until the slow potatoes, bubbling up, knocked loudly at the saucepan-lid to be let out and peeled.

"What has ever got your precious father then?" said Mrs. Cratchit. "And your brother Tiny Tim! And Martha wasn't as late last Christmas by half an hour!"

"Here's Martha, mother!" said a girl, appearing as she spoke. "We'd a deal of work to finish up last night and had to clear away this morning, mother!"

"Well! Never mind so long as you are come," said Mrs. Cratchit. "Sit down before the fire, my dear, and get warm."

"No, no! There's father coming," cried the two young Cratchits, who were everywhere at once. "Hide, Martha, hide!"

So Martha hid herself, and in came little Bob, the father, with at least three feet of comforter, exclusive of the fringe, hanging down before him; and his threadbare clothes

darned up and brushed to look seasonable; and Tiny Tim who bore a little crutch and had his limbs supported by an iron frame!

"Why, where's our Martha?" cried Bob Cratchit, looking round.

"Not coming," said Mrs. Cratchit.

"Not coming!" said Bob. "not coming upon Christmas day!"

Martha didn't like to see him disappointed, if it were only in joke; so she came out from behind the closet door, and ran into his arms, while the two young Cratchits took Tiny Tim.

"And how did little Tim behave in church?" asked Mrs. Cratchit.

"As good as gold," said Bob. "He gets thoughtful, sitting by himself so much. He told me, coming home, that he hoped the people saw him in church, because he was a cripple, and it might be pleasant to them to remember on Christmas day, who made lame beggars walk and blind men see."

Bob's voice trembled when he said Tiny Tim was growing strong and hearty.

Tiny Tim's little crutch was heard on the floor as he limped to his stool beside the fire; and while Bob compounded some hot mixture in a jug and put it on the hob to simmer, Master Peter and the two young Cratchits went to fetch the goose, while Mrs. Cratchit and Martha did all the rest.

Bob took Tiny Tim beside him in a tiny corner at the table; the two young Cratchits set chairs for everybody.

At last the dishes were set on, and grace was said. It was succeeded by a breathless pause, as Mrs. Cratchit, looking slowly all along the carving-knife, prepared to plunge it in the breast; but when she did, and when the long-expected gush of stuffing issued forth, one murmur of delight arose all 'round the board, and even Tiny Tim beat on the table with the handle of his knife, and feebly cried, Hurrah!

There never was such a goose or such a pudding for dessert.

Oh, a wonderful pudding! Bob Cratchit said, and calmly too, that he regarded it as the greatest success achieved by Mrs. Cratchit since their marriage. Everybody had something to say about it, but nobody said it was a small pudding for a large family. Any Cratchit would have blushed at such a thing.

At last the dinner was all done, the cloth was cleared, the hearth swept, and the fire made up.

Then all the Cratchit family drew 'round the hearth, and at Bob Cratchit's elbow stood the family display of glass—two tumblers, and a custard-cup without a handle.

These held the hot stuff from the jug, however, as well as golden goblets would have done; and Bob served it out with beaming looks, while the chestnuts on the fire sputtered and crackled noisily. Then Bob cried, "A merry Christmas to us all, my dears. God bless us!"

Which all the family re-echoed.

"God bless us every one!" said Tiny Tim, the last of all.

He sat close to his father's side, upon his little stool. Bob held his withered little hand in his, as if he dreaded that the child might be taken from him.

"Spirit," said Scrooge, "tell me if Tiny Tim will live."

"I see a vacant seat in the chimney corner, and a crutch without an owner," replied the ghost.

"Oh no, kind spirit!" said Scrooge. "Say he will be spared."

"If he is to die" returned the ghost, "he had better do it, and decrease the surplus population."

Scrooge hung his head to hear his own words quoted by the spirit, and was overcome with penitence and grief.

"Man," said the ghost, "it may be that, in the sight of Heaven, you are more worthless and less fit to live than a million like this poor man's child!"

Scrooge cast his eyes upon the ground. But he raised them on hearing his own name spoken.

"Mr. Scrooge!" said Bob. "Mr. Scrooge, the Founder of the Feast!"

"Indeed!" cried Mrs. Cratchit, reddening. "I wish I had him here. I'd give him a piece of my mind to feast upon! Imagine drinking the health of such a stingy, hard, unfeeling man as Mr. Scrooge. You know he is, Robert! Nobody knows it better than you do!"

"My dear," was Bob's mild answer, "It's Christmas day."

"I'll drink his health for your sake and the day's" said Mrs. Cratchit, "not for his. A merry Christmas and a happy New Year! He'll be very merry and happy, I have no doubt!"

The children drank the toast after her. But they had no heartiness for it. Scrooge was the ogre of the family. The mention of his name cast a dark shadow on the party for full five minutes.

After it had passed away, they were ten times merrier than before. The chestnuts and the jug went 'round and 'round; and by and by they had a song, from Tiny Tim,

356

who had a plaintive little voice, and sang very well.

They were not a handsome family; they were not well dressed; their shoes were far from being waterproof; their clothes were scanty. But they were happy, grateful, pleased with one another. When they faded from view and looked happier yet in the bright sprinklings of the spirit's torch at parting, Scrooge had his eye upon them, and especially on Tiny Tim.

It was a great surpise to Scrooge, as this scene vanished, to hear a hearty laugh. It was a much greater surprise to recognize the laugh as his own nephew's, and to find himself in a bright, dry, gleaming room, with the spirit standing smiling by his side, and looking at that same nephew with approval!

There is nothing in the world so contagious as laughter and good humor. When Scrooge's nephew laughed, his wife laughed. And their assembled friends laughed too.

"He said that Christmas was a humbug!" cried Scrooge's nephew. "He's a comical old fellow, and not so pleasant as he might be. However, who suffers by his ill whims? Himself, always. Here he takes it into his head to dislike us, and he won't come and dine with us. What's the consequence?"

"He misses a very good dinner," everybody answered.

"I was going to say," said Scrooge's nephew, "that I mean to give him the same chance every year, whether he likes it or not, for I pity him. He may rail at Christmas till he dies, but he can't help thinking better of it if I go there, in good temper, year after year, and say 'Uncle Scrooge, how are you?' If it only puts him in the mood to give his poor clerk a little money, that's

something; and I think I shook him yesterday."

After tea they had some music and played games.

Scrooge, wholly forgetting that his voice made no sound in their ears, sometimes joined in quite heartily.

At last they began playing a game called *Yes and No,* where Scrooge's nephew had to think of something, and the rest must find out what, by asking only questions that he could answer by yes or no. He was thinking he said, of an animal, a live animal, rather a disagreeable animal, an animal that often growled, that lived in London, not in a menagerie, and was not a horse, or an ass, or a cow, or a bull, or a tiger, or a dog, or a pig, or a cat or a bear.

At every new question put to him the nephew burst into a fresh roar of laughter. At last someone cried out, "I know what it is! It's your uncle Scro-o-o-oge!" Which it certainly was.

"He has given us plenty of merriment, I am sure," said Fred, "and it would be ungrateful not to drink his health." He raised his glass of mulled wine and said, "To Uncle Scrooge!"

"Well! To Uncle Scrooge!" they all cried.

"A merry Christmas and a happy New Year to the old man, whatever he is!" cried Scrooge's nephew.

Uncle Scrooge had imperceptibly become so gay that he would have thanked the unconscious company in an inaudible speech if the ghost had given him time. But the whole scene passed off in the breath of the last word spoken by his nephew; and Scrooge and the spirit were again upon their travels. Suddenly, as they stood together in an open place, a bell struck twelve.

Scrooge looked about him for the ghost, and saw it no more. As the last stroke ceased to vibrate, he remembered the prediction of old Jacob Marley, and lifting up his eyes, he beheld a solemn phantom, draped and hooded, coming like a mist along the ground towards him.

THE LAST OF THE SPIRITS

When the phantom slowly, gravely, silently came near him, Scrooge bent down upon his knee; for in the air through which this spirit moved it seemed to scatter gloom and mystery.

It was shrouded in a deep black garment, which left nothing of it visible save one out-stretched hand. He felt that it was tall and stately, and its mysterious presence filled him with a solemn dread. He knew no more, for the spirit neither spoke nor moved.

"Am I in the presence of the ghost of Christmas Yet To Come?" said Scrooge.

The spirit answered not, but pointed downward with its hand.

Although well used to ghostly company by this time, Scrooge feared the silent shape so much that his legs trembled beneath him, and he found that he could hardly stand when he prepared to follow it. The spirit paused a moment, as observing his condi-tion, and giving him time to recover.

"Ghost of the Future!" he exclaimed, "I fear you more than any I have seen. But, as I know your purpose is to do me good, I am prepared to bear you company. Will you not speak to me?"

It gave him no reply. The hand was pointed before them.

They scarcely seemed to enter the city, for the city rather seemed to spring up about them and encompass them of its own act. But there they were, in the heart of it, among the merchants who hurried up and down, and chinked the money in their pockets, and conversed in groups.

They left the busy scene, and went into an obscure part of the town, where Scrooge had never penetrated before, although he recognized its situation, and its bad repute. The whole quarter reeked with crime, with filth, and misery.

Far in this infamous resort, there was a low-browed shop, below a roof, where iron, greasy rags, bottles, and old bones were bought. A gray-haired rascal, of great age, sat smoking his pipe.

Scrooge and the phantom came into the presence of this man, just as a woman with a heavy bundle slunk into the shop. But she had scarcely entered, when another woman, similarly laden, came in too; and she was closely followed by a man in faded black. After a short period of astonishment, in which the old man with the pipe had joined them, they all three burst into a laugh.

"Let the charwoman alone to be the first!" cried she who had entered first. "Let the laundress alone to be the second; and let the undertaker's man alone to be the third. Look here, old Joe, here's a chance!"

The woman who had already spoken threw her bundle on the floor and sat down in a flaunting manner on a stool, and look-ing with a bold defiance at the other two, said, "Every person has a right to take care of themselves. *He* always did!"

"That's true, indeed! said the laundress. "No man more so."

"Very well, then!" cried the woman. "That's enough. Who's the worse for the loss of a few things like these? Not a dead man, I suppose."

If he wanted to keep 'em after he was dead, the wicked old miser," pursued the woman, "why wasn't he natural in his lifetime? If he had been, he'd have had somebody to look after him when he was struck with death, instead of lying gasping out his last there, alone by himself. Open the bundle, Joe, and let me know the value of it."

Joe opened the bundle, and dragged out a large and heavy roll of some dark stuff.

"What do you call this? Bed-curtains?"

"Ah! Bed-curtains! Don't drop that oil on the blankets, now."

"His blankets?"

"Whose else's do you think? He isn't likely to take cold without 'em, I dare say. Ah! You may look through that shirt till your eyes ache; but you won't find a hole in it. It's the best he had, and a fine one too. They'd have wasted it by dressing him up in it, if it hadn't been for me."

"What do you call wasting of it?" asked Joe.

"Putting it on him to be buried in, to be sure," replied the woman with a laugh. "Somebody was fool enough to do it, but I took it off him."

Scrooge listened to this dialogue in horror.

"Spirit!" said Scrooge, shuddering from head to foot. "I see, I see. The case of this unhappy man might be my own. My life tends that way, now. Merciful heaven, what is this!"

He recoiled in terror, for the scene had changed, and now he almost touched a bed —a bare, uncurtained bed—on which, beneath a ragged sheet, there lay a something covered up.

The room was very dark. A pale light, rising in the outer air, fell straight upon the bed; and on it, plundered and bereft, unwatched, unwept, uncared for, was the body of this man.

Scrooge glanced towards the phantom. Its steady hand was pointed to the head.

"Spirit!" cried Scrooge, "this is a fearful place. In leaving it, I shall not leave its lesson. Trust me. Let us go!"

Still the ghost pointed with an unmoved finger to the head.

"I understand you," Scrooge returned, "and I would do it, if I could. But I have not the power."

The ghost conducted him through several familiar streets, and as they went along, Scrooge looked here and there to find himself, but nowhere was he to be seen. They entered poor Bob Cratchit's house—the dwelling he had visited before—and found the mother and the children seated around the fire.

Quiet. Very quiet. The noisy little Cratchits were as still as statues.

" 'And He took a child, and set him in the midst of them.' "

Where had Scrooge heard these words before?

They were very quiet again. At last Mrs. Cratchit said, in a steady voice that only faltered once, "I have known him walk with Tiny Tim on his shoulder very fast indeed. But he was very light to carry, and his father loved him so that it was no trouble. And there is your father at the door!"

She hurried out to meet him; and little Bob in his comforter—he had need of it, poor fellow—came in. The two young Cratchits got upon his knees, and laid, each child, a little cheek against his face, as if they said, "Don't mind it, father. Don't be grieved!"

Bob broke down all at once. He couldn't help it.

"Spirit" said Scrooge, "Tell me what man that was, with the covered face, whom we saw lying dead?"

The ghost of Christmas Yet To Come took him to a dismal, wretched churchyard.

The spirit stood amongst the graves, and pointed down to one.

"Men's courses will foreshadow certain ends, to which, if persevered in, they must lead," said Scrooge. "But if the courses be departed from, the ends will change. Say it is thus with what you show me!"

The spirit was immovable as ever.

Scrooge crept toward it, trembling as he went; and following the finger, read upon the stone of the neglected grave his own name, EBENEZER SCROOGE.

"Am *I* that man who lay upon the bed?" he cried, upon his knees.

The finger pointed from the grave to him, and back again.

"Spirit!" he cried, clutching tight at its robe, "hear me! I am not the man I was. I will not be that man. Why show me this if I am past all hope?"

For the first time the hand appeared to shake.

"I will honor Christmas in my heart, and try to keep it all the year. Oh, tell me I may sponge away the writing on this stone!"

Holding up his hands in a last prayer to have his fate reversed, Scrooge saw an alteration in the phantom's hood and dress. It shrunk, collapsed, and dwindled into a bedpost.

The bedpost was his own. The bed was his own, the room was his own. Best and happiest of all, the time before him was his own, to make amends in!

THE END OF IT

"Oh Jacob Marley!" said Scrooge, "Heaven, and the Christmas time be praised for this! I say it on my knees, old Jacob; on my knees!"

He was so glowing with his good intentions, his face was wet with tears.

"I don't know what to do!" cried Scrooge, laughing and crying in the same breath. "I am light as a feather, I am happy as an angel, I am as merry as a schoolboy. A merry Christmas to everybody! A happy New Year to all the world!"

He was checked in his transports by the churches ringing out the lustiest peals he had ever heard. Running to the window, he opened it, and put out his head.

"What's today?" cried Scrooge, calling downward to a boy in Sunday clothes.

"Why, Christmas day," replied the boy.

"Then I *haven't* missed it!" exclaimed Scrooge. "The spirits have done everything in one night. Boy, do you know the poulterer's, in the next street but one, at the corner?" Scrooge inquired.

"I should hope I did," replied the lad.

"Do you know whether they've sold the prize turkey that was hanging up there? Not the little prize turkey: the big one?"

"It's hanging there now," replied the boy.

"Is it?" said Scrooge. "Go and buy it, and tell 'em to bring it here, that I may give them the directions where to take it. Come back with the man, and I'll give you a shilling. Come back with him in less than five minutes, and I'll give you half-a-crown!"

The boy was off like a shot.

"I'll send it to Bob Cratchit's! He shan't know who sends it," said Scrooge to himself.

The hand in which he wrote the address was not steady; but write it he did, and went downstairs to open the street door, ready for the coming of the poulterer's man.

It *was* a turkey!

"Why, it's impossible to carry that to Camden Town," said Scrooge to the man. "You must have a cab."

Scrooge dressed himself in his best suit and got out into the streets. He had not gone far when coming toward him he beheld the portly gentleman who had walked into his counting-house the day before and said, "Scrooge and Marley's, I believe?" It sent a pang across his heart to think how this old gentleman would look upon him when they met; but he know what path lay straight before him, and he took it.

"My dear sir," said Scrooge, taking the old gentleman by both his hands. "How do you do? I hope you succeeded yesterday. It was very kind of you. A merry Christmas to you, sir!"

"Mr. Scrooge?"

"Yes," said Scrooge. "That is my name, and I fear it may not be pleasant to you. Allow me to ask your pardon. And will you have the goodness"—here Scrooge wispered in his ear.

"Lord bless me!" cried the gentleman, as if his breath were gone. "My dear Mr.

Scrooge, are you serious?"

"If you please," said Scrooge. "Not a farthing less. A great many back-payments are included in it, I assure you. Will you do me that favor?"

"My dear sir," said the other, shaking hands with him, "I don't know what to say to such munifi—".

"Don't say anything, please,"retorted Scrooge.

He went to church, and walked about the streets, and patted children on the head, and questioned beggars, and looked down into the kitchens of houses, and up to the windows, and found that everything could yield him pleasure. In the afternoon he turned his steps towards his nephew's house.

He passed the door a dozen times before he had the courage to go up and knock. But he made a dash and did it.

"Is your master at home, my dear?" said Scrooge to the girl.

"Yes, sir."

"Where is he?" asked Scrooge.

"He's in the dining-room, sir. I'll show you upstairs, if you please."

"Thankee. He knows me," said Scrooge, with his hand already on the dining-room lock. "I'll go in here."

"Why, bless my soul!" cried the nephew, "who's that?"

"It's your uncle Scrooge. I have come to dinner. Will you let me in, Fred?"

Let him in! It is a mercy he didn't shake his arm off.

Nothing could be heartier. Wonderful party, wonderful games, wonderful happiness!

He was early at the office next morning just the same. If he could only be there first,

and catch Bob Cratchit coming late! That was the thing he had set his heart upon.

And he did it. The clock struck nine. No Bob. A quarter past. No Bob. Bob was full eighteen minutes and a half late. Scrooge sat with his door wide open, that he might see him come in.

Bob's hat was off before he opened the door. He was on his stool in a jiffy, driving away with his pen, as if he were trying to overtake nine o'clock.

"Hallo!" growled Scrooge, in his accustomed voice, as near as he could feign it. "What do you mean by coming here at this time of day?"

"I am very sorry, sir," said Bob. I *am* behind my time."

"You are!" repeated Scrooge. "Yes, I think you are. Step this way, sir, if you please."

"It's only once a year, sir," pleaded Bob. "It shall not be repeated. I was making rather merry yesterday, sir."

"Now, I'll tell you what my friend," said Scrooge. "I am not going to stand this sort of thing any longer. And therefore I am about to raise your salary!"

Bob trembled. He had a momentary idea of calling to the people in the court for help and a strait-jacket.

"A merry Christmas, Bob!" said Scrooge, with an earnestness that could not be mistaken, as he clapped him on the back. "A merrier Christmas, Bob, my good fellow, than I have given you for many a year! I'll raise your salary, and try to help your struggling family, and we will discuss your affairs this very afternoon. Make up the fires and buy another coal-scuttle before you dot another *i*, Bob Cratchit!"

Scrooge was better than his word. He did

it all, and infinitely more. And to Tiny Tim, who did *not* die, he was a second father. He became as good a friend, as good a master, and as good a man as the city knew. It was always said of him thereafter that he knew how to keep Christmas well. May that be truly said of all of us!

And so, as Tiny Tim observed, "God Bless Us, Every One!"

—Abridged.

Ring Out Wild Bells

By Alfred Tennyson

Ring out wild bells to the wild sky,
  The flying cloud, the frosty light;
  The year is dying in the night;
Ring out, wild bells, and let him die.

Ring out the old, ring in the new,
  Ring, happy bells, across the snow;
  The year is going, let him go;
Ring out the false, ring in the true.

Ring out the grief that saps the mind
  For those that here we see no more;
  Ring out the feud of rich and poor,
Ring in redress to all mankind.

Ring out a slowly dying cause
  And ancient forms of party strife;
  Ring in the nobler modes of life,
With sweeter manners, purer laws.

Ring out the want, the care, the sin,
  The faithless coldness of the times;
  Ring out, ring out my mournful rhymes,
But ring the fuller minstrel in.

Ring out false pride in place and blood,
  The civic slander and the spite;
  Ring in the love of truth and right,
Ring in the common love of good.

Ring out old shapes of foul disease,
  Ring out the narrowing lust of gold;
  Ring out the thousand wars of old,
Ring in the thousand years of peace.

Ring in the valiant man and free,
  The larger heart, the kindlier hand;
  Ring out the darkness of the land,
Ring in the Christ that is to be.

The Cataract of Lodore

By Robert Southey

How does the water come down at Lodore?
    From its sources which well
    In the tarn on the fell,
    From its fountain in the mountain,
    Its rills and its gills,
    Through moss and through brake,
    It runs and it creeps,
    For a while till it sleeps,
    In its own little lake,
    And thence at departing,
    Awakening and starting,
    It runs through the reeds,
    And away it proceeds,
    Through meadow and glade,
    In sun and in shade,
    And through the wood shelter,
    Among crags in its flurry,
    Helter-skelter—hurry-skurry.

How does the water come down at Lodore:
    Here it comes sparkling,
    And there it lies darkling;
    Here smoking and frothing,
    Its tumult and wrath in,
  It hastens along, conflicting, and strong,
    Now striking and raging,
    As if a war waging,
  Its caverns and rocks among.
    Rising and leaping,
    Sinking and creeping,
    Swelling and flinging,
    Showering and springing,
    Eddying and whisking,
    Spouting and frisking,
    Twining and twisting,
    Around and around,
    With endless rebound;

Receding and speeding,
And shocking and rocking,
And darting and parting,
And threading and spreading,
And whizzing and hissing,
And dripping and skipping,
And whitening and brightening,
And quivering and shivering,
And hitting and splitting,
And shining and twining,
And rattling and battling,
And shaking and quaking,
And pouring and roaring,
And waving and raving,
And tossing and crossing,
And flowing and growing,
And running and stunning,
And hurrying and skurrying,
And glittering and frittering,
And gathering and feathering,
And dinning and spinning,
And foaming and roaming,
And dropping and hopping,
And working and jerking,
And heaving and cleaving,
And thundering and floundering;
And falling and crawling and
    sprawling,
And driving and riving and
    striving,
And sprinkling and twinkling and
    wrinkling,
And sounding and bounding and
    rounding,
And bubbling and troubling and
    doubling,

Dividing and gliding and
  sliding,
And grumbling and rumbling and
  tumbling,
And clattering and battering and
  shattering;
And gleaming and steaming and
  streaming and beaming,
And rushing and flushing and
  brushing and gushing,
And flapping and rapping and
  clapping and slapping,
And curling and whirling and
  purling and twirling,
Retreating and beating and
  meeting and sheeting,
Delaying and straying and
  playing and spraying,
Advancing and prancing and
  glancing and dancing,
Recoiling, turmoiling and toiling
  and boiling,
And thumping and flumping and
  bumping and jumping,
And dashing and flashing and
  splashing and clashing,—
And so never ending, but always
  descending,
Sounds and motions for ever and ever
  are blending,
All at once and all o'er, with a mighty
  uproar—
And this way the water comes down
  at Lodore.

—Abridged

The Voyage of the *Hispaniola*

From TREASURE ISLAND

By Robert Louis Stevenson

The story of how Stevenson came to write this exciting book about pirates is in itself interesting. One day, just for fun, he drew a treasure map and named the place Treasure Island. As he looked at his drawing a whole yarnful of characters came to life in his mind. So he wove them together into a plot and wrote about their adventures in a great book, "Treasure Island."

The story is told by the boy it happened to, Jim Hawkins, whose mother ran the Admiral Benbow Inn. An old sea dog came to the Inn to hide, but a band of pirates ferreted him out and searched his papers. Jim snatched up a packet of them and found a map showing the location of a hidden treasure.

Thrilled by his discovery, Jim and his friends, Dr. Livesey and Squire Trelawney, set out on a ship, the Hispaniola, *to find the treasure.*

But among their crew was a one-legged pirate known as Long John Silver. Long John and his confederates were secretly planning to get the treasure for themselves.

The story tells about how Jim overheard their scheme, and warned his comrades, about the danger they were in and the bloody fighting that ensued, about the final capture of the treasure, and many other exciting adventures. One scene from TREASURE ISLAND follows here. We hope it will make you want to read the whole book.

THE VOYAGE

ALL NIGHT we were in a great bustle getting things stowed in their places, and boatfuls of the Squire's friends came to wish him a good voyage and a safe return.

We never had a night at the *Admiral Benbow Inn* when I had half the work; and I was dog-tired when, a little before dawn, the boatswain sounded his pipe and the crew began to man the capstan-bars. I might have been twice as weary, yet I would not have left the deck; all was so new and interesting to me—the brief commands, the shrill note of the whistle, the men bustling to their places in the glimmer of the ship's lanterns.

Long John, who was standing by, with his crutch under his arm, at once broke out in the air and words I knew so well:

"Fifteen men on the Dead Man's Chest—"

And then the whole crew bore chorus:

"Yo-ho-ho, and a bottle of rum!"

Even at that exciting moment it carried me back to the old *Admiral Benbow* in a second; and I seemed to hear the voice of the captain piping in the chorus. But soon the anchor was short up; soon it was hanging dripping at the bows; soon the sails began to draw, and the land and shipping to flit by on either side. And before I could lie down to snatch an hour of slumber the *Hispaniola* had begun her voyage to the Isle of Treasure.

I am not going to relate that voyage in detail. It was fairly prosperous. The ship proved to be a good ship, the crew were capable seamen, and the captain thoroughly understood his business. But before we came the length of Treasure Island two or three things had happened which require to be known.

Mr. Arrow, the mate, turned out even worse than the captain had feared. He had no command among the men, and people did what they pleased with him. But that was by no means the worst of it; for after a day or two at sea he began to appear on deck with hazy eye, red cheeks, stuttering tongue, and other marks of drunkenness. Time after time he was ordered below in disgrace. Sometimes he fell and cut himself; sometimes he lay all day long in his little bunk at one side of the companion; sometimes for a day or two he would be almost sober and attend to his work at least passably.

In the meantime we could never make out where he got the drink. That was the ship's mystery. Watch him as we pleased, we could do nothing to solve it; and when we asked him to his face, he would only laugh if he were drunk, and if he were sober deny solemnly that he ever tasted anything but water.

He was not only useless as an officer, and a bad influence among the men, but it was plain at this rate he would soon kill himself outright; so nobody was surprised nor very sorry when one dark night, with a head sea, he disappeared entirely and was seen no more.

"Overboard!" said the captain. "Well, gentlemen, that saves the trouble of putting him in irons."

But there we were, without a mate; and it was necessary, of course, to advance one of the men. The boatswain, Job Anderson, was the likeliest man aboard, and, though he kept his old title, he served in a way as mate. Mr. Trelawney had followed the sea, and his knowledge made him very useful, for he often took a watch himself in easy weather. And the coxswain, Israel Hands, was a careful, wily, old, experienced seaman who could be trusted at a pinch with almost anything.

He was a great confidant of Long John Silver, and so the mention of his name leads me on to speak of our ship's cook, Barbecue, as the men called him.

Aboard ship he carried his crutch by a lanyard round his neck, to have both hands as free as possible. It was something to see him wedge the foot of the crutch against a bulkhead, and, propped against it, yielding to every movement of the ship, get on with his cooking like some one safe ashore. Still more strange was it to see him in the heaviest of weather cross the deck. He had a line or two rigged up to help him across the widest spaces—Long John's earrings, they were called—and he would hand himself from one place to another, now using the crutch, now trailing it alongside by the lanyard, as quickly as another man could walk. Yet some of the men who had sailed with him before expressed their pity to see him so reduced.

"He's no common man, Barbecue," said the coxswain to me. "He had good schooling in his young days, and can speak like a book when so minded; and brave—a lion's nothing alongside of Long John! I seen him grapple four, and knock their heads together—him unarmed."

All the crew respected and even obeyed him. He had a way of talking to each, and doing everybody some particular service. To me he was unwearily kind, and always glad to see me in the galley which he kept as clean as a new pin, the dishes hanging up burnished, and his parrot in a cage in one corner.

"Come away, Hawkins," he would say, "come and have a yarn with John. Nobody more welcome than yourself, my son. Sit you down and hear the news. Here's Cap'n Flint—I calls my parrot Cap'n Flint, after the famous buccaneer—here's Cap'n Flint predicting success to our voyage. Wasn't you, Cap'n?"

And the parrot would say, with great rapidity, "Pieces of eight! Pieces of eight! Pieces of eight!" till you wondered that it was not out of breath, or till John threw his handkerchief over the cage.

"Now, that bird," he would say, "is maybe two hundred years old, Hawkins—they lives for ever mostly; and if anybody's seen more wickedness, it must be the devil himself. She's sailed with great Cap'n England, the pirate. She's been at Madagascar, and at Malabar, and Surinam, and Providence, and Portobello. She was at the fishing up of the wrecked plate-ships. It's there she learned 'Pieces of eight,' and little wonder; three hundred and fifty thousand of 'em, Hawkins! She was at the boarding of the

Viceroy of the Indies out of Goa, she was; and to look at her you would think she was a babby. But you smelled powder—didn't you, Cap'n?"

"Stand by to go about," the parrot would scream.

"Ah, she's a handsome craft, she is," the cook would say, and give her sugar from his pocket, and then the bird would peck at the bars and swear straight on, passing belief for wickedness. "There," John would add, "you can't touch pitch and not be mucked, lad. Here's this poor old innocent bird o' mine swearing blue fire, and none the wiser, you may lay to that. She would swear the same, in a manner of speaking, before chaplain." And John would touch his forelock with a solemn way he had, that made me think he was the best of men.

In the meantime, the Squire and Captain Smollett were still on pretty distant terms with each other. The Squire made no bones about the matter; he despised the Captain. The Captain, on his part, never spoke but when he was spoken to, and then sharp and short and dry, and not a word wasted. He owned, when driven into a corner, that he seemed to have been wrong about the crew, that some of them were as brisk as he wanted to see, and all had behaved fairly well. As for the ship, he had taken a downright fancy to her. "She'll lie a point nearer the wind than a man has a right to expect of his own married wife, sir. But," he would add, "all I say is we're not home again, and I don't like the cruise."

The Squire, at this, would turn away and march up and down the deck, chin in air.

"A trifle more of that man," he would say, "and I should explode."

We had some heavy weather, which only proved the qualities of the *Hispaniola*. Every man on board seemed well content. They must have been hard to please if they had been otherwise, for it is my belief there was never a ship's company so spoiled since Noah put to sea. Double grog was going on the least excuse as, for instance, if the Squire heard it was any man's birthday, and always a barrel of apples for any one to help himself that had a fancy.

"Never knew good come of it yet," the Captain said to Dr. Livesey. "Spoil fo'c's'le hands, make devils. That's my belief."

But good did come of the apple-barrel, as you shall hear; for if it had not been for that, we should have had no note of warning, and might all have perished by the hand of treachery.

This was how it came about:

We had run up the trades to get the wind of the island we were after—I am not allowed to be more plain—and now we were running down for it with a bright lookout day and night. It was about the last day of our outward voyage, by the largest computation. Some time that night, or, at latest, before noon of the morrow, we should sight the Treasure Island. We were heading S.S.W., and had a steady breeze abeam and a quiet sea. The *Hispaniola* rolled steadily, dipping her bowsprit now and then with a whiff of spray. All was drawing alow and aloft. Everyone was in the bravest spirits because we were now so near an end of the first part of our adventure. Now, just after sundown, when all my work was over and I was on my way to my berth, it occurred to me that I should like an apple. I ran on deck. The watch was all forward looking out for the island. The man at the helm was watching the luff of the sail and whistling away gently to himself; and that was the only sound excepting the swish of the sea against the bows and around the sides of the ship.

I got bodily into the apple-barrel, and found there was scarce an apple left; but sitting down there in the dark, what with the sound of the waters and rocking movement of the ship, I had either fallen asleep or was on the point of doing so when a heavy man sat down with rather a clash close by. The barrel shook as he leaned his shoulders against it, and I was just about to jump up when the man began to speak. It was Silver's voice, and before I had heard a dozen words I would not have shown myself for all the world, but lay there, trembling and listening, in the extreme of fear and curiosity; for from these dozen words I understood that the lives of all the honest men aboard depended upon me alone.

"No, not I," said Silver. "Flint was cap'n; I was quartermaster, along of my timber leg. The same broadside I lost my leg, old Pew lost his deadlights. It was a master surgeon, him that ampytated me—out of college and all—Latin by the bucket, and what not; but he was hanged like a dog,

and sun-dried like the rest, at Corso Castle. That was Robert's men, that was, and comed of changing names to their ships— *Royal Fortune* and so on. Now, what a ship was christened, so let her stay, I says. So it was with the *Cassandra,* as brought us all safe home from Malabar, after England took the *Viceroy of the Indies;* so it was with the old *Walrus,* Flint's old ship, as I've seen a-muck with red blood and fit to sink with gold."

"Ah!" cried another voice, that of the youngest hand on board, and evidently full of admiration, "he was the flower of the flock, was Flint!"

"Davis was a man, too, by all accounts," said Silver. "I never sailed along of him; first with England, then with Flint, that's my story; and now here on my own account, in a manner of speaking. I laid by nine hundred safe from England, and two thousand after Flint. That ain't bad for a man before the mast—all safe in bank. 'Tain't earning now, it's saving does it, you may lay to that. Where's all England's men now? Why, most of 'em aboard here. Old Pew, as had lost his sight, spends twelve hundred pound in a year, like a lord in Parliament. Where is he now? Well, he's dead now and under hatches; but for two year before that, shiver my timbers! the man was starving. He begged and he stole, and he cut throats, and starved at that, by the powers!"

"Well, it ain't much use, after all," said the young seaman.

"'Tain't much use for fools, you may lay to it—that, nor nothing," cried Silver. "But now, you look here: you're young, you are, but you're as smart as paint. I see that when I set my eyes on you, and I'll talk to you like a man."

You imagine how I felt when I heard this abominable old rogue addressing another in the very same words of flattery as he had used to myself. I think, if I had been able, that I would have killed him through the barrel. Meantime, he ran on, little supposing he was overheard.

"Here it is about gentlemen of fortune. They lives rough, and they risk swinging, but they eat and drink like fighting-cocks, and when a cruise is done, why it's hundreds of pounds instead of hundreds of farthings in their pockets. Now, the most goes for rum and a good fling, and to sea again in their shirts. But that's not the course I lay. I put it all away, some here, some there, and none too much anywheres, by reason of suspicion. I'm fifty, mark you; once back from this cruise I'll set up as a gentleman in earnest. Time enough, too, says you. Ah, but I've lived easy in the meantime; never denied myself o' nothing heart desires, and slep' soft and ate dainty all my days but when at sea. And how did I begin? Before the mast, like you!"

"Well," said the other, "but all the other money's gone now, ain't it? You daren't show face in Bristol after this."

"Why, where might you suppose it was?" asked Silver, derisively.

"At Bristol, in banks and places," answered his companion.

"It were," said the cook, "it were when we weighed anchor. But my old missis has it all by now. I would tell you where, for I trust you; but it 'u'd make jealousy among the mates."

"And can you trust your missis?" asked the other.

"Gentlemen of fortune," returned the cook, "usually trust little among themselves, and right you are. But I have a way with me, I have. When a mate brings a slip on his cable—one as knows me, I mean— it won't be in the same world with Old John. There was some that was feared of Pew, and some that was feared of Flint; and Flint his own self was feared of me. Feared he was, and proud. They was the roughest crew afloat, was Flint's; the devil himself would have been feared to go to sea with them. Well, now, I tell you, I'm not a boasting man, and you seen yourself how easy I keep company; but when I was quartermaster, *lambs* wasn't the word for Flint's old buccaneers. Ah, you may be sure of yourself in old John's ship."

"Well, I tell you now," replied the lad, "I didn't half like the job till I had this talk with you, John; but there's my hand on it now."

"And a brave lad you were, and smart, too," answered Silver, shaking hands so heartily that the barrel shook, "and a finer figurehead for a gentleman of fortune I never clapped my eyes on."

By this time I had begun to understand the meaning of their terms. By a "gentleman of fortune" they plainly meant neither more nor less than a common pirate, and the little scene that I had overheard was the last act in the corruption of one of the honest hands—perhaps of the last one left aboard. But on this point I was soon to be relieved, for, Silver giving a little whistle, a third man strolled up and sat down by the party.

"Dick's square," said Silver.

"Oh, I know'd Dick was square," returned the voice of the coxswain, Israel Hands. "He's no fool, is Dick." And he turned his quid and spat. "But look here," he went on. "here's what I want to know, Barbecue: how long are we a-going to stand off and on? I've had a'most enough o' Cap'n Smollett; he's hazed me long enough, by thunder! I want to go into that cabin, I do. I want their pickles and wines, and that."

"Israel," said Silver, "your head ain't much account, nor ever was. But you're able to hear, I reckon; leastways, your ears is big enough. Now, here's what I say: you'll berth forward, and you'll live hard, and you'll speak soft, and you'll keep sober, till I give the word; and you may lay to that, my son."

"Well, I don't say no, do I?" growled the coxswain. "What I say is, when? That's all I say."

"When! by the powers!" cried Silver. "Well, now, if you want to know, I'll tell you when. The last moment I can manage; and that's when. Here's a first-rate seaman, Cap'n Smollett, sails the blessed ship for us. Here's this Squire and Doctor with a map and such—I don't know where it is, do I? No more do you, says you. Well, then, I mean this Squire and Doctor shall find the stuff, and help us to get it aboard, by the powers! Then we'll see. If I was sure of you all, sons of double Dutchmen, I'd have Cap'n Smollett navigate us half-way back again before. I struck."

"Why, we're all seamen aboard here, I should think!" said the lad Dick.

"We're all fo'c's'le hands, you mean," snapped Silver. "We can steer a course, but

who's to set one? That's what all you gentlemen split on, first and last. If I had my
way I'd have Cap'n Smollet work us back
into the trades at least; then we'd have no
blessed miscalculations and a spoonful of
water a day. But I know the sort you are.
I'll finish with 'em at the island, as soon's
the blunt's on board, and a pity it is. But
you're never happy till you're drunk. Slit
my sides, I've a sick heart to sail with the
likes of you!"

"Easy all, Long John," cried Israel.
"Who's a-crossin' of you?"

"Why, how many tall ships, think ye,
have I seen lain aboard, and how many
brisk lads drying in the sun at Execution
Dock?" cried Silver. "And all for this same
hurry and hurry and hurry. You hear me?
I have seen a thing or two at sea, I have.
If you would on'y lay your course, and p'nt
to windward, you would ride in carriages,
you would. But not you! I know you."

"Everybody know'd you was a kind of
chapling, John; but there's others as could
hand and steer as well as you," said Israel.
"They liked a bit o' fun, they did. They
wasn't so high and dry, nohow, but took
their fling, like jolly companions every one."

"So?" says Silver. "Well, and where are
they now? Pew was that sort, and died a
beggar-man. Flint was, and he died of rum
at Savannah. Ah, they was a sweet crew,
they was! on'y where are they?"

"But," asked Dick, "when we do lay 'em
athwart, what are we to do with 'em,
anyhow?"

"There's the man for me!" cried the cook,
admiringly. "That's what I call business.
Well, what would you think? Put 'em ashore
like maroons? Or cut 'em down like that
much pork?

"Billy Bones was the man for that," said
Israel. " 'Dead men don't bite,' says he.
Well, he's dead now hisself; he know the
long and short on it now; and if ever a
rough hand come to port, it was Billy."

"Right you are," said Silver, "rough and
ready. But mark you here: I'm an easy
man—I'm quite the gentleman, says you;
but this time it's serious. Dooty is dooty,
mates. I give my vote—death. When I'm in
Parlyment, and riding in my coach, I don't
want none of these sea-lawyers in the cabin
a-coming home, unlooked for, like the devil
at prayers. Wait is what I say; but when
the time comes, why, let her rip!"

"John," cries the coxwain, "you're a
man!"

"You'll say so, Israel, when you see,"
said Silver. "Only one thing I claim—I
claim Trelawney. I'll wring his calf's head
off his body with these hands. Dick!" he
added, breaking off, "you just jump up, like
a sweet lad, and get me an apple to wet my
pipe like."

You may fancy the terror I was in! I
should have leaped out and run for it, if I
had found the strength; but my limbs and
heart alike misgave me.

I heard Dick begin to rise, and then some
one seemingly stopped him, and the voice
of Hands explained, "Oh, stow that! Don't
you get sucking of that bilge, John. Let's
have a go of the rum."

"Dick," I heard Silver say, "I trust you.
I've a gauge on the keg, mind. There's the
key; you fill a pannikin and bring it up."

Terrified as I was, I could not help thinking to myself that this must have been how
Mr. Arrow got the strong waters that destroyed him.

Dick was gone but a little while, and

373

during his absence Israel spoke in the cook's ear. It was but a word or two that I could catch, and yet I gathered some important news, for, besides other scraps that tended to the same purpose, this whole clause was audible: "Not another man of them 'll jine." Hence there were still faithful men on board.

When Dick returned, one after another of the trio took the pannikin and drank—one "To luck"; another with a "Here's to old Flint"; and Silver himself saying, in a kind of song, "Here's to ourselves!"

Just then a sort of brightness fell upon me in the barrel and, looking up, I found the moon had risen, and was silvering the mizzen-top and shining white on the luff of the foresail. And almost at the same time the voice of the lookout shouted, "Land ho!"

COUNCIL OF WAR

There was a great rush of feet across the deck. I could hear people tumbling up from the cabin and the fo'c's'le; and, slipping in an instant outside my barrel, I dived behind the foresail, made a double toward the stern, and came out upon the open deck in time to join Hunter and Dr. Livesey in the rush for the weather bow.

There all hands were already congregated. A belt of fog had lifted almost simultaneously with the appearance of the moon. Away to the southwest of us we saw two low hills, about a couple of miles apart, and rising behind one of them a third and higher hill, whose peak was still buried in the fog. All three seemed sharp and conical in figure.

So much I saw, almost in a dream, for I

374

had not yet recovered from my fear of a minute or two before. And then I heard the voice of Captain Smollett issuing orders. The *Hispaniola* was laid a couple of points nearer the wind, and now sailed a course that would just clear the island on the east.

"And now, men," said the Captain, when all was sheeted home, "has any one of you ever seen that land ahead?"

"I have, sir," said Silver. "I've watered there with a trader I was cook in."

"The anchorage is on the south, behind an islet, I fancy?" asked the Captain.

"Yes, sir; Skeleton Island they calls it. It were a main place for pirtates once, and a hand we had on board knowed all their names for it. That hill to the nor'ard they calls the Foremast Hill; there are three hills in a row running south'ard—fore, main, and mizzen, sir. But the main—that's the big un with the cloud on it—they usually calls the Spy-glass, by reason of a lookout they kept when they was in the anchorage cleaning; for it's there they cleaned their ships, sir, asking your pardon."

"I have a chart here," says Captain Smollett. "See if that's the place."

Long John's eyes burned in his head as he took the chart; but by the fresh look of the paper, I knew he was doomed to disappointment. This was not the map we had found in Billy Bone's chest, but an accurate copy, complete in all things—names and heights and soundings—with the single exception of the red crosses and the written notes. Sharp as must have been this annoyance, Silver had the strength of mind to hide it.

"Yes, sir," said he, "this is the spot, to be sure; and very prettily drawn out. Who

might have done that, I wonder? The pirates were too ignorant, I reckon. Ay, here it is: 'Capt. Kidd's Anchorage'—just the name my shipmate called it. There's a strong current runs along the south, and then away nor'ard up the west coast. Right you was, sir," says he, "to haul your wind and keep the weather of the island. Leastways, if such was your intention as to enter and careen, and there ain't no better place for that in these waters."

"Thank you, my man," says Captain Smollett. "I'll ask you, later on, to give us a help. You may go."

I was surprised at the coolness with which John avowed his knowledge of the island; and I own I was half frightened when I saw him drawing nearer to myself. He did not know, to be sure, that I had overheard his council from the apple-barrel, and yet I had, by this time, taken such a horror of his cruelty, duplicity, and power, that I could scare conceal a shudder when he laid his hand upon my arm.

"Ah," says he, "this here is a sweet spot, this island—a sweet spot for a lad to get ashore on. You'll bathe, and you'll climb trees, and you'll hunt goats, you will; and you'll get aloft on them hills like a goat yourself. Why, it makes me young again. I was going to forget my timber leg, I was. It's a pleasant thing to be young, and have ten toes, and you may lay to that. When you want to go a bit of exploring, you just ask old John, and he'll put up a snack for you to take along."

And clapping me in the friendliest way upon the shoulder, he hobbled off forward and went below.

Captain Smollett, the Squire, and Dr.

Livesay were talking together on the quarter-deck, and, anxious as I was to tell them my story, I dared not interrupt them openly. While I was still casting about in my thoughts to find some probable excuse, Dr. Livesay called me to his side. He had left his pipe below, and, being a slave to tobacco, had meant that I should fetch it; but as soon as I was near enough to speak and not to be overheard, I broke out immediately: "Doctor, let me speak. Get the Captain and Squire down to the cabin, and then make some pretense to send for me. I have terrible news."

The Doctor changed countenance a little, but next moment he was master of himself.

"Thank you, Jim," said he, quite loudly, "that was all I wanted to know," as if he had asked me a question.

And with that he turned on his heel and rejoined the other two. They spoke together for a little, and though none of them started, or raised his voice, or so much as whistled, it was pain enough that Dr. Livesay had communicated my request; for the next thing that I heard was the Captain giving an order to Job Anderson, and all hands were piped on deck.

"My lads," said Captain Smollett, "I've a word to say to you. This land that we have sighted is the place we have been sailing to. Mr. Trelawney, being a very open-handed gentleman, as we all know, has just asked me a word or two, and I was able to tell him that every man on board had done his duty alow and aloft as I never ask to see it done better. And if you think as I do, you'll give a good sea cheer for the gentleman that does it."

The cheer followed—that was a matter of course; but it rang out so full and hearty that I confess I could hardly believe these same men were plotting for our blood.

"One more cheer for Cap'n Smollett," cried Long John, when the first had subsided.

And this also was given with a will.

On the top of that the three gentlemen went below, and not long after word was sent forward that Jim Hawkins was wanted in the cabin.

I found them all three seated round the table, the Doctor smoking away, with his wig on his lap, and that, I knew, was a sign that he was agitated. The stern window was open, for it was a warm night, and you could see the moon shining behind on the ship's wake.

"Now, Hawkins," said the squire, "you have something to say. Speak up."

I did as I was bid, and, as short as I could make it, told the whole details of Silver's conversation. Nobody interrupted me till I was done, nor did any one of the three of them make so much as a movement, but they kept their eyes on my face from first to last.

"Jim," said Dr. Livesay, "take a seat."

And they made me sit down at the table beside them, and all three, one after the other, and each with a bow, drank my good health, and their service to me, for my luck and courage.

"Now, Captain," said the Squire, "you were right, and I was wrong. I own myself an ass, and I await your orders."

"No more an ass than I sir," returned the Captain. "I never heard of a crew that meant to mutiny but what showed signs before, for any man that had an eye in his

head to see the mischief and take steps according. But this crew," he added, "beats me."

"Captain," said the Doctor, "with your permission, that's Silver. I very remarkable man."

"He'd look remarkably well from a yard-arm, sir," returned the Captain. "But this is talk; this don't lead to anything. I see three or four points, and with Mr. Trelawney's permission I'll name them."

"You, sir, are the Captain. It is for you to speak," says Mr. Trelawney, grandly.

"First point," began Mr. Smollett. "We must go on, because we can't turn back. If I gave the word to go about they would rise at once. Second point, we have time before us—at least, until this treasure's found. Third point, there are faithful hands.

Now, sir, it's got to come to blows sooner or later; and what I propose is to take time by the forelock, as the saying is, and come to blows some day when they least expect it."

"Jim here," said the Doctor, "can help us more than any one. The men are not shy with him, and Jim is a noticing lad."

"Hawkins, I put prodigious faith in you," added the Squire.

I began to feel pretty desperate at this, and altogether helpless; and yet, by an odd train of circumstances, it was indeed through me that safety came. In the meantime, talk as we pleased, there were only seven out of the twenty-six on whom we knew we could rely; and out of these seven one was a boy, so that the grown men on our side were six to their nineteen.

377

"Peculiarsome" Abe

From ABE LINCOLN GROWS UP

By Carl Sandburg

Probably no other writer on Abraham Lincoln has given us so true and sympathetic a picture of the Great Emancipator as Carl Sandburg. His impressive six-volume biography, originally published as ABRAHAM LINCOLN: THE PRAIRIE YEARS and ABRAHAM LINCOLN: THE WAR YEARS, won him the Pulitzer prize for history in 1940. It has remained the classic biography of Lincoln ever since.

But knowing that young people would be chiefly interested in Lincoln's boyhood, and being, in addition, a writer of delightful poems and stories for children, Sandburg put the story of Lincoln's boyhood into a beautiful book for children, ABE LINCOLN GROWS UP. One chapter of it appears here. We feel that it gives a wonderful sense of the character of the boy Abe. We hope it will inspire those here introduced to Abe Lincoln to read more about him by his classic biographer Carl Sandburg.

THE FARM boys in their evenings at Jones's store in Gentryville talked about how Abe Lincoln was always reading, digging into books, stretching out flat on his stomach in front of the fireplace, studying till midnight and past midnight, picking a piece of charcoal to write on the fire shovel, shaving off what he wrote, and then writing more—till midnight and past midnight. The next thing Abe would be reading books between the plow handles, it seemed to them. And once trying to speak a last word, Dennis Hanks said, "There's suthin' peculiarsome about Abe."

He wanted to learn, to know, to live, to reach out; he wanted to satisfy hungers and thirsts he couldn't tell about, this big boy of the backwoods. And some of what he wanted so much, so deep down, seemed to be in the books. Maybe in books he would find the answers to dark questions pushing around in the pools of his thoughts and the drifts of his mind. He told Dennis and other people, "The things I want to know are in books; my best friend is the man who'll git me a book I ain't read."

And sometimes friends answered, "Well, books ain't as plenty as wildcats in these parts o' Indianny."

This was one thing meant by Dennis when he said there was "suthin' peculiarsome" about Abe. It seemed that Abe made the books tell him more than they told other people. All the other farm boys had gone to school and read *The Kentucky Preceptor*, but Abe picked out questions from it, such as "Who has the most right to complain, the Indian or the Negro?" And Abe would talk about it, up one way and down the other, while they were in the cornfield pulling fodder for the winter.

When Abe got hold of a storybook and read about a boat that came near a magnetic rock, and how the magnets in the rock

378

pulled all the nails out of the boat so it went to pieces and the people in the boat found themselves floundering in water, Abe thought it was funny and told it to other people. After Abe read poetry, especially Bobby Burns's poems, Abe began writing rhymes himself. When Abe sat with a girl, with their bare feet in the creek water, and she spoke of the moon rising, he explained to her it was the earth moving and not the moon—the moon only seemed to rise.

John Hanks, who worked in the fields barefooted with Abe, grubbing stumps, plowing, mowing, said, "When Abe and I came back to the house from work, he used to go to the cupboard, snatch a piece of corn bread, sit down, take a book, cock his legs up high as his head, and read. Whenever Abe had a chance in the field while at work, or at the house, he would stop and read."

Abe liked to explain to other people what he was getting from books. Explaining an idea to some one else made it clearer to him. The habit was growing on him of reading out loud. Words came more real

if picked from the silent page of the book and pronounced on the tongue; new balances and values of words stood out if spoken aloud. When writing letters for his father or the neighbors, he read the words out loud as they got written. Before writing a letter he asked questions such as: "What do you want to say in the letter? How do you want to say it? Are you sure that's the best way to say it? Or do you think we can fix up a better way to say it?"

As he studied his books his lower lip stuck out; Josiah Crawford noticed it was a habit and joked Abe about the "stuck-out lip." This habit too stayed with him.

He wrote in his sum book or arithmetic that compound division was "When several numbers of divers denominations are given to be divided by 1 common divisor," and worked on the exercise in multiplication: "If 1 foot contain 12 inches I demand how many there are in 126 feet." Thus the schoolboy.

What he got in the schools didn't satisfy him. He went to three different schools in Indiana, besides two in Kentucky—altogether about four months of school. He learned his A B C, how to spell, read, write. And he had been with the other barefoot boys in butternut jeans learning "manners" under the school teacher, Andrew Crawford, who had them open a door, walk in, and say, "Howdy do?" Yet what he tasted of books in school was only a beginning, only made him hungry and thirsty, shook him with a wanting and a wanting of more and more of what was hidden between the covers of books.

He kept on saying, "The things I want to know are in books; my best friend is the man who'll git me a book I ain't read."

He said that to Pitcher, the lawyer over at Rockport, nearly twenty miles away, one fall afternoon, when he walked from Pigeon Creek to Rockport and borrowed a book from Pitcher. Then when fodder-pulling time came a few days later, he shucked corn from early daylight till sundown along with his father and Dennis Hanks and John Hanks, but after supper he read the book till midnight, and at noon he hardly knew the taste of his cornbread because he had the book in front of him. It was a hundred little things like these which made Dennis Hanks say there was "suthin' peculiarsome" about Abe.

Besides reading the family Bible and figuring his way all through the old arithmetic they had at home, he got hold of *Aesop's Fables, Pilgrim's Progress, Robinson Crusoe,* and Weems's *The Life of Francis Marion.*

The book of fables, written or collected thousands of years ago by the Greek slave, known as Aesop, sank deep in his mind. As he read through the book a second and third time, he had a feeling there were fables all around him, that everything he touched and handled, everything he saw and learned had a fable wrapped in it somewhere. One fable was about a bundle of sticks and a farmer whose sons were quarreling and fighting.

There was a fable in two sentences which read, "A coachman, hearing one of the wheels of his coach make a great noise, and perceiving that it was the worst one of the four, asked how it came to take such a liberty. The wheel answered that from the beginning of time, creaking had always been the privilege of the weak."

And there were shrewd, brief incidents of foolery such as this: "A waggish, idle fellow in a country town, being desirous of playing a trick on the simplicity of his neighbors and at the same time putting a little money in his pocket at their cost, advertised that he would on a certain day show a wheel carriage that should be so contrived as to go without horses. By silly curiosity the rustics were taken in, and each succeeding group who came out from the show were ashamed to confess to their neighbors that they had seen nothing but a wheelbarrow."

The style of the Bible, of *Aesop's Fables,* the hearts and minds back of those books, were much in his thoughts. His favorite pages in them he read over and over. Behind such proverbs as "Muzzle not the ox that treadeth out the corn" and "He that ruleth his own spirit is greater than he that taketh a city," there was a music of simple wisdom and a mystery of common everyday life that touched deep spots in him, while out of the fables of the ancient Greek slave he came to see that cats, rats, dogs, horses, plows, hammers, fingers, toes, people, all had fables connected with their lives, characters, places. There was, perhaps, an outside for each thing as it stood alone, while inside of it was its fable.

One book came titled *The Life of George Washington, with Curious Anecdotes, Equally Honorable to Himself and Exemplary to His Young Countrymen. Embellished with Six Steel Engravings,* by M. L. Weems, formerly Rector of Mt. Vernon Parish. It pictured men of passion and proud ignorance in the government of England driving their country into war on the American colonies. It quoted the far-visioned warning of Chatham to the British parliament, "For God's sake, then, my lords, let the way be instantly opened for reconciliation. I say instantly; or it will be too late forever."

The book told of war, as at Saratoga. "Hoarse as a mastiff of true British breed, Lord Balcarras was heard from rank to rank, loud-animating his troops; while on the other hand, fierce as a hungry Bengal tiger, the impetuous Arnold precipitated heroes on the stubborn foe. Shrill and terrible, from rank to rank, resounds the clash of bayonets—frequent and sad the groans of the dying. Pairs on pairs, Britons and Americans, with each his bayonet at his brother's breast, fall forward together faint-shrieking in death, and mingle their smoking blood." Washington, the man, stood out, as when he wrote, "These things so harassed my heart with grief that I solemnly declared to God, if I know myself, I would gladly offer myself a sacrifice to the butchering enemy, if I could thereby insure the safety of these my poor distressed countrymen."

The Weems book reached some deep spots in the boy. He asked himself what it meant that men should march, fight, bleed, go cold and hungry for the sake of what they called "freedom."

"Few great men are great in everything," said the book. And there was a cool sap in the passage: "His delight was in that of the manliest sort, which, by stringing the limbs and swelling the muscles, promotes the kindliest flow of blood and spirits. At jumping with a long pole, or heaving heavy weights, for his years he hardly had an equal."

Such book talk was a comfort against the

same thing over again, day after day, so many mornings the same kind of water from the same spring, the same fried pork and corn-meal to eat, the same drizzles of rain, spring plowing, summer weeds, fall fodder-pulling, each coming every year, with the same tired feeling at the end of the day, so many days alone in the woods or the fields or else the same people to talk with, people from whom he had learned all they could teach him. Yet there ran through his head the stories and sayings of other people, the stories and sayings of books, the learning his eyes had caught from books. They were a comfort; they were good to have because they were good by themselves; and they were still better to have because they broke the chill of the lonesome feeling.

He was thankful to the writer of *Aesop's Fables* because that writer stood by him and walked with him, an invisible companion, when he pulled fodder or chopped wood. Books lighted lamps in the dark rooms of his gloomy hours. . . . Well—he would live on; maybe the time would come when he would be free from work for a few weeks, or a few months, with books, and then he would read. . . . God, then he would read. . . . Then he would go and get at the proud secrets of his books.

His father—would he be like his father when he grew up? He hoped not. Why should his father knock him off a fence rail when he was asking a neighbor, passing by, a question? Even if it was a smart question, too pert and too quick, it was no way to handle a boy in front of a neighbor. No, he was going to be a man different from his father. The books—his father hated the books. His father talked about "too much eddication"; after readin', writin', 'rithmetic, that was enough, his father said. He, Abe Lincoln, the boy, wanted to know more than the father, Tom Lincoln, wanted to know. Already Abe knew more than his father. He was writing letters for the neighbors; they hunted out the Lincoln farm to get young Abe to find his bottle of ink with blackberry brier root and copperas in it, and his pen made from a turkey buzzard feather, and write letters. Abe had a suspicion sometimes his father was a little proud to have a boy that could write letters, and tell about things in books, and outrun and outwrestle and rough-and-tumble any boy or man in Spencer County. Yes, he would be different from his father; he was already so; it couldn't be helped.

In growing up from boyhood to young manhood, he had survived against lonesome, gnawing monotony and against floods, forest and prairie fires, snake-bites, horse-kicks, ague, chills, fever, malaria, "milk-sick."

A comic outline against the sky he was, hiking along the roads of Spencer and other counties in southern Indiana in those years when he read all the books within a fifty-mile circuit of his home. Stretching up on the long legs that ran from his moccasins to the body frame with its long, gangling arms, covered with linsey-woolsey, then the lean neck that carried the head with its surmounting coonskin cap or straw hat—it was, again, a comic outline—yet with a portent in its shadow. His laughing "Howdy," his yarns and drollery, opened the doors of men's hearts.

Starting along in his eleventh year came

spells of abstraction. When he was spoken to, no answer came from him. "He might be a thousand miles away." The roaming, fathoming, searching, questioning operations of the minds and hearts of poets, inventors, beginners who take facts stark, these were at work in him. This was one sort of abstraction he knew. There was another: the blues took him; coils of multiplied melancholies wrapped their blue frustrations inside him, all that Hamlet, Koheleth, Schopenhauer have uttered, in a mesh of foiled hopes. "There was absolutely nothing to excite ambition for education," he wrote later of that Indiana region. Against these "blues," he found the best

warfare was to find people and trade with them his yarns and drolleries. John Baldwin, the blacksmith, with many stories and odd talk and eye-slants, was a help and a light.

Days came when he sank deep in the stream of human life and felt himself kin of all that swam in it, whether the waters were crystal or mud.

He learned how suddenly life can spring a surprise. One day in the woods, as he was sharpening a wedge on a log, the ax glanced, nearly took his thumb off, and left a white scar after healing.

"You never cuss a good ax," was a saying in those timbers.

I Hear America Singing

By Walt Whitman

I hear America singing, the varied carols I hear:
Those of mechanics, each one singing his as it should be,
    blithe and strong;
The carpenter singing his as he measures his plank or beam;
The mason singing his as he makes ready for work, or leaves
    off work;
The boatman singing what belongs to him in his boat; the
    deckhand singing on the steamboat deck;
The shoemaker singing as he sits on his bench; the hatter
    singing as he stands;
The wood-cutter's song; the ploughboy's on his way in the
    morning or at noon intermission or at sundown;
The delicious singing of the mother, or of the young wife at
    work, or of the girl sewing or washing;
Each singing what belongs to him or her and to none else,
The day what belongs to the day—at night the party of
    young fellows, robust, friendly,
Singing with open mouths their strong melodious songs.

America

By Sidney Lanier

Long as thine art shall love true love,
Long as thy science truth shall know,
Long as thine eagle harms no dove,
Long as thy law by law shall grow,
Long as thy God is God above,
Thy brother every man below,
So long, dear land of all my love,
Thy name shall shine, thy fame shall glow.